I0666942

THE BLESSINGS OF
SAINT WICK

BLUE BOX BOOKS

THE BLESSINGS OF SAINT WICK
WICK AFTER DARK
BOOK TWO

All Rights Reserved
©2018 K.A. Thompson

No part of this book may be reproduced or transmitted in any form or by any means without permission in writing from the publisher.

Published by Blue Box Books
www.blueboxbooks.com

ISBN 978-1-932461-54-1

Printed in the United States of America

THE BLESSINGS OF
SAINT WICK

MAX THOMPSON

Also by Max Thompson

The Emperor of San Francisco: The Wick Chronicles, Book One
Ozoo: The Wick Chronicles, Book Two
Forked: The Wick Chronicles, Book Three
The Space Between Whens: Wick After Dark, Book One
The Psychokitty Speaks Out: Diary of a Mad Housecat
The Psychokitty Speaks Out: Something of Yours Will Meet A
Toothy Death
The Rules: A Guide For People Owned By Cats
Bite Me: A Memoir (Of Sorts)
Epistle: A Love Letter
There Once Was a Cat From Nantucket

Visit Max online at his blog, The Psychokitty Speaks Out
http://psychokitty.blogspot.com
or on Facebook
http://facebook.com/thepsychokittyspeaksout

Books one of his people (K.A. Thompson) wrote

The Charybdis Novels:
Charybdis
As Simple As That
Finding Father Rabbit
The King and Queen of Perfect Normal
The Flipside of Here

It's Not About the Cookies
Rock the Pink

Visit K.A. Thompson online at her blog,
Thumper Thinks Out Loud
http://kathompson.blogspot.com

THE BLESSINGS OF
SAINT WICK

WICK AFTER DARK

THE BLESSINGS OF SAINT WICK

1

King Jackson walked the length of the room, hands clasped behind his back. He paused every now and then as he examined the cluster of machines that were hardwired together, making sure he didn't trip over cables, and his eyebrows knotted as he tried to understand what he was seeing. These small metal boxes each contained a dozen computing processors and a cooling system that operated so quietly he strained to hear the hiss and moan of parts clicking against one another. There were twenty computer clusters lined up along the right side of the workshop, and in the center of the room was a thirty-foot black square crisscrossed with thousands of thin silver stripes.

The quiet made Drew three kinds of anxious, and when he couldn't take it anymore, he blurted out, "This is a seriously rough prototype. Everything projects from the floor upward, so it won't feel real, exactly. The demo will be a less tactile experience than it will when we've integrated everything into a full room."

Jax nodded, and Will flipped the switch. Overhead lights dimmed and the floor hummed, the thin lines of silver glowing. A moment later, with a clattering of tiny metal clicks, a tree rose from the center of the black square, followed by another, and then a small cat appeared. It ran between the trees in a figure eight pattern, chasing its own tail.

"You can step onto the floor," Drew told the King. "That won't hurt anything. And if you're very deliberate about how you set your hand on them, you can feel the bark on the trees."

Jax was looking at the cat. "Nothing like Wick, eh?"

"Do we need another Wick?" Will asked dryly. He gestured toward the tree closest to Jax. "Give it a try."

Gingerly, Jax reached out and then ran his fingers down the tree's trunk. He jerked his hand back, looked at his fingers, and then touched it again. When he pinched his thumb and forefinger together, they met as if nothing were there. "That's damned impressive," he said, touching it carefully once again. "This is only a few weeks' worth of work. How the hell did you pull it off?"

"Got the right equipment," Drew said. "Will knew someone who knew someone...once I saw the original system, it wasn't a stretch to modify it. They had too many heat-generating parts crammed together. It still runs warm, but I'm not worried that it'll melt or anything."

Drew was being humble; the original military-grade holographic computer system, pulled out of operations decades earlier because it had the nasty habit of going up in flames, was a bastion of broken ideas and unfulfilled wishes. It should have worked; it was built on the foundation of half a dozen centuries of advanced computer technology, systems that had taken men to the moon, connected the world, and made it possible to build a colony on Mars. It was a simple enough idea that suffered from over-thinking, and once Drew had it in front of him and pulled it apart, he knew immediately how he would fix it.

He separated the banks of solid state hard drives and motherboards into clusters, used insulated casing with extra space for airflow, added a seventy-year-old cooling system, and hardwired it all together. When he was certain he could run them all at the same time and maintain relatively even temperatures, he added the ultra-miniature projectors and tested the electrical burden. When that didn't melt, he wrote the code that instructed several hundred thousand nanobots to work in tandem with the projectors, creating the illusion of a three-dimensional monitor.

Will and Drew started on the project just days after Will returned from his honeymoon, and a few weeks later Jax requested an informal inspection. He wanted a solid reason for

Drew's absences from dinner every night, something to appease his Queen. It was too much too soon, she'd complained; between school and playing with Will, he was never home, and she had a hard time believing they had that much to work on.

"Once he got going—" Will cringed at the sound of someone upstairs being slammed onto the floor "—there was no slowing him down. He is, however, at a point where he needs to refocus his effort to his studies and let the practical matters rest."

"But it's not going to be difficult to upscale this," Drew said. "I can build—"

"Not yet," Will said.

"Grades?" Jax asked Drew.

With a heavy sigh, Drew assured him that his grades were just fine. He hadn't forgotten his promise to the King: get a degree or don't marry Oz. He hadn't missed any classes, he was holding a solid 95% average, and he was making time for her. His days were long, but not unbearable.

The ceiling shook again.

"What the hell is going on up there?" Jax asked, looking up.

"Oz is tossing Zed and Jay around," Drew answered. "Zed, I think. Most of what she does to Jay involves chasing him across the room and threating to kick him in the nads."

Jax told him to go upstairs to let them know it was time to leave. Aubrey wanted everyone home for dinner, and they were not disappointing her.

When the door to the stairwell clicked behind him, Will turned to Jax and said, "I don't think they realize what today is. They've undoubtedly felt it looming, but I'm not certain they've clued into the actual date."

Oz has. I heard her crying this afternoon. She hid in the bathroom so no one would hear her. When I went in to check on her, she was looking in the mirror at the scar on her chest.

He didn't pass that along to Jax.

It had been a year, exactly, since Will fled with Oz, Drew, and Zed, to a safe house in Denver. The First Minister of Florida was hell-bent on killing Drew in order to bring his mother—Queen Shazia of Midlam—to her knees, and he had no qualms about destroying Oz to get to him. It didn't matter that Oz was his granddaughter; if she were in the way, he'd end her life as easily as he would blink.

I was sure Drew remembered the date, too, but he kept himself distracted with getting everything ready to demonstrate the computer system to Jax.

"This date is etched onto Aubrey's soul," Jax told Will. "Hell, mine, too. I will never forget watching the shuttle doors close, wondering if I would ever see my kids again. You. Wick. Drew. I swear to God, it was like everything we loved was in that—"

Will stopped him before he could get footing on that path. "And it's over. The kids are all upstairs in Oz's dojo, and in an hour the noise at dinner will be so loud that you'll wish they would stop talking for two minutes."

"Not tonight. I want it noisy." Aubrey didn't want them to remember the date; she wanted her dining room filled with laughter and everyone talking over each other. Jax wanted that for her more than just about anything, and he asked Will to not remind them. "Reclaim the day for ourselves. Write over the memory of that shuttle door closing with one where our entire family is laughing so hard that someone is bound to throw up."

Will's nose scrunched up. "I don't have to be there for that."

"You do, and you will be. Your wife is already there helping Aubrey get everything ready. No excuses." He turned back to look at the black square again. "He hasn't taken it back to military specs yet, but damn, Will. This is impressive."

"He doesn't understand the science yet," Will said. "He simply has an amazing ability to look at things and understand how they should work. When the components were delivered, he took ten minutes to pick apart one of the arrays and knew the changes he needed to make." Will went to the closest cluster and set a hand on it. "It's fifty percent larger yet runs ninety percent cooler. And I can hear the gears inside his head turn. He's close to forming a picture of how he can retain the cooling capabilities while decreasing unit size."

"And yet, you already know how he could do it. You could do all of it."

"I understand the science—"

"You understood the science when you were six years old," Jax guessed. "When the Elysium project fell apart, you could have told us how to fix it, couldn't you?"

"It was not mine to tell."

"And now?"

"Now? I'm not dead, Jax. And while I still won't give you all the answers, I have no issue with providing Andrew with the materials he needs to succeed with this. But he needs to create the framework himself and discover all the small bits on his own."

Drew came back into the room, Zed and Jay right behind him. "Jesus, Will, are you fondling the computer?"

"I am." Will left his hand on it. "It does things for me."

"If I come in here some morning and find an empty wine bottle and snuffed out candles, I'm telling your wife."

Will shrugged lightly. "You're assuming she wouldn't be here with me."

Jay groaned. "Come on. Just, no. That's my *mom*."

Zed pushed Jay toward the door. "Pretty sure he's fondling your mom, too."

The groaning continued as the door swung closed behind them. Will finally took his hand off the computer case, a slight grin playing on his face. "He does not object to displays of affection as much as he would like you to think."

"Yes, and how do you feel every time your parents hint at their sex lives?" Jax asked, not expecting an answer. "Where's Oz?"

I hear her on the stairs. She's not moving.

Drew started toward the door, but Jax stopped him. "Head for home with Will," he said. "I want a few minutes alone with my daughter."

Before he could protest, Will nudged him toward the door. He held it open for me, expecting me to follow, but I went over to the stairwell door instead.

Will said I was a nosy little shit, and to not let them leave without me.

Jax climbed the six stairs to get to Oz and sat next to her. He didn't say anything. When she took a deep breath, he kissed the side of her head and waited for her to speak. When she didn't, he dangled his hand between his legs and crooked his pointy finger, beckoning me to come up and purr for her.

When I jumped onto her lap, her hands went to my back. "I know what today is, Dad. I know why Mom wants the big family dinner. I'm not sure I can do it. I get the point, seize the day and all that, but in my head today is the anniversary of the day that started turning everything...wrong."

"I know."

I curled up on Oz's legs and purred, hard.

"How can we turn it into a reason to party?" she asked. "We got into that shuttle and didn't know—"

"No, we didn't know," Jax said. "We didn't know that sending you off with only a heartbeat's notice would pull you so close to Will and Drew and your brother that you all became this...thing. A unit that no one else will ever be a part of. We didn't know that Will would hone you into a damned fighting machine and make you more formidable than I ever imagined possible. We didn't know that you would all find that *thing* that deep down makes you remarkable."

She sighed and leaned her head against his shoulder.

"Today marks one year since you climbed into a shuttle and headed off to a place where you learned more about yourself than you would have in a lifetime of staying home, Ozzy. And it will be weeks before you face the anniversary of the day your grandfather declared war on you."

"He was never my grandfather."

"That's fair."

"And not your point."

He kissed her again, sliding his arm around her shoulder. "I will never truly understand what you went through, but you beat the bastard. And when you had the chance to kill him, even his avatar, you were the better person and let him live."

"Not the same thing, Dad. It wasn't Munson in the simulator, just someone who looked like him."

"Someone who looked like him by design. Someone who poked you with the sharp ends of every doubt you had. You didn't cave. I would have."

"I don't think so."

He pulled away, just enough to look at her face. "Without a doubt. And if Will offers to take me into that simulator to face him, I'll kill him as many times as I can. I'm not tough enough to let him live. You're not only that tough, you're that compassionate. You lived. You won. So if you need to, turn today into a giant fuck you to Levi Munson, and in a few weeks when the day he took you rolls around, stand on the Golden Gate and spit into the ocean. Have Drew whip it out and pee on the bastard's grave. Just don't let him own any part of you, not today, not the day he sent his men after you, or any day after that."

"Huh." She took a deep breath. "We gave him the entire Pacific as a grave. Why the hell did we throw his ugly ass into something that magnificent?"

"To let the beauty wash him away."

She was quiet for a minute or so. "I can't ask Drew to pee off the Golden Gate, Dad."

"He'd do it."

"Yeah, but then the net would activate and it would all just splash back, probably all over me." She lifted me up and started down the stairs. "It would help if I could focus on the positives. Right now, all I can think about is how twitchy I feel."

"All right." He closed the stairwell door behind us. "Consider this—this is the date you got onto a shuttle and headed for a place where the boy you've always loved became the man you'll always love. You went to the place where he asked you to spend the rest of your lives together and then worked so hard that he was able to fulfill his promise to not let anything stop him from getting to you when you were lost. Today is not the day you stepped away from home into horror, Oz. Today is the day that Oz and Drew began to truly mature and made it possible for me to not only see that boy as your husband but to look forward to the day when you marry him."

She set me down before she grabbed him in a tight hug.

"I would trade every nightmare you endured with a dream if I could, Ozzy. But one of the truths is that without the war, I still might not be ready for the two of you to be together. I still might not see Drew in the light he deserves."

"You've always loved him," she said against his shirt.

"As the son of my friends, and as the boy who is always welcome in my home." He reached down for me and nodded toward the door. "I don't see him as a boy anymore and I respect him more than you realize. I love him as if he were my son. Try to keep that close to you, turn today into the anniversary of the day the two of you truly became Ozoo."

2

I lounged on the counter closest to the table—Jax noticed and glared at me, but he didn't tell me to get down because Aubrey would remind him they owned plenty of bleach and then promise to clean up after me later—and watched the madness Aubrey wanted as it unfolded. There was organized chaos as everyone helped set the table and bring food in from the kitchen. She threatened Jax with her bright red spatula once because he dared to stir the gravy without asking first, and she raised an eyebrow when Will added nearly a pound of butter to the potatoes he was mashing, but she didn't chase anyone out of her kitchen, and when everyone sat down together, she didn't have to ask for the sudden snap of quiet that happened when she reached for Jax's and Will's hands.

Zed didn't huff and roll his eyes when the prayer began, and both Finn and Jo lowered their heads, even though they didn't believe in God and considered prayer to be nothing more than fairy wishes. With the possible exception of Jay, everyone at that table knew what day it was, and they weren't taking from or mocking the thing that gave Aubrey the most comfort. She wanted a prayer of thanks over the food she and Aisha had prepared, gratitude for their lives together, and they were giving it for her.

I couldn't see Will's face, but I knew his eyes were closed. He'd once been as much an atheist as his parents, but over the years Aubrey had given him hope that there was something else out there. He thought he was more of an agnostic now, willing to entertain the idea that there was a God or at least a life after this one. When the prayer was over, his *amen* was clear, not the rote whisper of his younger years when Jax begged him to go along with her request to pray before the meals they shared, and he leaned toward Aisha to plant a kiss at her temple.

It took less than the beat of a heart for the chatter to begin. I tried to pick one conversation to follow, but they were loud and I only managed to catch snippets. Oz, Zed, and Jay had two classes together and answered parental questions about the workload. Finn picked Aisha's brain about a math problem that was eluding him, and Jo poked at him because it was something he should be able to figure out. Jay mentioned a girl named Zara, and that caught both Will and Aisha's attention. Aubrey was grateful that they'd all been doing homework at her kitchen table most afternoons, though she still didn't see as much of them as she liked.

Drew was the only quiet one. He half-listened to the talk swirling around him, but his attention drifted, his brain retreating to a problem that wouldn't leave him alone. He was quiet through dinner and well into dessert when he realized there was a bowl of cherry Jell-O in front of him. He picked it up and looked at it curiously, turning the bowl around, squinting as he examined it.

The chatter became a murmur. Drew lowered the bowl a bit, and then stuck his finger into the center of his dessert, wiggling it a bit before pulling it back out. He turned the bowl again and stuck his finger back in, pulling it out and pushing it back in, until Aubrey threw a dinner roll at him.

He blinked rapidly, unsure of what had just happened.

"Stop finger fucking your food," Jax said. "The Queen finds it obscene."

She kicked him under the table.

Jax, not Drew.

"I wasn't—" He sighed and set the bowl down. "It stays cool. Slide your finger in, and you feel a layer of warmth, but then the coolness seeps through."

"Uh huh," Jax grunted. He leaned his elbows on the table and was obviously trying to not laugh. "I generally prefer the things I stick appendages into to remain warm."

"Oh my god, Dad," Oz groaned, while Zed and Jay snorted.

With a sigh, Drew looked at Will. "I was considering its cooling properties."

"It would liquify if exposed to heat long enough," Will said.

"This particular structure. But if we could get a similar substance and tweak it? A double whammy of staying cool while being conductive?"

"Yes, but perhaps now is not the time," Will said gently. "And really, stop sticking appendages into your dessert."

"You should talk," Jo mumbled.

"Really, Mom?" Will leaned forward to look past Finn so he could see her. "Now?"

She had everyone's attention and I was hoping she would rat him out, but Aisha knew what she was talking about and hurriedly asked Jay if he had any homework, sparing Will from his mom.

"We all have homework," Jay grumbled. "Major test this week."

"Sophia and Zara are coming over later to study," Zed said. Then, as if it suddenly occurred to him that he hadn't mentioned it before, he asked Aubrey if that was all right. "We can go down to the staff kitchen and stay out of the way."

"No, we can't," Jay said. "Zara can only come if there are going to be parents around."

"Seriously?" Oz asked. "She's your age, right?"

Jay nodded. "A little older, actually. Her dad is super protective."

Aisha remembered her from an algebra class. "Her father is the consummate hovering parent, but he's not unreasonable. He lost his wife and another child when Zara was still in grade school, and he's just...terrified." She looked at Jay. "If he needs one of us nearby, then we'll be near."

"Still," Oz grumbled. "She's eighteen."

"I get it," Jay said. "He's not a dick about it, either. I mean, he asked if we'd have parents here. It's not like he snapped and ordered us to drum up supervision."

"But she won't come if there isn't," Zed pointed out.

"Yeah, well, she gets it, too."

Drew forgot about his dessert. "So. Girlfriend or just a friend?" he asked Jay.

"Just a friend. So far. I think."

Zed snorted. "They have lunch together every day. They study together between classes. And he shows up for her gym class even though he's not actually taking the class."

Jay shrugged. "It's a jogging class. They run around campus. I run with them. The instructor doesn't care."

"He runs with her the whole time, but he can't always keep up," Zed said, laughing. "He's *literally* chasing her."

"Says the guy who's taking an intro to piano class just because Sophia is."

"Really, Zed?" Aubrey sighed. "You've been playing for years."

"Just padding my GPA."

Jax reminded Aubrey that he once took a class in the history of the modern royal family. "There was this smoking hot post-grad student taking the class who flirted with me outrageously, and I knew I wouldn't mind how easy the course would be."

"You nearly drove a professor to quit his job, Jackson. I don't think a week went by when you didn't challenge his version of events. He was a nervous wreck by the semester break."

"Well, he was wrong a lot."

Aubrey turned back to Zed. "Take the class, but don't be obnoxious. Don't work ahead of everyone else, and don't show off."

"How far into your relationship was it?" Oz asked.

"Year and a half?" Jax answered. "We were already engaged and planning the wedding."

"Good thing, too," Aubrey said. "If I had seen that arrogant side of you before, we might not have gotten that far."

"You knew he was an insufferable ass, Aubrey," Will said.

"You both were. Really, why did I stick around?"

Jax grinned and raised an eyebrow.

"Don't you dare," she said, jabbing her pointy finger at him.

"We already know he was a horndog, Mom," Oz said. "Not a surprise if you were sleeping with him by then."

"And not something we're discussing!"

"We could go back to whatever Will was doing," Drew said. "Jo? You were saying?"

"Sure, go down that road," Will said. "But remember, I know more about the two of you—" he pointed to both Drew and Oz "—than you likely want shared with the masses."

Oz scowled and turned to Drew. "What the hell have you been telling him?"

"He's bluffing."

"The whipped cream slide," Will said.

"Oh, good lord," Aubrey huffed, ignoring Oz's and Drew's laughter. "I miss the days when you were all little and the worst thing I heard was that Drew threw something at Oz or Zed peed down the stairwell."

"Who says I haven't done that lately?" Zed asked.

With that, Aubrey declared dinner over and said that everyone over twenty-one was invited to sit on the balcony to drink Jax's expensive scotch. Anyone not old enough to drink was clearing the table and doing dishes. Even though I was technically old enough to go onto the balcony, I couldn't drink, so I stayed in the kitchen and waited until Jax was out of sight, then jumped onto his empty chair and sniffed at his plate.

You won't tell on me if I lick some of his gravy, will you?

Drew slid a clean bread plate toward me and drizzled some gravy out of the bowl onto it. "No reason you should have someone else's scraps, Wick. You can have some chicken, too. None of us will tell Mr. B that you ate at the table. Or at his spot."

They fed me bits and pieces while they cleaned up, and when the dishes were done and after Sophia and Zara arrived, Drew moved me to the breakfast bar where I could see. He sat in Jax's chair so he could hear if I said anything.

He wasn't going to repeat it because he didn't want to freak Zara out—Zed had told Sophia that Drew could understand me but wasn't sure she believed it—but he still wanted to make sure I was heard.

"Your dad's okay if there's not an uber-adult hovering?" Zed asked Zara. "One of them will sit in the living room where they can see us if you want. It might be Will's dad, but he counts."

"This is fine," Zara said. Her cheeks flushed, almost the flaming color of her hair, but she laughed.

The idea of Finn as their supervisor amused Oz. "Finn is not a supervisor. He's more of a friend than he is Will's dad."

"My dad just wants someone responsible close by, that's all. It's not like he wants someone standing by the table, watching every move we make."

"Will would do it," Drew said. "He'd be happy to sit here and stare at us, quietly correcting any mistakes we made in our studies, and if biology was one of the subjects, he would draw a disturbingly realistic human model. Guts, gonads, and all."

"He doesn't embarrass easily, does he?" Zed mused.

Jay chuckled. "Understatement. I've asked him things that my dad would run screaming from. Hell, things my mom would answer if she could without dying from embarrassment. He just answers, like it's no big deal."

"What the hell kind of things are you thinking about, Jaybird?" Zed asked, laughing.

"Well, there was a question about spontaneous, unwanted erections. He was pretty sympathetic and surprisingly helpful."

Sophia groaned, "Jesus, Jay."

"What? It happens."

Zara's cheeks flushed again. "At least you can talk to him. I asked my dad a pretty basic question a few years ago and he's still sputtering. His little girl can*not* be thinking about those things."

"Given the sheer amount of sex going on in our apartment, it's hard to avoid thinking about those things. Jesus, my mom..."

"Newlyweds," Oz chuckled.

"It's not like it's nonstop banging. And seriously, hearing them in the next room laughing their asses off with each other is a hell of a lot better than having to hear my dad and George rage-fuck in the next room. Will and my mom are having fun and seriously laugh a lot. I just pop my headphones on and go to sleep."

He'd thought living with Will would be awkward, but within a couple of weeks realized he was more comfortable living here than he'd been living downstairs from George and his father. "Mock me if you want, but there's a lot of love here. I never feel like I'm in his way. Hell, every morning before he leaves, he kisses me on the cheek, kisses my mom, and tells us both that he loves us. And it doesn't feel weird."

You guys better not make fun of him.

"I keep telling Will he'd be a great dad," Drew said.

"He is. Well, I haven't given them any real crap to deal with yet, but he didn't lose his shit with me before they got married, when I called him an asshole or when I tried slamming doors in his face."

"You didn't," Zara said.

"I had a difficult month or two," Jay admitted.

"Your dad and George were splitting up right at the same time your mom was getting super close to Will," Oz said. "Everyone understood how hard the summer was for you."

Over the summer, Will took Jay to his own When for major surgery, things that Oz and Drew and Zed knew Jay didn't want known. I mentally awarded Oz a few points for giving him a reason other than being a jerk.

"Yeah. Anyway. You're right, Will's a great dad, and it would be great if they popped out a kid of their own."

"Will keeps saying he's just looking forward to all of us having kids," Oz said.

"You hop on that, all right?" Zed snorted. "Get married in a couple months, pop out the first one before your first anniversary."

"Yeah, no." Drew pretended to shiver. "No."

"Come on, have a kid," Zed urged. "You have help here. You could still finish school."

"I know," Oz said. "And don't think we haven't talked about that. But we really want to be the kind of parents we had, and for that I think we should wait a few years. When we're not still stupid."

"Come on," Zed sighed. "If you wait until you're not stupid, I'll never get to be an uncle."

That made her laugh. "Well, screw you, too."

Drew pointed right at Zed. "I don't know what you two are planning, but don't wait to cover your own asses. Get the implant. If you don't think you can go to your dad, then go to Will. He'll hook you up with Mass." He turned to Jay. "That goes for you, too. Do it before you need it."

"Hey, you're not my mom," Zed said, chuckling.

Jay blew air through his half-closed lips. "Fuck, I haven't even kissed a girl, Drew. I'm not exactly..." He half shrugged and looked at Zara. "There. That's a thing you know about me. I'm seventeen, and I haven't so much as held a girl's hand."

Zed jumped in before Zara could respond. "Nothing wrong with that. Some of us wish we'd had a little more self-control when we were younger."

"Younger," Sophia snickered. "Zed, you're young *now*."

"I know, but...yeah, you and I have to talk soon."

She cocked her head a little to the right. "I know you've dated. That's not a huge shock. I wasn't expecting the virginal prince and you damn well better not expect that from me, or we have a major problem because I had a *hell* of a lot of fun in high school."

"Maybe now's the time to tell you what an ass I was."

"That could take all night," Sophia teased.

"You have no idea." Zed grumbled, but he got up and held his hand out to her.

When they were in the living room, with Sophia on the sofa and Zed perched on the coffee table, Drew's phone rang.

"My mom," he said as he looked at the screen. "She's on video."

He and Oz went into Aubrey's office to take the call. That left Jay and Zara alone at the table, so I jumped over and headbutted him on the chin. If they had me to focus on, maybe he wouldn't feel awkward about telling her he'd never kissed anyone.

After a minute of petting me, without looking at him she said, "If it helps, I've never kissed anyone, either."

He perked up. "Really? But you were pretty popular in high school."

"Think about those guys, Jay. Are there any of them you could see me with? I only liked one, and he was too shy to even look at me most of the time."

"Lots of assholes in our class," he agreed. "I seriously couldn't stomach another year there."

"I hated the way they treated you and I wonder who they're picking on now. I mean, it wouldn't have been you if you'd gone back. You're not a tiny target anymore."

Jay turned in his seat. "You were always nice to me, even when it meant taking shit from other people for it. I noticed, you know."

"Really? I didn't think you had." Her eyes crinkled at the corners when she smiled at him. "There was a reason, and not just because I was nice to everyone."

He blinked.

"Too shy to look at me," she said.

"What? Me?"

"I had a crush on you going all the way back to seventh grade. Back when you actually would talk to me."

He blinked again. A lot.

"Are you still shy?" she asked.

"Um. Yeah, a little. Why?"

She set her hand on the back of his chair. "First kiss," she said simply. "I didn't want to waste it on anyone. But I'd like it to be you."

His eyes went wide. "Now?"

"We're alone. Unless you don't want—"

"HellyesIdo."

Great. Neither of you knows what you're doing. There's going to be a lot of slobber, and I can't even hand you a napkin.

I backed up a few inches, just in case. It was a nice kiss; they didn't bump noses or teeth, and it wasn't a hurried peck. It lasted just long enough for him to need a breath, and by then Oz was coming out of the office.

"We have gotten absolutely nothing accomplished here," she said as she sat down, pretending she hadn't seen anything. "Well, study-wise. Zed at least seems to be doing all right."

"I can't believe he's telling her about Rhonda while the rest of us are here to witness the potentially ugly end result."

"*Rhonda?*" Zara was surprised, but she kept her voice soft.

"Seriously? Zed's always been so sweet, I can't picture the two of them doing *anything*. Jay, did she ever, you know, zone in on you?"

He shook his head. "I don't think she's into guys that look like they're still twelve. I doubt she even noticed I was there."

"Well, she would have noticed you this year."

"Let her notice. I'm not interested."

"Good for you," Oz said.

"I'm not judging her," Jay said. "But Zed is my best friend, and I would never do that to him."

"Would Zed even care?" Zara asked. "It's not like Rhonda has actual boyfriends. Just...toys."

"He might not care, but I would."

Sophia must not have cared, either, because she grabbed the front of Zed's shirt and pulled him in for a long kiss.

"Oh, he needs to hurry up and turn eighteen," Oz said under her breath.

Jay laughed and asked why.

"Right now those two hooking up is technically illegal because of the age difference, but now that he's laid his cards out on the table—seriously, Jay, push him to see Mass and get the damned implant. He might want to be an uncle but I sure as hell don't want to be an aunt yet."

"I can try, but he's not gonna want to go into Mass's office and have that wind up on the news."

"Why?" Zara asked.

"Mass is a gender medicine specialist. People are idiots and will talk."

"He's the new family doctor," Oz said. "If it hits the news, that will be the first response released by PR. Mass heads up the practice with *all* the doctors and nurses currently vetted to treat members of this family. That goes for you, too, now. Mass is more than Will's friend, he's your doctor now."

"Yes, Mom."

"Jay."

"Fine, he's yours, too. Do you really want to go see him for a sore throat knowing what he has in his hands all day?"

"He washes his hands," Zara mused.

"Just saying."

"Who washes his hands?" Drew asked as he exited the office.

"Mass. After he handles peoples' junk."

"Huh. He didn't wash his after he whipped my dick out of the way and then grabbed your hand, did he?" he asked Oz.

"Wait," Jay said. "What the hell?"

"He refilled my implant, and then poked Oz's finger for a blood test."

"And he didn't actually handle you," Oz said.

"I could feel his breath on my nuts, Oz. That counts."

Zara giggled. "You guys get really personal with each other, don't you?"

"Yeah, sorry," Jay said.

"It wasn't a complaint. But you'd never hear my sister and me talking like this."

"It comes with having a brother," Oz said. "And a Jay."

"And Will," Jay pointed out.

"Will is never intentionally crude," Oz said.

Jay scoffed at that. "You've never overheard him in the next room with my mom. I mean, he's not any *good* at it but it makes her laugh and I think that's what matters to him."

"He's definitely happier than I've ever seen him," Oz said. "Your dad still okay with you moving here?"

"I think so. He's dating his fucking head off. I'm not even trying to keep up because every time I'm there he's with someone new." He scratched at his whiskers. "Most of them women, believe it or not."

"Whatever makes him happy," Drew said.

"Happy. Hell, if we ever encounter aliens, my dad will be the first one in line to hump one. Male, female, it won't matter. If he can figure out where all the parts go, he'll do it."

"God, don't tell my dad that," Zara said. "He's a little...stuffy."

"Oh, but I'd like to be at that introduction," Oz said. "'Mr. Hendricks, this is my dad, James. Alien humper.'"

"Yeah, no, we all know what Jay would say instead of humper," Drew snorted.

"Hey, I'm working on that. I promised Will I'd try to clean up my language a little. He's worried I'll offend the Queen."

Will's voice snapped at them from the entry. "How are we offending the Queen tonight?"

"Trying not to," Jay said. "I'm working on my f-bombs."

"Good." He went over to the sofa and poked Zed's back and told him to get the hell off Sophia. "You're supposed to be studying."

"I am," Zed said. "Biology."

"Then I suggest you change the course matter. Your mother was already upset once tonight by Drew engaging in inappropriate relations with his dessert."

"I had an idea," Drew protested. "It made me think about—"

"No," Oz said. "You're not thinking about work things anymore tonight. Once we're done here, I want your undivided attention for the rest of the night. No talking about nanobots or nanoprobes or heat dispersion. Leave work at, you know, work." She pushed away from the table. "In fact, come on. We're going to make my dad twitch and go into my room and sit at the window and watch people on Union Square, and we're not talking about anything remotely scientific."

"Just keep the door open, and your dad will be fine," Will called after them. He turned back to Jay. "If you want time to walk Zara home before her curfew, you'd better get going. If you don't think you have enough time to get there, ask the guard up front to call a car."

Jay thought they had plenty of time to walk there. Zed and Sophia left with them, but they'd left their tablets on the table. Will peeked at them—it was just untouched history notes—and turned them off.

They didn't study at all.

"Zed seemed to be mapping Sophia's dental work."

He told her about that girl from last year. She kissed him, so I don't think she's mad about it.

"Good for him."

And Drew wants you to take Zed to see Mass.

"I would prefer he asks his father."

*You know he won't, and he won't go on his own. And Jax gave
you permission.*

Will sighed. "What do you know about Jay and Zara?"

*He kissed her tonight. It was his first kiss, did you know that?
It was hers, too, and she said she'd waited because she wanted him
to be her first kiss.*

"Did you sense they want more?"

Not yet. I think Jay is shy about that.

"Probably not for long."

*Did you know that Jay likes hearing you make Aisha laugh?
He also wants to be a big brother.*

"Did he actually say that or are you inferring again?"

*He said it would be nice if you and Aisha had a kid of your
own. And that he thinks you're a great dad.*

"Huh. I think I would be a passable dad."

*No, he thinks you already are a great dad. To him. So don't
screw it up.*

*

After Zed and Jay left, and Oz had dragged Drew into her
bedroom—okay, he went willingly as long as she promised to
leave the door open and keep her pants on—I wound up on the
balcony. Jo and Finn were leaving, because it was dark out and
they were old; Jo declared that people their age needed to get
to bed early, but she pinched his butt when she said it so I don't
think she planned on going to sleep, and Will pretended not
to see that even though he thought it was both funny and a bit
disturbing.

He'd taken a fresh bottle of scotch outside. I took a sniff
to see if it was scotch to be savored or scotch to get drunk on;
this was something they were savoring. It smelled old and rich,
a bottle bought to share with friends, not something to get
hammered on for the hell of it.

Jax spun the ice cubes around in his glass and mused that
it was almost time to teach Drew how to appreciate fine scotch.
He was only a couple of months from turning 21, and Jax was
looking forward to dragging Drew to Fuzzy's on occasion.

"Ah, he'll never be much of a drinker and I don't want to push him," Will said. "Perhaps the focus should be on teaching him to drive. Then we can make him chauffeur us to bars outside the city center."

"He loves the cinnamon whiskey," Aisha reminded them.

"As much as I hate to say it," Aubrey said, "of the two of them, Oz is the one who will go drinking with you."

Jax nodded. "And I will enjoy that. But I would like to pull Drew away from here and from her every now and then. I know the boy well enough, but I'd like to get to know the man."

"When did that happen?" Aubrey scowled, though she didn't sound upset. "He was this goofy teenager and now he's so grown up."

"It happened somewhere between Denver and the Colorado-Kansas border," Will said. "He was almost there while we were in the safe house, but by the time we crossed in Kansas, that teenager only existed in his shadows. Zed is nipping at his heels. He often seems older than seventeen."

"And look at them now," Jax sighed. "It's making me feel old."

Zed told Sophia about that other girl.

"I know, Wick," Will said.

I bet Jax wants to know that.

"Then Zed will bring it up."

"Might as well tell me," Jax said. "What does Zed need to tell us?"

Will tapped the top of my head with his middle finger. "It's less a matter of need than it is that you would want to know. He told Sophia about the girl from last summer. She does not seem deterred by it. At least, when I walked in, they were unquestionably...close."

This time Aubrey sighed. "It's going the distance with those two, isn't it?"

"He does seem to be approaching this relationship with consideration."

"You know already," Jax grumbled.

Will shook his head. "No, I really don't."

"Yeah, yeah, everything has changed, anything can happen. Fine. Did future me have to put up with Governor Lopez for the rest of his life?"

Will shrugged lightly, but he didn't smile.

"Well, that's as noncommittal as it gets."

"Greet your future as it comes, Jax. I could recite the lengthy history that I was taught as a child, but it means nothing now. As I told Drew when he asked about his progeny, he might have sons, he might have daughters, he might have a puppy. I don't know."

No dogs. Tell him to get a cat.

"Wick, the offer is still open. I'll get you a cat of your own if you'd like."

"Another cat might have been preferable to the hover cart," Jax said. "And warning that he *had* the hover cart would have been appreciated. Do you know what it's like to walk down the hall at four in the morning and suddenly have Wick screaming toward your face? I actually shrieked."

Will picked me up and set me on his lap. "Are you riding around in the middle of the night?"

No one can yell at me to slow down in the middle of the night.

It amused Aubrey. "The morning after your wedding, I was in the kitchen making breakfast and all the sudden I felt Wick sniffing at my ear. It was disconcerting, to say the least."

"He's also been teasing the guard," Jax said. "He hovers at the foot of the stairs, staring at the door. I've come out of the elevator more than once to find a guard blocking it, telling him he's not allowed outside on the cart. Last week he was there, so I shoved him into the elevator and sent it upstairs—two minutes later he was zooming down the stairs heading right for the door guard. I was right outside and heard the poor kid shriek 'you can't go outside, the King will kill me!'"

I wouldn't really take it outside. You told me not to.

"Then why torment the guard?" Will asked.

Because it's funny.

"All right, then. He does it because it amuses him."

"They disabled the sensors that automatically open the

door because of him," Jax complained. He wagged his pointy finger at me. "Stop teasing the guard. They need to know they can count on you to follow the rules, and if you do get out by accident, they'll be running after you. They know you're more than a pet. Respect that."

"Twenty-five years ago," Aubrey said to Aisha, "did you ever imagine that the men we married would have arguments with the cat? Or even long conversations?"

"Hon, I never thought that *I* would be having conversations with a cat. Even when Will's not around, I spend a lot of time talking to Wick."

She guesses right at what I'm saying a lot. It's impressive.

"Guessing that you want something to eat is not impressive, Wick. It's expected."

Be nice, or I'll tell you what she says about you. And how did we go from talking about how grown up Drew is now to picking on me?

"Because picking on you is more fun than discussing Drew's current level of maturity."

Jax leaned forward in his chair. "All right, cat. Something I've wanted to know since Will admitted he understands you. How frustrating was it for you when I was little and had no clue what you were saying? You were a mouthy little thing until I was twelve or so. I think you gave up."

I thought you didn't like me. Then Will showed up and told me that you were like all the grownups. You didn't know how to understand.

"I'm sorry, Wick." He looked at Will. "When did you tell him?"

"Initially, after the bridge incident. I held your backpack while your mother tried to smother you. I peeked inside and told Wick he was all right, and he told me that he'd tried to tell you climbing the bridge was a bad idea. I explained it as quickly as I could. I needed to remind him a few years later."

I was already starting to forget you then, the day on the bridge.

"I know, Wick. It had been almost four years for you since

you'd made your way through the portal in the closet. Finn warned me that you might slip into a gray area."

"What?" Jax leaned back. "What closet portal?"

"There's a small one in the back of Oz's closet. Wick used it for a time, making sure he knew how to move through a portal on his own when the time came."

That was your closet, too. Does he know that?

"You did quite well," Will said, ignoring the question.

"Well," Jax said as he refilled their glasses, "it's a good thing we stayed friends all these years. I'd hate to have to battle you for custody of Wick, even though I would win."

"Ruling in your own favor would be cheating."

"So?"

Good thing you plan on staying here.

"Indeed, Wick. I have no desire to pick up and move."

"You're moving upstairs," Jax reminded him. "Should be ready just before Christmas."

"Have you told Oz and Drew that you also renovated the other guest suite?"

"No, and we're not going to," Aubrey said. "They can have it after they've been married for a while."

Jax nodded. "When Zed is ready for his own place, they move upstairs, he takes your old place. Jay takes Drew's. Or swap, whatever, I don't care. Whoever needs the most space."

"Roommates," Aubrey said.

That made Aisha chuckle. "We're planning their lives without their input."

"They don't have the luxury of some decisions," Jax said. "Here, they're protected. I won't force them to stay, but I will strongly encourage it."

Sure, keep the entire royal family in one convenient spot for someone to blow up.

Jax scowled when Will told him what I said.

"He's not wrong," Will said.

Jax leaned over and looked me in the eyes. "No one moves until I'm ready for them to move. And when I'm ready for that kind of change, it will probably be Aubrey and I. Across the street, where I can spy on them all."

Will lifted his glass to that. "Father of the year, right here. There's not a thing creepy about that."

*

Jax and Aubrey headed off to bed, leaving Will and Aisha on the balcony alone. They moved to the bench seat but weren't sitting too close and their hands were in full view, so Drew felt comfortable coming out and taking Jax's vacated seat. Oz had fallen asleep, so he was going to enjoy some fresh air for a bit before heading downstairs.

"Jax won't have you beheaded if you crawl into her bed," Will said. "He probably wouldn't notice."

"I would. I made him a promise. I'm sticking to it."

"Just a couple more months," Aisha said.

"That presumes I don't piss her off too badly before then. If I could get my brain to shut up for an hour or two…"

"Now I know where my father gets it," Will mused. "His brain runs a full ten minutes ahead of himself. And he's easily distracted by the shiny objects that new ideas bring."

Drew wanted to laugh, but it wasn't funny. He didn't like the distractions, and he was aware that Oz was becoming increasingly frustrated by it. "The stupidest things set me off. We can be talking about something and all the sudden I have these notions that are just tickling the back of my mind, but they won't come forward and I can't seem to stop myself from trying to pull them out."

"Hence, the molestation of your dessert tonight," Will said.

"Seriously. I had this flash in my head, picturing a dish filled with the nanobots, and something about the Jell-O made me think of…something. Hell. It was the temperature. Stick your finger in, and it's cool. Leave your finger in, and it's slow to warm up."

"Leave it in long enough and the heat from your skin will liquify the gelatin."

"I know. But there was still something about it."

Aisha moved her hand from Will's leg to his arm, and subtly tapped the back of his hand. His eyebrow twitched, but he didn't turn to look at her, and Drew didn't notice.

"You've been focused on bringing down the operating temperature of the computer array," Will reminded Drew. "And you accomplished that. Perhaps worry less about heat and more about school."

"And sleep," Aisha said. "Drew, you're exhausted. Your days have been longer than they need to be. Go get some rest and try to think about anything other than work."

"Easier said than done. I've started dreaming about the freaking nanobots." He sighed and got up. "But, yeah. I'm going to bed."

When he was down the stairs, Aisha said, "How close is he to connecting the gelatin to the nanobots?"

"Closer than I thought," Will answered. "And yes, you're right, we need to tell Jay to not overly explain the surgical tank to Drew. Or anyone else for that matter. Drew is aware that Jay was floated in a tank for his surgery, but he doesn't have the specifics, and this is something he needs to pursue without any helpful suggestions."

She slipped her fingers between his. "I owe Jay's surgery to Drew, don't I?"

"The substance in the tank was not Jell-O," Will joked.

She leaned away from him. "No. Really?"

"Ah. I detect sarcasm."

That made her laugh. "I just meant...look, he's focusing on all these tiny details, and to me they all add up to the same things I saw when Jay was in that tank. The nanobots, the way Drew talks about using them to not only help create the holograms, but aid in computing power, and he was looking at the Jell-O like, 'this is it. I don't know what it will do, but it's going to be important.' Jax poked at him for what he was doing to it, but all I saw was the moment when the spark was lit, and that will eventually become the thing that gives my son the life he deserves. Just tell me the truth, Will. I owe that to Drew, don't I?"

"The world will owe Drew credit for many things. More than I know of. And he's years ahead of where he was, in my timeline."

"How so?"

"He'll never become Midlam's King," Will said. "He doesn't have the distractions of a protracted war. All bets are off, and I truly cannot wait to see his notions come to fruition."

3

"Will locked me out of the workshop," Drew explained to Finn. "Oz is with her mom doing wedding things, and I've studied so much today that my brain hurts." He side-glanced at Will, who was leaning against the island in the center of Finn's lab. "Since you were planning a video conference with my Dad?"

"Didn't come to visit me," Finn groused lightly. "I see how it is. Fine, use me."

Finn led them down the metal staircase to the third level, where the prototype for the transporter lived. There were four different versions of it, and they all resembled the one we'd seen in Richard's Dayton lab. A circular metal gate rose from the center of a twenty-foot-long shiny platform, with wires and lights and things that beeped and made my ears hurt.

"You," Finn said to me, "no going anywhere near those. Every time we send something through, it comes out the other side broken. I don't want you taking any chances."

Drew, on the other hand, was allowed to walk around the largest of the gates. "This is a lot like the one on the bridge, isn't it?"

Will nodded.

A little over a year ago, thirty-year-old Finn popped up with a solid case of amnesia, and Will pretended he had no clue. Once Finn had spotty memories of who he was and When he belonged, Will conceived of the gate and used it to send his father home. It functioned as a time portal without being on the path of the portal tunnel, and Finn was sure it was the key to developing the first useful transporter.

Drew's father, an engineer, was helping him. He was on the

receiving end of Finn's efforts, which so far included a disturbing number of inverted bowling balls.

Richard called right on time; Drew waved at him from behind Finn but waited quietly while they discussed their next trial, and while they talked he examined the control console. It looked like every other panel I'd seen; lots of buttons and levers, and a monitor off to the side. There was nothing special about it, but he still had to resist the urge to press buttons for no reason other than to see what might happen.

We might go -boom- so stop looking.

When he heard Richard tell Finn that the math was all fine, Drew snorted and whispered to Will, "Maybe they should have Aisha double check it."

"Already did."

"I can hear you back there," Richard said. "How's your own work going, Drew?"

"I can make a tree that feels kinda real," he said, stepping back to the monitor. "And a cat. That's progress, I suppose."

"He's developed texture. He's working on depth," Will added.

"Texture's a step further than anyone else I know of." Richard looked at Finn. "He's making better progress than we are."

"Your project is more complex," Drew said. "I mean, if it wasn't, transporters would have been a thing a couple hundred years ago. People have been working on them for about half a millennium, haven't they?"

"Off and on," Finn said. "There have been periods of technological stagnation."

There had also been times, Richard said, where single atoms were thought to have been successfully transported into space, but there was no supporting evidence. And the truth was that it might be a dead end; no one managed it in Finn's lifetime, which told Richard they might be barking up a dead tree.

"Or just taking the wrong approach," Drew said. "And anyway, what about the moral implications?"

"How so?"

"To do what you want to do, you have to disassemble a person and then reassemble them on the other end. Basically, you're killing someone and gluing all the bits back together, counting on it being the same person."

Richard nodded. "And there you have the crux of stagnation in research. It's also the main reason we're focusing on inanimate matter. Who cares if we kill a thousand bowling balls?"

"Why bowling balls?"

"There was one lying around," Finn said with a shrug. "It's also a multilayered substance, something that let us know right from the start that it was turning inside out."

Drew turned to Finn. "You pretty much transported through a gate. Why not do it that way?"

"That requires a transponder and an enormous amount of power. And in the end, it's still pushing something through time, not space. I left here on the bridge and arrived home on the bridge."

Drew glanced at the gate. "All right. How does a portal work? It moves someone through time, right? But there's also space involved. You step into the portal, wind up in the space between, and then out the other side."

Finn went over to a desk and grabbed a sheet of paper and a well-chewed-upon pencil, and he poked a hole in the paper. He showed Drew the little flap that was left behind and told him to imagine that the hole was the portal, and the flap was time. He then curled one end of the paper under itself and used the pencil to show him the simplest way a portal worked.

"The pencil is you. You step through the portal—" he pushed the pencil through, and then moved it in a loop to the other side of the paper "—and come out the other side. The flap closes behind you, for all intents and purposes, until you make the return trip."

"But how?"

"The portal is essentially a tear in the fabric of time," Will said. "You don't really step through it, so much as time bubbles around you at that point. It's more that you're warping time around you, not that you're moving through it."

"Except you can stop in the tunnel. You got stuck there."

"Because there was nowhere else for me to go. Essentially, the flap had closed, leaving me...incomplete."

"But still. I don't get why they just can't do it the way you got Finn home. I mean, yeah, there's all that power needed, but nothing says stuff needs to be transported outside a ship. Use the gates, stick transponders in them, and change the parameter from time to space. Or even add it, just time shift for like a second or two. If you can bounce things off null space in time, surely you can navigate direction, too."

Finn folded his arms. "We're attempting direct point-to-point transport. Null space has not been part of the equation. That technology technically doesn't exist yet."

"So invent it. You're gonna do it someday anyway. Jump on it."

"Is that possible?" Richard asked Finn. "I know you've been wary about bringing data from your own time to this one, but is it outside the realm of feasible?"

Finn's eyebrow's knotted together.

"Anything's possible now, Dad," Will said. "We've already veered from the course time had laid out. Do what you want, see what happens."

As long as what happens isn't blowing us all the hell up.

"We'd have to tighten the security here," Finn mused. "If I bring anything from home to help us here...it can't leave this lab. I won't risk it."

"Say the word," Will said as Drew took a few moments to say goodbye to his father. "I'll arrange for guards."

Outside, on Union Square, Drew suddenly stopped.

"What did I just do? Did I just say something that puts them ahead of us? You wanted to nail down personal transporters first, and I opened my big mouth."

Will shrugged it off. "Yes, you nudged him along farther than I would have, but we have other things to focus on. If we drop the transporter project along the way, it won't matter."

"He's already got it, Will. You said when you were stuck in the portal that you were incomplete. That portal freaking transported you. He just needs—"

"I know."

"It'll occur to him. I didn't mean to screw up the one thing you wanted to do."

"What I want," Will said, prodding him toward home, "is for you to develop a better sense of focus. Concentrate on the nanobots, and for god's sake, stop finger fucking your food in front of the Queen."

"I'm never living that down, am I?"

"Not a chance."

Instead of heading across the Square and to home, they went to the little corner bakery. Will wanted coffee that Aisha had not made— "I love her, but I swear, I need to find a gentle way to ban her from the kitchen" —and Drew was too twitchy to go home and not work.

"Read a book," Will suggested. "Get your mind off the things your mind is stuck on."

Drew had tried that; he'd opened several different novels but couldn't get past the first chapters. The words in front of him would blur, his brain would click into motion, and he stared at the page for long stretches of time before realizing that he was pondering possibilities and not reading.

It was a new problem for him; he'd always been able to fall into a book. He'd also never had a problem focusing on the things Oz was talking about, but in the last couple of weeks she was expressing more and more frustration that he was sitting right there with her while his mind was off somewhere else.

He pressed fingers to his forehead. "I swear, I'm making an effort to stay present and I'm making time for her, but I just can't turn my damned brain off, and I'm afraid I'm going to blow it."

Will wanted to tell him he wouldn't, but he knew how close his own parents came to parting over Finn's obsessive work habits.

Tell him about them.

"About who?" Drew asked me.

"Your grandson," Will said with a sigh. "You know Finn has issues with getting lost in his work."

"I thought they worked it out."

"They did. But it took my mother admitting to me that she felt him slipping away and in turn I showed him what happened to their future selves. She would have eventually left him, Andrew. I know I told you to chase rabbits down holes in order to find the things you want to work on but stay away from that particular one. Oz comes first. Oz, school, work, in that order."

"I'm trying."

Try harder.

"That's helpful, Wick," Drew groaned. "It'll get better after we're married. If we're living in one place without—"

"No," Will said. "Living together will make it easier to take for granted that she's there and that there's always later to engage."

"Personal experience?"

"Observation." He hesitated. "Not for Oz's ears, understood?"

Drew nodded.

"I watched for too long as her grandfather made that assumption. He needed to be there for his wife far more than he was, and he always assumed there would be more time. One day turned into another, and then yet another, until their marriage became more days apart than together. There *should* have been more time. He understands now that had he been able to take days at a time, hours every day, he would have seen the changes in her and understood that more was going on than marital boredom."

"And it wouldn't have been too late. How does anyone die from cancer, anyway? Pop a few pills, and you're fine."

"When found early enough, depending on the type. A month sooner, I think, and her brain would have been repairable. She failed to recognize the symptoms and Eli didn't note changes in her behavior. None of us did."

You did. But you were afraid to say anything.

"She and I had a complicated relationship, Wick. And we're getting off point. Don't make the mistakes that Eli and my father have made. Figure out how to make Oz your ultimate priority, Andrew. You need her more than you need an understanding of nanotechnology, and Oz needs to know she matters to you more than work."

"Yeah, but—"

"No buts. She understands that you're trying to lay the foundation for a career to support your family. She'll be patient for a while, years even. But by then it becomes habit, and it's a hard habit to break."

"Now you're speaking from experience."

"Limited experience, but yes. I feel hardwired to move when the King needs something. It's what I've done since I was your age. Aisha comes first now, and it will take effort to tell Jax no every now and then."

"Are you even allowed to do that? I mean, I know he's your best friend and all that, but he's still King."

"We're both feeling our way through these changes. He understands."

He's jealous, too. He wants to be able to say no and stay home and play with Aubrey.

"Indeed, Wick. He never wanted to be King. He only wanted to be Mr. Blackshear, history teacher."

"Yeah, I get that."

Will leaned back in his chair. "Be honest. Is the fact that you're not going to become Midlam's King the reason why you're so anxious to immerse yourself in this project? You don't need to feel guilty about that. It's what you and Oz wanted."

It was what they wanted, but none of it happened the way they expected, and everything had changed. "She doesn't want to be Queen any more than I wanted to be King. But she accepted that it was going to happen, and she's never complained about it. She's sucking it up and honoring her promise, and I feel guilty that I was so willing to step away from the one I made. And the end goal has changed. Part of why we wanted to end the monarchy was to keep our kids, whether we had them with each other or not, from being stuck the way we were."

"It's the burden royal children have had to bear throughout known history."

"Yeah, and a lot of them were either total dicks about it or they abused the position. We've studied our family histories, Will. We know that none of the royalty born from the former US came into this wanting it. King Norval didn't run for the job, but he was elected anyway. In Midlam, Queen Sariah ran, but reluctantly. That made everyone after them held to a position they might not want. There could have been another way."

"There could have been, but this is the choice the people made. Norval could have refused but understood why he was pressed into service. Sariah agreed to run because she knew it was the best thing for Midlam. The people wanted parity, and they knew in them it could be achieved. And your choice could still be to end it."

"After talking to the older versions of us? It feels like a selfish choice. We'd walk away and have the private life we want, and the people suffer. It did sound like too many suffered, Will."

They were quiet for a while. Drew sat with his elbows on the table and head in his hands, and Will sipped at his coffee, studying the man who would become his great-grandfather. The silence wasn't uncomfortable; they had reached the point where they could sit together and not say a word, and it was fine. Still, I felt like Will had more to say, but was giving Drew time to stop feeling sorry for himself.

"Have you ever wondered why I'm so involved in how Pacifica is run?" he finally asked. "Why Jax has me sit in on meetings that are otherwise so tightly secure than only those who absolutely need to be are included? Why I bounce from one agency to another, and why he consults me on matters that are only his to rule upon?"

"You're his advisor."

Will nodded. "But have you ever known another King or Queen to have an individual so deeply involved? Your own mother had no counterpart. Even your father was never as involved in Midlam's rule as I am in Pacifica's. My involvement goes beyond his desire to have someone upon whom Oz can rely if something happens to him."

Well, now you're just bragging.

"I guess I never really thought about it." Drew sighed and sat up straight. "You're the Emperor."

"Nonetheless, mixed in with all the little reasons, Jax has one fundamental purpose for giving me such wide access."

"He's lazy," Drew said lightly.

"Well." Will grinned. "Perhaps. He understood, before Eli abdicated, that he never wanted to spread himself so thin that he would fail to give Aubrey the attention she was owed. He knew his father was kept from being with his mother as often as he wanted because of the job. By sharing his responsibilities with me, allowing me to take care of the smaller details, he has a bit more time for her and for his children."

Drew didn't get where Will was going with it.

"The other versions of you had no Emperor, Andrew. They had no one to share the responsibilities of ruling two countries, and they did rule two, for many years. Their Jax did what he could, but he was burnt out by war and grief, and Aubrey needed him. You and Oz won't have two countries with fundamentally separate governments to juggle, and you won't have to do it alone. If Oz chooses to keep the monarchy, I'll be here to help in any capacity she needs, and her father will be more available. And that's presuming he steps down. He might not."

"So Oz might not become queen."

"She will, eventually. It might not be until you're both very old."

"Has Mr. B hinted that he's not abdicating in the next decade or so?"

"We haven't discussed it in anything but abstract terms. I do think it's safe to assume that because the circumstances are different, he'll hold the throne for quite some time."

"If he dies as King, he'll be the first since Norval."

Will nodded.

"I'm not sure if I want to hope for that or not. I mean, he wants a life with just Mrs. B for a while, doesn't he? A real retirement?"

"He'll carve out time as he eases Oz into the position and gives her more responsibilities. What he wants most is for his children to have normal, happy lives. And you can help him with that by not becoming my father. You have time for all of this, Drew. There's no hurry to invent the better hologram, nor a hurry to get to anything else we've discussed."

"Except beating your dad to the transporter."

"I'd happily give that up if it means you learn better time management. As I am learning, it's not always easy to keep focus at home, but I'm also learning it's very much worth the effort."

Drew nodded again.

"Good. Now, tell me what's been swirling around in your head. Get it out of your system now, before Oz and Aubrey come home."

I curled up on the table. Drew was off like a shot, and it was going to be a long conversation.

*

Drew was still talking when Aisha took the chair near Will's. I'm not sure how long it had been—it could have been an hour, it could have been three; I slept through most of it—but Will didn't look bored. I had a vague notion that he'd been asking questions of Drew, trying to help him pull ideas from the back of his brain, which meant that he was at least a little bit interested and not just being polite. Aisha kissed Will before she sat down and said she didn't want to interrupt, even though I think she really did.

"Drew was explaining some of the things he wants to explore," Will told her. "He may have come up with a way to utilize data sharing among several computers to enhance his projections without multiplying lag time and without creating additional heat."

"This is going to go right over my head," she mused. "I'll pet Wick while you two make me feel unintelligent."

"I think I told him everything already," Drew said. "The problem is how I get from the theoretical idea to being able to implement it. I feel like I actually have to invent something to get from point A to point B."

Will raised an eyebrow. "Or perhaps you need to concentrate on your studies. The answers are probably there. Someone else may have invented the one thing you need most."

"Always comes back to school for you, doesn't it?" Drew grumbled.

"Oz, school, work." Will ticked those off on his fingers. "Don't give her a reason—"

"I know, I know." He pushed away from the table and stood up. "I'm not doing anything to make her change her mind about me. God, if she did? My heart would shit all over itself."

"Well, there's a pleasant image," Will said as Drew headed for home. "How did your meeting go?"

She'd left the apartment early in the morning for work things, even though it was the weekend and there wouldn't be any kids to teach. She wasn't happy about it—why the hell did they schedule in-service meetings at seven in the damned morning on a day off?—but she seemed excited now.

"The in-service was a waste of time," she said. "It was the meeting after that I need to tell you about."

He turned his chair so that she knew she had his attention.

"All right, you already know that when Jay and I moved back to San Francisco one of the first things I applied for was a position at the university. There weren't any openings, but I've renewed the application every year and have kept my CV updated in their system."

There were fifteen applicants for three newly-opened teaching slots in the math department. "I want this job, Will. Hell, I need this job. If I stay at the high school, sooner or later I'm going to clock one of those little bastards."

Every day that ticked on, she was more annoyed with her students. She stood at the front of the class filled with disinterested teenagers, many of whom were complicit in tormenting Jay throughout the three years he'd been there. "Most of the kids are fine, wonderful even, and I know they had nothing to do with how picked-on Jay was. But so many others *were*, and the majority of my students are only there because they need another math class in order to graduate. They don't care about what they learn, which means it's hard as hell to get them to listen, and I'm tired of it."

Will leaned over and kissed her. "You'll get the job. I have no doubt."

"Don't you dare use any influence you might have to get it for me."

"I have no influence anywhere in the school system, regardless of the level. You're a good teacher, I've heard that from more than one source. And you don't have to keep teaching high school if it no longer makes you happy. Quit. Find something else if you want to do. Or not. Retire if you like."

"I have to work, Will."

"Only if you want to."

"I have a son to put through school. I'm not dropping all that on James."

"We can afford his tuition and anything else he needs."

"I—"

"We," Will insisted. "I'm not keen on the notion of separate finances, Enzo. Jay's expenses are our expenses. School, food, clothing, anything he needs and things he simply wants. And to that matter, he needs an allowance."

She leaned back in her chair, arms crossed. "One thing at a time. We've never discussed money, Bilbo. I just assumed I'd continue to pay for Jay's needs and pop for a fair share of the groceries."

"Then we need to discuss finances. You need to know where everything we own is, how much, and how to access it."

She snorted. "I have a cash account, that's it. One. I'll add you to it. Go wild at the bookstore...for about five minutes."

"Your money is at greater risk if I peruse the Kovlov's catalog. What about an allowance for Jay?"

"James and I talked about it a few times, but it's been easier to give him money as he needs it. He doesn't ask for much and what he does is reasonable."

Will didn't think that was enough and that he might not ask. "He's now in college, with college-level needs...and a potential girlfriend on the horizon. You've already told him you don't want him working until he's gotten through at least a year of school, so he has no other options. He won't ask for the kind of money he'll need for social obligations."

"I can talk to—"

"Do we need permission from James to do this? It's a simple enough matter. We sit down with Jay and determine how much he'll need each month and expect him to learn to budget his money. Does this need to become anything more?"

"He'll want to contribute."

The look on Will's face was pained. "Please, just let me do this. I understand, James is his father, and by all means tell him about it, but give me this one thing."

She leaned over to kiss him. "All right, I get it."

"Good. I'm not sure I do, but still."

"Sweetheart—" another kiss "—you're stuck between your promise to not get between James and me where Jay is concerned and being a real parent to him. So yes, you get this one. James can suck it up."

"Thank you. And if James feels pushed aside, tell him that eventually Jay's going to need a car. He can do that. Get the car."

"Sure, that'll go over well. 'James, we're giving Jay five hundred a month for the hell of it. Now you need to drop three times as much on a car he'll drive a grand total of four miles a day.'"

They play-argued about it for half an hour. Will was most animated when he was advocating on Jay's behalf; Drew was right, he'd be a great dad. I knew deep down he wanted to be. The key wasn't making sure he grasped that. The key was making sure he knew he was ready for that.

4

After dinner, Jay went upstairs to study with Zed. Will collected his financial information and set it on the table; Aisha pulled her account up on her tablet and handed it to him, mumbling that it wasn't impressive, but teachers don't get paid much. Teachers with kids feel it even more.

She glanced at his tablet and told him he needed to divide them up because she had no idea what she was looking at. He pulled up a page on his tablet and then handed it to her, telling her it was the base summary.

"Ninety percent of my income comes from investments," he said. "Salary is on top, real estate second line, stocks and other investments third, fourth, and fifth." He went on, and her eyes widened. "Left column toward the bottom are trust funds set aside for Andrew, Oz, and Zed. That's money I don't touch unless I need to move something to a better yielding investment. The right column is cash savings." He swiped to another page. "Cash-ready accounts. You can do whatever the hell you want with these. Well, you can do whatever the hell you want with any of it, except for the trust funds. And I would appreciate prior discussion if it's property you want to dispose of."

She blinked a few times. "How the hell, Will?"

"I haven't had anyone else to spend it on," he said. "I'd also like to open a trust for Jay with an amount commensurate to what the other kids already have."

She began shuffling through the information, her eyebrows knotted together. "These properties," she said. "Rentals?"

"Most of them. A few are used for shelter purposes and don't incur income. And I bought the apartment Eli put me in when I was a teenager, mostly because of its sentimental value."

She glanced up. "Anyone living there?"

"Currently, no."

"Oh, we are so going there and doing nasty things to each other. Please tell me that odd, oversized bean bag chair is still there."

"It's in storage, but it probably smells like twenty-five-year-old funk."

"Yet you kept it."

That apartment was the place he felt he'd grown up. It was the first place he felt comfortable in his own skin. He'd gone through heartbreak, and he'd learned to accept the life thrust upon him while living there. It was a place Jax and Aubrey used on occasion to be together, when they were worried that Queen Donna would kick down the door to Aubrey's apartment and yell at Aubrey for doing things to her baby boy.

It was where Eli told you that you were a good man and that he trusted you with not just Jax's life but his own.

"Indeed, Wick. It was the place I realized the old King truly trusted me."

He loved you.

"Yes, he loved me, but I didn't realize that."

"He terrified me," Aisha snickered. She slid her tablet toward him. "This isn't anywhere near what you've earned over the years. I have one cash account, that's it."

He picked the tablet up. "It's not an insignificant number."

"We've had the same number of years to accumulate money, Will. And our base salaries aren't that far apart. Really, how?"

He cheated.

"I didn't cheat, Wick, not exactly."

"You've gone back in time to invest, haven't you?"

He shrugged lightly. "I have made use of information learned in the past. And perhaps a few of the savings accounts were started when I was much younger."

"Well, now I don't feel so inadequate."

"There's nothing inadequate about this," he said, setting the tablet down. "And I truly had little in the way of expenses. I had no children to support and I live rent-free at the whim of the

King. Whether I invested my earnings or not, the money would have accumulated."

Except for your clothes habit. You like spendy clothes.

He had to give me that one. He didn't shop off the rack; almost everything he owned was tailored by the Kovlov's. Even his underwear.

"Everyone has an indulgence," Aisha said. "And trust me, I appreciate the tailored underwear."

What's your indulgence?

"Shoes," she replied. "Not that I buy many, but the ones I do are not cheap. If I have to stand in front of classes all day, I want my feet to feel like they're being hugged."

"That's a necessity," Will said. "And investment in your overall health."

She considered it and then said, "Fine. Remember that the next time I go shopping." She slid the stack of tablets toward him and added, "I'm working, Will. Even if I'm not contributing much, it matters to me."

Remember what you told Drew about Oz's school? The effort?

"Equitable contribution of effort," he said. "Enzo, you can do anything you want. Continue to teach or not. Open your own business or not. Take up yoga and open a studio. Run for public office. Wait, no, don't do that. I understand the need to work, but we could both quit tomorrow, and we'd be fine."

You can't quit. Jax won't let you.

"Jax wouldn't be able to stop me, Wick."

"You'd never quit," Aisha said as she got up. "If not for Jax, you'd stay for Oz."

"I would quit if the circumstances dictated it would be better for *us*. My loyalties to Jax are absolute, except where you are concerned."

She bent over to kiss him. "I'll never ask you to quit, Bilbo. Now come on and help me wash the dishes. If you do a good job, I'll take you out for ice cream."

"You could just say you want to go out for ice cream," he said.

"Fine. We're doing the dishes and then going out. And mister, you're going to suck it up and actually have ice cream. It won't kill you."

*

This is too adorable. You don't have to share, you know. You're allowed to each have your own ice cream.

"I don't want my own, Wick," Will said. "I'm content with a few bites."

"They serve bananas," Aisha told him. "If this is torture for you, get one."

"It's not torture." He spooned up a small amount of ice cream with a tiny smear of chocolate sauce. "You truly don't want me to eat much of this."

He'll fart all night long.

Wait, have you farted in front of her yet? I told you, it's not true love until you fart.

"Stop it, Wick. It's true love even absent...that."

"Are you two still arguing about farting?" she asked. "Wick, I'm pretty sure we've sealed the deal, though I couldn't tell you when."

Will could probably tell her, but the door to the shop opened and Zed and Jay came in with Sophia and Zara. Instead of looking annoyed that there were parental type people who could end their fun on a whim, they crowded around the end of the booth to say hello.

"There you are," Jay said. "I tried calling to tell you we were going out, but you didn't answer."

Aisha patted her front pants pockets. "I left my phone at home."

"Mom says if you're upset, blame her," Zed said. "She told Jay it was fine."

Will leaned back. "You're all old enough to go out, Zed."

"And old enough to know it's common courtesy to let the parents know where we'll be." He checked his watch and added, "And we only have an hour until Zara has to be home, so..."

Will touched Jay's arm to get him to linger while the others went to the counter. He handed Jay his bank card and said, "Pay for Zara, too."

Jay glanced at Aisha, looking for permission to take it, and as he slid the card into his pocket, he reminded them that Zara wasn't his girlfriend, exactly, so she wasn't expecting that.

"Do you want her to be?" Will asked.

Jay grinned.

"Then pay."

"That was sweet of you," Aisha said as Jay left the table. "But next time you lend him your bank card, give him a spending limit. Tonight might cost you a hell of a lot more than you expect."

"It's fine."

"He could unintentionally do a lot of damage with that card."

"Twenty thousand daily limit on that card. If those kids can eat that much ice cream, more power to them."

"Fine, but if they try, you get to clean up the fountain of vomit later."

"We'll spray him down with a hose."

"Jax redux," she snorted. "Alcohol-free, but still."

Are you ever going to tell me about that?

"He was drunk," Will said. "Too drunk. We had gone to—"

Jay returned and slid Will's card toward him. "Thanks, I appreciate it. She was surprised."

"Hang onto it for tonight, just in case."

Dammit. I'm never gonna find out.

They sat at the table behind us; Zara slid as close to Jay as she could get without bumping elbows, and the chatter and laughter coming from their table was loud. Aisha moved closer to Will so that they could still hear each other over the noise, and I resigned myself to sitting across from them without my own ice cream, unable to make sense of their conversations.

This is rude, you know.

I was half a minute from jumping up on the table to sit on Aisha's lap—I could hear more than noise from there—when the door opened, and the noise dropped to a rumble.

What happened?

Will shrugged; Aisha whispered, "Rhonda Jones."

"Ah."

I turned to look at her. She was petite and blonde, her hair tied back in a ponytail, and she had a splash of freckles across her nose and cheeks. Her hands were stuffed into the pockets of a bright blue windbreaker, and she was wearing white slacks that were rolled up an inch or two at her ankles, showing off a blue sock on one foot and a yellow one on the other.

She doesn't look like a whore.

Will gave me The Look.

Rhonda smiled warmly and gave a little wave to Aisha, and said, "Hey guys," as she passed Zed's table. Zed nodded in return and they all started talking again, but it was softer, and no one was laughing.

Actually, I'm not sure I know what a whore looks like.

Have I ever met one?

Is there a uniform?

"Wick, I'm going to start leaving you at home," Will whispered harshly. "And remind me to have a frank discussion with Zed regarding the way he speaks about others."

Rhonda went to order and began flirting with the kid behind the counter; she leaned against it and had her head tilted just a bit to the right while she giggled at whatever he was saying. I stretched to get a look at Zed, to see if he was watching her, but he'd already turned his attention back to Sophia. They weren't as loud as they had been, but she was smiling, pushing hair that wasn't really there away from his eyes.

Aisha did that to Will a lot, just to touch him. I decided it was human petting, a concession to the real thing because they couldn't get away with stroking each other in public.

A minute later, Zed slid out of the booth to answer his phone. He stepped away from the table, close to a guard who waited across the shop, the one pretending to be a customer even though he wasn't touching his ice cream. Zed's expression went from happy to pained, and he looked over at Sophia, disappointed.

When he was done with the call, Will waved him over to find out if everything was all right.

"Work," he said. "They got a call about a guy in the ER at University Med. He's not going to make it, and I need to get over there."

"He's alive, and they're calling you?" Aisha was puzzled.

Zed hated the idea of someone dying alone. "If I can be there, at least they have someone pulling for them. Most of the time they know they're dying and just don't want to die alone. And sometimes I can find out what they'd like done in their memorial." He managed a wan smile. "There's always a song. Even though I warn them I don't sing well, like, at all, they ask me to sing it for them one more time. People should get their last wish."

Will got up. "I'll go with you."

Aisha got up, too, which meant I was going to the hospital. She told Jay where they were going and reminded him he could ask the guard to get him a car to take Zara home, and if we were going to be late, she would call him.

The hospital was less than a quarter mile away, so we walked. Aisha was quiet—this was new for her, she'd never gone with Zed on a work call and didn't know what to expect—but Will was used to Zed's job and knew he might want someone to talk to. He asked about the man we were going to see, if they'd been able to tell him anything.

He was an unknown, a John Doe with no identification, and the person who called Zed couldn't tell him what the cause of death would be. "He stumbled into the ER a few hours ago, that's all I know. The police have already gotten prints and DNA, but the guy is unresponsive and can't tell them anything. That's all I know."

Half a minute after we arrived, a woman at the front desk nodded toward the double doors to the right and held up three fingers. He gave her a slight nod in return and we went through, and on the other side there was a man in surgical pajamas who looked at us and opened his mouth like he wanted to tell Will I wasn't allowed to be there, but he knew who Zed was and decided against it.

It was a small room. There were beeping machines at the head of the bed with flashing lights and lines that connected to the headboard. There was a sonic faucet on the other side of the room with a hand sanitizer connected to it, but there were no chairs for anyone to sit in. The lighting was intentionally dim. It was clearly not a regular hospital room, one where someone could wait with their ill loved one, where hope could walk through the door poised on the tongue of a doctor or nurse. This was a room where people exhaled one last time and their hearts stopped beating; the man in the bed was bathed in the low light of a thousand tiny bulbs that had been set to imitate dusk.

His face was a mask of pain, head tilted back, neck muscles strained as if he was trying to tear himself away from everything that hurt. There was a nurse—or a doctor, I didn't ask who he was—putting medication into a tube that went into his arm, and when he was done, he stepped out of Zed's way while he jotted notes onto his tablet.

Aisha stayed to the back of the room, away from the bed and the pain that was painted in twilight hues, but Zed and Will went right to it. John Doe was a conflux of old and young; his hair had receded and thinned, and his face had tight lines at his eyes and mouth, but his skin was young and smooth. His hands were balled into fists and pushed hard against his chest, but he didn't move and didn't cry out.

"Hey, bud," Zed said softly. "My name is Zed, and I'm here with the Emperor. I know you don't know me...I'm Prince Zealand, so you might have an idea who I am. I came so that you didn't have to be stuck here alone."

One clenched hand unfurled, just a little bit. Two of his fingers extended, an invitation to touch. Zed set his hand on his but didn't squeeze, just in case it would hurt.

"I know you're in pain and talking is the last thing you want to do, but if there's any way you can let us know what you need, we'll make sure you'll get it."

Will stepped over to the nurse while Zed continued to talk to him in quiet, soothing tones. "What happened?"

"No clue. There's no sign of injury and no detectable disease. Yet his heart is barely beating, and nothing we've done has increased cardiac output. We haven't been able to control his pain. When he came in he was babbling incoherently, and he collapsed less than ten feet into the ER—at the rate of his cardiac decline, he'll be gone within half an hour. That's really all we know. He's not in the database and we don't know who else to call on his behalf."

But they called Zed. Dude is in pain, but that doesn't mean dead.

"We'll stay with him," Will said. He watched as the nurse left the room, making sure he was out of earshot, and then stepped back to the bed. He whispered to Zed to let him speak, and when he did his voice was not as soft as Zed's and was a bit demanding. "Sir, I'm Will Blackshear. I believe I can help. If you will permit me to touch you, I'll be able to tell the doctor who you are and what your medical issue is. Understand, this requires that I listen to your thoughts. I'll endeavor to not pry and will only take the information you want me to have. If you understand, tap a finger."

There was no reaction, but his eyes fluttered.

"I know When you're from," Will said, this time softly.

It took effort, but he extended his pointy finger on the other hand and tapped his chest.

"If I have your consent, tap again."

The finger tapped.

Will carefully set his hand on the man's forehead, and Zed gently pulled his away to make sure he didn't confuse things. As thoughts sped into Will's head, he bent to get closer, to listen better. The man's eyes opened, partway, and his lips parted, but he couldn't speak.

"It's all right," Will said out loud. "It's not too late, I don't think."

Eyes closed. He opened his mouth again, and wheezed, "Why is this happening to me?"

"Call Mass," Will told Zed. "Tell him it's an emergency, and we have someone we need to get home immediately. If he can't get here in five minutes, I'm picking the patient up and taking him to the OR portal, and I don't care who sees."

*

The man's name was Tucker Lee. Will made sure Mass knew what it was before he bolted into the ER; with the name on his lips and the insistence that this was his patient, he was aware of his medical issues, and he was taking him to the OR, no one would bother to question him. He arrived with three of his team, the people who slipped between Whens with him, and they rushed him upstairs and had him through the portal before anyone else from the ER could follow.

Mass returned a minute later, six days after he left.

"He's still tanked and is slow in recovering," he told Will. "Did you get anything other than his name? Maybe family we can contact?"

Will hadn't searched for much information when he touched Tucker. He was looking for a name because he suspected he was adrift in the wrong When; all he wanted was confirmation. He hadn't asked about family or poked through Tucker's memories to find anything about them. It hadn't seemed prudent or timely.

Mass understood Will's sense of urgency. "We'll just wait, then. Once he's healed up enough to come out, we can find family then."

"What about his anchor here?" Zed asked. "Is there someone else in the city about to croak because whatever kept them together broke?"

That was something else Will hadn't listened for.

"Look," Mass said. "I know Finn has had his minions bouncing around, looking for people who were moved and they're being given the chance to go home, but this might become a serious problem going forward. The largest numbers were dropped off in a sixty to seventy year time frame, thirty years back and then beyond. As that population ages out and as accidents occur, there could be a hell of a lot more people suffering the effects of being alone in the wrong century."

"Duly noted," Will said, though he wasn't particularly worried. Finn once said that he'd made sure the numbers were small enough to not attract attention in any given decade. He'd spread twenty thousand people throughout time; an epidemic was not likely. Mass left without refuting that, but Aisha looked dubious.

"Will, someone from your century trying to navigate the twentieth would draw attention just trying to figure out cars and toilets. Drop them in ours, and the similarities will carry them through, which was probably something Finn considered and why he left so many clustered around now. Mass might not be wrong. If Finn could hide a lot of people here and carry that through for the next thirty to forty, there might be a hell of a lot of refugees in crisis soon."

Finn wrote down who went where, right? He can send people to find them.

"He's trying," Will said. "I have to trust that he can handle it."

He's turning bowling balls inside out five times a week.

"His difficulties with his current work have no bearing on his ability to direct a recovery operation."

"I think Wick means you need to keep on Finn about this. He gets distracted. He might forget, and accidents happen."

5

I went home with Zed. Will wanted to go talk to Finn, to tell him what had happened and remind him about how many people might still be waiting for a way home. We rode home in the back of one of the guard's cars, and when we got there he spied Sophia sitting on the steps at Union Square, waiting for him.

You could have been out all night, dude. That's one patient woman.

I rode on Zed's shoulder as he crossed the street to sit with her, and then slid onto his lap.

Is she cold? Ask her if she's cold. She might want to go inside.

Sophia rubbed my head near my ears the way I liked and then asked Zed how it had gone.

"He wasn't seriously almost-dead," Zed said. "Just a little bit almost-dead. Will called Mass, Mass knew what to do for the guy, so instead of watching the poor guy die, I got to see the moment when he realized he was going to live."

"That must have been incredible."

"Seriously. Anyway, I'm sorry I had to take off, especially with Rhonda right there. Did she do anything?"

"We actually had a friendly conversation," she said. "She was sweet, and I saw the appeal. I was expecting her to be, I don't know, gross. Maybe a little crude."

"She has her moments. I'm still sorry, and I hope leaving didn't upset you."

She slid on the step until her side was pressed against his. "Take a good whiff, Zed. Do I smell angry?"

By reflex, he inhaled deeply. "You smell like cherries and vanilla, but I don't think that has anything to do with how you're

feeling. But yeah, no. You don't smell mad or upset. You smell...
amused."

They'd invited Rhonda to sit with them while they finished
their ice cream. She teased Jay about finally having the nerve to
look twice at Zara and told them she'd wondered if they would
ever get together—she'd seen them watch each other in the
hallways, obvious in their hopes and oblivious to each other, but
never understood why neither would just go ask the other one
out. They talked about school—she was on her last chance if she
didn't get it together this year she was being shown the door—
and admitted it was time because she was about to set a record
as the oldest graduate of San Francisco's secondary education
system. Her uncle had removed her from an uneasy home life,
given her a place to live, and she could stay as long as she made
an effort...and it might be easier this time around because all of
the boys were jailbait and that didn't amuse her. "Rhonda was
nice to be with tonight. And easy to talk to."

"She was a colossal mistake, Soph. I don't blame her, though.
I blame me."

She didn't understand why. As far as she was concerned, a
harmless fling was just that—harmless. If she was willing and he
was willing, there wasn't anyone to blame. "You had fun and got
laid. Don't apologize for it."

"A year ago, I would have agreed with you."

"Then what changed?"

He had to think about it. "I changed. Oz happened." He huffed
through his nose. "Ozoo happened. Seeing what Levi Munson did
to my sister changed everything. I mean, he didn't—" He sucked
in a deep breath. "Being cooped up with Will for weeks on end
and then all those miles we walked to get to her? I spent every
waking hour with Will and Drew, and it was like, goddammit,
they have their shit together and neither of them would *ever* use
someone like that. Drew, holy fuck. He wanted to be with Oz *so*
badly, but he waited. And even after we were home and she was
healed up, he waited. And every day he waited I realized that's
what I wanted."

"To wait?" she asked lightly.

"Sex is easy. But it also becomes this *thing*. You start too soon, and that's all the relationship becomes. Being patient and cultivating that relationship? I don't think that's half as easy, but they've proven that it's worth it. And I want that with you, I really do. I want to be totally okay with the idea that we'll go out, and the night will end with a kiss, and I won't be disappointed or upset. When we started talking online and calling each other all the time? Soph, all I wanted was for us to be the kind of friends that they were. And then when—if—we became physical, it would be the right thing. Not the convenient thing."

Sophia snaked her arm around his shoulders and then kissed him on the cheek. "And here I was hoping to jump your bones tonight. I thought we were pretty much there. I did move here with you in mind, after all."

"Tonight?" He fought the smile tugging at the corners of his mouth. "Planning something?"

"I don't know. I was hoping you'd walk me home, I'd ask you to come in and have a drink or something, and we'd just... go from there."

He started to say something, but before he could blink there was an extra tongue in his mouth. For the next few minutes, there was a lot of heavy breathing and smooching sounds, which annoyed me because I hadn't considered I was going to have to suffer through the start of yet another relationship. And then there was twitching. I wanted to run across the street and go home, but Zed probably wanted me to stay right where I was to hide that from her.

"Don't make me wait too much longer," she said when they finally parted.

"I won't," he promised. "Maybe another week?"

"A week," she laughed. "What will a week matter?"

"I should get an implant first," he said.

Another kiss, then she took his hand and set it on her arm, telling him to feel the ridge near the bendy part. "Ovatron rod," she said. "I came here prepared. You don't need an implant."

Get one anyway, dude.

He brushed his fingers over it. "Well, now I wish we'd walked Zara home."

"I'll settle for making out on the steps for now."

"So, when it's clear it's going to happen…consent?"

"Given," she said. "Consent?"

"Given."

Holy hell.

I'm not happy. Clearly, you are, but I'm not. And what if the Queen looks out the window? She won't be happy, either. She'll go out onto the balcony and yell at you, and she'll use your whole name. Zealand Marcus Blackshear, get your tongue out of that poor girl's face and take poor Wick off that erection! It's not polite!

"Fucking hell, Wick. What's your problem?"

You're poking me.

"Can you stop with the fussing? People are going to think I'm hurting you."

Can you stop with the foreplay? People are going to think you're about to do her right here on the steps. And I'm not sure that you won't.

I heard footsteps behind him and stretched to look over his shoulder. Oz and Drew were close by, walking across the Square, holding hands.

I need help, Drew.

"Zed, are you giving Wick a hard time?"

Yes, and I'm sitting on it.

"I don't know what his problem is," Zed said. "He started yapping his head off a couple minutes ago, and I have no idea why."

"Wick?"

Take a guess. He's way too happy.

Drew reached to scoop me off Zed's lap, and I braced for a tug of war over my poor body, but then Zed was no longer quite as happy and he handed me off.

I should get treats for putting up with that.

"Hush, Wick," Drew whispered to me as we crossed the street. "It's not like he was doing something to *you*. You could have moved."

He gave me a treat anyway. While Zed and Sophia plopped down on his sofa to talk to Oz, Drew chopped up little bits of leftover hamburger and put it in a dish on the floor along with a dish filled with gravy covered cat food. I happily ate both, savoring it slowly, and when I was done I went into the living room to thank him, but he and Oz were gone and Zed was sucking the remains of Sophia's dinner from her back teeth.

I sat on the floor in front of them.

Where did Drew go? I have things to tell him.

Zed ignored me and went right on slobbering all over the poor girl.

Is this like Oz and Drew grinding in the back seat of Will's car? Because you're doing it wrong.

They weren't going to stop at grinding.

Sophia pulled her shirt off and tossed it on the floor, and less than ten seconds later Zed unhooked her bra and threw it on top of the shirt. There was a flurry of clothes being discarded, and before I knew it, they were on the floor, which seemed terribly uncomfortable.

There wasn't even a nice, furry rug to cushion things.

They didn't need me. When I was sure of that, when I knew Zed wasn't going to break anything and that she was right where she wanted to be, I left.

I decided to go find Drew. Zed didn't need anyone's help but Sophia's, which was a bit of a relief. If he didn't need help, I didn't need to stick around for the grand finale or any encores they had in mind.

*

Oz and Drew were upstairs, in the kitchen. There were playing cards stacked on the table and Aubrey was taking cookies out of the oven; Jax had four beer bottles in hand, and I thought he intended to get Oz and Drew drunk, but then Will and Aisha came in, and Jax handed them each a beer. "Aubrey made cookies and Drew wants to learn to play poker."

"I never said that," Drew said.

"You meant to. I'm good at reading people. You desperately want to learn five-card stud and are so confident that you want to play for cash."

"Yeah, no, I don't think so."

"Come on. It's easy."

Drew folded his arms. "I'm not gambling with someone who can glance at me and tell if I'm bluffing or not." He looked at Will. "Do you ever win?"

"I do. Frequently. He bluffs as well as a six-year-old."

"Will can lie and not let it show," Oz said. "I'm still trying to figure out how."

"You've seen my lie color," Will said.

"Not often."

"Sociopath," Jax grumbled. "Where's Zed?"

"He and Sophia are downstairs," Oz said. "Watching a movie, I think."

"A movie. Is that what you kids call it now? Whatever happened to just making out?"

"Why not both?" Drew mused.

They aren't watching a movie.

Drew and Will both heard me but ignored me.

Well, they aren't. But Sophia almost died tonight. Seriously, I was there.

Will's eyebrow twitched, and Drew couldn't resist. "Say what, Wick?"

"Don't encourage him," Will said, popping the top off his beer.

No, really. She was super close to being dead. She yelled out 'Oh God, I'm coming' and she would have, too, if Zed hadn't held her down.

Beer shot out Will's nose.

It was awesome.

Drew bit his bottom lip and stared down at the table, but his shoulders were shaking, so he was either laughing or crying.

"What the hell did that cat say?" Jax asked.

Drew shook his head—he didn't want to look up—and Will was too busy soaking up the beer with a napkin.

"Well?" Jax pressed.

"I truly cannot repeat it," Will finally said. "It was…obscene."

"Wick's first dirty joke," Drew said with a giggle.

"And we will not offend the Queen," Will said. "Understood?"

Drew finally looked up. "Of course not."

Jax reached for the cards. "I hate you both."

Drew leaned toward Oz and whispered, "I'll tell you later. But no, your parents don't want to hear it."

Jax would laugh.

"No," Will said, "he wouldn't. Jax and Aubrey are far more mature than the rest of us."

That made Aisha laugh.

"Fuck you, Emperor. I'm mature, but I enjoy a good dirty joke every now and then," Jax grumbled.

Aubrey pretended to smack the back of his head as she sat down. "Jackson, I don't ask much, but I do ask that you watch your language."

"Fine." He pushed away from the table. "If I can't swear at them, I'm drinking something stronger. Then I'm taking all of Drew's money. Will's, too."

Oz grabbed two cookies and said she was going to save Drew from the humiliation. He'd have more fun sitting out on the balcony watching people on the Square than he would coughing up his lunch money, and if she played, she was cheating and watching every color flicker and flare around each of them.

"I see it better than you do, Dad," she said. "You wouldn't stand a chance."

I went out on the balcony with them. When Drew realized I was following him, he grabbed a sweatshirt—one with the pouch re-sewn so that I could sit in it—and put it on so that I wouldn't be cold.

This is why I like you. You cater to my whims.

They snuggled on the bench seat. There weren't many people to watch down on the Square so they leaned back and watched the stars instead, mulling over Elysium and what it could eventually become. It was meant to be a place where people lived and vacationed, a multicultural, multigovernmental oasis, but now that it was in Pacifica's hands, anything could happen.

Drew wanted it to become residential and entertainment space; he liked the idea that in twenty years he might take his kids there on vacation. What he didn't want was for it to become a playground for the military. Oz recognized its potential for just that: planetary defense against the hordes of volatile aliens surely racing toward earth to strip it of its minerals and its thick, juicy human meat-treats.

Somewhere out there was the race that would see humankind as cattle. She wanted to be able to blow them to tiny pieces before they got anywhere near close enough to be a credible threat.

I waited for the inevitable eat-me jokes, but those never came. Oz spent the next two hours pumping him for his ideas about making Elysium a reality. She didn't want him spending all his time with his brain on his work things, but she was interested in the bigger picture. Their future was tied in with Elysium, she was sure of it. If not for them, then their kids and grandkids.

Future Will could spend part of his childhood there instead of being isolated in Finn's lab. Drew thought that if he got it right, if all the little ideas in his head came together, then one day Will might come live in this When, but not because he had to, but because the information in the Old Mint told him he had a life waiting here.

"But first, we start our own lives. Our own careers."

"I don't even know what career I want," Oz said. "I'm leaning toward teaching, but then Dad is bringing me in on meetings more and more. Even if he doesn't retire, he's still grooming me for government work."

"You okay with that?"

She set her head on his shoulder. "I don't mind. Most of it is interesting and eye-opening, but I'm not sure it's what I'd choose for myself."

"Then don't. Tell him. You want to teach, the same way he did, the same way your mom does."

Will wanted to teach.

He wound up doing what King Eli wanted him to do.

"And Will might be why my dad is pulling me along. He can see for himself that Will might step away from the job sooner or later. Aisha changed everything for him. And that's a good thing, not a complaint."

"Still."

"I agreed to this when I was sixteen," she reminded him. "I stood in front of the entire country and accepted the position of being next in line. I don't really mind, Drew."

"But you wish he would ask what you want, don't you?"

"It would be nice."

"Is he letting you make any decisions yet?"

She lifted her head to look at him "Not yet. Why?"

Drew gestured in the direction of the Square. "He put an end to the First Friday concert thing when the war started. I'd like to see it come back."

"I bet he'd listen to that request."

The door squeaked open, and Zed and Sophia came out with Jay right behind them. "What request?" Zed asked.

"Friday concerts," Oz said. "We miss them."

Zed pulled chairs up and sat near Drew. "That'd be cool." He popped Drew on the arm. "And thank you."

"Thank your sister. I was going to say no."

"He was not." Oz leaned forward to look at Sophia. "I feel like I shouldn't be aiding and abetting my little brother, but hell. It's not like you couldn't drag him off to your apartment."

Sophia laughed. "That was actually my plan tonight. I'd hoped he would take me home, and then stay for a while."

"Yeah, something you should know," Drew said. "Wick outed you to Will. It was the funniest freaking thing he's ever said, and you need to be damned glad Will and I are the only ones who can understand him."

"What the hell did you tell them?" Zed asked me.

After making sure Sophia was all right with being the subject of my crudity, Drew repeated my observation. She howled along with Oz and Jay, and I thought Zed was really mad, because his pointy finger got super close to my face, but then he tucked it under my chin and scratched. "You're a furry little pervert, aren't you?"

No. I'm never staying again. I only watch when I'm not sure if help is required.

"Still helping Will?" Drew asked.

He fell off once. I think I need to.

"Holy hell, I don't want to hear that," Jay said. Then, "How could he just fall off?"

"Wick says your mother is, uh, enthusiastic," Drew told him. Jay groaned.

"Didn't you say the other day that you're *glad* they're so active?" Zed asked.

"Doesn't mean I want to know anything about it."

"Our parents all have sex," Oz said. "If Mom chases Dad around the bedroom a dozen times a week, good for them."

Drew nodded. "I rarely see my parents touch. Trust me, I wish they were as openly affectionate as your parents are." He leaned over and kissed Oz, right at her temple. "I swear, our kids will be as mortified by us as Jay is by them."

"I'm holding you to that. And to your promise to not get lost in your work."

"We'll kick his ass if he turns into a lab rat," Zed said.

"You gonna tell your kids that you were each other's one and only?" Jay asked.

"I suppose, if they ask," Oz said. "Why?"

"Because I have no clue about my mom," he said. "I know she's been with my Dad and with Will. She hid it if she dated anyone else in between. Well, there was the one guy I met for like ten seconds, so I *know* she did, but I never saw it and don't know if she slept with him or anyone else. And I'm curious."

"Not really your business," Zed said.

He shrugged. "I don't need the details or anything. I just wish I knew if she was lonely all those years or not. Like, Zara and I were talking. She has no clue if her dad has ever dated or not. It bugs her, too. Like, we might have been dicks about it, but it was still important to see. I want to know that Mom was happy."

"Tell her that," Sophia said. "But I know what an unhappy relationship looks like. You'd have felt it. My dad is on his third marriage and he's happy for the first time."

"She's happy now," Jay mused. "I mean, it's obvious." He was quiet for a moment and then said, "I really wish they'd been able to stay together when they were our age."

"Will doesn't," Drew said.

Jay's eyebrows knotted. "Why the hell not?"

"Because if they'd somehow worked it out back then, you wouldn't be here now. And he's told me straight up, he wouldn't trade you for anything. In a thousand lifetimes, Jay, he'd break up with her every time, just to make sure you were born."

"He really said that?"

Drew nodded. "You know enough about Will's life to know how big a statement that is."

"Yeah, don't fuck it up," Zed snorted.

"Don't put that on him," Oz said. "Their marriage is not on you, Jay. She and Will are capable of making it work even if you're a total ass to him."

"I won't be, though."

Sophia sighed. "It's not always easy when your parents remarry. I know how it feels. If you ever have that thought thunder in your head that you want to scream at him that he's not your dad...it's okay. You're allowed to be mad every once in a while, even if you like the guy."

"I already did that," Jay snorted.

"Still want to?" Zed asked.

Jay shook his head. "Will fucking named me as his own. He didn't have to do that. My mom never asked him to. If I could name him as my dad without hurting my actual dad? I would."

"Bonus dad," Oz said. "That's how we think of Will."

"I still want something better for him." He got up. "I'm gonna go say goodnight to them and then head downstairs."

"You want Will to get it?" Oz asked before he opened the door. "Just tell him you love him. He doesn't need a new name to answer to, but every now and then he might like to hear that you love him."

As the door shut, Drew said, "He's going to march into the middle of a half-drunk poker game and announce his undying love for his stepfather."

"There are worse things he could do," Oz said.

"He has the right idea, though," Sophia said, checking her phone. She tapped at it a few times and then told Zed she'd sent for a cab. "Your parents would probably not be happy to find me here this late."

"I can take you home," he said.

"And you'd stay. Let's not let them know about this just yet." She leaned over and kissed him, and it was a really good kiss, too. "Stay here. I can find my way to the front door on my own."

He didn't want to, but he did what she asked. When the elevator door closed and she was on her way down, he thanked Drew again.

"Just tell me you changed the sheets."

"Never made it that far," Zed snorted. "Your living room floor was *royally* abused, though."

"Not the first time," Oz said.

"Why are you all right with this?" Zed asked her. "After last year, not what I expected."

"You're not the same kid you were last year. None of us are. Hell, if she had told you she didn't want to have sex for at least a year, you'd have been all right with it, wouldn't you?"

He nodded. "Yeah, but once she told me tonight she wanted to…one way or the other, it was happening."

"Yeah, not the same kid who borrowed Will's car to screw around with Rhonda. That kid wouldn't have been happy if she'd wanted to wait. Totally understandable that she didn't."

He told them about running into Rhonda at the ice cream shop. "Sophia says they talked after I left. She kind of liked Rhonda and understands why I did what I did, but damn. That really could have gone the other way."

"You in love with Sophia?" Drew asked.

He seemed surprised by the question. "Man, if I'm not? Holy hell. I don't know how the two of you don't just explode all over the place. If this isn't love, I don't think I'd survive the real thing."

He got up and went in to take a shower, leaving Oz and Drew the way they'd been earlier, cuddled up and looking for hints of their future in the sky.

6

Oz went into her own room and Drew headed to his apartment—sometimes they did that because Jax had asked Oz to spend a night every now and then in her own bed—so I followed Will and Aisha downstairs. He grumbled about the lack of actual poker being played, and she poked back at him: all he really wanted was his quarterly batch of warm chocolate chip cookies, and no one else was fooled by his bitching that they'd never gotten around to the cards.

Jay was already in bed, music bleeding through the spaces around his door. It was a nightly ritual: turn on a fan, turn on music, read for half an hour, put headphones on, then lights out. I went in to check on him every now and then, and most of the time he also had a t-shirt over his eyes, trying to block out the little bit of light that bled under the door.

They didn't bother turning on the lights in the living room. Jay had left his bathroom light on for them to navigate by, and Will flicked it off as they walked past. They went into the bedroom, and Will sat on the edge of the bed while Aisha went into the bathroom.

I watched as he pulled his socks and shoes off, and then as he stared at his feet.

You didn't grow new toes, did you?

"No, I didn't grow new toes. Why?"

You're looking at your feet like there's something new.

"Just thinking." He stood up to take his pants off. "I have a bedtime routine now, Wick. I've never had that, not that I can remember."

You did when you were little. After dinner you had your bath, then you cuddled up with Jo and she told you stories. Sometimes, she asked you to tell her one. Your stories were always about the Emperor.

"I'm surprised you remember that."

I'm surprised you don't. You did it until you were ten or eleven.

"I remember. But I was also allowed to stay up reading if I wanted. It was less a bedtime routine and more like an end of day routine unless we were in the lab."

Same thing.

"Not really. I didn't have to stay in bed."

You don't have to stay in bed now. Sometimes you get up.

"You're just being argumentative, Wick."

Just pointing out the facts. The fact is that you had a routine when you were little, and you're kinda doing the same thing now. Except Aisha doesn't tell you stories. She just does things to you.

"Not every night."

Lots of nights. Most nights. And she's always the one to start it.

That gave him pause. He pulled his shirt off and tossed it across the room to the hamper, but he was thinking about it.

"Always?"

I've never seen you make the first move. I mean, you kiss her like a million times a day, but if it goes beyond that, it's all on her.

He twitched when he heard the shower go on and I think he was about to ask to get in with her when the door opened and she stuck her arm out, curling her pointy finger and beckoning him in.

Maybe next time.

"Let's not argue with the current results," he said, though that might have been to himself and not to me.

*

I slept in the living room. Will didn't need me; by the time they came out of the bathroom they were done with whatever bouncy-type things they were going to do, and all I saw happening was cuddling and pillow talk. I curled up on the sofa and snoozed until Will shuffled down the hall before sunrise.

He was only half dressed, shorts and nothing else, and he went straight for the kitchen where the coffee lived.

Work early?

"She rolled over and kneed me in the back. Not hard, but here we are."

Could have been worse.

"Much worse." He turned the coffee maker on and sat at the table, resting his chin on his hands. "On the plus side, I was actually sleeping. I have a vague notion of dreaming, too."

You dream.

"But I rarely remember them."

I have a hard time catching you in dreams, but if you want, I can pay attention and listen.

"That's all right, Wick. I'm quite content with simply being able to sleep more."

Me, too. I don't miss you sitting on the floor begging the sleep fairies to come do things to you.

"I'm sorry. I didn't realize you'd ever had to witness that."

You were desperate sometimes. I wonder why I could always sleep easy but you couldn't.

"You're a cat. Sleep is hardwired into your DNA."

Maybe.

"You're also capable of remaining awake and aware for lengthy periods. More than most cats, I think. You sleep, but perhaps not as many hours as is the feline norm."

I've evolved.

"That must be it."

I hear Jay. He's up.

Jay headed into the bathroom, but instead of going back to bed when he was done, he shuffled out and sat at the table with Will.

"It's only four-thirty, Jay," Will said. "Go back to bed."

"I woke up an hour ago and sleep isn't happening anymore. Probably not until my second class today."

Will got up to pour his coffee and offered to run water through the heating element so Jay could have tea. "Something particular keeping you awake?"

Jay shrugged.

"Girls? School? That warrant out for your arrest in Vegas? I told you, I have influence. I can help with that."

"Yeah, sure." Jay managed a tired grin. "My drug-running days are over. No worries there."

"Then girls or school."

Jay hesitated. "George."

"Is not your problem anymore," Will said as he sat back down. "He has no way to return, and no one on the other side of the portal will help him if he asks."

That wasn't what Jay worried about. He accepted that George was lost to home and family in this When. He had no expectations that he could return. "I worry about him anyway. He looked like he was nearly dead when Mom yanked him back home. I just want to know that he's all right."

"After everything he did?"

Jay nodded.

Will leaned back and considered it. "My father made sure he got help, and I know he found members of George's family. If there were issues, he would have told me."

"Yeah, but..." He sucked in a deep breath. "Can I see him? Can you take me there for just a little while? A couple hours, max."

"I can't promise that, Jay. This is something I need to discuss with your mother."

He gave a slight nod. "But not my dad, all right? Because he'll freak out if he knows I've seen George. And the whole Other When thing—"

"That is not for his consumption."

Jay was quiet for a long time, and Will sat there, waiting, stirring his coffee even though he took it black and the only thing that did was make it swirl up the sides of his mug.

"I know he tormented you when you were kids," Jay finally said. "I get that you don't want to see him again. I shouldn't even ask."

"You can ask anything of me, but I may not always be able to do as you wish. I feel comfortable giving you permission to go somewhere with Zed or to stay out a little late, but bigger things I need to run by your mother. This is one of the bigger things."

"Yeah, I get it. Can I ask you something else?"

Will nodded.

"It's none of my business."

"That's fine. I'll decline if it crosses a line."

"Why did George think you were a freak? It's not like the time travel thing bothered him because that's how he got here. But he was weirdly upset by something about you. Zed and Oz know, but they won't tell me, and—"

"It's all right," Will said. "I'll tell you, but it may upset you as much as it upset George."

"Come on. I'm getting used to the oddities around here. You carry on conversations with the cat. It can't be much weirder than that."

"It's intrusive, Jay. And understand, it's something I had no control over when I was a child, but I do now." He waited a beat, and added, "It's also why I walked away from your mother so many years ago. I had no control then, either."

"Damn, if this is like some kind of weird sex thing—"

"Yes, when I was four years old I terrified George with some weird sex thing."

"Oh. Yeah. No."

"It will be easier for me to show you—and I promise you, I will *never* do this without your permission."

Will reached across the table and told Jay to set his hand on his. When he did, he looked confused, and said, "Yeah, I know, I love you, too, but I still—" His eyebrows arched. "I heard that inside my head. You were talking inside my head."

Will pulled his hand back. "The other issue is that if I listen, I can also hear what you're thinking. I can see your memories. Feel your fears and hopes. But I swear, I will not."

Instead of being freaked out by it, Jay was amazed. "That's an *awesome* superpower. Can you do more than speak and hear?"

"I can place a thought into your mind as if it were your own," he said. "Admittedly, that's a new skill."

"Why did that freak George out? Man, I would have become your best friend and gotten you to do all kinds of weird shit."

"It's not as wonderful when you consider the damage I can do. Without control, no one I touch can keep secrets from me. I have access to every truth, every lie, everything good or bad someone has done. George realized this very early on, and he assumed I would use it against him. To him, I was a freak of nature. And in a manner of speaking, I am."

"Not a freak," Jay said. "Evolution, maybe. I mean, I know what Zed can do, and Oz is your great-grandmother, and she can see sound. Maybe your family line is where humanity starts to change. A thousand years from now, you might be the norm."

Notice he didn't say normal.

And a thousand years from now, there will be dragons.

"Wick that was in a simulator. I don't think we'll have dragons."

"Someday I want to go meet Wick's dragon," Jay said. And then, the thought suddenly flooding into his brain and out his mouth, "Huh. Wait. Do you and Mom talk in your heads when you don't want anyone else to hear?"

Will grinned but didn't answer.

"How does she know you're going to? You have a signal or something?"

With that, he took another sip of his coffee, raising his eyebrow.

Jay thought about it for a while, and then his eyes went wide, "Holy crap, there are times that has to be fucking fantastic."

"And that," Will said, getting up, "is not a topic I am willing to discuss."

Jay laughed. "It's not like you guys are super quiet, Will. But being able to, you know, give directions without having to say it?"

"Directions." He rinsed out his cup. "What time is your first class?"

"Nice change of subject. Abrupt, but acceptable. And it's not until nine."

"And I will discuss taking you to see George with your mother after school. I don't want to upset her before."

*

We waited for her at the corner bakery on Union Square. There was bacon to be had—the girl who worked the counter in the afternoon always had a slice for me—and he picked at a sandwich, digging out all the meaty bits and leaving most of the bread.

Half a dozen pigeons waited patiently on the ground because they saw the bread and had high hopes he would shred it into bite-sized bits and toss it to them. I was nervous and upset because there were enough of them to form a cat-hating gang.

"They won't hurt you," Will said. "If they get too close, all I have to do is stand and they'll hop away."

They'll come back.

"Look at them. They're huge. I doubt they can even fly more than a few feet. They're not going to grab you and fly off."

Jax should ban them from Pacifica.

"And how would he do that, Wick? Round all of them up and put them on a shuttle to Florida?"

I'd be in favor of that. Red might like having pigeons in Florida. He can paint them white and pretend they're doves and get religious or something with them.

"Doves are pigeons, Wick."

No, doves are pretty.

"They're from the same family, Columbidae. Sorry to burst your bubble."

Fine. Then Red will be happy to get a million not-white doves. He can paint them himself.

If he had something to say to that, it left his head when he spotted Aubrey walking toward us. He got up—he still believed in getting up when she walked into the room or if she was headed in his direction—and when she was close, she kissed him on the cheek.

"You really don't have to get up every time you see me, William."

"In public, yes, I do. One does not sit in the presence of the Queen."

She sat in the chair he pulled out from the table for her. "Then your legs are going to get very tired."

He could stand there for hours if necessary, and she knew it. Once she was seated, though, he went to get her some coffee, and then sat down.

"Tell me something," she said as she stirred sugar into the coffee, "do you pop up every time your wife walks into the room?"

Parts of him do. It's kind of disturbing.

"I did until she yelled at me. Apparently, a simple acknowledgment of her presence is enough." He laughed at himself. "I never did that for my mother. I don't know why it's so ingrained."

"I do appreciate it in public, but you can stop at home. Jax doesn't get up. Why should you?"

"Because," he said evenly, "aside from being my friend, you're my Queen. Even at home."

"Your Queen is making a formal request, William. She wishes her brother-in-law to relax and abandon formalities at home. And our apartment is part of *your* home."

"Brother-in-law."

"You know Jax speaks of you as his brother to everyone now, don't you?"

I heard him refer to you to someone on the phone as 'My brother, the Emperor.'

"Oz is not calling me Uncle Willie," he said. "Whatever Jax calls me, just, no."

She can call you Bill.

"No, Wick, I don't wish to be called 'Bill,' either."

Aisha calls you Bilbo.

"Yes, and she's the only one who can." He explained to Aubrey, "Aisha sometimes calls me 'Bilbo.' That, I don't mind, but only from her."

"And you call her?" Aubrey prompted.

He grinned sheepishly. "Enzo."

I wanted to call her Bob, but they didn't like it.

"Wick, we're never calling her Bob. If you want a Bob in your life so badly, I'm still willing to get you a kitten."

"Oh, let's thrill Jax and get Wick three or four kittens. Wick could teach them to line up on the counter and stare at him during breakfast every morning."

They would be my minions. Bob One, Bob Two, Bob Three, and Bob Four.

The idea amused Will. "Well, Wick? Do you want your own little feline army?"

I'll think about it. Training them sounds like work.

"The day we stop asking him is the day he'll decide he wants his own pet," Will told her. "And we're on the hook for it, because we've already promised him."

"He's holding out for babies." She reached over to tickle me under the chin. "Me, too, Wick. I hope Oz and Drew don't wait too long."

"She's not even twenty yet, Aubrey."

"I know. And it's selfish of me. But when they thought they were pregnant, I realized I'm looking forward to grandkids more than just about anything else. Can you imagine? That house filled with kids? If they have two or three, and Zed has two or three, and Jay—" She laughed lightly and said, "And you."

I wanted to tell her that he wanted one. He just didn't know it yet.

He also needed to know he was ready for it.

I want a lap. Give me a lap.

"Think you can keep them all living there?" he asked as he backed away from the table enough to make space for me.

She was hopeful. Will and Aisha's upstairs apartment, along with the remodeling of the adjacent guest suite, would be done soon. After that, they intended to remodel Drew's apartment and open the unused space behind it for another. "If everyone goes along with it, they'll each have their own apartments, big enough for growing families. And that includes Jay. I hope he understands he's not on the fringe of this family. He's as much in the middle as Oz and Zed and Drew. Jax and I realized recently that every time one of us utters the words 'the kids' that we always think of Jay as one of them. I think it started on your honeymoon, even."

"It may take him some time. He still feels pulled between life here and life with his father. He feels guilty for enjoying living here and immersing himself in family life, and he feels guilty when he's with James and wants to come home. He feels guilty for having fun with James and feels guilty for wanting to sometimes take off to see him when it's not James' weekend. It's a process."

He comes home early from his dad's a lot.

I jumped off his lap to the ground and circled around the table.

"Then he's lucky you're the man he comes home to," she said, patting her lap to invite me up. "If anyone understands the guilt of feeling pulled between two places, it's you."

He nodded. "I'd like to say I'll never make him feel bad about wanting to leave here to go there, but I can see it coming. Sooner or later Aisha will have a day when she needs him to stay at the same time James is pulling him to go. I know which side I'll fall on."

"He's nearly grown, Will. By the time that happens, he and Zed might be sharing Drew's old apartment, and he'll figure out for himself what he needs to do."

Will scowled. "I forbid him to be nearly grown. The rest of you might be ready for that, but I am not. I just got him."

She laughed. "Sweetie, he's growing up whether you like it or not. Those four kids together remind me so much of the three of us at their ages. And Jay? He's the Emperor at eighteen. Thoughtful and serious, but so much fun."

"I don't recall having his language issues."

"You're the reason the List exists, Will. Only now you're the one who mostly respects it, and Jax abuses it to no end. But still, for a boy who grew up without knowing anything about you, Jay was certainly raised to be very much like you."

He leaned back, folding his arms. "You think that was intentional?"

I climbed from Aubrey's lap to the top of the table. And plopped down dramatically, making sure my tail swished across Will's coffee cup.

"I think Aisha had the ideal man stamped on her heart, and whether she realized it or not, she molded her son in his image." She glanced past him. Aisha was coming across the Square. Aubrey got up. "I won't faint if he swears in front of me. But the list stands."

You're why the Bad Word List got put in writing. That's awesome.

"I thought it made me sound more adult. I was wrong."

Jax swears more than you do.

"Now. But at eighteen and nineteen, I was just as bad about it as Jay is."

"What were you bad about?" Aisha asked before she kissed him and sat down.

While she smooched him, I rolled onto my back and wiggled closer to Will.

"Swearing. Aubrey reminded me of the origin of her list."

"Hm. The mouth that roared." She made him kiss her again. "I'm sorry I'm late. I had a meeting that ran long."

"Irate parent?"

"Persistent interviewer." She took a deep breath. "Today was round two of university interviews."

He sat up straighter. "And?"

"And I'll know in a few days. But the interview went well, Will. I mean, *really* well. I'm afraid to get excited about it, but unless the other candidates are overqualified, I have a shot."

"Get excited about it. I'm excited."

"I'd have to leave my job at the semester break. It'll piss off the board."

He shrugged. "Not your problem." When I flicked my tail in his face, he batted it away. "Wick, what the hell?"

"There's Jay, too."

"What about him?"

"Does he want his mom following him to college?"

"Yes, he does. Don't overthink it, Enzo. You're getting the job, you're quitting the high school, and you're becoming the hottest professor at the university."

Oh, we're not bringing up George, are we?

"Indeed, Wick. We're going to celebrate."

"I don't have the job yet, sweetheart."

"Then we celebrate the interview, and today having been a wonderful day."

"All right. How was your day so wonderful?" She raised a playful eyebrow. "I know it started off nicely."

"My day actually started before that. Jay was up at four-thirty, and we had a nice conversation. I imagine he'll be grouchy later from lack of sleep, but this morning he was quite pleasant."

"You sleep less and you're not grouchy."

Yes he is.

"I'm used to it. But, he asked me point blank what is it about me that George was so afraid of, and the answer didn't upset him. He was intrigued and deemed it an awesome superpower."

"It's handy every now and then," she said. "Did you tell him or show him?"

"A demonstration seemed appropriate. I think he was surprised that it wasn't something worse. And his mind went directly to the occasions when it might be...helpful."

"How so?"

He set his hand on hers, and a couple of seconds later her eyes lit up, and she leaned over to kiss him.

"Ah. He might be right. We should do that more often."

"My concern is that I would lack enough control in the moment to only listen to the things you're asking me to do. Or worse, I would hear a random stray thought of 'God, finish already and get off me.'"

She was laughing, but said, "Never."

"All right then. 'What, already?' My ego would be wounded."

He was focused on her and not on my twitching tail. Since that no longer annoyed him, I rolled back to my side, kicking his coffee cup over with my back paw. He caught it before it flew over the side of the table, which was both impressive and disappointing.

"This goes both ways, mister. There have been a couple times when I haven't jumped in the shower first and worried that you're thinking things like 'but it's not actually supposed to taste like fish.'"

"Wouldn't matter. I like fish."

Well, now you have me thinking about fish. I'm hungry. Can we have fish for dinner?

I didn't get an answer. Instead, he kissed her again and then got up to get her something from the bakery, and she was still giggling about eating fish when a guy in a business suit walked past, stopped suddenly, and backtracked.

"Aisha?"

Her eyes flashed brightly, recognizing him. "Scotty?"

I'm Wick.

Since we're doing introductions.

And she's married. Her husband can break people with one hand, you know. While sneezing.

"Long time," he said, ignoring me.

"Summer after high school." She gestured to the chair on the other side of the table and asked him to sit for a bit. I moved and plopped down in front of her, to make sure he knew she was not available. "How was Harvard?"

"Not what I expected," he said as he sat down. "I actually had to work. How was UC?"

"More fun than it should have been."

Will came back with coffee and hesitated before he sat down.

She seemed excited for them to meet. "Will, this is Scotty. We went to high school together. Scotty, this is my husband, Will."

Oh, good, now he knows you're married.

"Emperor," Scotty said. He pointedly did not offer his hand. "Nice to see you again."

"You know each other?" Aisha sputtered.

Will reached out and offered his hand, ignoring Scotty's surprise. "Indeed. Scott and I have met on several occasions."

"And until recently, I didn't know your name," he said. "There was a rumor running through the shelter's office that you didn't have one."

Will grinned. "Yes, and I was bred in a loom along with other alien life forms."

"So, we now know you have a name."

"You can put that part of the rumor to rest, then."

"All right," Aisha said. "I'm not the one who should feel out of the loop. Scotty, what is it you do that has you meeting with my husband?"

Will raised an eyebrow. "Clearly, he's part of a secret organization of men and women who sit around and start rumors about the Emperor of San Francisco."

"That's only part of what we do," Scotty said. "I'm just a lawyer. Once in a while I represent the shelter."

"He sits on the board," Will explained. "Elected to its head three times."

"You wanted to be a minister once," Aisha said.

"I went into law instead. People tend to believe in law. In God, not so much."

"What changed your mind?" Will asked.

"There was a girl," he answered. "Even though we parted ways, she made me believe I could do a hell of a lot more good in the world if I used the brain and the talents God gave me to find my passion in life, and then go after it. She was right, too. I think I've done more fighting for the disenfranchised in court than I ever could have as the minister of a local church."

"Smart woman," Aisha said. "Glad you listened to her."

"So am I. I still think about her now and then, hoping her life turned out as well as mine."

With a soft smile, she said, "It's been everything she hoped for, and more. Please tell me you found the right one, too."

He nodded. "I did. We met in grad school and have three incredible daughters. You might want to keep an eye out for my youngest, though. She has a horrible crush on the Emperor."

"I gave her my popcorn once," Will said. "She promised to marry me when she grew up."

"Competition." Aisha was laughing. "How old is she now?"

"Eight," Scotty said. "So you have a while. But it's been four years, and she hasn't wavered."

"Does she know that I'm married now?" Will asked.

Scotty got up. "The whole world saw your wedding, Emperor. She's both thrilled that Daddy once knew the bride, and positive that you're just biding your time until she's older. I may let you be the one to break her heart later."

He said his goodbyes and left for the meeting he'd been headed to.

"Small world," Will said as Scotty walked across Union Square. "I had no idea he was the high school boyfriend. I've known him for at least fifteen years."

"Probably because you never want to know anything about my premarital social life."

"Fair enough. But him, I would like to know about. I gather you parted as friends?"

"Funny enough, we planned our breakup months in advance. He was going to Harvard and I was staying here, and we both understood that long distance was not in the cards. We tried to keep in touch as friends, but—" she set her hand on his arm "—I met this adorable and strangely moody young man, and it wasn't long before I just kind of tucked Scotty away into the back of my mind."

"A moody young man who wouldn't touch you and wouldn't say why."

"A moody young man I loved. And yes, you can ask me about my relationship with Scotty. Even if you don't think it's any of your business."

"It's not. But, still. How long were you together?"

"I think I was thirteen?" she said, uncertain. "It was the spring before we started high school, tail end of middle school. We were both new here and moved into the same building. Oh, and I didn't tell my aunt about him. I knew she wouldn't approve."

"Of you dating?"

"Of him living down the hall. Too close for comfort. As it is, I'm pretty sure she died thinking I was still a virgin. We were sneaky little shits."

"I have a hard time imagining you being quiet about anything. Then he was..."

"The first?" She nodded. "I hope that's not a problem for you, Will. Sitting across from him in some meeting, trying to not think about that."

They'll greet each other with it. 'Hey, you saw my wife naked.'
'Hey, your wife once sucked my—'

"Wick!"

Aisha didn't know what I'd said but it still made her laugh and she tickled me on my chin.

"It won't be an issue," Will said. "But, thirteen?"

Why not? Jax was humping everything in sight at thirteen.

"Oh, god no. We dated for a couple of years before we got that far. It was a good thing we waited, too, at least we had deep enough feelings for each other. Otherwise, I might have run off because that was some really horrible sex."

"As I often remind myself, it takes practice."

"You have nothing to worry about. But oh my God, Will, neither of us had a clue what we were really doing. Fumbling around with clothes on didn't teach us a damned thing about what we wanted when it came to actually *doing* it. I wasn't ready, so it hurt even more than it would have. He was done in, like, nothing, and we both freaked out over the surprising amount of blood there was." She chuckled. "He thought he'd broken me and wanted to rush me to the ER. I had to stand there and tell a scared, naked sixteen-year-old boy what a hymen was, and then to take off the damned condom already because it was looking seriously stupid just hanging there half shriveled."

Will thought for a moment and then said, "Well, now I truly do feel like I didn't actually blow it the first time."

"Sweetheart." She kissed him, her lips lingering a bit. "It was wonderful. You want honesty?"

"It's been just long enough that I think my ego can stand the criticism."

"No criticism. The truth is that I wasn't expecting fireworks the first time with you. I thought it would be over in about ten seconds, and I was fine with that because I wanted to be with you so badly. So, imagine my surprise when it wasn't over with before I could blink, and I still came before you did. You were pretty damned good right from the start, and you've only gotten better."

I think he had something to say, but he couldn't because she kissed him, and it was a really good one.

Reluctantly, he pulled away. "Keep this up, and we'll make the news."

"Bilbo, I think if you stand up right now and there's a photographer anywhere near, you'll at least make a gossip site or two."

I am not sitting on your lap to hide the evidence.

Do you know how many boners I've hidden in the last year?

Too many.

"How many, Wick?" Will pressed. "Come on. You complain a lot, but I think you exaggerate."

Drew. So many times for Drew. And you. And Zed. Jax even put me on his lap last week because he didn't want Aubrey to know how happy he was that she was dusting the top shelves in the living room. And it didn't even do any good because she looked down and asked if he was peeking up her shirt to look at her boobs and he admitted it, and the next thing I know I'm on the floor and she's on the footstool, and it's a good thing no one else came home because she did some very unhygienic things to him, and—

"Take a breath. You're not obligated to stay on someone's lap, even if they're using you to hide an erection."

"Poor Wick," Aisha said with a laugh. "That was a long-winded complaint."

"Apparently at some point recently he was witness to Aubrey doing...things...to Jax."

"Leave the room when it bothers you, sweetie," she told me. "You don't need permission."

Sometimes it feels like I need to be told I can leave.

"Are you sure you want him to leave?" Will asked. "He has been known to offer stellar suggestions."

"Like the pudding and handcuffs? Which you still have not been willing to try."

He shrugged.

"All right. What part of it do you have an issue with? Being tied up, or tying me up?"

"The latter seems unnecessarily aggressive and somewhat disrespectful. I have no problem with the pudding or the play, it's using handcuffs on you that I take exception to."

"All right. Then you don't cuff me or tie me up. I'm not pushing you out of your comfort zone. And you don't have to use pudding if you don't want. Find something else." She leaned in close, resting her chin on his shoulder, one hand on his chest. "But, sweetie, trust me, I won't mind one bit if you tell me to lie still, and then you lick me clean from stem to stern. I promise you, at some point, I will be begging you to fuck me, and fuck me hard. While you're busy licking and sucking and using your fingers just *so*, I'll be trying to get my legs around you and get you inside me, and once you're in, I will come harder than I ever have."

Yeah, he couldn't get up after hearing that.

7

I waited on the stairs by Drew's front door. It would have been more comfortable if I'd gone inside to curl up on his sofa, but he sometimes went upstairs with Oz after school and I didn't want to miss him. The guard at the front desk kept glancing at me, trying to figure out what I was waiting for. He even offered me a piece of meat out of his sandwich, I think to make me go away.

It was good meat, too, sliced from a roast Aubrey had made and then left in the staff kitchen for the guards. I didn't like that I was making him uncomfortable, but I had no way to tell him I was waiting for Drew and wasn't intentionally trying to make him squirm.

It wasn't like I was taunting him with my hover cart, threatening to bolt out the front door. I was just waiting. And not blinking.

The guard was visibly relieved when Oz and Drew walked through the door, and he scooped me up, but I waited until we were out of earshot before I said anything.

Oz needs to tell Aubrey that someone needs to invite Jay for dinner.

"No one needs an invitation," Oz said. "He can just show up. He knows that."

Then someone needs to tell Jay to just go upstairs when he gets home, and I'll tell Will where he is.

We headed upstairs.

"All right, cat," Drew said. "I'll bite. Why can't Jay go home?"

Because Aisha said things to Will that made him about eight and a half inches of happy and I don't think they'll even notice if Jay comes home.

"Eight and a half inches? Seriously?"

I'm guessing. I've never measured.

"All right. I'll text Jay and tell him to come up here. He and Zed should be home soon."

"Unless they're out with Zara and Sophia," Oz said.

Text him and ask. Just tell him not to go home yet.

"You're a good wingman, Wick," Drew said. "Are you going back downstairs? I know you worry about Will falling off."

Not yet. I think they're tying each other to the headboard. They can only fall so far. Besides, chocolate syrup is involved so he might squirt off the other side of the bed and splat against the wall, but I don't think that counts as falling.

Drew handed me to Oz and brushed past Aubrey, speeding toward the balcony.

"I don't know," Oz said before Aubrey could ask. "Wick said something, and Drew's trying not to laugh at it, I think."

"Wick, sweetie," Aubrey said as she reached out to pet me, "it must have been awful for you all those years when you didn't have anyone to talk to."

I talked. Not that anyone understood me.

"He survived. And change of subject, but according to Wick, Jay will be here for dinner. Jay doesn't know it yet, but Wick doesn't think he should go home or he might see things he's not ready for."

Aubrey brightened. "Zed is bringing Sophia home for dinner. Call Jay and tell him to invite Zara, too. We might as well have a houseful."

It was a noisy houseful. Jax couldn't make it home for dinner, so Aubrey was glad to have them all there, and she sat back and listened as they talked over each other. I waited on the counter closest to the table—no King to frown at me and tell me to get down for the five thousandth time—and she snuck little bites to me.

When dinner was over, Drew got up and started clearing the table and told Zed and Jay they were going to help. He suggested that Oz and the Queen take everyone else out onto the balcony to enjoy the evening while they did dishes, which earned him a kiss on the cheek from Aubrey and a pat on his butt from Oz.

"What are you sucking up for?" Zed asked.

"Screw that," Jay said before Drew could answer. "Why the hell can't I go home?"

"Because Will is pile driving your mom into oblivion, and Wick thought it might be better if you came up here instead. You know, in case oblivion turns out to be happening on the sofa. Or the living room floor."

"Ugh. Do they know where I am?"

"I assume. Wick?"

I know. Go downstairs and make sure they haven't broken each other and tell them where Jay is.

I don't get paid enough for this.

"I'll give you something meaty when you come back," Drew called after me.

Yeah, yeah, yeah. I heard you tell Oz the same thing and she's still waiting.

"Furry little asshole!" he yelled across the room.

There was a trail of clothing in the hallway, but the bedroom door was closed, which meant I had to use the cat flap. It opened behind the nightstand, requiring me to squeeze through and turn uncomfortably in order to get around it.

I made a mental note: ask Will to move that a few inches.

They were still on the bed, but no one was struggling to get loose from too-tight bindings. Will's leg dangled over the side of the bed and I was pretty sure they hadn't heard me come in, so I pressed my nose against his skin and waited for him to jump.

He sucked in a sharp breath and hissed, "Son of a bitch, that had better be you, Wick."

No. Drew got a dog when you weren't looking.

I jumped up onto the bed. Will was on his back and Aisha was cuddled against him, but I wasn't interrupting anything.

Jay is upstairs, and he had dinner already. I don't think he's coming down until you call him and tell him you're not naked anymore.

Aisha lunged across Will to grab her phone from the nightstand. "Will, it's almost seven o'clock."

"That explains why I'm hungry." He waited a beat. "For food."

"Sure about that?"

He grabbed her wrist before she could grab onto him. "The little emperor is exhausted, Enzo. And the big emperor's stomach is growling."

"Fine. I'll make us some dinner." She started to get up, but he lunged for a kiss.

"Let's just go out. Fresh air would do me good right now."

You just don't want her to cook.

After another kiss, she went into the bathroom, and he started getting dressed. "I never said that, Wick."

But that's what you meant.

He smiled and didn't deny it. "You can come with us if you like. I'll make sure we go somewhere that serves Wick-friendly food."

Drew promised me meaty things. And I think Aubrey would like company. Jax is still at work.

"That's very considerate of you."

"Hot date tonight, Wick?" Aisha asked as she came out of the bathroom.

"He's going back upstairs to keep Aubrey company until Jax gets home."

And get meaty things. Drew promised.

I promised to have Drew tell Jay that his sensibilities wouldn't be offended if he came home and that they were going out, and then headed up the stairs. Everyone was on the balcony, except for Aubrey. She had spent some time with them and then begged off to soak in the tub with a book and soft music. I checked on her—she was absorbed in whatever she was reading and didn't even notice me there—and then went back to the balcony.

Drew's lap seemed safe. They were all loud enough that the pigeons weren't going to swoop in and bother me, and if I needed him to he would get a sweatshirt and let me warm up in the pouch.

They were talking about Rhonda again. Sophia insisted she understood why she'd been a thing for Zed, and she'd enjoyed their short conversation. Zed insisted she was tricky like that; there was a reason she racked up the numbers she did.

"People can change, Zed," Drew said. "Maybe she's tired of being the punchline to so many really crude jokes. Or maybe she's just matured."

"She got the fuck away from her parents," Jay pointed out. "Her uncle expects more. Could be that's what she needed."

Zed allowed for the possibility but cautioned them against expecting him to help or even befriend her. "And before you start spouting Willisms, I get it. Decide what kind of man I want to be and be it. That doesn't mean I should surround myself with my own mistakes. Because if I did, and she really hasn't changed?"

Oz nodded. "Your ex-girlfriend could be a PR nightmare."

"She wasn't my girlfriend."

"Your fuck buddy?" Sophia said, amused. "Even if that got out I don't think it would be more than a blip on a remote gossip site. You all—" she gestured to Oz and Drew and Zed "—are essentially the best behaved royal kids in the last couple of hundred years. No one will care if Zed spent a few weeks sweating on the back seat of a car with a willing classmate, no matter what her current circumstances. She was having a good time. That's not illegal."

"It really doesn't bother you?" Oz asked.

"I haven't been sitting at home waiting for Zed to grow up," she said. "I've got a few mistakes of my own."

Zed leaned back. "Oh, yeah? Somehow I think your mistakes are gonna be way more interesting than mine."

"Maybe." She laughed again and added, "Grosser, anyway."

"All right. Now I have to know."

"Are you sure you want to? It involves an aborted handjob and is *really* gross."

"Hey, everyone knows about my mistake. Unless you're embarrassed, why the hell not?"

She wasn't embarrassed. I had the feeling not much embarrassed her.

"All right. Junior year, there was a new guy. Kind of cute, but in an awkward way, like he had no idea and couldn't believe anyone would be interested in him. We had a couple classes together and I flirted a little bit, but we barely talked until just before the holiday break. By then, he had a little bit of confidence and didn't run when I asked him to the winter dance."

"Prom light," Oz snickered.

"It's Texas. We do things big. The winter dance came with all the expectations of prom," Sophia said. "And we had a great time, I mean for a shy kid he could dance, and he was super attentive, so yeah, I figured why the hell not just go for it? At the very least, find a quiet spot and fool around, see what kind of kisser he was and let it go from there."

"Floppy tongue guy?" Zed asked.

"No, the kissing was really good. So I let him know I was open to more, and hands were all over the place. I mean, we weren't going to actually have sex in a closet, but somewhere along the line I figured a hand job wasn't out of the question, so I went for it. Unzipped his pants and got them down his hips a little, and it was like...damn, son, what the hell is up with your dick? I mean, the head was huge and gnarly red. Like a baby arm with a big fist at the end. But still, you know, who am I to judge? Maybe it was a birth defect or something, and I wasn't going to make an issue of it. He was hard, I got my hand around him, and he shrieked like I'd stabbed him."

"How fucking hard did you grab him?" Zed asked.

"Not hard at all. But he sucked in a sharp breath when I stroked forward, and it was the backstroke that got him. Son of a bitch had never pulled back his own foreskin, so it was super tight, which meant he'd *never* cleaned under it."

Zed and Drew were already groaning.

"I pulled it back and I know it hurt like hell, but this massive chunk of...cheese...popped out and splattered on the floor. Oh my god, the smell. He's screaming because his frenulum tore, I'm trying to not vomit while I'm digging around for something to wrap that sucker up so the bleeding would stop. And I got a better look...oh god, his glans had all these little angry-red, slimy-wet craters, and I have no idea how I didn't smell it before, or that boy was even alive it was so infected. Then the closet door yanked open and one of the chaperones was there, the smell hit him in the face, and he was trying to not throw up. So the door is open, and everyone can see in, and I'm trying to wrap a piece of cloth around this poor guy's penis... I don't think I looked at another guy for *months*."

Jay slowly crossed his legs. "I really feel like I need a shower now."

Zed was laughing hard. "Well, now I know why you asked straight up if I was circumcised and seemed a little disappointed that I'm not."

Zara was more grossed out than the rest of them. "Forget that. All I want to know now is if you guys, you know, wash *everything*."

"Slowly and deliberately," Zed said, still laughing. "Couple times a day sometimes."

"How could anyone over, like, four years old not know to pull the damn thing back and clean it off?" Drew asked. "By the time I was three my dad was making me do it myself during bath time."

"I wasn't going to ask," Sophia said. "After that, he wouldn't even look at me. Never spoke to me again."

There was uncomfortable quiet, until Zed mused, "How the hell did that poor slob jerk off?"

"Stop showering, report back in a year," Oz said.

"I will pin you down and go at it with a washrag if you even think of that," Sophia warned him.

"Promise?"

"Great," Drew sighed, "we're all getting inspected for the next week or two until they're satisfied that we actually do bathe."

"That could go both ways," Oz said. "In fact, I highly recommend it." She got up and reached for his hand. "Come on, let's go...study."

Put me down. I don't want to help.

Drew set me on Zed's lap.

"Well, that wasn't subtle," Zed mumbled.

"I'd help you study, too," Sophia said, "but it's getting late, and Zara and I need to get going before her Dad starts pacing the hallway in front of my door."

Zed and Jay started to get up, but Sophia patted Zed on the chest and reminded him that she knew the way out, and she would call for a car on the way down. When they were in the elevator, Jay shifted uncomfortably and sighed.

"What?"

"Personal shit."

"So? We were just discussing our dicks with them. We can do personal."

Jay grunted and folded his arms. "Should I tell Zara?"

"That you have a dick?" Zed snorted. "Fuck all if I know. Maybe if it looks like she's about to dive for your crotch, ask her to be gentle and swear you just showered."

"No, I meant about everything."

"Why would you?"

"I dunno. Maybe she should know that the guy she's interested in used to be a girl."

Zed folded his arms, suddenly serious. "You were *never* a girl. You were a male born with the wrong junk, that's all. It's been fixed. It's not like you have to explain to a partner about scars and shit, right? You're one hundred percent, down to the DNA, male. That's good enough."

Jay shrugged.

"What if Zara suddenly announced she was post-surgical trans? Would it matter to you?"

"No, but that's different. I've been through it. I get it. If she doesn't—"

"Jay, she's your first girlfriend. The chance that she'll be your last is pretty slim. Don't rock the boat. Just enjoy the ride."

"Yeah, if I ever get to ride. Man, that poor son of a bitch."

"Come on, Soph seriously embellished that story for our entertainment. It was gross, and she knew it would make me laugh."

"Still." Jay got up. "Ugh."

He headed down the stairs—no elevator, Will had trained him not to—and Zed took me inside where there were no pigeons. Without any prompting, he went into the kitchen, mumbling that Drew had promised me food and hadn't delivered.

This was new.

I liked it.

If Sophia was the reason why, he needed to keep her.

*

Jax came home while I was eating, and Aubrey set her book aside to heat up dinner for him. I stayed long enough to make sure he wasn't going to go back to work—if he was, I would stay and keep her company—and then went downstairs. Jay was the only one in the building who was alone—technically Zed was alone but once he had given me food he went to take a shower and I knew after that he would call Sophia to tell her goodnight and thanks for the sex—so I figured he might need my company more than anyone else.

He was at the dining room table with his homework. There were two different computer tablets and an electronic notepad that he was scribbling on, and he was too focused to notice when I jumped onto the chair across from him. I sat quietly and watched him because talking would interrupt him and that would be rude. School was hard enough without my interference.

I waited with my chin resting on the table for twenty minutes before he realized I was there. "Anyone ever feed you?" he asked. "Go into the kitchen if you're hungry. I'll open a can."

I'd had a snack but that wasn't a meal, so I went into the kitchen.

"It must suck to not have thumbs," he said as he spooned food out onto a plate. "You're smart. If you had thumbs and could open your own cans, you wouldn't need us."

Sure, I would. I need someone who has money to buy the cans.

"I need a brain like yours, Wick. You're good at figuring things out. I suck at it."

You figured out that I might want food. I think you're a freaking genius.

"I'm barely squeaking by in school, you know. I know all the stuff, but I blow it on the tests. I'm going to suck as much in college as I did in high school. I'm a fucking waste of tuition."

Ask your mom for help. Or Will. Or Zed. He's taking the same classes. He's a good student.

He went back to the table while I ate. "Like this. Pacifican history. There's all this stuff about how our government is structured, and I *know* it. The King rules, but he has advisory councils. The military is separate, but he's its head. Yet there's nothing about why we don't have a parliament like England, and I know that'll be on the test. The teacher doesn't lecture on it, she just reads from the textbooks. But she'll fucking well expect us to all pull the answer out of our asses."

There's no parliament because it was voted against when the United States split up and Pacifica began. Fewer politicians meant less political posturing.

"You know this stuff, don't you?"

Sometimes Will won't shut up. I hear a lot.

"Why can't I find the answers to the things I know she'll ask?"

It was probably covered in an earlier chapter. You've just forgotten. I know how that feels, I've forgotten a lot.

I jumped onto the table and sat near him, where I could see his tablets. He had a chart of the government on one and a textbook open on the other. He was reading about the chain of command, and how the monarch essentially has the final word but can also be overruled by the Supreme Court in certain cases, but there was nothing about why things were the way they were.

I touched my nose to the screen and found the table of contents, and then looked for the chapter that would tell him about the days when the government was being formed, when King Norval argued against his own candidacy, and how the political convention in charge of writing the charter that would become the constitution explained their choices.

They were tired of political parties looking out for their own interests. A brilliant democratic republic became a mentality of us versus them, and it put party over country. They thought if the right King or Queen was elected, then everything would work out. And so far it mostly has. The Supreme Court has only overruled the monarch three times, I think.

"Fucking aces, Wick," he muttered. "You can read."

Surprise.

"Goddamn, I wish I could understand you. You'd be an awesome tutor."

I'll still help you if I can.

Sometimes, you just have to remember the things you learned for one test but then shoved aside for the next.

He flipped through the information and scribbled notes on the other tablet.

"All right, smart guy," he muttered after a while, "what do you know about girls?"

Be nice to them. They smell good and are squishy in all the right places.

He blinked rapidly and then saved the document he was working on so that he could open a blank one. "If you can read, you can probably write. Can you type?"

My paws are too big to hit all the right letters. I lifted a paw and hoped he'd understand.

"Use your nose. It can be short answers. But will you try? Just, I dunno, type your name."

My nose left wet smears on the screen, but I hit the right letters in the right order. W I C K.

"Hot damn. Okay, what's your favorite snack?"

D E A D T H N G S.

I missed a letter and hoped he didn't think less of me for it.

He chuckled. "I meant, specifically, but that's all right."

S T E A K.

"Jesus fucking—I know it's work for you, but we can talk, Wick!"

O Y A Y.

"Sarcastic little shit, aren't you?" He looked up as the front door opened, and Will didn't get three feet inside when he squealed, "Wick can type!"

I get snot all over everything, but yeah.

They both came over to see. Will wasn't especially surprised, but Aisha was. "What made you think of trying this?" she asked.

"He opened a chapter in my history book and showed me the information I needed. I figured if he could read, he could type, and he fucking did it."

I don't enjoy it.

"Wick's incredibly intelligent," Will said, "but don't abuse this ability. He's not a party trick, and he doesn't particularly enjoy the process."

Jay looked a little deflated. "Damn, I'm sorry."

I T S O K I W N T T T A L K Y O U.

Will pointed out how long that took me to type out. "If you need answers from him longer than a word or two, come get me or Drew to translate. It's easier on him."

Make sure he knows I really like having conversations with him even when he doesn't know what I'm saying.

"He talks back a lot," Jay said. "I figured if he hated it, he'd just leave."

"Unless he deems it to be important, he might. Wick will suffer for the sake of the people he loves." He bent over to look me in the eye. "Thank you for being the messenger tonight. And I apologize for making you uncomfortable."

I think Jay was more uncomfortable.

At the same time, Jay huffed, "Him?"

Aisha kissed the top of his head and said, "I'm sure having dinner upstairs was a hardship for you."

"Yeah, *that* was the uncomfortable part." He was trying not to laugh. "I don't know what exactly Wick told Drew, but the message I got was that I couldn't come home because Will was pile driving you into oblivion. Possibly on the sofa."

"Wick, you didn't," she said with a sigh.

No. I said that Aisha said things to make Will eight and a half inches of happy and that Jay might not want to go home.

"He did not," Will said. "And I would prefer we change the subject."

"Fine." Jay turned his tablets off. "Did you talk to her yet?"

George. In case you forgot.

"I have not. There wasn't an appropriate time."

"What?" Aisha asked.

Jay grimaced and looked down at the table.

"He asked me to take him to see George," Will said simply. "A short visit, so that he can see for himself that George is all right."

She sighed and folded her arms, but she didn't look angry about it. Her temple twitched as she ground her teeth together, but the look in her eyes was soft and understanding. "All right."

Jay's head snapped up. "Seriously?"

"I don't like it, but I've expected this." She pulled a chair out and sat down. "I don't want you alone with him, sweetheart. We'll take you, but you are absolutely not going anywhere with him."

"That's fine. I just want to see for myself that he's gotten better."

Will sat down, too. "I'll ask my father to arrange something. But be prepared for George to decline the invitation, Jay. He may not be ready to face you."

"Would it be like the same amount of time for him as it's been for me?"

Will nodded. "Finn takes great care to keep his movements consistent. He wouldn't want to risk going much further forward than he would if he still lived there."

"Cool." He got up and picked up his tablets. "And thanks."

Aisha watched him go into his room. "You don't have to do this, Will. If Finn can make the arrangements, I can take him."

"If Jay can willingly face George, so can I. I admire his compassion, even if I don't share it."

"Oh, hon, I have no idea where he gets it from. I'd still like to kill the bastard. I have such a visceral reaction to even the thought of his stupid face."

"Then perhaps you shouldn't go. Why tempt yourself?"

"I'm going. And Wick should be there, too. One look at how angry I am and the furry little attack monster staring him down, George won't dare to breathe wrong."

I won't have to bite him again, will I?

"I doubt you'll need to bite him, Wick," Will said. "But by all means, if you think the situation calls for it, you're free to do anything necessary to protect Jay."

Then you better be near something I can use to get the taste out of my mouth. Bacon works. Make sure you have bacon.

They fell quiet for a long time, looking at each other. Will slid his hand across the table and reached for hers, then said, "Neither of us has to go, Enzo. I'm not sure we should. I just gave Wick carte blanche to hurt someone, and we're both okay with the idea."

"Because it's George."

"I know. I still want Wick to go, but perhaps we should ask Oz and Drew to take Jay instead." When she looked puzzled, he added, "I'm not rational where George is concerned, and neither are you. Jay needs to see that he's all right, and he won't be if we're there."

She didn't want to send Jay two hundred years into the future without a parent.

"Finn can supervise, on the periphery. They can use the hospital portal, and they can meet George in the cafeteria. The location is controlled, and they'll be safe."

"You really think you'd hurt George?"

He said he wasn't sure, but I knew what he really worried about. He was afraid she might, and if she was successful, she'd never forgive herself.

8

Drew yanked his door open and jumped back a step, not expecting my face to be right in front of his face. He rolled his eyes, unimpressed with my new trick, and then stepped aside to let me in.

"He's figured out how to use the hover cart to knock on the door," he told Oz.

I would use a paw, but it's too quiet and you might not hear it.

Oz was on the sofa, tying her shoes. "Just wait. When we're living in Will's apartment and he has the hallway to play with, he'll come screaming toward you in the middle of the night, and you'll scream like a little girl. He's already done it to my dad a few times."

"Oh, the hover cart moves upstairs with Will."

"Wick will find a way." She got up and headed for the door, stopping long enough to kiss him. "My dad should be in his office upstairs. Take Wick with you. He can have fun doing circles around the desk and driving Dad nuts."

I would enjoy that.

Drew had a new toy to show Jax; It was a scaled-down holographic generator, built on a computer that was no larger than the palm of his hand. He had it connected to his phone, running a program that would allow him to change the display with a simple touch to the phone's screen.

"It's definitely a toy," he told Jax once it was set up on the desk. "But it's allowing me to tweak things before really tackling the computer array, and I've been able to write better code—sometimes the end result looks pretty freaking real."

He had more to say about it, but there was a knock on the open door, and General Myers came in. Jax asked him to wait a minute; he wanted to see what Drew had been working on.

Drew turned it on, tapped at his phone, and a bouquet of roses in a crystal vase appeared, hovering over the base.

"That's incredible." Jax touched a petal. "That feels real. And if not for the computer casing at its base, I'd never guess I was looking at an image."

With another tap of the screen, the flowers shifted and became an arrangement of wildflowers.

General Myers leaned in to get a better look. "My brain is telling me I can smell them. What sort of projectors are you using? I don't think I've ever seen a holo so complete. There's no opacity, no static, no light bleed."

Drew started to answer, but closed his mouth when Will entered and snapped, "Turn it off."

Jax looked confused and Drew hesitated until Will repeated it. "Drew. Turn it off."

He turned it off.

"Problem?" Jax asked. "He was just demonstrating—"

"I know what he's doing." Will watched the display fade. "Andrew, if you want to share your newest work, do it upstairs, where you're showing it to your father-in-law. Bringing it here is showing it to your King. There's a difference."

Jax nodded. "Wasn't thinking. I'm sorry, Drew, but he's right. I'll take a closer look later."

Myers settled into the chair near Jax's desk, and the look he gave Will was harsh. "It's a toy, Emperor. What's the harm? I'd like to know more about how he accomplished that."

"Indeed."

"Come on. Those flowers looked real. He didn't get that sort of resolution using standard projectors. I'm interested."

"As one would be."

The temperature in here just dropped, didn't it?

"I can leave," Drew said. "I'll leave." He picked up the small computer and slid it into his back pocket. "Uh. Yeah. Later."

"Is that kid just smart, or is he goddamned brilliant?" Myers asked. "I'm curious."

"Brilliant, but he has no idea," Will said. "Give him time before you start poking your nose in his work, Anthony. He's just getting started."

"But that was damned impressive—"

Jax ended the discussion before it could get rolling. "Not why we're here. What's up, Will?"

"Our seated representative to the Consortium is retiring," Will said. "She's given nearly a years' notice, but you'll need to name her replacement months ahead of the vote on Florida's inclusion."

"Suggestions?" Jax asked.

"The only qualified candidates I know of wouldn't want the job," Myers said, looking pointedly to Will.

"And no, I will not take that seat," Will said to Jax. "There's time. But you needed to know."

"Put feelers out," Jax said. "That includes you, General."

General Myers reminded Jax that the Consortium was part of the U.N. and not Pacifica's military; anyone he could recommend came with the baggage of a commitment to service. "And don't look at me, either," he said as he got up. "Only other job I'm remotely interested doesn't exist. Get Elysium up and running, and I'll be more than happy to serve as an ambassador on it."

"Now that job, I might fight you for," Will joked.

"No need to be mean," Myers said as he headed for the door.

When Myers left, Jax turned to Will and asked, "All right, what's the real issue with Drew's demonstration?"

"Anthony Myers," Will said simply. "Drew's work is not something the General should be aware of yet, and Drew needs to understand the difference between presenting something to you, personally, and to his King. Oz's father can brush it off as an amusing endeavor. His King, when presented with another viewpoint on it, will have to take that very seriously."

"Myers will underscore the military applications," Jax said. "Understand, Will, even if Drew shows me all the neat tricks at home, if I determine that what he's doing can be utilized—"

"It can't be," Will said firmly.

"Not yet," Jax guessed. "If he does what I think he will, it could become a valuable tool. And once he works out his computer issues, we'll be interested in terms of what he can do for Elysium. He knows that already."

All Will wanted was time. He wanted Drew to be able to work without the government looking over his shoulder and without the threat that they would swoop in and take over. He especially wanted time for Drew to file and be awarded the patents on anything he created.

"This is for Oz, too, Jax. He desperately wants to be able to provide for her in a way that allows her to follow her own interests outside of learning to follow your rule. Give him that."

"All right, I'll take the king hat off when he's showing me things."

"Crown, Jax," Will said dryly. "It's a crown."

*

I floated behind Will as he went down the stairs. We were on our way to see Drew, to make him feel better about being ordered to turn his computer off and to ask him to take Jay to see George.

You have to say you're sorry for kicking his metaphorical puppy.

"You grasp metaphors."

I read.

His door was open. The computer was on his table, and he was on the sofa staring at his tablet, jaw set and eyebrows knotted. Will hesitated at the door, so I zipped past him and sped toward Drew's head.

He startled nicely.

Will threatened to take the hover cart away, but I knew better.

"An explanation may be in order," Will said after Drew nudged my cart away from his face. "My intention was not to upset you."

"I figured."

"And yet, I did. I apologize for that, and it's my fault for having never stressed the appropriate times for sharing information with Jax." He considered it for a moment. "Taking new developments to him in his office is essentially offering the project for government consumption, especially when someone like Anthony Myers is present."

"It's a prototype. A toy."

"It's an advanced toy, Andrew. Myers surely recognized that you've utilized technology he hasn't seen before, and if he'd had more information, he would have understood that what you've already accomplished is valuable to the military. We don't want them touching it, not until you're far enough along to secure patents and trademarks in your own name."

"He wouldn't yank this out from under us."

"No, Jax wouldn't. King Jackson, on the other hand, might feel he has no other choice, especially if pressured by the General."

"But Mr. B already knows what we're doing."

Will nodded. "Theoretically. And I'm not asking you to hide anything from him. Simply be judicious in when and where you offer him information about your progress. Never in his office, and especially never in front of those with whom you are not already close."

"All right, I get it. I'm not sure I agree with it, but I got it."

"Andrew—"

"No, I see where you're coming from, Will. But Mr. B has already seen most of the work we've done, and he's mentioned more than once that he wants whatever cooling system we design to be used on Elysium. You've outright told me that's where we're headed. The King is already aware of what's coming Pacifica's way."

But the General isn't.

He could take your stuff and change it to make things go -boom-.

"You can't make a bomb out of a hologram, Wick."

Nanothingies. They can be taught to bite.

"You think he'd exploit the nanotech?" Drew asked Will.

"If he has a sense of the possibilities, yes. He'd have little choice."

Drew sighed and then nodded. "At some point, I won't even be able to share anything with him."

"Jax has far more latitude, but we should consult before offering him future demonstrations."

"All right. I get it." He got up. "I told Oz we'd meet her to work out after her class. She wants you to scare the crap out of Jay today. Spar with her, let him see you go after her, then tell him he's next."

He told me to dock the hover cart if I wanted to go with them; I still wasn't allowed to take it outside, even if he was with me. Drew grabbed a sweatshirt that I could ride in, and I bounced off his stomach as they power-walked toward the workshop.

"I have a significant favor to ask," Will said when we were halfway there. "Jay wants to see George. Aisha is willing to allow it, but—"

"She's afraid she'll kill the son of a bitch on first sight."

"Indeed."

"I don't mind taking him as long as you're okay with me using a portal again."

They want Oz to go, too.

"Not from a lack of trust, Wick," Will said. "She's the muscle. I have no doubt that you can manage getting Jay to the right time. You'll use the portal in the hospital and will meet George in the cafeteria. Finn will wait nearby."

"Yeah, sure. Why not. But if he does anything, I'm unleashing Oz on him."

That was understandable. And if it came to that, they were in a hospital. Surely someone could save George when she was done with him.

9

I wound up going home with Jay and Zed, and once we were home, I scrambled behind Jay as he called out for Aisha. He bolted up the stairs two at a time; she wasn't in the apartment, so they ran, hoping she was upstairs.

She was on the balcony with Aubrey, enjoying the cool afternoon, an open bottle of wine on the little table between them.

"First off, he's okay," Jay said as he threw the door open. "I mean, he said he was okay, and he was walking so I think he is, but there was blood. Not a lot, but still. Blood."

"Take a breath," Aisha said as she turned to look at him. "What happened?"

Zed snorted. "Oz nailed Will in the gut with a wicked spinning side kick. She launched him halfway across the room."

"Yeah, but he popped right back up," Jay said. "It took a minute for it to really hurt, and then he started bleeding. Drew took him to see Mass, just in case."

Aisha started to get up.

"He said for you to stay home and not go running after him. Oz and Drew are with him, and if anything is broken, they'll call."

"He really did seem okay," Zed said. "Might have twisted an ovary, but he'll live."

He didn't throw up this time, so that's something.

I jumped in her lap and head-butted her chin.

"All right," she said with a heavy sigh. "I'll wait here. I don't like it, but I'll wait."

That was all the excuse Aubrey needed. Jay and Aisha were staying for dinner, and Will could join them when he got home.

Aisha didn't argue. She knew that feeding everyone was Aubrey's happy place and it was less an invitation than it was an order.

I waited in the living room, where I could see both the elevator and the head of the stairs. Jax came home not long after Zed and Jay, and he helped set the table while Aubrey finished cooking. A guard came out of the elevator looking for Jax, but he only had a question and his intrusion annoyed me because it felt unnecessary. Just before dinner was ready, the elevator door pinged and Will shuffled out, trying to not grimace, with Oz and Drew behind him.

"It's just a hell of a bruise," he said before Aisha could freak out. "No broken bones. I'm going to be stiff for a few days, but it's fine."

"Still not apologizing," Oz said as she brushed past.

"As well you shouldn't," he said, just before he sucked in a sharp, ragged breath. He didn't argue when Aisha led him to a chair at the table and ordered him to sit, or when told him she would get his drink and anything else he needed. If dinner had been something other than stew, he probably would have let someone cut his meat.

Did she jingle your bells?

Drew laughed. "Close, Wick. His bellybutton might be hung up on a vertebra."

You should have blocked.

"Thank you for the suggestion," Will grunted.

He was quiet through dinner, wincing every now and then. Before dessert, Jax got up to get a bottle of scotch and poured a triple for Will, declaring it to be medicinal.

"First time in his life, he's having to take a few hits," Drew said. "He's not used to being on the ouchy end of the kick."

"It's been quite some time," Will agreed. "I am duly impressed that she did this much damage with such controlled technique. I never want to be on the end of a full-force kick."

After dinner, he got up slowly, even though the scotch had taken the edge off, and excused himself. Aisha scrambled after him and asked if he needed help; he shook his head but whispered that he needed to talk to her on the balcony in a few minutes.

Puzzled, she waited for him out there. I was near the double seat and watched her peek over the edge, looking at the people on the Square. When he came out, she reached for him and helped him sit down.

"Be honest. How badly did she hurt you?"

"It's not from the kick," he said. "Not entirely." He lifted his shirt to show her the growing black and purple bruise, and a three-inch sealed incision near his navel. "She destroyed my implant. When her heel connected, the flesh around it split, and it partially slipped out. The tube disconnected and shifted." He winced again. "Right into a testicle."

"Ow." She carefully touched a finger just below the incision.

"Mass said he had no choice but to remove it. The implant, not the testicle."

"I can imagine."

"He also said he could place a new one on my left side."

She looked up. "I don't imagine you'll need one for a week or so, but when?"

"He could have done it today." Will took a deep breath. "I asked him not to, not until I could talk to you."

"You don't need my permission, sweetheart."

"I think I do, if my choice is to not replace it."

She let that sink in. "What are you saying, Will? Do you want us to have a baby?"

He trailed a finger along her jaw and then let his arm rest on the bench behind her. "I at least want to open the floor to discussion. Enzo, until he was prepping to replace it, I didn't realize how badly I wanted him to tell me I had to heal first. I at least want the possibility."

I jumped onto her lap, just because.

"Sweetheart, I told you *months* ago that if you wanted a child of your own to tell me."

"We can't have one simply because I have this paternal itch. We both need to want this."

"He doesn't get it, does he, Wick?" she asked me. "Will, when I told you to ask me, it was because I already knew. You changed every notion I had about having more kids. I thought you were waiting a bit, that's all."

"I thought I was, too. And I'll continue to wait if you're not certain. Don't say yes because you now know I want this."

"I want this, Will." She leaned in to kiss him. "If only you weren't so sore right now."

"I won't be by the time you ovulate."

She raised an eyebrow.

"I keep track. You're absurdly regular. I know when you'll dig the heating pad out to help with cramps, when you'll bring home cupcakes with a disgusting amount of chocolate frosting heaped on top, and when you'll mumble about wondering how the hell I can find such a mess attractive. And I'll tell you the absolute truth. You're beautiful, no matter how cranky you are."

"But we could practice," she said against his lips.

"Give me a few days, Enzo. She kicked me hard enough that it's going to get worse before it gets better."

There was a lot of kissing, but it wasn't the kind that leads to bouncy things. It was gentle and sweet, and I stayed on Aisha's lap.

"A couple things," she said when they parted. "The obvious, we tell no one, all right?"

He nodded.

"The other—we can't let our sex life become all about conceiving. We have a hell of a lot of fun and I don't want to lose that. No tracking days, all right? I don't want to make love with you on a schedule."

"If it happens, it happens," he agreed.

I won't say anything. But I get to be there when you tell everyone, all right? When it's actually going to happen?

"I hope you don't mean you want us to announce it every time we have sex," Will said to me.

No, they'll think you're bragging. I want to be there when you tell everyone after she's pregnant. I kinda married her, too, you know.

"Wick," Aisha said, planting a kiss on my head, "you'll be the first to know. But both of you need to keep my age in mind. It might not be as easy as it was with Jay."

"How long did it take then?"

"Oh, hon, I blinked and was pregnant. We decided one week, and the test was positive the next. At my age now? I don't know if I still ovulate every month. I could get a testing kit, but..."

"You're not that old, but still. We'll have fun with it for a while."

You should go thank Oz. Well, if you were telling people.

"How's that, Wick?"

Who knows how long you would have waited to tell Aisha you want your own sticky person? You owe Oz since she broke you and made you think about it.

"I'll thank her eventually."

"I'll bake her some cookies," Aisha said.

But we like her.

Will laughed and refused to tell her what I said. She threatened to poke him where it hurt, but then Jax and Aubrey came out with glasses and a bottle of scotch, and she couldn't because it would have made her look really mean.

"What's the real damage, Will?" Jax asked as he poured the scotch. "I've never seen you move like a three-hundred-year-old man with a hernia."

"No real damage," Will answered. "Oz is getting very, very good. When she focuses, she's formidable."

"And if she doesn't?"

"She occasionally second guesses herself. There have been moments of micro-hesitation when I've gotten too close for comfort, and she senses that her options are few." He took a small sip and winced. "I changed the soap I use, Jax. Drew admitted to me privately that it was too close to how Levi smelled and sometimes jolted her out of the moment. She recovers quickly, but it means something."

"I'd give anything if the process were easier for her," Aubrey said.

"It could be, if she'd allow it. The residual pain, the angst—"

"You'd take her forward," Jax guessed.

"I've offered. She chooses to give therapy more time."

"That will never erase the pain," Aubrey sighed.

"She won't allow brain remapping, either," Jax sighed.

Well, this took a turn. We were happy and kissing. One of you needs to kiss.

"Wick wants me to kiss you," Will said to Jax. "I am declining."

"Your loss," Jax said.

I jumped over to Aubrey's lap and patted her lips with my paw.

"I'm not kissing Will, either, sweetie. That would upset Aisha. Is it enough if I give one to Jax?"

I jumped back to Aisha's lap so that Aubrey could lean forward to give Jax a quick kiss. They made fun of me for a minute or so, wondering what brought that on, but after that, they stopped talking about sad things and started talking about the wedding, which made them all happy.

"It will be a colorful wedding," Aubrey said. "I hope the boys don't mind wearing red. Oz wants a lot of it."

"Does that include the best man?" Will asked, not sounding at all thrilled with the idea.

"You're one of the boys," she answered, amused. "Red tux, white shirt, black shoes. And that was a concession, William. She wanted you all in red high-topped sneakers."

"Please tell me the father of the bride is not included in that," Jax groaned.

"Luckily for you, she's fine with your official uniform."

"Did she ever pick a maid of honor?" he asked.

"Zed. She wants her brother to stand with her." Her eyes got a bit teary. "She thinks that next to Drew, no one else has ever been as good a friend or had her back the way he does. She wants to buck tradition. No bridesmaids, just Zed and William standing with them."

"If I can stand by then," Will said with a grimace. "One of you may have to carry me to the elevator tonight."

"Eh, we'll roll you down the stairs," Jax said.

Will reached for the bottle of scotch and said if that was happening, he wanted to be significantly anesthetized. While he poured, Aisha's phone rang, and she stepped inside to answer it.

"Drew's birthday next week," Will said. "Are we taking him to Fuzzy's for his first legal drink?"

"If we can get him to drink, sure," Jax said. "And if we can get him to leave Oz at home for a few hours."

"Not on his birthday," Aubrey said. "They probably have plans."

"Day after, then. Boys night out."

"I hope you enjoy cinnamon—" Will started. Aisha came back and looked a little flushed, and he stopped to make sure she was all right.

"I got the job. That was the head of the math department. He made the offer, and I sign the contract tomorrow." She sounded surprised. "Damn, Will, I got the job!"

"Never a doubt." He wanted to jump up to hug her but settled for tilting his head back to kiss her. "Congratulations, professor."

Jax and Aubrey offered their congrats as well, and I jumped back onto her lap to give her chin a headbutt.

"Congrats to you, too," Jax said to Will. "The closest you'll ever get to sleeping with a co-ed."

Aubrey smacked his arm, and probably not for the last time that night.

*

Will was too sore to pull his own clothes off, prompting Aisha to wonder out loud if there was more damage than he was letting on, and questioning whether to call Mass again or wait until morning. He swore it was only bruising and the incision that hurt, and after he kicked his shoes off, she pulled his t-shirt over his head and then unzipped his jeans.

"This should be going much differently," he mused.

His pants were around his knees when Jay came out of his bedroom. "Damn, guys, you have a door, you know."

"He can barely move," Aisha told Jay. "I'm just helping."

Will didn't even try to cover up. "Apologies for the nudity. It was not intentional."

Jay turned around and headed down the hall, but he was laughing and not offended by the sight of Will naked with his pants around his ankles.

She could have left your underwear on, you know.

Aisha helped Will into a pair of shorts, and they followed Jay into the kitchen. He grabbed a bottle of root beer and sat at the table and asked if he was in trouble for something. Will was very slow to sit across the table from him, grimacing a bit as he shook his head. "Your mother has news," he said.

Aisha grabbed the never-ending fruit platter from the refrigerator and a drink for Will and sat next to him. "It's good news for me," she said. "Maybe inconvenient news for you."

"What? I have to stay with Dad an extra weekend or something?"

Will leaned back. "You say that as if it's a bad thing."

Jay sighed. "I didn't mean it like that. But if you guys are going somewhere, I can stay here alone, you know. It's not like Dad is home much now anyway, and if he is, he's never alone."

"Really?" Aisha was surprised. "He's dating already?"

"If you can call it that. He's...I dunno. Getting a bunch of shit out of his system, I guess. He brings home someone different every night. I don't think he minds that I've skipped out early the last couple of his weekends."

"I'd say that doesn't sound like him, but it does. I'm sorry, sweetheart. He shouldn't be parading a line of men in front of you."

Jay snorted. "Yeah, no, most of them are women. Like I said, he's working through some shit."

"And not what we intended to discuss," Will said abruptly.

Aisha told Jay about the job. "The downside for you is that I'm following you to school. I don't imagine you had this in mind when the school year started."

"Fuck, who cares about that? This is awesome. Congrats. When?"

They talked about the start of the next semester, and Jay assured her that they could co-exist on the same campus. It was a big place, and if she didn't want anyone to know his existence was her fault, well, different last names would help cover that up.

"Stop," she said, even though he was clearly teasing. "But I won't be following you around. We probably won't see much of each other."

"Unless you drive him to school," Will said.

"I don't need to learn to drive, Will!"

"Yes, you do."

"I can drive her," Jay offered. "If you let me use your car, anyway."

"There," Aisha said. "I have a chauffeur."

"He didn't say I could use his car," Jay reminded her.

"You can use my car anytime you want to," Will said. "I would appreciate it if you didn't abuse the privilege the way Zed did, but I rarely need it. The fob is in the drawer of the stand by the door."

Jay glanced in that direction. "Seriously? Sweet. Thanks."

"Get a parking permit first," Aisha said. She turned to Will and said, "James was not on board with the idea of getting him his own car. If he can use yours—"

That surprised Jay. "You actually asked Dad about that?"

She nodded. "It's complicated. He wasn't abrupt about it, but he doesn't think it's necessary."

"Doesn't think it's necessary or doesn't want to be the one to pay for it?" Will asked.

"Don't," she said quietly.

"It's all right," Jay said. "Dad's kinda right, I don't *need* a car. And if I can use Will's every now and then, that's good enough. I really don't mind walking most of the time."

Will looked angry for a fraction of a moment. "And to that end, we also discussed an allowance for you."

"Let me guess. He said no to that, too. You look kinda pissed, but that's fine, too. He's always just given me money when I've asked. He doesn't see a need for it."

"I—we—want you to learn to budget," Will said. "We'll open an account for you, and deposit funds weekly. Use it for daily expenses and recreation, and if the amount is insufficient, we can make adjustments."

"What, like for everything? Food, clothes, stuff like that?"

"We don't expect you to grocery shop," Aisha said lightly. "Lunches, clothing you want but don't need, and—" she took a deep breath "—dating."

"Why not just let me get a job? You shouldn't have to pay my way on a date."

"As I keep telling Drew, school is your job," Will said. "Finish this year and see how it goes."

Jay sounded disappointed when he said, "Fine. Don't flunk out and *maybe* you'll let me work come summer."

"Take the time to find the things that matter," Will suggested. "Explore the possibilities for your future. You have a lifetime of work ahead. Now is the time to learn."

"Speaking of the future," Aisha said. She took another deep breath. "Tomorrow you're heading into it. George wants to see, you, too."

10

Their plan to stay behind ended ten seconds after we met Mass near the portal. He'd seen Finn off, and when he saw how sore Will still was, he told Aisha it didn't matter what Will wanted; they were going to his office on the other side, where he could repair the bruising and muscle micro-tears in less than half an hour.

Oz and Drew would still go with Jay, but there was no reason for Will to stay behind, in that much pain, not when it could be fixed.

"You can stay here and hurt for another week or go with me, and this afternoon you can let Oz kick you in the cojones again."

Aisha took hold of his arm. "You're going."

He went.

Once we were through, Mass herded them toward his office, and Finn led the way to the cafeteria. He warned that we were a little early; George wouldn't be there for another fifteen minutes.

They won't care once they get a look out the window.

Ten seconds after Finn opened the cafeteria door, they were plastered to the giant wall of window, stunned into jaw-dropping silence by the sight of people taking flight from the launch pad across the street. Drew plastered both hands flat against the glass, his nose a hair's breadth away from it, his breath fogging the glass.

Oz pointed to a bike idling just five feet below. "What the hell? How is it just hanging there?"

"Doesn't rely on magnets," Finn said. "Ask him nicely, and Will might show you how stupid he used to get on these." He drew a loop in the air with his finger. "I think I had a heart attack that day. He was twelve."

Drew looked at Oz. "Didn't he tell us he never rebelled as a kid?"

"He said that?" Finn chuckled. "His memory is probably impaired from all the alcohol Jax poured down him before he was even twenty."

"You know about that?" Oz asked, glancing at him sideways, keeping an eye on the bike.

"Your father has been a fountain of information regarding the years I missed with him." He leaned against the window on his shoulder, arms folded. "He wasn't breaking a confidence. He thought I needed to know that Will had an actual adolescence."

"We should go spy on teenaged Emperor again," Drew said. "Knowing who he is? We'd look at him completely differently than we did last time."

"Speaking of that." Finn turned away from the window. "You know the rules. If you get access to a computer, you won't look for information about yourselves. Or your friends."

Oz shrugged. "Times changed. It wouldn't really be us, anyway."

"Still."

"What about me?" Jay asked. "You think my future has changed, too?"

"Undoubtedly," Finn said. "But leave it alone, just in case."

A deep voice rumbled behind us. "I could be bribed. I've looked you up."

George stood ten feet away, hands shoved into his pockets. I wouldn't have recognized him, other than by his voice. His hair had grown back, thick and dark, and he didn't look so beaten down. The wounds on his face had healed and left no scars, and the pressure of time no longer forced him to hunch over. There was no twitching, no swatting at bugs that only he could see.

He was also at least twenty years younger.

Finn went to wait at a table close to the door, and Oz said that she and Drew would be nearby, but far enough to give them privacy. "Take all the time you need," Drew said, "but signal if necessary."

George sighed. "Sit next to him, if it helps. Aisha needs you close, and I understand."

Oz looked at Jay, who shrugged.

Give him space. He wants it even if he doesn't know it.

"Look how tall you've gotten already." George reached out and brushed fingers across Jay's cheek. "Not even fuzz. Stubble."

"Puberty fucked me hard," Jay said. "In a good way, not the life-sucks way."

They sat at the table nearest to the window and Drew guided Oz to one that was closer than they'd planned but was still far enough away to give Jay a sense of privacy. I jumped onto Jay's lap because that's where Will wanted me to be. I had a good view of George, and if I needed to hiss at him he would see all the sharp points on my teeth.

If I hissed, he would remember what it felt like to have those points sink into his scalp and my claws dragging down his face.

"You look great," Jay told him. "Like, this is probably where you're supposed to be. You got better pretty fast."

George was certain that Aisha had saved his life. If he'd gotten his way, convincing Jay to run off with him, he would have lived an hour or two more at best. "The last thing I remember, she'd kicked me in the groin. The next thing I knew was in the hospital and two weeks had gone by. Blackshear's medics rushed me here and stuck me in a recovery tank. It was programmed to the age I should have been based on my date of birth, so yes, I'm where I would have been if I'd stayed here all along." He thought for a moment. "The tanks. They're hard to describe. It's almost like an aquarium—"

"I know what it's like." Jay gestured to himself. "That's how this happened. I spent four days floating in one."

"I'll be damned," George said softly. "If I'd known..."

"You still would have been against it."

He nodded. "But not as adamant or vocal. I wouldn't have understood the hurry, but if I'd known bringing you here was possible I would have yielded. The surgery is reversible here, Jaime. You could have seen for yourself without the risk of life-long regrets."

"Jay," he reminded George. "And I don't have regrets. Seriously. I have never felt more like myself than I do now."

"Jay," he repeated. "It's reflex, I'm sorry. In here—" he tapped his forehead with his pointy finger "—I do think of you as Jay. I speak of you to my family as Jay. And as male. Every day I wonder how you're doing, and if your life is good."

"I'm living with my mom and Will most of the time now, and it's been great."

"And it's your senior year," George said, grinning.

Jay shook his head. "High school sucked, so I took the exit exam. I just started my first year at UC."

"I'd like to say high school is always awful, but it was one of my personal highlights. How's your dad?"

Jay took time before he answered. "Surrounded by people all the time, but lonely as hell. He's got shit to work through."

George knew what he meant. "I'm sorry. Sorrier still that you see it happening."

"You know how he is."

"I would give anything—" He sighed hard. "I miss him. If you tell him you saw me and he asks, I miss him."

"I'm not sure I'm allowed to tell him, but if Will says I can, I will."

George visibly deflated.

"Will's a decent guy, George. If there's a way to tell Dad anything, he'll help me figure it out. I still don't get why you hate him so much."

"He's just...unnatural."

"Yeah, well, who he is isn't his fault. The things he can do aren't his fault."

"You know about him?"

"Yeah, and I think it's pretty fucking amazing."

"He can suck secrets out of your brain with a touch, Jay. It's intrusive."

"He doesn't do that."

"But he *did*."

Jay flinched. "That's not like Will."

"It was, when we were children. Accident or not, he learned more about our classmates than anyone should have a right to know. One bump on the playground, and he knew the worst of the things I wanted no one else to hear."

"And?"

"And he asked questions. He knows things—" George swallowed hard. "William Blackshear can ruin a man if he wants to. That kind of power should never go unchecked."

"What's he got on you?" Jay asked. "How bad could it be? You were, what, four? Five?"

"Fine. You need a reason to hate me, I'll give you one." George looked across the room to Finn. "He's around here somewhere, isn't he? Go get him. It's time we ended this."

"I thought it was over when you came home," Jay said as Finn left.

He couldn't explain it. His hatred for Will was ingrained so deeply that it felt like it was hardwired into his brain. He couldn't remember a time in his life when he didn't hate Will or wasn't afraid of him. He'd hoped that by living in Las Vegas so far ahead of where Will was that he'd never see him again, never risk being seen, but karma bit him in the ass while kismet kicked him in the balls.

Will came into the cafeteria without Aisha and without Finn. He hesitated at the door—he didn't want to be there, and if not for Jay, he wouldn't be—but he crossed the room and sat next to Jay, staring at George without saying a word. Whatever George wanted, he had to ask for it. Will wasn't offering anything.

"Tell him what you know about me," George said, nodding toward Jay. "Tell him the awful things you learned when you ran into me on the playground."

Will had no idea what he was talking about.

"You know exactly what you heard, Blackshear. You asked me about it. You wanted details." When Will still claimed to not know what he meant, George looked at Jay, eyes burning with rage and fear, and said, "I killed my baby sister when I was three years old. He knew. He saw it in my head. He could have told everyone."

Jay's heartbeat pounded against my back.

"I waited for that shoe to drop," he went on. "When will Blackshear rat me out? What the hell will he want for his silence, and will my parents give it to him? Will they even bother protecting me? Or will they just hand me over, grateful to finally be rid of their little bastard? But then the other kids realized he knew things about them, too. At least by then I had them on my side. They were just as afraid of him as I was."

Will blinked a few times and then remembered. "You didn't kill your sister, George. She fell and hit her head on the edge of the bathtub. You had nothing to do with it."

"It was my fault," he said evenly.

"No, it truly wasn't."

George gripped the edge of the table, his fingers turning crimson under the pressure. "I remember it. I remember being *screamed* at because of it. I did—"

"You're looking back through the haze of six decades of memories," Will said. "I have it as an entire image in my head, every detail I saw in your mind that day. I can show you if you'll allow it." He held his hand out. "You weren't at fault. I won't listen to anything you're thinking about now, I'll only place the memory back into your mind. Undisturbed, unaltered."

"You're out of your goddamned mind."

"Perhaps. But I am not a liar. I'll only show you what you need to remember."

"He can control it now," Jay said. "I swear."

If not for Jay, George would have run from the room. Instead, he slowly reached across the table, fingers trembling, and let Will touch him.

It only took a moment. When Will pulled his hand back, George crumpled under the weight of the memory Will had returned to him and he set his head on the table, sobbing. In a flash, he saw himself standing in the bathroom as his little sister, just two years old, stood in the bathtub and slipped. Her head cracked into the side of the tub as she went down, blood splattered the wall and the floor, and his mother scrambled to get to her from the other side of the room. Her terrified scream for him to go get help slapped at him.

Three-year-old George stepped over to the doorway where he stood rooted, terror cementing his feet in place. He stared down the hallway to the living room where his father was, but he couldn't make his feet lift from the floor and he couldn't call out. It was his mother's screams that finally propelled his father down the hall, shoving George out of the way.

He sat in the hall and waited, watching as she was pulled out of the tub and placed on the floor, blood oozing from her head, a thin red line seeping into a crack that slowly inched toward him. He stared at that crimson sliver as his father's sobbing pulsed in his ears and he swallowed whole his mother's guttural scream when medics carried that tiny, unmoving body out of the apartment. Hours later, he was still sitting in the hall staring at the thin line of dried blood, waiting for someone to tell him she was all right, and that she was coming home. His sister's complete silence echoed all around him, a bubble waiting to pop, a scream that pulsed inside his head.

His parents left, an aunt came to stay with him, and he waited, the last thing his mother said to him before she left ringing in his ears. '*Why didn't you do something?*'

"Her death was not of your doing," Will said quietly. "You were the victim of abrupt grief, not the perpetrator of something horrific. If I asked you about her and why, I am truly sorry. Neither of us had filters then, George. Neither of us knew better. But I am sorry."

Should I go purr on him?

Will shook his head, very slightly.

George was quiet for a long time.

"I tried to kill you," he said, after some time, without looking up. "More than once. I wanted you dead for what you knew. Jesus, the pool..."

"I am aware."

It took several more minutes before he could sit up. He brushed tears from his face and took a deep breath. "I still think you're—" Another deep breath. "I can't begin to understand why you are the way you are."

"I am aware."

"All those years, I thought you were just waiting to tell the world that I was a murderer."

"You were four years old in preschool," Jay said. "Just a baby."

"Doesn't matter." George spoke softly, his sorrow threaded around every word. "She was bathing in water because I'd convinced her it was more fun than a sonic scrub and she begged to be allowed to try it. She stood up because I was teasing her. I told her if she stayed in the tub too long, a monster would slither out of the drain and nibble on her toes. I know my mother heard that. They let me think it was my fault. My parents. They knew I blamed myself. They blamed me." His breath hiccupped. "You're positive this is the exact memory you took?"

Will nodded. "My own memories can be fuzzy with time and distance, but the things I take from others remain intact."

From the other table I heard Oz whisper, "Oh, God, Drew, the things he heard me think about doing to you…"

"I don't care what your parents said," Jay murmured. "That was a fucking accident. You didn't do anything to her. It was just teasing. Brothers and sisters tease each other all the time, even I know that." He sat up straighter. "That's why you always yelled at Dad when he told me I was going to shrivel up like a raisin or that I would get sucked down the drain if I didn't get out before he pulled the plug. And when we moved to San Francisco, you had the bathtub removed. Your apartment was all sonic, there wasn't even an option to use water in the shower."

George nodded. "I wasn't losing you the way I lost her."

"Damn," Jay breathed.

"And yet, I lost you anyway." He turned to Will. "Your mother wanted to slap the daylights out of me not too long ago. If she still wants to, I'll stand there and take it. What I did to you—"

Will started to get up. "Don't make her the offer, because she'll take you up on it." He planted a kiss on the top of Jay's head. "We'll be in Mass's office when you're done. Take your time."

Before Will was all the way across the cafeteria, George called after him. "Don't make Jay go home right after this." He gestured to the window. "Let them see this world. I always wished he could know where I came from…show him some of it. All of them." Then, as if he was choking on the word, "Please."

"Perhaps," Will said as he left.

They could barely look at each other.

I crawled onto the table and sat between them, trying to figure out what I could do. George didn't like cats, but he was in pain. Jay was tongue-tied and didn't know how to help him. I could sit there and purr hard enough that they would both hear it, but they needed to feel it.

The quiet began to hurt. It felt like panic bubbling in my belly, and I didn't know how to stop it.

Oz sighed hard and then announced, "Jay has a girlfriend. She's kind of hot, too. Start there."

Jay rolled his eyes, but it made George laugh and he asked about her, then about dating and learning to drive and peppered him with questions about school. When they finally exhausted the conversation and had shared everything they wanted each other to know, after George gave Jay his contact information in case Will ever brought him back, Jay hugged him for a long time.

"You're one hell of a fuckup," Jay said, "but I still love you. And I hope you can get over hating Will. He's so damned good for Mom, and he loves me, too, you know."

"I'll try. For you, I'll try."

They watched him leave, and as soon as the door shut, Jay asked, "You think we'll get to stay for a little while?"

Drew shrugged, and Oz was about to answer when Finn came back to show them where Mass's office was. The door was only open a few inches, so Finn pointed to the chairs lining the hall a few feet away and said they could wait. Since I knew I could slide between the door and the wall, I went in.

They weren't clustered around his desk the way patients often did when they met with their doctor. Instead, Will and Aisha were together on a short sofa in the corner and Mass was in a comfy chair, a coffee mug in hand. His office here was a lot brighter than the one back home; these walls were covered with pictures of family and hand-drawn anatomy posters. The bonus: there were no silicone models of people-junk strewn about like discarded toys.

"If that's the only issue," he was saying, "hell, I can get you pregnant in about two minutes."

"I wouldn't brag about that," Will said.

"Ha. No, it would actually take about twenty. Specimen from you, injection for her to cause spontaneous ovulation, I work some magic and boom. She's pregnant. No muss, no fuss."

"No fun," Aisha said. "We'll go at it the old-fashioned way, but if we're still not pregnant in a few months, we might take you up on that." She rubbed Will's arm and snickered. "If we keep coming back here, though, we might want help sooner. That cult is still out there, and they want your babies. Me first."

"They're a myth," Will said. "Besides, I think they believe I'm somewhere around Portland. And over two hundred years old. Two-hundred-year-old me might be willing."

I jumped onto Will's lap.

Can Mass give me back my fun bits? I might like to find a girl kitty and have a litter.

"We're not asking Mass to de-neuter you," Will said. "I'm really not sure we want you reproducing."

Mass leaned forward to look at me. "I could do it, you know. You'd have to spend a day in the tank, and the surgical gel would stick to your fur badly enough you'd need a long bath, but I could do it."

"Don't help him," Will said.

I'd get wet?

"Wet and sticky. The bath would require soap and a considerable amount of water."

I'll think about it, then. I'm not sure it would be worth the trouble.

"It would be funny to see." Will picked me up. "Remember, not a word to anyone else, Wick. We don't want this laid bare for inspection."

No worries. They don't even care why you're in here. They just want to know if they get to stay and see things.

"Do we want to show them around a bit?" he asked Aisha as we left the office.

She thought it was fine, but not fair to Zed. Finn offered to go get him, and then offered the apartment for the night. "Plenty of room for everyone. The fridge isn't stocked right now, but I can give you my cash card so you can feed them. Take them out, let them have a good time."

He said he'd meet us on the Square and darted through the portal before Will could tell him no.

"You have a choice," he said as he prodded them down the hall. "We can show you the wharf park, or I can borrow a couple of flight packs from the lab and you can spend some time trying to fly."

Drew looked like he was going to explode. "The wharf park, that's the one with the bubble and Northern Lights?"

Will nodded.

"Flying," Jay said. "Come on, when else will we have a chance like that?"

Oz looked at Drew. "You know what Zed will vote for."

He knew, and he tried to cover his disappointment. Will walked next to him and said quietly, "The park is a spectacular honeymoon location. I would be more than happy to escort you back and leave you there for a couple of days."

He brightened until he realized they'd already made plans.

"Andrew," Will said, trying not to laugh, "you can do both. Spend two nights in the park, go home, and still make your reservation."

"Oz will like it?"

"She'll love it."

"Good, because I think she's only going to Disneyland for me."

"She's talked about going back for years, Drew. Don't let her fool you. She and Zed have only been once because it's difficult to justify the inconvenience to the general public when the park is overtaken by security. Your honeymoon is finally a good enough reason. She's simply allowing herself to be seen as the mature one."

Drew chuckled. "If we come here for the first couple of nights, maybe she'll be open to bringing Zed and Jay along to Disney. I know they want to go."

Oz turned around and walked backward. "Who's going to Disney with us?"

Drew shrugged. "Everyone?"

She shrugged in return. "Cool."

"Wait. Are you really okay with that?"

"It'll be more fun with them," she said. "I'll still get time alone with you, hot stuff."

"Goddammit," Will grunted with pretended upset. "You both just walked me right into that, didn't you?"

"Told you I'd get you to go back someday!" Oz said as she turned back around.

As Drew jogged a few steps to catch up to her, Aisha took Will's hand and leaned into him. "Come on, it'll be fun. Jay's never been, and if there's a chance I'll be waddling my way around life next year, it would be nice for him to have one last big thing before he turns eighteen and becomes a big brother."

That didn't make Will feel any better. "In six or seven years, I'm going again, aren't I?"

"Oh, sweetie. For the next eighteen to twenty years, you're going a whole bunch of places you don't want to. And for the first couple of years, you'll do it on no sleep."

That, he was fine with. He was used to not sleeping.

11

People streaking over Union Square had to wonder about the four teenagers gawking at them. They clustered in the center of the square, mouths open—except for Oz—and they shrieked when a kid on a hoverboard went screaming past. Oz had seen enough of other Whens to keep her composure, but deep down, she was probably squealing, too.

"Everything looks so different," Zed said. "But it's also kind of the same. If that makes sense."

"Fuckton of traffic," Jay muttered. "If this means anything, people are gonna start breeding like damned rabbits in the next couple hundred years."

"Longer life spans now," Oz mused. "Even if most people hold to one or two kids per family, the fact that they live longer here means a higher population."

They finally stopped gawking at random people when Will and Finn came out of the lab, each carrying two packs.

"People here really live around a hundred eighty years?" Jay asked Will.

"That's the average lifespan. Some live longer. Some don't."

Zed looked at Finn. "Other versions of you went back in time and stayed there. You could look up the last one and see when he died, right? And get an idea which side of the average you're on?"

"He wouldn't look," Will said as he slipped into the flight pack harness.

Finn shrugged. "What makes you think he's dead?"

That stumped Will. "You looked him up."

"Time is a tricky thing, William. Maybe I didn't have to. Maybe he came looking for me instead." Even though Will didn't need the help, Finn reached over to tighten the straps that went around his legs and waist. "Watch Will carefully. He learned using a three-step process. Pay attention to his knee before he leaps, and his arm positions."

"Should we be doing this here?" Oz asked. "It's kind of crowded."

"It's fine. This is a common launch spot for new fliers," Finn said. "Lots of controls in the area."

"Nets," Oz guessed.

"Similar," Will said. "I'll show you."

He flicked the pack on, took three fast steps and jerked his knee upward for leverage, and he was in the air, heading toward the statue on the far end of the Square. He didn't slow down, and when he was three feet from it, a light flashed and he bounced away softly. The rebound was slow enough that he was able to regain control without falling, and he switched direction, gliding over our heads with his feet trailing a bit behind him.

He circled the Square, and then he hovered, one knee bent toward his waist. As he slowly lowered his leg, the pack brought him down.

"You've seen how Wick maneuvers his hover cart," Will said as he and Finn helped Zed and Jay into packs. "Directing your path isn't much different. Twitch your shoulders in the direction you wish to go and control your speed with your legs. Both knees slightly bent will move you forward. One leg straight and the other bent allows you to hover."

"What happens if we bend both knees?" Zed asked.

"Don't do that," Will said.

Finn shrugged into the remaining pack. "You could show them."

"Absolutely not. Zed, you're with Finn, Jay is with me. Just do what we do and try to stay within arms' reach."

Finn reminded them to count their steps. On three, bring your knee to waist level, and your shoulders toward your ears. He and Zed jogged in tandem, and Zed shot right up, fast enough that Finn had to grab him by the ankle to keep him from going too high.

Jay didn't get enough speed going, so Will hovered a few feet above, and talked him through a second try. When he still didn't get airborne, Will lowered until he could reach Jay's hand, and yanked him up. "Being up here is more important than how you manage it," he said. "Finn had to drag me along more than once."

"When you were six," Finn said. "And if I recall, the first time I grabbed you I sent you tumbling."

"And I wanted to do it again," Will said. "Tumbling is fun until you throw up."

They floated around the Square, slowly, until Zed and Jay felt comfortable. Will let them go up a bit higher, and they took off, heading up Powell Street.

Aisha is holding her breath. She's scared.

"Will won't let anything happen to Jay," Drew said. "Besides, you flew on a dragon a few months ago. There weren't any safety nets, and it was a hell of a lot more dangerous."

"That was different. This is my son *and* my husband."

She knew Will had flown in these packs when he was little, and she knew there were invisible nets all over the place. That didn't make her feel any better, and when they finally came back, it took effort for her to not scoop Jay up and hug him.

"Seriously," Oz whispered to Drew, "Jeff was a hundred times riskier, and she loved Jeff."

Neither of them needed as much instruction. Oz took off before Finn could, and both Will and Drew went up at the same time and sped after them. They circled the Square faster than Zed and Jay had and were down the street going twice as fast. Jay watched, his mouth open, and Zed laughed loudly.

"Hell, yeah, showoffs!" he called after them.

Finn came back first. He was tired—it took him more effort to handle the pack than it used to—and he offered it to Aisha.

"Oh, hell no."

Finn slipped it off. "Come on. When Will comes back, he'll want to take you up."

She argued; this was for the kids, and she didn't need to fly across the city. Finn was almost convinced to let it be, until Jay said, "Come on, Mom. Do it for Will. Let him show you this. It was part of his childhood. This is fun for him."

Finn was tightening her straps when they came back, and Will broke out into a wide grin. He promised her they'd go slow, just around the Square, just long enough for her to get a sense of how they worked.

He held her hand as they circled overhead, and for part of it he flew backward so that she could see his face. Halfway around, the fear melted, and she started laughing. When they'd made a full circle, he showed her how to hover, and they stayed fifteen feet above for a long time, whispering to each other.

"God, they're gonna kiss," Jay groaned.

He wasn't wrong.

They hovered there long enough to attract attention. Three women who had only marginally paid attention when Oz and Drew had taken flight watched intently as Will and Aisha flew together. The first of them to notice popped the other two on the arm and then pointed as they hovered, whispering, and especially when Will kissed her.

"Come on," Oz said to Jay, "that was sweet."

Those ladies over there think so, too.

"I think they're looking at Will," Drew said, and I think he was going to stand there and watch them watching Will, but before he could even blink, Will's foot brushed past his face, missing his nose by less than an inch.

"All right," Will said when he landed. "You've got the basics. Stick to the Square, where we can see you, and no peeking into windows."

"Killjoy," Oz muttered as she slipped the pack back on. "I was going to jump on the balcony to see what's there now." She gestured in the general direction of the building that stood where the royal house had once been. "It's obviously not the same, but still."

"Someone lives there," Will said. "Be nice."

When they were in the air, moving toward the corner, Finn asked Will, "Not telling them that's home?"

"Not until I know if we're staying the night."

"Stay," Finn urged. "Let them have some fun. After they're done with the flight packs, take them to Bounce and then out to dinner." Sensing Will's lack of enthusiasm, Finn added, "It's not like they're missing school or work for this. Get them used to having feet in more than one When."

"That implies bringing them back."

"Will. It's going to happen. Oz and Drew especially. Ease them into it and make it fun. Don't wait until Eli is a teenager and itching to move on."

"He didn't itch. Mom needed him to go, but that shouldn't happen this time around."

"He'll go, and Oz and Drew need to be prepared for it, even if it means preparing them without them understanding what you're doing."

Aisha reached for Will's hand. "Sweetie, we can stay. Finn's right, they're all speeding into grown-up lives, and it would be nice to give them a purely teen-centered evening. They can't do that at home, not as easily as other kids. Here, they can."

"Fine," Will said. "But you're participating at Bounce."

Finn laughed, gave Will his cash card, and said he'd see them later. He was heading home to have lunch with Jo.

"What did I just press you into agreeing to?" she asked.

"Bounce is a variable-gravity jump house. You float, you fall, you tumble, and half the time, you vomit."

*

Aisha's argument for not stepping into the room with the padded walls and ceiling: "Someone has to stay with Wick."

Will said it was bullshit, but he laughed so that meant she could poke him in the ribs and not feel bad about it. She declared that she was too old to free float and reminded him that she had personal parts that could give her a black eye in the absence of constant, adequate gravity.

"That's not how—"

"They bounce too much, they get sore. They get sore, you're not playing with them later."

That was enough reason for him to sit in the observation room with her. He'd rented a private space and there were snacks in the room, so he sent everyone else in to have fun and settled onto a little sofa with her.

He also accidentally on purpose failed to tell them what to expect. They went into the game room and moved to the center, looking up and around, waiting to see what would happen, when Will flipped the switch that engaged the anti-gravity engine. It was no more than a hum, but enough to startle Zed and enough to make Oz turn sharply, looking to Will with a "What the hell?" expression.

They floated. As the engine cycled, there would be varying degrees of gravitational pull in the room; they could move around once they figured out how, but they also had no idea when and how fast things could change.

One second, you're bouncing off a wall, heading for the other side of the room, and the next your feet are stuck to the ceiling.

"There's an entire sport built around this," Will said as Zed collided with Jay. "Three players to a side, twenty-one balls of varying colors, with six very small slots at differing heights throughout the room. Each colored ball represents points, and the goal is to get all the balls into the slots before time runs out. First team to twenty-one points wins."

She watched Drew tumble as he tried to get some sense of up and down. "They can't even find their own asses. Throw balls in there, and someone is going to get hurt."

"Which is why I opted for a private room and not a public one. I didn't think it would do their egos any good to have eight and ten-year-old kids screaming past and around them, yelling to get out of the way."

"Let me guess. You were a yeller."

"Indeed. But I was also limited to doing this with the technicians from my parents' lab. I was young and wiry, and they were not, relatively speaking."

Drew spiraled past Oz, reaching for her. She slapped his hand away and laughed, watching as he crashed into the wall.

"Your parents' employees spent a lot of time with you, didn't they?"

"When they could. I was a ready-made excuse to indulge in things like this. The workload was formidable, but every now and then someone would remind my parents that I needed to do something fun and it wouldn't hurt to take an afternoon off. I am grateful for it. While I didn't have the experiences of a normal childhood, I was gifted opportunities to do normal things."

He sat back, arms folded. "I'd forgotten that, really. They used me as an excuse for group excursions but included me wholly in the things we did. When I was eight or so, there were two female techs who used to chase me around the bounce room, threatening to hug me. I squealed and scrambled away, but truthfully, when they caught me?"

"You let them, didn't you?"

"Perhaps." He grinned. "They knew of my issues, and yet none of them were afraid of me. I suspect they understood that I needed contact, even if I was reluctant to let a girl near me."

"Aw, was little Will afraid of cooties?"

"I might still be."

Just as she decided to swap a few cooties with him, Jay slammed into the window. He couldn't even fall to the floor and get sympathy from anyone because he started to float back up.

"Aside from that," she said, "they look like they're getting the hang of it."

"We can't have that." Will reach over and turned a knob by the switch that started it all. Everyone was sucked upward, and just before they would have hit the ceiling, they plummeted. The cycle repeated four times, and on the fifth, when they were close to the floor, they grabbed hands and formed a circle, and spun their way back up.

"There we go," Will said. "Use each other."

"If you're trying to make one of them throw up, I think it's wasted energy. They're enjoying it too much."

"Good. If they overdose on fun, they won't ask to come back for a while."

Bouncing off walls and spinning around upside down wasn't enough to quell anyone's appetite. We stopped for dinner on the way—Will chose a restaurant with outside seating so they could watch bikes speed past and hear the pulse of the city notch up as night began to fall—and afterward, Will led the way home. He still hadn't told them where they were going, just "home."

Halfway there, Oz called out from behind us, "Define, 'home,' Emperor. Did you live down in—"

Aisha let go of Will's hand and spun around. "You can't call him that, not here. The last thing we want is for anyone to know who he is."

They all looked confused. Even a lady walking behind us stopped abruptly, surprised by the sudden outburst. She tucked a strand of red hair behind her ear and then darted around us, probably hoping to avoid whatever Aisha was about to dish out.

"I'll explain later," Will said. "And no, I didn't live in the lab, if that's what you were thinking. Not exactly."

"How does one 'not exactly' live in a lab?" Zed asked.

"I spent more time there than I would have liked. But we did have an apartment nearby, and my parents still keep it for the times they spend working here."

"Jo works here?" Oz asked.

"Infrequently, but she has been coming with Finn more often. She has friends here and has begun a project of her own."

"Was Finn serious when he hinted that he might still be alive right now?" Zed asked. "His other self? I'm trying to wrap my brain around it. That Finn would be around two-seventy, wouldn't he? Or older?"

Will wasn't sure if Finn was serious or pulling their legs, but he would be very, very old. It wasn't impossible; the typical lifespan in this When was 180, and 220 wasn't unheard of. The oldest person Will knew of had lived to almost 300 and died when his boat overturned in the bay.

"The news report suggested he was fighting with a sea lion over his catch. When the boat overturned, he was trapped under it and couldn't swim his way out. Still, he was healthy and active, and could have lived many more years."

"Then that guy is alive now, in our When. Like, he's already an adult. An old one."

"I haven't done the math, but one would assume."

"Damn," Drew breathed. "And I thought making it to, like, one-twenty was impressive."

"It is," Will said. "That still meets the average for your generation. Average is not a failing, not in living."

We turned the corner and were on the sidewalk in front of the old royal house.

"I'm happy being average," Zed said.

Jay snorted. "We're talking lifespan, not your di—"

Aisha's head snapped so she could glare at him. "Jay!"

"Average is fine there, too," Zed said, laughing. "Too far under, and there's massive disappointment on both sides. Too far over, and there's not enough lube in the world. Right in the middle? Everyone's happy."

"Bullshit," Jay said. "You'd kill to be over average."

Aisha sighed and turned around.

"Human vagina is only so long, Jaybird. It doesn't do any good to be that much over."

"Human as opposed to what? What the fuck are you doing that you'd have to qualify that?"

"Can we change the subject?" Aisha asked.

"We can," Zed allowed, "but why?"

Will stopped at the door. "Because she asked you to."

When he opened the door, Aisha went in, but everyone else stayed on the sidewalk and stared, until Oz sputtered, "Here? You lived here?"

"It stayed in the family," Will explained, ushering them in. "Upstairs, same floor on which you currently live."

They bolted up the stairs. It was an entirely different building, and the floor plan wasn't identical, but there was a balcony, and the bedrooms were relatively close to where they expected them to be. The floors were worn and the furniture old, but none of them seemed to notice. They were too busy being blown away by the idea that it was still their family home, even after a couple of centuries.

"How?" Oz sputtered.

"There was a Queen," Will said. "She gave up the throne, and the people gifted her the only home she'd known. It's been rebuilt since she lived here, but the essentials are the same. All the apartments you'd expect are still in the building, with a few extra. The roof is still a well-used refuge. And the Hall of Remains...remained."

"Our stones?" Zed asked, looking a little creeped out.

"You will not visit that floor," Will said.

Oz was intrigued, not creeped out. "Did you ever? Your stone would be there."

"I have, but only with my father. The Emperor's stone is surely there, but he never allowed me to see it. I am curious... I've always assumed it would be black. I'd like to know."

"Absolutely not," Aisha said. "I don't even want to think about it."

"But those people really aren't us," Oz said. "Not anymore."

Will understood what she was saying; from the moment he lived, their lives changed. Fundamentally, the people memorialized in the Hall were different. From Jax onward, their lives were not the same.

"We've met those people," Will said. "We've spent time with them. Celebrated with them. They are, perhaps, no longer you, but to us they are still people we love and people we will visit again." He hesitated. "You've met them, Oz. They cared enough to advise you, and you may yet see them again. Don't put the last of them into your head."

"You met you?" Zed blurted.

"On Oz's birthday," Drew said. "I don't think we appreciated it the way we should have. I'd like to talk to them again and take more time to really listen."

"And you guys," Zed said, gesturing to Will. "How did you celebrate with them?"

He wasn't sure he should answer. He and Aisha had gone back to spend Jax's birthday with them. They sat on the roof drinking very old Scotch, swapping stories about Oz and Drew and Zed, musing the different paths the younger versions would take. They hoped for less heartache for Zed—but still wouldn't tell me what had happened to him—and for young Eli, the Eli who had not yet been born, to find his way to Harper, so that Finn would still be born.

Will and Aisha had stories they could not tell, things that would lead to questions they couldn't answer. He sucked in a deep breath and said, "Years will not erase the love between your parents and me. We need to leave it at that. But suffice to say, I have visited them, and I will again."

"Do they know that?" he pressed. "I mean, our parents, in our When."

Will nodded. "They are aware."

"Let it go," Oz told Zed.

He let it go. Will told them to explore but not intrude—this was still his parents' home and wanted their privacy protected—and to choose rooms for the night. "But not your own room," he told Oz. "That's mine."

"Hey!"

"It was my boyhood bedroom," he said. "I have the most current claim."

"We don't want to sleep there, anyway," Drew said to Oz. "Think about it. Take a black light in there, and, ew."

For that matter, if you open the fridge and there's a whole bologna with a hole dug out, don't eat it.

Will pointed at Drew. "You will *not* repeat that."

"I have no idea what it means, but I can guess, and holy hell, Will."

Oh, look. He's flustered.

He showed them where the video monitor was—it blended in with the wall when it was turned off—and reminded them to go choose rooms for the night. He was going out to pick up a few groceries. I needed cat food, and he was sure they would all want something to snack on before going to bed.

"He's gonna buy cardboard protein," Zed said. "Tiny little cubes of despair."

"I'll go with him," Aisha said. "It might still be healthy, but you'll be spared the cardboard."

Will pretended offense and reminded them to stay in the apartment. The balcony was not off limits, so while he and Aisha walked down the stairs, they headed out and leaned over the edge to watch as they came out the door.

I can't see. But don't pick me up.

"There's not much to see, Wick. Will put his arm around her and they're walking super close together. Nothing embarrassing. Oh, wait. She just grabbed his ass."

What else is down there?

"There are a few people on the Square, still. Some kid on a hoverboard is grinding down the stairs. And there are guys unloading stuff from a...truck, I guess. That looks like a truck, I think."

Big black or blue egg with an open back?

"Kind of."

Delivery truck.

"That's a freaking Christmas tree," Zed said. "Or pieces of one. Is the whole thing in that one truck? Cripes, it's like they fit a forty-foot tree inside a twenty-foot long truck."

"That time of year," Oz mused. "Ours should be going up this week. And the ice rink opens soon. We should try it this year."

"Us and the guards?" Drew said, laughing. "There won't be room for anyone else on the ice."

Zed didn't think they would have to skate. "They can surround the outside of the rink and stare."

"Maybe yours," Oz said. "I know at least two of mine will use it as an excuse to slap some skates on. If they know ahead of time, a couple of off-duty guards will show up. They never get to have any fun, they'll want to take it while they can."

If I had money, I would pay to see that old guard with the weird mustache ice skate.

"Tiptitch?" Oz asked. "God, that would be funny as hell, and he would do it, too."

Tiptitch—Tip—was ancient; he'd been one of Jax's guards when he was a boy, and he'd been more relaxed with the rules than most. Jax got away with things he shouldn't have because Tip turned a blind eye to much of it and he let Will handle a good part of keeping Jax reined in. He stepped back from family guard duties when Oz turned thirteen; he told Jax that he was getting too old to chase teenagers around, but the truth was that he understood Jax wanted someone less lenient to serve as her head guard.

He loved Tip; he didn't want Oz to have those kinds of feelings for the people whose job it was to dive in the line of fire. Tip moved on to a training position, and he kept the kids' guards in line. He got what he most wanted: to know Jax's kids as almost-friends, and to be responsible for keeping them safe.

"I thought he was going to retire," Zed said.

Oz nodded. "He was pretty broken up when Axe turned traitor," she said, speaking of her former head guard. "He blamed himself. I think Will was the one who talked him out of quitting. He convinced Tip that there was one more generation left in him, and he needed to train his replacement."

"So, we get him to skate."

"Damn, Zed," Drew said, "The guy is creaky-old. He'd break a hip or something."

He's sturdier than you think. He can rip a phone book in half.

Drew's eyebrows knotted. "What the hell is a phone book, Wick?"

Oz pulled her phone out and was going to look it up until she realized it wasn't going to work. "We're stuck in a tech-rich environment with no way to use it."

There's a computer connected to the Internet in the living room.

"Will would be pissed off if we started looking things up."

"Yeah, but he did show us how to get broadcast stuff," Jay said. "Maybe there's some news. We can find out what's major in the world today."

Zed found a site that looked like it was newsworthy, and they crowded onto the sofa to watch. There was a talking head droning on about the stock market; it had taken a hit when the President of Kryzistan appointed two of his sons to his national security council and his eldest as his public spokesman. The sons were, the talking head declared, as dim as Elysium on a power holiday, prompting Drew to ask, "Where the hell is Kryzistan?" and Zed to wonder what a power holiday was.

Oz surmised that the former was somewhere in the middle east or Asia, and the latter was energy conservation, though it was just a guess.

A new talking head appeared; she looked upset and gazed into the camera as if she were relaying horrible news to her best friend while enjoying every awful second of it. She reported from east Texas, where a shuttle containing food stores meant for Elysium had exploded minutes after lift-off. There was a scroll across the bottom of the screen, 'select green for optimum viewing,' and Zed pushed the green bar on the remote.

The picture filled the room, surrounding us on all sides as the shuttle exploded, debris tumbling around and overhead; the sound of metal shearing and fuel igniting came from the ceiling like rain.

Zed jumped to his feet, yelling, "What the actual fuck?!" as Jay dove for the floor. Neither Oz nor Drew startled, but he reached for her hand.

Push the green button again. That was just an enhanced broadcast.

Drew took the remote and pressed it again, and the picture faded back to the monitor. "A little warning about that would have been nice."

"Is this the kind of shit you're working on?" Zed asked Drew. "Because that was seriously freaky. The whole damned thing was like *right here.*"

It can be fun when it's entertainment. News can be scary.

"What kind of entertainment?" Drew asked me.

Nature shows are fun. Will used to put them on so I could chase birds around the living room.

"Huh. That's probably where Finn got the idea for a full-scale simulator."

Zed's eyes got wide, and he grinned. "Imagine porn on this."

"Ew." Oz screwed up her face. "You're kind of disgusting sometimes. I don't want to sit back and watch some guy's three-foot-long penis flopping toward my face. The scale on this would be frightening."

"Yeah but think of the boobs."

Drew cocked his head as if he were considering it. "Forget the boobs. Think of it as an educational tool. At this scale, if you can't find a woman's cl—"

"What the hell have you been watching?" Will asked as he stomped into the room.

"The news," Zed said, truthfully.

They discovered the green button.

"Ah. I should have warned you about that. And really, Drew? If you haven't found it by now? Why is she keeping you around?"

Aisha sighed. "Just put the groceries away and be nice."

"No, really," Zed said, "why *is* she keeping you?"

"I really hate you all," Drew grumbled.

Aisha took the remote and turned the monitor off. "Stop. If you're hungry, there's fruit, sandwich meat, bread, milk, bacon, eggs, and cookies."

"And we can guess who picked what," Zed said.

"Leave the bacon and eggs," Will said. "We'll have breakfast before we head home."

He and Aisha headed for his bedroom, and I followed. They wanted to cuddle on the window seat before going to sleep, and I wanted a break from the adolescent insults.

How did you know what Drew was going to say?

"I heard Zed mention porn as we were on the way up," Will said. "It wasn't a leap to figure out."

"They aren't wrong," Aisha said. "Porn in surround imaging?"

"No, thank you."

She laughed as she snuggled against him. "Still don't want to go there, eh?"

"I have no opposition in theoretical terms. My issues arise from the objectification of the participants in the industry. I accept that it's a legal enterprise and the actors initially enter into their contracts willingly, but I doubt they remain out of choice, and from what I know, it's difficult to walk away from."

"That's slick, mass-produced porn," she said. "There's an entire amateur genre created by ordinary couples, uploaded online as free entertainment. It's a hell of a lot more popular, too."

"Why would anyone do that?"

She pulled his arms around her a little tighter, toying with the ring on his finger. "I've never asked anyone who's actually done it. I suppose it's a thrill. They enjoy the idea of others watching them, getting excited. And I meant what I said before. I wouldn't judge you if you let your curiosity get the better of you."

"Unlike someone we know, I don't see myself searching out instruction online," Will said lightly. "No matter how much it seems like I'm trying to devour an ice cream cone."

"Come on, that was sweet of them. They were just looking for ways to make each other happy."

"I know." He sighed. "Would it make you happy if I gave in on this, and watched something with you? I'm not comfortable with it, but I understand I'm passing judgment without the experience to form an opinion."

"No, sweetheart. I've seen my fair share of porn. I could go the rest of my life and not miss it. But if you're ever curious, I'm there. It might be different seeing it with you."

He hesitated, but then said, "I am quite content with things as they are."

"I hear a 'but' in there."

"Not 'but' so much as, I realize that as physical as our relationship is and as much as I enjoy that, I am never the one to initiate. And I'm not sure I know how to."

"You initiate," she said. "More often than you realize."

"I can't recall once—"

"Bilbo." She pulled his arms away from her so that she could turn to see him. "Every day. It starts first thing, when I wake up and you're there, and no matter how tired you are, you smile like you're *so* happy to see me. And in so many moments after that? Every stray kiss, every undemanding touch. While I get ready for work, you make breakfast. When you're on your way out the door, you kiss Jay and then kiss me, and it's not some rote thing done out of habit. It's like it makes you happy."

"It does."

"And that's just it. You make me feel wanted from the moment I wake up. You touch me just to know I'm there. You sneak up and plant kisses on my neck, without expecting anything more. You love my son, and he sees it. Every day, Will. I see this all unfolding, and by the end of the day it's all I can do to not jump on you. Sweetie, you initiate sex with me all damned day long."

He kissed her, and it was really long and kind of sweet. "Thank you for that," he said softly. "Yet I still feel as if I should learn to be more direct in those moments when all I want is you. I have no idea how without seeming...selfish."

"Ah, you mean like that day a week or so ago, when I was grading tests and you kept bringing me tea and cookies and lingering at the door like you had something to say?" She laughed lightly. "I knew what you wanted, sweetheart, but I had to get those tests done. By the time I finished, you had gone out for a run."

"Then what should I have done?"

"Put the tea on the desk, kiss the back of my neck, whisper that you want me. You'll wait, but you want me. Or ask me to take a break. Tell me you love me, and just want to be with me."

"That seems within my skill set."

"You have a wonderful skill set." She kissed him again, setting her hand on his chest, and then added, "But for god's sake, don't set the tea down and push your erection against me. I like direct, but not that direct."

"And I was just about to do that."

"Ooh. Well, right now I'd enjoy that. We didn't actually have sex the last time we were here. I was too stressed out."

"And now?"

"Oh, hon, if I'm any level of stressed, I'm counting on you to just pound it out of me."

"All right. I was only kidding about the erection before, but another kiss and I'm there."

Her hand started to slide from his chest, but she stopped on his stomach when someone knocked on the door.

"Damn well better be important," Will called out.

"Three stinky boys," Oz said. "They all want showers, but none of us can figure out how the hell to make it work. There's a lot of humming, but no water and I can't find the switch to take them off sonic."

Will sighed hard. "All right, just a minute," he said.

Aisha patted his chest and told him to sit tight and keep thinking about her. "I'll show them how to work the showers. I think I remember how to switch it to water."

"And set the drain to recycle," he reminded her.

I'm not sure where to sleep. You're going to do bouncy things. Drew and Oz are probably going to do bouncy things. Zed and Jay are probably going to stay up talking about bouncy things.

"Curl up on the sofa in the living room."

I could.

"You can stay here, Wick. Sleep on the window seat. We'll be quiet."

I stared at him.

"All right, I will endeavor to keep her quiet. Oz and Drew are in the next room, she'll hear how thin the walls are. But it's going to happen, so you either need to sleep through it, be all right with it, or go into another room. I'm not entirely sure what your problem is, though."

Says the guy who doesn't want to watch porn.

That gave him pause. "Touché. Fine. I get it. Do you want me to go find something for you to watch on the monitor in the living room? I have no idea what passes for entertainment now, but I'm sure I can find something."

That's all right. I'll find something to do once you don't have much blood in your brain.

He reached out and scratched behind my ears. "I'm sorry you have to put up with so much."

I don't mind it, really. I like that you have her. And I like when it's after, and you're all gooey and you lay there and talk with your noses close together and giggle if one of you gets snot on the other.

I'm just uncomfortable with the bouncy parts because it feels private and I should go away.

"Aisha has no issue with you being in the room, Wick. And truly, I don't even think about it."

Fine. We'll call Oz and Drew in so they can grade you.

"That's different, and you know it."

You're just afraid they'd point and laugh.

"Possibly," he said, humoring me. "I have improved. I think."

So has Drew.

"I don't need to know about that."

He would want you to know. He can't tell you he's getting good at it, but deep down he wants to brag.

"All right, I understand that. He doesn't have someone his own age he can discuss it with." He leaned back against the window frame. "I often wish he was closer to his brother. And could talk to him about his life."

Carter is a douche. Drew needs someone who doesn't think with his dick.

Maybe Zed. Zed is getting less teenagery.

"Perhaps. I can't choose Drew's confidants, regardless."

Aisha came back and closed the door gently, laughing. "I have never seen anyone as fascinated with bathing as those four are now. Drew had a dozen questions and I couldn't answer any of them, and Jay just might spend the next hour switching back and forth between sonic and water."

"I know which he'll prefer," Will said. "The sonic is... tingly. Far more so than the ones at home. Did they sort out the bedrooms?"

"Oz and Drew are next door. I think Zed and Jay are sharing a room, even though they don't have to." She sighed. "Another year and those two are going to want to move out and share an apartment. I won't be ready for that."

"They'll take Drew's apartment." He got up and met her halfway across the floor. "Jax said he wanted to blow out the back wall and make it bigger. He probably sees the move coming, too."

Aisha raised up on her toes to kiss him, even though she

was nearly as tall as he was and didn't have to. "As long as we can keep Jay close."

He didn't respond to that. He trailed his fingers over her shoulders, down her arms, and when she asked what he was thinking, he said, "My brain has disengaged."

Her fingers traced over the spot where Oz had kicked him. "All better? I don't want to hurt you."

"Not even a twinge."

I curled up and tried to go to sleep while they undressed each other. Even if I drifted off, I would notice when they were quiet again, whispering to each other in the dark. I intended to stay where I was, but knew I'd peek, because seeing Will content and happy was the best part of my day, and I didn't want to miss it.

*

Before they even got out of bed, Will and Aisha were planning how to get everyone else down to the Square and through the portal without any discussion about taking the morning to sight-see or even taking an hour to play with the flight packs one last time.

"I especially don't want Zed to get a look at Treasure Island," Will said.

"You don't think he'd get a little over-excited that he gets his castle?"

"I think," he said, sitting up, "that if he sees the castle and learns what it's for, that he'll feel tied down to the work he's doing now. I can feel him pulling away from it—"

She grabbed his arm to make him lay back down and curled up against him. "Not ready to get out of bed," she said. "And why would you want him to pull away from it? I thought he was destined to change so much about how we deal with death."

The Zealand Blackshear that Alcatraz was re-named for, the man whose work the castle was built to accommodate, was someone Will did not want to come into being. "In a few years I fully intend to interfere in the timeline," he told her. "There's a deep well of heartache that spurred Zed into immersing himself into his work, and I refuse to allow it to happen this time around."

Tell us what happens to Zed.

"I can't, Wick. I can't risk that you'll slip up and tell Drew, I'm sorry."

Well, screw you, too. I don't tell.

"You never tell on purpose. But sometimes you say things that lead to an understanding...please don't be offended."

Well, Zed doesn't die young, I figured that much out.

"No, Zed will not die young. He will live a long and very productive life."

I stomped up the bed, climbing on Aisha to get close to Will's face.

Old Oz said that her Zed lived for his kids and his work. But she didn't mention his wife. Zed loses a wife, doesn't he? And he never gets another one. Just tell me.

"Wick, sweetie," Aisha said, patting my front leg, "Your claws are digging in, and Will likes my boobs. I'd like them to remain unpunctured."

Will sat up, giving me space to slide onto the mattress. He sighed, hard, and then said, "All right, Wick. Yes, that Zed lost his wife, and it happened when they were both far too young. He spent his remaining years swimming in grief. He raised his children, and by all accounts, never so much as looked at another woman. He was a good father, he was dedicated to speaking for the dead, and then an incredible grandfather. But his heart was shattered. I can stop it from happening, and I will."

Aisha sat up and put her arms around him. "You warned me you would change time if it meant saving the people you love. Just tell me what I can do, and when."

It was still years away, and for once it didn't mean going back in time. He only needed to be there in the moment, to keep her from stepping out onto a busy SOMA street on a cold autumn afternoon. The date and time were etched onto his brain, and no matter what, he would be there.

They got up and dressed quietly, and while she was putting her shoes on, he went out to the kitchen to start breakfast.

He rushed out there so you wouldn't cook, you know.

"I'm hurrying, Wick. I'll still help."

Please don't. I never imagined anyone could turn bacon into rubber, but here you are.

"You're insulting me, aren't you? I'm starting to recognize the tone in your voice when you're snarky."

It's not an insult if it's the truth.

She sat on a stool at the breakfast bar while Will fried bacon, and one by one the others came out of their bedrooms, sleep sliding from them in reluctant wisps. Drew offered to help and was told to sit down, it would be ready soon, and the others followed his lead. When Will was ready to pour the scrambled eggs into the skillet, Aisha got up to bring glasses of juice and water to the table.

Jay's eyebrows knotted when he looked at her. "Something wrong, Mom?"

She glanced at Zed, and her eyes teared up. "I'm fine," she said. "Just tired."

PMS, dude. She just wants to go home and cuddle with a heating pad.

When she turned to go back into the kitchen, Drew leaned toward Jay and whispered to him. Jay's lips formed a silent "Oh," and he left it alone.

Before he put the plate full of bacon on the table, Will crumbled a piece for me and picked me up, setting me on the breakfast bar. He whispered, "thank you" as he put the plate down, and then turned to push Aisha's chair in for her, even though she was perfectly capable of doing that herself.

"Can Wick have eggs?" Jay asked. When Will nodded, he got up and spooned some of his eggs onto my plate. "I didn't salt them yet, buddy. If you want more, just...well, tell Will. You can have another bite of mine if you want."

"Don't give him too much," Drew said. "We'll all suffer if he eats more egg than he should."

"Not something you want to find out at three in the morning," Oz grumbled.

"Little shit crawled under the blankets and cut loose." Drew pointed at me. "You're sleeping with Will tonight."

"If Jay keeps feeding him, he's sleeping with Jay," Will said.

Like I'm giving you people a choice.

Still, I got another bite of egg and enough bacon that I didn't want any cat food while they did the dishes. When the last one was put away, and the trash sorted and placed in the recycle and incinerator bins, Will told them they were heading straight home. He might bring them back some time if they got him drunk enough to agree.

Zed was poised to make a case for staying for a little while longer, but Oz nudged him with her shoulder and gestured toward Aisha, who had slipped her arms around Will for a sleepy, take-me-back-to-bed hug.

"What time of day are we heading for?" Drew asked just outside the portal. "If we go back to the minute after we left, Zed might run into himself."

We followed Will. He aimed for a few minutes after Finn had left, hoping Union Square wouldn't be crowded and we could slip in unnoticed.

A dozen guards were milling around the portal opening, acting as cover, and waiting impatiently, bouncing on his toes, was the King of Pacifica.

12

Jo was already on her way to Scotland; Finn waited for Will, hoping that they could get there before Jo's mother—who had been in a fragile state for several years, and who was the reason he and Aisha spent part of their honeymoon in Glasgow—gave up the fight. There was no root cause of the failing of her health; it was as if one day she simply decided it was time, and the steady decline began.

Will didn't pack for the trip and told Finn not to bother taking his bag. When Jax told him why he was waiting for us on Union Square with a dozen of the royal guard, Will blinked and made up his mind: she was not going to die. It was that simple. She hadn't even reached one hundred years and should have almost as many to look forward to. Dying was unacceptable, and he intended to tell her that.

"You." He pointed at me. "You're going with us. She misses you."

All right, dude, but I'm not staying for years on end. If she needs me that much she's gonna have to move here.

He was all right with that idea.

Jax offered Will a government hyper-speed shuttle; it would get us there in under two hours, landing just after Jo. He warned Finn as they strapped in that he might feel a bit nauseated because of the speed, and if he did, there were barf bags in the little drawer in the dashboard.

What if I barf?

"Wick, if you throw up, you're just going to have to deal with it until we land. And then you're getting a bath."

I endeavored to not hork up my back claws. I was in my plastic tomb on the seat behind Finn; if I aimed right I could vomit between the slats and bounce bits of chewed up bacon and egg off his head, but I didn't want to risk any splash back. The high-pitched whine when Will fired up the engine cut through my head and made my whiskers twitch, and when we launched, I was pressed against the back of the tomb hard enough that I was certain I'd reached a two-dimensional state and could be peeled up like old tape. Once we were fully airborne, my insides settled, and my breakfast didn't feel like it was about to plaster the sides of my tomb.

"If this thing goes any faster, we'll get there two days in the future." Finn pulled a barf bag out, just in case. "Pacifica has had the answer to portal-free time travel all along, haven't they?"

"Indeed," Will said. "One flick of a switch and I'll open a wormhole to the next century. Think of all the work that would save you."

"What would be the fun in that? Though if you have the tech, I'd like to play with it. Maybe we can access a parallel universe or two."

"Maybe we already have." Will raised an eyebrow, teasing Finn. "Somewhere out there is the universe where I never left home. Another where I married Aisha in my twenties. Infinite possibilities."

Finn considered it. "More likely there's the universe where you became an insufferable asshole and were thrown off the Golden Gate Bridge by the infuriated masses. I love you, son, but leaving home when you did probably saved your humanity."

He's not wrong, you know.

"No helping him, Wick."

Then quietly, Finn said, "I hated every moment of it, Dash. All those years—I've lost track of how many times I resisted the urge to bolt through a portal to be with you. I missed you horribly."

"I know you did. I missed you, too, but I understood the reasons."

"My logic was fundamentally flawed, you know that, don't you? We were so focused on keeping my identity secret and making sure you were there when my idiot younger self showed up...I could have sent Jo to meet me there on the plaza, I would have recognized her and listened to her. She could have gotten me home—"

"Let it go, Dad," Will said. "Whatever the reasons, flawed or not, letting me go was the right thing. Look at the life it gave me."

"What about the life you could have had?" Finn asked, sounding small.

"A life without Jax and Aubrey? Or Oz and Zed and Drew? Losing those two years of my teens when Aisha was everything to me? No thank you. I wouldn't trade that part of my family for anything. If you feel guilty, stop. I honestly wouldn't want my life any other way."

And now you have Aisha for real.

"Exactly, Wick. Now I have Aisha and Jay. I'd kill the man who tried to take them from me."

"But I wish I had known when you were younger—"

"Wishing won't change anything, and this is where we're supposed to be right now. I'm serious. I wouldn't change a thing."

Finn nodded.

"Were you serious about still being alive in your third century? I honestly could not be certain that you weren't kidding."

"Do you want to meet me?" Finn asked.

Will turned away from the control panel. "You weren't kidding. How did you find him?"

"There was some confusion over paperwork in my thirties," Finn said. "I had applied for a grant, someone else with my personal identifier had applied for a previous one with another department—it got complicated. Long story short, he showed up at the lab to straighten it out. We've had several encounters over the years. So, yes, the previous version of me is alive and mostly well in my home When, and honestly...he hates me."

That made Will laugh. "I'd probably hate my younger self after two hundred years, too. And yes, I would like to meet him."

"If you see him once, you're forming an obligation. That man lost his son and has been alone far too long. For years I didn't know why, but now I get it. He hates me because he knew what I was going to do."

How do you feel about him?

"Frankly? He's an arrogant ass. Very bitter. Like Scrooge, but without the ethereal epiphanies."

"So now you know where I got it from."

"I always assumed from your mother's side. Craig is a very constricted sort of man, you know."

"Ah, don't go blaming Gran," Will said. "I didn't see much of him until you moved him to this When. I've treasured my semi-annual visits to see him and Gram."

"You were afraid of him when you were a boy. When you were ten, you decided he was creepy, because all he did was cross his arms and stare at you. Occasionally, he growled."

See, he's just like you. Ask Drew.

"Fine, Wick. But unlike Drew, I never hid in a closet to get away from him."

Finn laughed. "No, you hid under the bed."

"I did not."

"Dash, you were terrified of him until you hit fourteen or fifteen." The smile faded. "Fifteen. After we knew."

Fifteen was the year Finn realized who Will would grow up to be. It was also the year Will began spending more time away from home, leaving in graduated steps, until he realized he had to leave for good.

His grandparents left their own When after that, landing in San Francisco before he did—time travel is fun to play with—and King Eli helped Finn get them to Scotland and settled there, so that Will would have family he could travel to see. They didn't want to stay in Pacifica because if they did, they would be in his way. Finn felt like Will needed to have a sense of adulthood and didn't want them hovering, but he also wanted Will to have family roots in his new When.

Will visited twice a year, staying just long enough to feel the effects of not having his anchor with him. He'd missed two visits after the war started, and it was then his grandmother seemed to have given up. Craig kept Will apprised; she'd long stopped eating enough and was a shell of who she should be, but the long absence seemed to pick away at her.

They were quiet the rest of the way. Will handled the controls, and as we neared Glasgow, his fingers began tapping on the panel, as deftly as Zed playing the piano. The landing was not as disconcerting as the takeoff, and when he shut the engine down, he congratulated Finn on not vomiting.

We landed in a field on the outskirts of the city, not far from the road where Will's grandparents lived. The old King waited beside a car parked on the street, leaning against the back door. He looked tired and worn, but he smiled and hugged Will, patting him on the back when he did.

Jo had already landed and was on her way to see her mother, and Eli waited to give us a ride. He lived across the street from them when he wasn't traveling and spent most afternoons with Will's grandfather. They explored Scotland together, got drunk in pubs together, and when his wife decided enough was enough, they apologized to her together.

Henryetta Ferguson was as formidable as Jo could be, and she took none of their nonsense. She wasn't afraid to scold them as if they were wayward little boys, and she had no problem holding them accountable to their random acts of misbehavior. But mostly, she loved that they had each other, and loved Eli like a brother.

"She keeps telling me I have to be here for Craig to lean on," Eli told Will. "As if I would abandon him."

"She's not going to die," Will said flatly. "I don't care what she wants. It's not time."

"Emperor, she can barely sit up. She sleeps more hours than she's awake. I don't think you have a choice in this. She wanted you here to say your goodbyes."

"Well," Will said as he climbed into the car, "we don't always get what we want."

*

I hadn't seen them since Finn took me from home and left me with Jax. I'd seen pictures over the years and had been there every now and then when Will called with a video chat, but this was the first time in decades that I could smell them and taste the air around them, and when Will brought me into the house, I wiggled and squirmed to get down.

Henryetta was sitting in an oversized comfy chair with a fuzzy blanket draped across her legs, and once her scent tickled my nose, I wanted nothing more than to sit on her lap and purr. I raced across the floor, but before I jumped up, I thought better of it and turned to Will to ask permission.

"Gram? Wick wants to sit with you, but he's afraid he'll hurt you."

She patted her lap and invited me up and didn't mind when I crawled halfway up her chest to sniff her face.

"Aye, I missed you, too, Major Wick. Oh, and you're as soft as I remember." She put an arm under me to hold me close, and with her free hand, she petted my head. "Such a brave boy, you are. Always have been."

From her, I'd take that. I tucked my head under her chin and purred hard, hoping that would get down to her heart.

Will stood near the footrest. He put his hands on his hips and said, "What's this I hear about you wanting to die? You're too young, Gram. You'd miss too much."

"Major Wick, he thinks I have a choice."

"You do, and you know it," Will said. He ushered Finn and his grandfather out of the room, and when the door clicked shut, he dragged a chair across the room and sat close, where he could hold her hand.

Her heart sounds okay. Her breath isn't sweet or sour. I don't hear anything wrong inside her, other than she's fighting a burp. She should just let that sucker fly.

"Tell me why, Gram," he said. "You give me one good reason why, and I'll give you one good reason why not."

"I hear home calling for me," she said, her thick burr threaded around every word. "All the reason I need."

"Home doesn't mean dying. And if you died, you would miss the best years of my life. I want you here for that."

"There's only one home left to me, Liam." She sighed, half serious, full drama. "Craig and I were never meant for this world.

It's filled with rain and sorrow, and even you can't chase those clouds away."

"It's Scotland," he reminded her. "You wear the rain like a second skin. That's not a reason."

"I want to go home."

"Then I'll take you home. But you're not dying, not yet."

She lifted me up a bit. "He thinks it's so easy. I made up my mind. I'm ready."

Burp and you'll feel better. I promise.

"You met my wife. Did you like her?"

"She's lovely, Liam! Of course, I like her. I love her, she's sweet and strong, and isn't afraid of Eli."

That made him laugh. "You haven't met her son yet. He's an amazing young man, Gram. I love that boy as if he were my flesh and blood and I know you would, too."

"I'm sure," she said, placating him.

"Gram, if you die—"

"Go home," she said.

"If you *die*, you'll never meet him. But if you let me take you home, to your real home, I'll bring him to see you often. In fact, we've just come from there. He loved it, and I know he wants to see more." He rubbed his thumb over the back of her hand, gently. "He has no grandparents of his own. Your living would be as much a gift to him as it would be to me."

She closed her eyes and huffed out an exasperated sigh.

"Gram. Look at me."

She barely opened her eyes, looking at him through her eyelashes, until he cocked his head and said, "I was raised by a stubborn Scottish woman. I know how to play the game and win."

"Fine."

"If you let me take you home, not only will you get to know Jay, you'll have time to get to know my child, too."

At that, she perked up. "Liam."

"Not yet, but soon, I think. Aisha has no family, Gram. No mother, no grandmother. If you die, our child will grow up without having what I did. She would never know the sweetness of being showered with your kisses, and Gran frowning and scowling, then making her giggle until she thinks she's going to wet herself."

He lifted her hand, thin, wrinkled skin folded over bones, and pressed his lips onto delicate fingers. "Longing for home isn't the same as wanting to die. I can have you home in two hours. You'll have sunshine and warmth, and you'll see me often. I promise, I will visit more than I do now, and when our child is born, Aisha and I will bring her to spend time with you."

"Major? What do you think?"

I stood with my paws on her chest, her breath tickling my nose. When she bent her head to look into my eyes, I reached up with a paw and stroked her forehead, hoping she would feel my words.

I think you should go home because if you die right now, he'll be sad and then he won't do bouncy things, and then we'll never get a baby.

"Aye, that would be like him, wouldn't it?"

Will let go of her hand. "You understood him."

"Not the words. Wick exhales blessings sometimes, you know." She sighed again, and then lowered the footrest of her chair. "All right, then. Take me home, Liam. I won't be the reason you wait to have a child."

He didn't wait to see if she had second thoughts. He jumped up and yanked the door open and began barking orders.

"Gran, go pack for both of you. Anything you need for a short time. I can arrange to have everything else sent. Dad, call Mass and ask him to meet us in front of the house, and tell him he needs to have medical waiting on the other side of the hospital portal."

They scurried off without arguing, and Jo pushed past Will to help her mother. Eli looked confused at first, and then asked what he could do.

"Go pack your own things. It's time for you to go home, too, Eli. Learn to live with your ghosts and stop running away. Call your son and tell him you're coming with us, and that you're staying." When Eli scowled, he added, "You're going. Period."

"You'd speak to your King like this?"

"You're not my King. You're—"

Bonus dad.

"Exactly. You're more than my King, you're my...bonus dad, and you're damn well going home."

"I'll go when I'm ready to go, Emperor. I have things to do here."

"There's no point in staying. I'm taking my grandparents home, and if you stay, you'll be alone."

Eli softened. "She wants to live, then?"

"She never wanted to die, but I'm also not giving her a chance to reconsider. Go pack. If you're on the shuttle, it's one less thing for her to worry about."

"She knows I'm capable, Emperor. She won't worry about me."

"Worry is what she does best," Will argued. "I will no' let your precious ego give her one moment of trouble. Don't be the reason she thinks about staying. She would do it for you, and you *know* that."

"She can't stop you from taking her, you can *see* that. Just pick her up and take her home and leave me be."

Will stood uncomfortably close to Eli. "Don't you dare do that to your son. Don't you dare make him stand there, waiting for everyone to get out of the car, and have you not be among them. You'd break his heart, Eli. I won't allow it."

Eli wanted to push him back, create space between them, but he wasn't used to Will allowing even a quick touch. He gritted his teeth and growled, "Step aside, Emperor."

"You're coming with me."

"Fine." He started for the door. "I'll go, ya dobber, but don't expect me to be nice about it."

"Can't have that now, can we?" Will said under his breath.

Go pat Gram on the back. She needs to burp. For real. Make her burp, and she'll feel loads better.

"What would we do without you?" he asked as he headed back into the living room.

Well, some of you wouldn't burp when they need to. So, you're welcome.

Only three people were waiting out front when we arrived. Mass had a car ready to take Henryetta to the hospital and then home, where she would be placed in a tank for a couple of days, just in case there was something wrong. If there were, he would fix it. Jax waited for his father, and Aisha waited for Will.

There was little talk as Will lifted grandmother from the shuttle. He placed her in the front passenger seat of the car and kissed her cheek, promising that he would come see her soon. She kept her arms around his neck and wouldn't let go, not without making him promise that she was living for all the right reasons.

He whispered his promise. "It's between you and me, Gram. Our secret. But you know I would never lie to you. I want my child to know you better than I ever have."

Finn helped Craig into the back seat and then held the door for Jo, and when they were gone, Will reached for Aisha. Eli handed Jax his bag— "I don't care if you're the King, you're damn well carrying my crap." —and then stomped inside.

I looked up. Oz and Drew were on the balcony, cuddled together, but they didn't wave or act like they were watching. In another minute, Eli would come out of the elevator and they would go inside to see him, leaving Will and Aisha alone.

"She looked happy," Aisha said. "Whatever you whispered to her, it made her light up."

"She agreed to live, at least."

Aisha leaned back to see his face. "Was she planning on just willing herself away? Or worse?"

She'd refused to eat and had barely had anything to drink for several days. Will thought that at some point, she would have been too weak to refuse intervention in spite of not truly wanting to die, but her spirit would have broken and the end result the same. This way, at least, she wanted to stick around, if only to see if Will held up his end of the bargain.

"Be angry with me if you need to be," he said, "but to push her in the right direction, I told her that we wanted a baby. And that we would bring the kids to visit her, often."

"She'll tell Jo and Finn," Aisha said.

"Perhaps, eventually. Hopefully, by then we'll have something to announce."

Mass is gonna tank her. She'll feel loads better then.

"Indeed, Wick. Time in the tank with proper nutrition may help her understand what she truly wanted."

"Mass said he wanted to put Craig in a tank, too. Keep them on equal footing."

They'll be younger. He'll make the tank take some years off.

"That will come later, Wick, perhaps in another week or two. And they deserve it. They came here for me, to give me family to keep in touch with. And selfishly, I want the extra years with them."

"We need to start some kind of planner," Aisha said. "Something to keep track of who to visit and when."

"It is becoming increasingly difficult," he said.

His phone pinged; it was Jax, telling him to get upstairs. There was a bottle to open, and a drink to be had with Eli.

They lingered for a few more minutes, holding onto each other, the quiet broken only by the sound of breath and lips touching.

*

The bottle was on the table, unopened, and Eli stared at it as if it were poison he'd been asked to ingest. His arms were folded against his chest and he scowled, refusing to look up when Will and Aisha entered the room.

Jax sat at the other end of the table, tired and confused.

"Temper tantrum?" Will asked.

I jumped onto the kitchen counter, to be out of the way in case Eli picked up a glass and chucked it at someone.

"No idea what the problem is," Jax said. "He's pissed off and won't say why."

Aubrey grabbed two wine glasses and a bottle from the pantry and suggested to Aisha that they should go out onto the balcony and leave the boys to their pissing contest. Half of me wanted to go outside with them because they would be reasonable and kind, but the other half really wanted to be there if Eli started throwing things.

Will sat down and reached for the bottle of Scotch. He poured a little bit into each of their glasses and ignored that Eli refused to look at him. "His royal highness's dick is in a knot because I gave him no choice about coming with us. I used his love of my Gram to get him on the shuttle, and then he didn't get to go home with them."

"Ah. You took away his playmates."

"Temporarily. He can go see them when they're ready." He looked at Eli, but Eli was still refusing to budge. "The important thing was getting Gram on that shuttle. If he wants to piss all over himself because I put him on the spot, that's his problem."

Jax cringed a bit and braced for his father's anger.

Will didn't, and he didn't flinch when Eli pounded his fist on the table and shouted, "You treated me like a goddamned child, Emperor. You used my grief against me. She would have gone with you regardless."

"He just wanted you to come home, Dad," Jax said.

"Home?" He got louder. "I was at home, Jackson. I live in Glasgow. Pacifica isn't my home anymore. My life is in Scotland."

"Fine." Jax shoved his chair away from the table and then stomped down the hall. He swung the bedroom door closed, but it closed with a click instead of a slam, which probably ticked him off even more.

"When did you get so mouthy?" Eli asked, reaching for his Scotch.

"Somewhere around three years old."

"What's got him upset? That I don't think of here as home anymore?"

"Oh, that's just the tip of the iceberg, Eli. But it's those last five words that cut through him, I think."

"Eh." He drained his glass in one long swallow and then reached for the bottle. "What the hell. What did I say?"

"'My life is in Scotland.' When just a few months ago, you were speaking of coming home. To Pacifica."

"To visit, not to stay. I have a home in Glasgow. Friends. I can walk the streets, visit the pubs, sit with friends and talk until night is done, and none of it comes with the baggage of who I used to be. I'm just Eli there."

"Girlfriend?"

"What? God, no."

"Then what's holding you to Glasgow, Eli? And don't repeat that sad little litany that suggests your life here would be awful. If you go back to Scotland, your closest friends won't be there, and they're not coming back. You'll have a quiet house and noisy pubs, and what else?"

Eli glared at him over the rim of his glass.

"Peace from the ghost that walks these halls? You'll never truly get that, you know. She's with *you.* She's not haunting every corner here, waiting for you to return so that she can swoop from the shadows and poke at you for your absence. You can run back to Scotland, but she'll go with you, and you'll never address the real issue."

"Fuck you, William."

He shrugged. "Fine. Be angry with me. I really don't care. But the specter of your dead wife isn't why you can't stay here, and you know it."

Eli reached for the bottle again.

You're getting him drunk. You might not like him when he's drunk.

"Whatever you're saying, cat, shut up. He doesn't need your help."

See?

Will leaned back in his chair, and he turned his glass to make the ice cubes spin. He did that over and over, listening to the swirl of liquid and ice.

"Once upon a time," he said, setting the glass down.

"Oh, fucking don't."

"There was a youngish king, not quite middle age, who could not crawl his way out of the fog of grief. He sat on the throne and saw nothing but pain, and his most consuming thoughts were of his overwhelming loss. He chewed on that loss like a gristled piece of meat until it settled in his throat, choking him. He announced—without discussion—that he was abdicating into retirement and that he intended to see the world before he was too old to appreciate it. And his people applauded because they loved their king and wanted him to be happy."

"What's your point?"

"The King," Will went on, ignoring him, "was so fascinated by his own fog that he failed to see what lingered at its fringes. His son waited there, expecting to catch his father when that fog lifted, so intent on being there that he had not properly grieved the loss of his mother. He was focused on holding his family tight to him, soaking up their sorrow, waiting for the day when his father would blink, and the fog would thin and then be gone. Only then he would feel comfortable enough to hit his knees and cry, he would feel able to mourn without worrying that he'd be multiplying his father's pain.

"But that never happened. His father handed him the crown and left, leaving the new young king to abandon his own life plan to assume a position for which he was neither ready nor properly trained. But he didn't complain. He left the job he loved and took on the one he did not, and he promised himself that he would be a kind and compassionate leader, as well as a present and attentive husband and father. He stepped into a life without friends, with little social interaction, because it was the lot in life to which he had been assigned. He did not complain because he didn't want to add to his father's pain. He didn't want to be a point of guilt.

"What he continued to hope, however, was that his father would find peace enough to come home, this home, and be a grandfather to a young princess and prince because they loved him without question and he knew they would be better people for having had him in their lives. But time did what it always does. It moved forward without regard to the old king's grief and the young king's wishes, and now the princess and prince are adults. He's still trapped in a job he never wanted but fully expected to take on when he was much older, and his father is still running away from the one thing that didn't stay behind.

"You may live in Scotland, Eli, but your life is here."

Eli said nothing, glaring across the table.

"Name me one thing more important in Glasgow than Oz and Zed, or Jax and Aubrey." He got up and drained the last of his Scotch. "Your body may reside there, but your heart beats here, in this house, and the longer you stay away, the more broken it will be."

He headed for the balcony, and I scrambled after him.

"Get back here, you son of a bitch," Eli barked.

Will stopped at the entryway. "For what? You laid an entire kingdom at your son's feet and walked away. It's time someone laid the truth down at yours and left you with it long enough to truly see it. Jax has done everything expected of him, and he has done it well. The only thing he wants in return is for you to come home for longer than it takes breath to fade from a mirror and mean it."

You should have taken the bottle. He might drink it all.

"He's a big boy," Will said as he pulled the balcony door open. "If he does, it's his choice."

"Whose choice for what?" Aubrey asked.

"Eli's, to get incredibly intoxicated." He sat on the double seat with Aisha, and I jumped onto Aubrey's lap. "I have upset your father-in-law. Wick is concerned because I left him with a nearly full bottle of very good scotch."

Aubrey waved it off. "He's been in a snit for years. Except for your wedding, I think everything has rubbed him the wrong way."

"Jax is also upset. He stomped off to hide in your bedroom."

"He'll be fine. Won't he, Mister Wick?" She lifted me up and nuzzled her cheek against my head. "How was your grandmother, really?"

"Not as dead as she wanted everyone to think," Will said, lightly. "She decided years ago that she didn't want to outlive me and announced that she fully intended to be gone shortly after I was. I don't think Gran believed her, but she began eating barely enough to survive on and that act of defiance has taken its toll over the years."

"But then you lived," Aubrey pointed out.

"By then it was habit." He knew she never intended for it to go so far; she'd never been truly happy in this When, but she was determined to make it work long enough to see him through to the end. His grandfather was happy, owed largely to Eli's friendship and near-constant presence, but she'd never integrated into the community and had no close friends.

The loneliness was killing her as much as her want of not outliving Will.

"She would never admit it, but I truly believe she just wanted to go home. It's not something she could have asked of Gran, not as content as he's been here."

"So you gave her an excuse." Aisha nudged him to put his arm around her. "You begged her to go, and she can't tell you no."

"I gave her reasons to live," he said. "Mass will make sure she's healthy, and when she is, they can come back if they want. I'm hoping that with my parents here, they'll want to visit here but not return to Glasgow."

"If they do, it's a short trip there," Aisha said.

"But if he stays here, Eli has essentially lost his friends and neighbors," Aubrey said. "And he blames you."

"Partly. I may have also held him accountable for leaving Jax in the lurch when he left. And given him a list of reasons why it was wrong."

Aubrey knew what he meant. "Those reasons are why Jax will hold on until he can no longer do the job. He wants Oz to have the life he missed out on. He thinks if he's lucky, she'll be an old, old woman before she takes the crown."

"She's beginning to understand that," Will said.

"I know. But I also know she's spent her life expecting Jax to abdicate when she hits thirty. I don't think she knows exactly what she wants to do, other than marry Drew."

"She's mentioned teaching," Aisha said.

"Only because it's all she really knows," Aubrey said, sighing. "I've been teaching fifth grade her entire life, and she remembers when Jax taught history. I don't think we exposed her to any other possibilities, and we should have."

"I've certainly not been a good example," Will chuckled. "I suppose if she wants to take my job, I can retire and allow her to become the King's babysitter."

"She's not old enough to go to bars, William."

"He is grooming her, regardless. If something happens, he doesn't want her floundering as she tries to navigate her way."

"She'll have you, I hope," Aubrey said. "And no pondering life without Jax. I can't bear the idea."

"Fair enough. Where are the kids? I thought I saw Oz and Drew out here a while ago."

"In her room. We're not telling Jax."

"I promise you, the only things going on in that room involve things to which he would not object. Drew is determined to honor the promise he made Jax."

She waved it off. "Oh, I don't care. If I had my way, he'd move up here again, and they'd stay until they needed more space."

"You'd just remodel the entire floor until there was room for all the kids and grandkids," Aisha said.

"When Oz was born," Will told Aisha, "Jax and Aubrey made a firm declaration of 'adult at eighteen.' They were determined that their children would be fully functional adults, living on their own. Now look."

"Stop teasing me. They're ready. But I want my family with me."

"I think I may have held Jay back a little too much," Aisha said. "One day he'll want to leave, but I'm not sure he'll be ready."

"*I* won't be ready," Will said. "Whatever plans you and James made, I won't be ready for Jay to leave anytime soon. I'll stand in the doorway and growl at him if I have to."

"He's not in a hurry, sweetheart. Jay is one of those kids who sees the free rent and food, and he's not about to walk away from that. I have a feeling we have him until he graduates."

"Then we need to encourage a graduate degree."

They're all gonna live here, anyway. You guys will have to move before they will.

"Plenty of room to expand in this building," Will said. "But first up, if Jax can convince Eli to stay, he'll need his own space.

Your plans to move Oz and Drew into my apartment may have to change."

"They can't stay in that tiny apartment we stuffed Drew into."

Will reminded her that the guest suite across from their new apartment had been remodeled, too, and Eli might take comfort in living where his family began. And if he knew that, if right from the start he understood he would still have his own home and not just a room in his son's house, his irritation might abate.

"Go check on him, Wick," Will told me. "If he's still at the table drinking, I'll go back and apologize."

He wasn't at the table.

I looked down the hallway; Jax's bedroom door was open again, and I could hear their voices rumbling. I wasn't sure if Will wanted me to go listen or not, but I decided it was private and didn't require my input, so I told him where Eli was, and then went into Oz's bedroom, where I hoped there was less drama and no bouncing, and I could get a quiet nap.

*

The entire window seat was available to serve my napping needs. Drew was at the desk using Oz's computer, and she was stretched out on the bed, on her stomach, reading. It was a quiet kind of normal that I welcomed as I curled up, but just as I was drifting off Drew abruptly pushed the chair away from the desk.

"We just had an amazing experience, and here we are going about our normal stuff like an old married couple."

Oz barely glanced up. "It was fun. I'm not sure it was amazing. I mean, there were no dragons or giant cats, and I didn't get to throat punch anyone *or* stand in front of a thousand men with my boobs flopping in the wind."

"How jaded will we be in five years? We went stupid far into the future, and it's like, yeah that was fun, but nothing...I dunno, special."

She turned her tablet off. "Maybe if Will hadn't had to run off right after, we'd still be freaking out about it. Zed probably is. This is all really new for him."

"He's had chances to travel all his life, hasn't he?"

"Dad offered over and over to take him somewhere. Until Finn popped up, he had zero interest. Now I'm waiting for him to ask why I was given a transponder when I was a baby, and he wasn't."

"Why *did* they give you one?"

"Not sure. Unless it was the Emperor's idea. He knew I would go back to snoop. But then Dad also got one when he was a baby. So I don't really know."

Finn gave Jax one because Eli thought they might go places together, like a secret bonding thing. Donna didn't know about it.

"Really," Oz said after Drew repeated it. "Grandma didn't know he could use the portals?"

She didn't know about the portals. She didn't know about any of it. Not until just before she died, when Will showed her.

"How could your grandfather keep it from her?"

He didn't tell her about lots of things. She didn't want to know how hard it was for him to be King. So they didn't talk about that stuff.

Oz rolled over and sat up, scooting to the edge of the bed. "You and me? We are not going to be like that. If your work gets hard, tell me. If you get excited about something, I want to know. No secrets."

"All right." He rolled the chair toward her. "I'll try to not be obsessive."

"You can be, a little. And I'll try to be enthused."

"Like your dad is when your mom starts talking about some kid who finally grasps long division? I have a hard time not laughing at how hard he's trying to pay attention."

"Exactly like that. And if I ever figure my own shit out, you get to do the same thing."

"Rethinking teaching?"

"No, I want to teach, but I flop around about what. It's like the dojo. I love working with you and Zed and Jay, but the idea of adding other students? I'm not as enthused about that. It's like

I was excited for twenty minutes, but now it's just...meh. Every time I think I know what field I'm most interested in, it turns into that. And I know I need to just pick something and stick with it."

"Why? Indulge your whims, Oz."

Chase a rabbit or two.

"Exactly. Will keeps telling me to chase rabbits down holes, to see where that takes me. Do that. Chase one, and if you don't like where it goes, chase another. Take a class on art appreciation. Music. Literature. You have time to figure it out."

She patted the bed, inviting him to sit next to her. "We're getting married in less than two months. I should have some kind of plan, don't you think?"

"The plan is we finish school, and while we're at it, I keep working with Will and you keep shadowing your dad. He's trying to teach you the job, let him. For now, that's enough."

"You work, Drew."

"I'm not sure you can call it work. I get to play with toys and see if I can turn them into something different."

"You still get paid."

He leaned back on his hands, tilting his head as he looked at her. "Is that it? We're not gonna be rich, Oz, but we'll do all right. We have a place to live, and Will's paying me enough to put food on the table."

"Like my mom's going to let us get out of family dinners."

"It's just an expression," he said, sneaking a kiss, "The point is that you have plenty of time to find the thing that makes you excited."

"Now that, I already have." She pushed him back onto the bed. "Happy and excited. Want to see how excited?"

"I do, but not here."

Her fingers were on the zipper to his jeans, and he was so distracted by her kissing that he didn't notice. I was unhappy about losing the spot I'd warmed up for my nap, but I jumped over to the bed and planted myself on Drew's chest.

No means no.

"My knight in shining armor." Drew laughed and held onto me as he sat up. "She wasn't going to take advantage of me, Wick."

"Just groping." Her hand brushed over the front of his pants. "All right, I might have tried a little more. We haven't really done anything in here."

He got up and set me on the bed beside her. "And we won't, not until we're married. After that, if you want to sneak up here and fuck on every solid surface there is, I'm down with that."

Her nose crinkled. "I'm not liking crude Drew. I don't mind hearing 'fuck me' once in a while when we're actually *doing* it, but, ew, no. Not like that."

"I'm sorry." He reached for her hands and pulled her up. "Wanna go make out on the balcony? That won't upset your dad and who knows, someone snooping might get a great picture of it."

They were too late.

Will and Aisha were still there on the double seat, fishing for each other's tonsils. I hoped they'd waited for Aubrey to leave, but I wasn't discounting the possibility that one of them started sucking spit from the other while she was sitting right there. Face it, Will was pretty much like a sixteen-year-old who just got to second base for the first time. He was six feet of hormones, and after observing Oz and Drew and Zed in their teens, I thought he probably wasn't thinking with his brain most of the time.

Oz pushed the door open and said, "Gross. They're *kissing*, Drew. I think tongues are involved."

I jumped into Will's lap.

I think they just got started. He's not happy yet.

"Don't you have an apartment you could go to?" Will asked.

"Don't you?" Oz dropped into the chair Aubrey had vacated. "Is Grandad feeling social yet? He looked like he wanted to murder someone when he got here."

"He's upset with me. He'll get over it."

"Why didn't he just follow them through?" Aisha asked. "If he's that upset with his friends leaving him behind, he could have just gone with them."

He wasn't given the option; Will knew what Mass's plans were, and Eli would have been waiting there just as much as he was waiting here. And reminding him he could pop through that portal any time he wanted gave him another direction to run.

"He needs to stay here for a bit. He owes Jax that much."

"He was just here," Oz said. "He came for your wedding."

"And left right after. Your father needs him for more than a few days, Oz. That's all he's gotten in the years since your grandmother died. A few days here, a few days there, with no time for them to truly connect."

Is that why you always stayed with yours for two weeks?

Will nodded. "I would have stayed longer if I could have. They came here for me, they deserved my time and attention."

"If they came here for you, why did they settle in Scotland?" Oz asked.

"To give me a life of my own. I had family, but no one hovering. I often wished they would move here, but looking back, I understand why they didn't."

"Finn would have recognized them when he showed up," Drew thought. "I still don't get why he felt like he needed to get his memory back on his own, though."

"Knowing what he knows now? I think he would have handled it differently. And the notes left in the Old Mint will warn future versions."

"Future versions will just build the gates, won't they?" Drew shrugged. "Hell, future you might not be sent here. No need."

"There will be notes left regarding that, as well. And the recommendation to follow through and send me, assuming I'm born. I might not be."

Oz turned to Drew. "You know, we talked for years about ending the monarchy. We could just go back and stop the United States from fracturing in the first place."

"Sure, we'll do that on our honeymoon." Drew looked to Will. "Which When would that be?"

"Late twentieth century," Will said. "That's where it all began to crumble. One could argue that the decline began in the nineteen nineties with the rise of the Moral Majority and the efforts to interject religion into government."

Oz grunted. "I'd rather go to Disneyland."

"Did you tell her?" Will asked Drew.

"That everyone is going with us?" Oz asked. "I know. It'll be fun."

"No, something else," Drew said. "You know that park in Will's When I told you about?"

"The one that excites you more than Santa bringing me invisible lingerie?"

"That one. We're spending our wedding night there. In the park, under the stars and northern lights."

"We'll get arrested for public indecency. I don't care where we are, Drew, it's our wedding night. I'm doing nasty things to you. Witnesses might not stop me."

"Now who's gross?" Will said. "I'll reserve a private space for you. You can do whatever you like, and no one else will be watching. Nor can they hear anything."

"You can literally spend a couple days stark naked in the great outdoors," Aisha chuckled. "Though technically it's indoors. You might not want to leave."

"Want to go back?" Will asked her. "I promised we would at some point."

"You're taking us there," Drew said. "If it's private space, I don't care if you're in the next...room or whatever it is. And then we can stop on the way back and pick everyone else up to go to Disneyland."

"Better make reservations there, too," Aisha said.

"Already done," Oz said. "We reserved the entire concierge floor of the main hotel. The one below it, too. That was a safety thing, but the rooms are paid for. The more, the merrier, really. I just wish Mom and Dad would go."

"They probably wish they could go, too," Will said. "That would result in the park shutting down to the public, and your parents wouldn't do that. Why do you think I was the one to take you and Zed when you were small? They wanted to, Oz, but they hate inconveniencing the masses."

"Have they ever taken a real vacation?" Aisha asked.

"Not since Jax took the throne. Even before then, the short trips they took could hardly be called vacations."

"Honeymoon?" Drew asked.

"They did have a honeymoon. Two weeks in Australia and New Zealand. If Jax could run away, that's where he would go. The only thing he would enjoy more would be a private island."

"Tear down Alcatraz," Drew said, mostly kidding. "Build the castle Zed wants, but give it to the King and Queen."

Will shook his head. "Not warm enough. Or private. Jax would want complete privacy, and his own beach to lay on."

"If you say totally naked..."

"Probably not. Your father has common sense, Oz. He's not risking sunburn to anything he might wish to play with later."

"Ugh, you really are gross now."

"Says the young woman who just admitted she planned on nasty public things with Prince Andrew."

"That's different."

"I'm sure it is." He handed me off to Drew, and got up, holding his hand out to Aisha. "At the risk of offending Oz's clearly delicate sensibilities, these two interrupted something I'd like to finish."

"It had better involve chocolate, a back rub, and a heating pad," she said. "'Night, you two."

"I'm not sure I feel like making out now," Drew said. "They sucked the wind out of my sails. And they got old people hormonal funk on our chair."

She reached over and patted his leg. "That's all right. We should go in and see if Grandad is over his snit."

I offered to go see, but they wanted to go inside, anyway. Eli had gone to bed—at least the guest room door was closed—and Aubrey and Jax were in the kitchen. He was backed up against the counter, his arms wrapped around her, face buried against her shoulder. If they heard us, they pretended not to. When Jax took a shuddered breath, Oz poked at Drew and whispered that they should just go downstairs.

I could have followed; they wanted to give Jax and Aubrey privacy, and so did I, but I didn't feel quite the same way about Eli.

If he wanted privacy, then he needed to block the cat flap.

He was stretched out on the bed, fully clothed except for his shoes. His scratched and dinged shiny blue suitcase was near the door, still packed, the shoes perched neatly on top. I jumped up on the bed, stomping on the mattress so that he would know I was there.

"What do you want, Wick?"

You're being kind of a dick.

I learned that from Zed. You don't look like one but you're being one.

"You're judging me, aren't you? You've always been a little shit."

You didn't used to be mean.

"Ah, I'm not pissed at you. I'm just pissed. I don't need to be here, you know. There's a bar stool back in Glasgow waiting for me."

There are bar stools here. And nice booths at Fuzzy's.

"The Emperor could have just told me that Jackson needed me. Hell, Jackson could have told me. Guilting me into staying? That's bullshit."

He did tell you he needed you here. You brushed it off and went back to Scotland.

"He was ready to be King, no matter what he thinks. That boy has always been adventurous, and he has nerves of steel. A backbone better than mine. And he had what I never did, he had the Emperor. What I would have given for them to have been true brothers."

He patted his stomach, inviting me to stretch out there.

"I loved that boy from the moment I laid eyes on him. He was a scrawny little thing, pale as a ghost. His eyes? Finn had explained the family line, but when I saw him? He had Donna's eyes. The same shape, the same color. The same sorrow. I wanted to scoop him up and bring him home with me, to raise alongside Jackson. My gut told me I'd get my chance one day, but I didn't do well with it, did I?"

He thinks you did fine. Will, I mean. I don't know what Finn thinks.

"Is he right, do you think? I've been running away? All these years I've told myself I stayed in Glasgow for Craig and Henry, not that I was avoiding home."

Last time, you said it was hard to stay here. You hear her everywhere. I think you do. I think she's whispering "stay."

"You know, when I speak of them, it's 'my boys.' Not just Jackson. People ask, I tell them I have two sons. And I bubble with pride over my boys, Wick. Why is it so easy to stay away, with friends, rather than to stay home with the ones I would die for?"

Because of reasons? I don't know.

Maybe you're still upset with yourself because you left Jax with a job he was kinda young for and you knew it was selfish.

"I could stay for a while, I suppose. Glasgow isn't going anywhere."

It was okay to be selfish back then, you know. When she died, it skinned the knees on your heart. You get to cry when that happens.

"I could spend a few months here, a few weeks there. Let my ghost give me a good talking to. I know she wants to. After all these years, I imagine she has a lot to say."

Probably just wants to know if you're okay.

"Ah, I shouldn't have snapped at those boys. William knows the buttons to push, and Jackson just wanted me to want to stay here. Surely, they know they *are* my life. I didn't mean to imply they weren't."

Maybe you should go say that to them. I could tell Will and he could pass it on, but it wouldn't be the same.

"Can I tell you something, Wick?"

You're going to no matter what my answer is.

"Jackson has been a far better king than I would have been, had I held on. Maybe he didn't feel ready, but he was meant to have that crown."

Tell him that.

"I know, I know. I should go talk to him. With any luck, it'll go better than it did an hour ago."

He might be groping Aubrey in the kitchen, but okay. I'll run ahead and warn them to zip up.

13

At five the next morning, Will and Jax were on the balcony, skipping their planned run in favor of hot coffee and cold air. Jax had only slept for a couple of hours; he'd stayed up until after one with Eli, sitting on the sofa with the rest of the Scotch and a bowl filled with dry popcorn on the coffee table in front of them.

It had taken two more shots of scotch for Eli's wall to crack. Jax only needed to tell his father that he loved him no matter where he felt he needed to be, but he missed him terribly. "There are only two things absent from my life that I long for. My dad, and grandchildren. I can wait for one of those, but the other, not so much. My heart hurts every time you leave because I honestly don't know if I'll ever see you again."

Eli blinked, the wall cracked, and then it crumbled. "Jackson, if I stay, if I let myself stay, I get everything I wanted in life before she died. I don't have to rule over so much as a card game, and I get my boys. I get to love you both, and I can let the world see how much and how hard. And that would have hurt her. She didn't understand the Emperor and I couldn't explain. I thought if I had, if I had shown her the portals and taken her to meet Finn and Jo, it would have terrified her badly enough to break us. But now I wonder. She saw the Emperor stay the same while you grew, that was one of the things she couldn't understand. She felt there was an otherworldliness about him, and his refusal to touch only cemented that feeling.

"I should have told her. I shouldn't have kept those secrets from her. She was fond of the Emperor even when she feared him, and I robbed her of the chance to love him. Ah, and she would have. If she had known he was our distant grandson, if I had not presumed she was too delicate for all the truths of my life—I fostered that distance, Jackson. I allowed the secrets to become this...thing...between us. And without that thing, maybe I would have seen—"

His confession of guilt poured from him in the same gush as the scotch from his glass when he tossed back the last shot. If he'd been honest, there would have been nothing to keep him from seeing her suffering, and she might still be alive.

"I don't deserve the life I have here. If I stay, I have everything I denied her. My boys. My time. Our grandchildren. Leaving has always been my penance. How can I stay?"

Jax knew there was no convincing him that he was wrong. All he could do was ask him to stay. If not for him, then stay for Oz and Zed. Learn to love Drew and Jay and Aisha the way he did his sons.

"Your penance has long been paid, Dad. Now you stay for her. This is what she would want, her grandchildren having you in their lives."

When Eli finally went to bed, Aubrey got up to cuddle with Jax, which I thought was going to lead to kissing and groping, but all they did was talk until she was too sleepy to stay up.

"He says he'll stay put for six months, as long as I don't mind him taking a few days here and there to go see your grandparents. After that, no promises. He doesn't think he's seen enough of the world and feels like he's running out of time."

"He's home," Will said. "He's staying for a bit. Let's just be grateful for that."

"For now."

The only way to keep him home, Will thought, was if he had something else to stay for. "He stays in Scotland for Gram, I think. If he had something equally important here, other than you, he might come home more often."

Give him a job. Maybe he misses being King.

Any job Jax could think of, Eli would dismiss as being busywork. His pride would trump the tasks; unless there was something essential, he didn't see his father jumping at it.

"The Consortium," Will said. "Eli could be the one to shake things up and influence the vote. There's not a standing member of it or the U.N. that doesn't respect him. He would understand that his influence is critical if we want Florida admitted."

"It's definitely not busywork," Jax mused. "But would he see this for what we intend? A way to tether him to home?"

"He might. But he'll also see the bigger picture. The world is not ready to be done with his leadership. He already knows our Consortium representative is retiring before the vote. Asking him to fill the position makes sense, Jax. It would make sense even if you weren't looking for a way to convince him to stay."

It wouldn't keep him home. Taking the job meant Eli would travel often, but his base would be in San Francisco, and he would return often out of necessity. "I'll ask him and hope he believes he really is needed, but I'm not sure how he'll feel having to answer to me. It's only just dawned on him that we're not teenagers anymore. He looks at us and sees the kids who kept stealing his beer."

"Don't laugh. That will be you and me sooner than we would like. Oz and Drew, Zed and Jay—when they're our age, we'll still see them as kids."

"The boys, maybe. Oz will always be my little girl, but she's becoming one hell of a woman."

"You'll still look at her in wonder, trying to figure out how your little girl has such a commanding grip on life. I imagine Eli has the same problem. His son is not only Pacifica's King but became Midlam's as well. You're far more involved in the world than he was and have earned quite a bit more respect in a very short time. That must befuddle him a bit. How can the boy who thought it was a good idea to speed down California Street on an antique bicycle be the same man who commands the world's attention and makes them all want to listen?"

"Eh, don't try to flatter me. I'm still not putting you in my will."

"Shame. I put you in mine."

"No one wants your collection of twentieth-century miniature stuffed animals, Will." He took a sip of his coffee and then sighed. "Anthony Myers requested a meeting today. He didn't say it outright, but my gut says he wants an official, closer look at Drew's work."

"And the answer?"

"Your brother will stall him and wants you to hide as much of your data as you can, and he doesn't want to know where. Your King may have no choice but to take his request seriously."

"I understand."

"He'll want a demonstration. It would be a shame if one of the components happened to overheat and go up in flames."

"Has he given you an indication of what he might like to see? Drew's desktop toy or his initial work with the full-scale interactive display?"

"I don't think he knows about the array, but he's not stupid. He saw that small hologram and grasped the power it takes to generate something that realistic. He made the leap. He knows Drew has made forward progress where our people stalled."

"Forward progress does not equate adequate function, Jax. Nothing we have now is worthy of the military's attention."

"Myers is doing his job," Jax said. "If he thinks there's a remote chance that you have a tangible idea that can be used militarily, he has to jump on it. It's not personal, and it's not greed."

"I know that. I'm saying he's jumping too soon."

"And that's what the meeting is likely about. What does Drew have, is it advanced enough to warrant tightening the security around it, and should the government take claim and insert their own engineers and researchers?"

"I won't allow that to happen."

Jax got up. "Let's hope the King doesn't see it that way."

*

Drew's hair was half plastered to his head, half sticking straight up, whiskers dotted his chin and upper lip but were barely splattered across his cheeks, and the only thing he had on was a pair of wrinkled shorts. Will noticed none of that; when the door opened, he greeted Drew with, "How many of the portable projectors did you build?"

"It's six freaking o'clock, Will."

"I know. Good morning. How many of the portable projectors did you build?"

He waved Will in. "Three. Why?"

"Where are they? Here or in the workshop?"

Drew dropped onto the sofa, trying to blink himself more awake. "One in the shop, it only sort-of works. Two here, both mostly functional."

"I need the two you have here," Will said. "We'll store them in my safe. And if General Myers asks, the only one in existence is the one in the shop."

That woke him up. "He wants it."

"Minimum, he wants a closer look at it." Will related his conversation with Jax. "We need to take several of the hard drives out of the array, and most of the projectors need to go dark."

"Easy enough," Drew said. "Flip a few switches, and the hologram won't display at even a quarter resolution. But if we take more than two clusters out of the array, the primary panels may overheat."

Jax said it would be a shame if one of them went up in flames.

"We can replace individual units," Will said. "But I want Myers believing that you truly are mucking about with this. He needs to see the portable as a toy and the larger unit as a pipe dream."

"Mr. B already knows—"

"I don't think he'll tip our hand. He sees the bigger picture. He wants the cooling system perfected for Elysium. But the King? He'll have no choice but to grant the General the inspection he wants."

"I really put him between a rock and a hard place, didn't I?"

"That issue is moot right now, Andrew. But I would like to get moving on this before Jax and the General are done speaking."

Oz is awake. You might wanna be looking the other way if she comes out of that room naked.

"Oz is not modest, but Wick makes a fair point," Drew said as he pushed himself up.

Will decided to leave before he could embarrass her. "Bring the portables and knock when you're ready to go. Don't bother making yourself pretty, it's a lost cause."

"The sense of humor is new, isn't it?" Drew asked, looking down at me. "He needs practice."

Are you sure he was joking?

"Furry little asshole," he muttered, heading into the bedroom.

I waited in the living room, just in case Oz was ready to pounce on him in the bedroom. It wasn't the bouncy things that bothered me; I didn't want to see her disappointment. Or joy. For all I know, she might be happy if he told her he had to leave. He'd say, *Oz, I have to go now*, and she'd be all, *Well, finally, I can snoop through his stuff without him knowing*.

I wondered if that had ever occurred to him, so when he came back out, still looking sleepy but with actual pants on, I asked him.

What if Oz looks through all your stuff when you're not here?

"What if she does?"

It's rude.

"I'm not hiding anything from her."

"What aren't you hiding from me?" She came out, dressed in his shorts and an old t-shirt. "You're allowed secrets."

"Wick's worried that you'll poke your nose into all my crap while I'm gone."

"Oh, yeah, because your stash of computer porn is so worth finding."

"You're welcome to it if you find it." He kissed her, and then picked me up. "You going with us today, or staying here and helping her look?"

I don't want to see your porn, either.

"Nanobots gone wild!" he called out as we left. "You're gonna love it!"

*

After he walked the perimeter of the computer array and the attached floor panels, Will decided that physically detaching components would be too obvious. Because it was the prototype, all the lines and wires were exposed, and a disconnect would stick out; Myers would make note, ask for repairs, and would then want another demonstration.

"Re-write some of the code, then," Drew proposed. "Interrupt the power flow after the second drive, and power down half the nanobots. Functionally, that would do the same thing. If he gets close enough to any of the projectors, they'll still appear to be working, but the only thing coming through most of them will be light that bleeds over from the others."

I could pee on something, short it out.

"I appreciate the offer," Will said. "We'll manage without, though."

"Hell, we could all pee on it," Drew mumbled as he lifted the portable from the table. "Treat the general to the wonderful aroma of fried ammonia."

While Will rewrote code and Drew tweaked the hardware, I hopped up on the window perch they'd made for me and watched people passing by. Some days I was noticed; women, especially, would stop and tap on the window to get my attention, rarely bothering to see what was going on behind me. Small children sometimes pointed and squealed, which meant I had to sit up and paw at the window because ignoring them would be rude. Other days all I saw was a stream of air bike riders looking for parking and unhappy people heading to work.

Waiting was boring, and there was nothing either of them were doing that would distract me, so I napped. I had a sense of time passing, though it could have been as little as an hour when I heard a van coming down the street. It parked across slots reserved for air bikes; the van was painted in Pacifica's colors and had the general's star displayed on the front side panel.

He's here. He needs to learn to park better. If anyone had left their bike there, he would have squished it and I bet you'd have had to pay for it.

Will spun his chair around and grabbed a tablet, pulling up a rough sketch of the portable's schematics. When the door opened, he was peering into the tiny open side of display platform, and Drew was fiddling with the controls on his phone. Myers stepped inside, followed by his aide, but he waited to be invited all the way in.

"Anthony," Will said, glancing up. "Something I can help you with?"

That was all the invitation he needed. His aide stayed by the door, but he came in and went straight to the hologram deck.

"I assumed you'd already spoken with the King," he said, peering over Will's shoulder.

"At five this morning, over coffee. I was made aware that you'd asked for a meeting with him, that's all. Oddly enough, he doesn't tell me everything."

"I would hope not." He crossed to Drew's side. "I just wanted a better look at what the boy is working on. The little I saw was impressive. If he can replicate it on a larger scale, we may release the components sitting in storage to him. He can use those materials to build on."

The boy is right here, he sees that doesn't he?

"Don't be too impressed," Drew said. "You saw this being operated before it warmed up. Right now, I can't get it to do shit."

"It worked fine in the King's office."

"Cold," Drew said. "Well, that and I added a few new parameters. Something went '*zzzt*' after that. I think it's because there's too much data being exchanged too quickly over a board that isn't cooled well enough."

"When it functioned, how did the hologram work?"

Drew pointed to the tiny projectors lining each point in the grid. "It's just a projection. Like a video monitor, without the monitor. The more projection modules, the more refined the image is."

"Until it overheats," Will grunted.

"And this?" Myers gestured to the panels on the floor. "A bigger version?"

"Someday," Will said. "Essentially, it's the system you abandoned years ago. Drew multiplied the power sources, but heat is still the core issue."

"Does it work?"

"It turns on," Drew said. "The display is kind of disappointing. Well, it was exciting at first because I got more imaging than I expected, but the resolution sucks, and I can't really do anything with it yet. It's really just something to look at for now."

He wasn't lying. That impressed me.

"What's your end game?"

Drew looked to Will before he answered. "Reality-level holograms. Something you can interact with. Like, having an avatar." He moved to the control panel and flipped a few switches. "All I have right now is a couple of trees. Those seemed easy because the structure is instantly recognizable, even if the details aren't quite right."

The platform hummed to life, and in the center of the floor rose the outline of two trees, with spotty color and no branches in the half-formed canopy. Myers walked the perimeter and seemed more impressed than someone looking at third-grade artwork should be.

"More computing power would give you the resolution you want."

"I know. But multiplying the computing power tends to overheat the system. Like, don't touch anything in the array, or you'll get burned."

He wanted to. His hand twitched toward the first case in the line, but he could feel the heat rolling off it and took a step back.

"And your avatar idea? How would that play out?"

This was the point when Drew usually got excited and began talking as fast as he could think. This time, he managed to dial it back. "All right. Say, you're an in-demand teacher of an obscure subject. The history of ancient Peruvian underwater basket-weaving. You can only teach in one place at a time, right? Teaching via video transmission works, but students tend to be less engaged. They treat the experience like watching broadcast entertainment and allow themselves to read other material or do other homework. But if you could appear in multiple locations at once, as if you were physically there? You're in Lisbon, but your avatar is in classrooms from Japan to Pacifica, teaching thousands at once. And it all feels real to the students."

"Feedback? Could this theoretical avatar see what his students see?"

Drew shrugged. "Eventually, I suppose."

"So my avatar could be on the battlefield, seeing everything unfold, while I was in a room in San Francisco."

"If the battle took place in a room, General. The technology to make this *that* portable doesn't exist yet. And for what you propose, all you need is someone on the field with a panoramic camera and a three-sixty display in your own location. This isn't something you'd use for battle."

"Shoot my avatar, no one dies. Shoot my cameraman?" Myers looked at Will. "Couple hundred years from now, does this thing work?"

"Not in the way Drew proposes. And before you ask, no, I cannot make it work the way you wish. I don't have that knowledge base."

"Does your father?"

"You'd have to ask him. But given that he's still mutilating bowling balls, I'm not sure he'd be up to the task of figuring this out."

Myers signaled for Drew to turn the platform off. "Hard to believe that in two hundred years, no one solved the issue of transporting."

"It's entirely believable," Will said. "It's something science has pursued for the last five hundred years. That in two hundred more it still might not happen is not a stretch. If he manages it, *that* will be the stretch."

"Then there'll be the moral argument," Drew said. "If you disassemble someone down to individual molecules and then reassemble them, did you kill the person or not?"

"We'd test it on animals first," Myers said. "That cat would go before you or I would."

"Touch Wick and I'll sic Oz on you," Drew said.

Myers looked at Will. "No one told me he was mean." He nodded to his aide, who opened the door. "I'm impressed, gentlemen. When you smooth out the kinks, I'd like to see it again. And if you progress as much as I think you will, I'll open our data banks to you and hand over the big toys."

"You're not taking this?" Drew asked, surprised.

Myers blew air through his lips. "Why waste my resources when I can waste yours? I know what you're thinking, I'll kick down your door and confiscate everything. It won't happen." He looked at Will. "You're already a major gear in the government works, Emperor. You get to keep your own projects, but I ask that when this is ready, we have the first crack at it."

"That's years down the road, Anthony."

"I know. But I suspect it's not as many years as you want me to think." He turned back to Drew. "You have my word, we won't take your research, nor will we insinuate ourselves into it. But we all know this leads to Elysium, holograms or not. Apply for the appropriate military grants and the King will sign them."

They watched him leave. Drew was too surprised to say anything, and Will wanted to be sure he got in the van and left before he opened his mouth.

He only believed about half of what you said, you know.

"I know, Wick," Will said. "He only needs to believe the half in which this is not ready for military consumption, even on the most basic levels."

"Did he?"

Will nodded. "The heat rolling off that first part of the system was enough to convince him we have major cooling issues. He saw what happened when the military's version went online. That's not a risk he'll take, not yet."

"But eventually, he will."

"I will do whatever I can to stand in his way on this, Andrew. As soon as we have a feasible working model, we need to secure the patents. I can't take his word, not completely. I can't prevent the military from co-opting your work, but having the patents will protect your interests and allow you to continue on."

"I really had avatars in mind," Drew said as he put the portable's base back together. "I mean, Oz was the first thing that came to mind, but yeah, I thought about military training. What I don't want is for this to be weaponized."

"Anything can be turned into a weapon," Will said. "And over time, I will have the necessary discussions with Jax."

"I really don't want to hide stuff from him." Drew's shoulders hunched, and he leaned against the table with his hands. "I have to, don't I? I can't really share much more of this with him."

"He understands how this works. It's not personal, and he won't take it as if it is."

"But if General Myers decides that any part of this is worth taking and turning over to the military's engineers, he'll go along with it."

"If Myers can justify it, he'll have no choice." As he powered down the rest of the equipment, he added, "You won't be working on this again until after your wedding. I'll make sure the general understands that."

"The wedding." Drew sighed. "You're going to be in a bright red tux, you know that, right?"

"We'll match the bride, then. I will not, however, wear those horrible ankle-high sneakers she seems to prefer."

"Like hell, you won't. If Oz wants us in high tops, we're wearing high tops."

Do I get a new collar?

"Wick," Will said as he opened the door, "she'll probably make you wear shoes, too."

Fine, as long as I don't have to wear pants.

"Tell her that, and she'll probably have a tiny tuxedo made just for you," Drew said.

I considered it.

I would be quite handsome in a red tux.

Well, now I'll be disappointed if I don't get one. She probably doesn't want me upstanding her, though.

"That would be the reason," Will said. "No one should look better than the bride. Remember that when all you get is a new bow tie. You're too handsome."

I know when I'm being mocked. I let him have that one, though.

I mean, he wasn't wrong.

14

"Twenty-one," Will said, raising his glass. "I am honored to be here and to be the one buying your first legal drink."

Drew had a mental vision of how his 21st birthday would go: dinner, then birthday cake, then a quiet evening with Oz on the roof, listening to music and dancing under the tent of lights that had been left up after her birthday. He hadn't wanted a party because the only friends he had in San Francisco were also Oz's younger friends and he thought a birthday spent with them would make him miss his friends from Chicago.

He wanted dinner at home, with family, and then time with Oz, but after dinner, Jax declared that Drew could do horrible things to Oz on the roof later. He and Will wanted Drew's company for a couple of hours. They were taking him to Fuzzy's, where he was having a drink.

No one asked Drew if that's what he wanted, but that's what he was doing. Oz urged him to go, promising that Jax wouldn't bite, and he only had to have one drink. He didn't even need to finish it—it was symbolic. "Just let Will buy you a drink. He's been looking forward to your birthday more than you have."

That was enough to propel Drew out the door without whining about it. Will had always presumed he would be nine months gone by Drew's 21st birthday; letting him buy a drink was more of a gift to him than a milestone for Drew's age.

Will ordered for all of them. He knew Drew would fall back on the cinnamon whiskey he liked, so before he could order for himself Will promised he would like what he was getting, and then ordered Long Island Teas for each of them.

Drew took a tentative sip, grimaced, but then the taste settled and he decided he liked it.

"First of many," Jax said. "And I mean a night out, not the drink. It's about time you were old enough for us to drag you over here."

"Without Oz, he means," Will said.

"Boys' night out," Jax declared. "I'm looking forward to Zed and Jay being old enough, too. Will's getting boring."

"Well, fuck you, too," Will snorted.

"They can come in here, Mr. B," Drew said. "Oz comes in. They just wouldn't be able to drink."

"I love my son and enjoy the time I spend with him, but I'm not ready for him to hang around the bar. And you're an adult now. Call me Jax."

"Um, yeah." Drew set the glass down. "I'm not sure I can."

"He had the same problem using my name," Will said. "Just refuse to answer him when he calls you anything else. He gets mad, but it works."

Go hiking together. That's when he stopped having problems with it.

"There we go. Take Drew on a hundred-mile hike. By the end of it, he'll remember your name and he'll be using it along with expletive-laced sentiments."

The idea didn't put Jax off but finding the time did. Even a few days, hiking through the Sierras or sitting on a beach in San Diego, anything where he didn't have to be himself, sounded good. He was tired; his attention was constantly pulled in a hundred different directions by a hundred different people in a dozen different countries.

"Not one complaint from Aubrey," he said. "I think the last time we went anywhere alone was on our honeymoon, and she's never said a word about what we might be missing out on."

"She understands," Will said.

"That doesn't make it right. And even if we found the time, we'd have to deal with guards and reporters and curious onlookers." He pointed at Drew. "You. Make time. I don't care what else you have going on, make time at least twice a year. Go off alone with her and leave the world behind."

"Until we have kids," he said.

Jax shook his head. "Even then. You have built-in babysitters. If Aubrey and I can't watch them, Will and Aisha can. If they can't, Zed or Jay will. Make the time, son."

"You know," Will said, swirling his drink, making the ice bang against the glass, "the portals haven't gone anywhere. We talked about Vegas not too long ago. You could still do that. Or go somewhere else. You could stay away as long as you needed, and no one would be the wiser."

"Go to Will's When," Drew said. "I mean, if you're just looking for some downtime with Mrs. B."

"I can arrange that," Will said. "Free accommodations, even."

Jax reminded him that Aubrey had a condition attached to any future portal trips. "And I'm not sure I want to do that."

Will laughed. "She was adamant that she's not having more kids, Jax. Get it done. Never again worry about getting the implant refilled." He glanced sideways at Drew. "Hell, go see Mass and ask him to take you forward to do it. It'll be painless."

"Would he float in a tank the way Jay did?" Drew asked. "I'd kind of like to see that. Well, not you specifically. Just someone getting surgery."

Will didn't want Drew to see the tanks; he didn't want to give him the idea for the surgical nanogel. "It's not a spectator event, Andrew. And I ask that you not make the request of Mass. He might feel obligated when the truth is that he would be uncomfortable."

"That didn't answer his first question," Jax pointed out. "Would I be floating in anything?"

"I'm not sure. I've never had a vasectomy. I did have a fracture repaired when I was young, but there was no floating involved. I simply sat in a tub-sized tank and read a book until it had healed. It was no more than four hours."

"Not bad," Drew said. He blinked rapidly, staring into his mostly empty drink, and said nothing when Will ordered him another. "Beats the hell out of how Oz's broken bones were healed."

"Does she remember?" Jax asked.

"Little bit. She tries not to. And her nightmares are easing up some. I think talking to someone else is helping."

"How the hell did I have a kid that fucking strong?" Jax asked, not expecting an answer. "And why the hell didn't I have Munson eliminated the day after I took the throne?"

"Your wife asked you not to," Will said. "As horrible as Levi was, he was still her father, and she worried about the effect his assassination would have on her siblings."

"Still."

"How did he die, really?" Drew asked. "I mean, I won't tell Oz, but I don't think she believes he was killed by another inmate."

"Pacifica did not have him executed," Jax said. "I swear to that."

Drew shrugged. "I'm okay with it if you did. I'm okay if you arranged for someone else to do it. The son of a bitch tried to have me killed, too. Twice. And after what he did to Oz? I kind of regret not doing it myself."

"Andrew," Will said, softly.

"I know. But goddamn, I don't have one iota of sympathy that he died the way he did. Trussed like a mother fucking deer during hunting season. He deserved that."

"He's drunk," Jax said, chuckling.

"Well, then drunk me wants to know who to thank for ending that miserable son of a bitch."

"Russia," Will said. "They're likely responsible, but there's no concrete proof."

"Weren't they on his side?"

"He didn't deliver what he promised," Jax said. "He was supposed to draw the war out, bring them in as Florida's allies, and use them to take both Midlam and Pacifica. In exchange for their aid, he would have given them a large chunk of the west coast and some incredible trade agreements."

"He really screwed up when he took Oz, didn't he?"

"He let his personal bias get in the way," Will said. "It's almost a shame he didn't live to see the things Red is doing."

Jax snorted. "Just the sight of Bree in pants would have given him a heart attack. The idea that education has opened to women through the university level? That they can drive and hold jobs beyond the menial? He would have exploded."

"Bree," Drew said, letting her name fall off his tongue. "Was she named after Mrs. B?"

"Yep."

"You know, she calls and emails Oz a lot. I think she has a little bit of a crush going on."

Oz was Bree's most visible example of freedom and strength, Will surmised. She was a friendly and open little girl growing up in a land of oppression; that her own father presented Oz as someone she could aspire to become, and someone she could admire, made her appealing. "Oz will be the one she opens up to. She may ask things of you as well. As annoying as that might be, remember, she's the future of Florida and she needs your honesty."

"She's adorable. I can't imagine not wanting to talk to her. Wanting not to talk to her. What? I'll talk to her."

"She also doesn't need to know what a monster Levi was," Jax added.

Drew nodded.

"More cheerful topic," Jax said as he signaled to the server for another drink. "My son. What's he doing with Sophia Lopez?"

"Ummm. He's pretty serious about her. Like, I mean, I don't think he's told her he loves her, but he does. At least he thinks he does. I kinda think so, too. He's been *really* careful with her feelings and all."

Jax sighed. "I'm stuck with Lopez, aren't I? Even if he doesn't get re-elected, I'm stuck with him."

"Zed is seventeen, Jax," Will said. "He may have several true loves before he settles down."

"Liar."

"But you know," Drew said. "Would it matter if we did?"

"Let Zed meet his life as it comes to him," Will said. "Don't give him any expectations. If I were to tell you anything about him, whether intentional or not you might nudge him in that direction."

Jax took a long sip of his drink. "Yeah, I'm stuck with that blowhard. At least he's not an asshole."

"What about Jay and Zara?" Will asked, trying to deflect.

Drew leaned back, crossing his arms. "So that's what this is? Interrogate the tipsy guy? As far as I know, he's only kissed her once. He thinks he's totally out of his element when it comes to girls and dating, but he doesn't mind all her dad's rules and thinks they're a small price to pay for being able to hang out with her. The rules give him an excuse to go super slow, and he wants to go slow because he's still adjusting to his body and he's a fucking gentleman. Is that enough?"

"Not interrogating you, Andrew. This truly is what we talk about. Kids and parents."

Jax sighed hard. "Speaking of parents. I know we promised you Will's apartment, but I don't think that's going to happen. My father is staying, at least for a while, and he needs his own space. And like it or not, he wouldn't do well in your apartment."

Drew shrugged. "That's fine. I like my place. It's cozy. We can live there."

Jax shook his head. "We've already made plans to have it remodeled, and the demolition begins in January. Aubrey wants another three-bedroom apartment down there, for Zed or Jay."

Drew shrugged again. "Then I suppose you're gonna have Oz and me living in her bedroom. Which I'm cool with. I mean, we'd get a place of our own in the city, but Mrs. B has been pretty vocal about us not straying far. Or at all, really."

"You're staying in the building. No one is ready for the two of you to leave. You can take Oz's room if you want. Hell, we'll open the wall between her room and Zed's and move him into the guest room, but there's another option. One we planned on offering you in a few years."

"Camping on the roof? That one I might have an issue with. Unless you're putting a toilet up there."

"They might actually enjoy that, Jax," Will said.

"Are you kidding? We'd have to ask their permission to use the roof if we did. Look, by the time you get back from your honeymoon, the other guest suite remodel will be done. Those are your choices. Live with Aubrey and me, or take the brand new, five-bedroom apartment that you'll get to furnish to your own tastes. But moving out of the building is off the table because it would break Aubrey's heart."

"Yeah, just Aubrey's," Will snorted.

"I admit, I would miss my daughter."

"Fuck that, you would miss having us to do the dishes every night because if we don't, Mrs. B is gonna slap an apron on your ass and make you do it." Drew snorted, hard, and added, "Probably in *just* the apron."

"How much has he had to drink?" Jax asked Will.

Drew's second glass was still half full. "Eh, he's still a lightweight. I think if he finishes this one, we can cut him off. Unless you'd like to ruin the rest of his evening, and Oz's as well. One more and he'll have performance issues. Throwing up as well."

"Now why would I care if he can't get it up tonight?"

"Ruin his birthday?" Will ventured.

"Phfft. That ship sailed by eight this morning," Drew said. "She woke me up and yelled 'Happy Birthday!' and the next thing I know—"

Will set his arm on Drew's. "Perhaps now is not the time to share this particular story."

Drew leaned toward Will and whispered loudly, "But it was *really* good."

Jax picked up his glass and muttered, "Well, like mother, like daughter," and slugged the rest of the drink back. "Aubrey's fiftieth. Make the arrangements, Will. She'd like nothing better than a weekend the way it was twenty-five years ago. The four of us on the beach, or in a park, fuck it, just walking around the city without worrying about who's watching or following. I'll give up wild fun in Vegas if I can give her that."

"Should I also make you an appointment with Mass?"

He nodded. "You know, after Zed turned ten, I approached Jacobsen about getting it done. He strongly hinted that Aubrey did not share the same contentment with the size of our family and may have asked about the risks of carrying more children into her later forties. And I bought it, every word. If she wanted one or two or, fuck it, even five more, fine. She'd jokingly said that forty-five was it, if I wanted another I'd better hop on it, but I had that in the back of my head. She'd asked him about having a baby in her later forties. So I waited."

"And then this summer when she flat out told you to get fixed, it hit you."

"It hit me."

"You want more?" Drew asked, slurring a bit. "That would be fun."

"No, I really don't. Not now. Grandkids, yes." He wagged his pointy finger at Drew. "No hurry on that, you little hornball. Finish school first."

"I already know how happy you'd be if we popped out a kid next year."

"I would love my grandchild more than you understand, no matter when. But *your* lives will be easier if you wait."

"Easier doesn't mean better," Drew said. "But, yeah, we've talked about it. A lot. Like, a lot of a lot. We still feel bad about not having the baby we thought we were having, but we really do want a couple of years to be stupid with each other. Go places. See stuff. You know."

"You could do all that with a child," Will said.

"Don't help him!" Jax blurted.

"Merely making a point. There is nothing they wish to do that couldn't be accomplished with a child. And you yourself have made the point that there will always be willing babysitters on hand." He turned to Drew. "Don't overthink it. If the two of you decide tomorrow that you'd like to start your family, have at it. You damn well know that every single person in your life will be nothing but thrilled."

Except for the cat.

"You'd be happy, Wick," Will said.

Happy for them, *sure, but not thrilled. Not when the sticky little monster starts to crawl and is chasing after my tail.*

"Not once did you have issues with Oz or Zed catching you or pulling your tail."

Fine. Let them have babies. Triplets. Triplets can chase each other instead of me.

"You're mean." Drew looked at Will. "Please tell me we only have one at a time."

"I'm not telling you anything. Hell, I'm still holding out for the puppy."

No. Puppies are not acceptable, either.

"You don't get a vote," Will said. "And we got off track. I'll arrange for us to use Finn and Jo's apartment. We can spend as much time as you wish there."

"I think people would notice if I suddenly looked a few years older," Jax sighed. "A week will do. And I would appreciate it if you would contact Mass so I can get this done. You know there's no way in hell I'm taking Aubrey somewhere and then staying off her."

Drew closed his eyes and groaned.

"Welcome to adulthood, Andrew. The grownups fuck like bunnies, too. I would think that would make you happy, given that you are one now."

"But you're old."

"And I have a hot wife," Jax countered. "And shut up."

He shut up. Mostly because he was laughing too hard to get another word out.

*

I rode on Will's shoulder during the walk home; he and Jax had to keep Drew steady, and I didn't trust myself to not dig my claws into Drew. They each took an elbow to steer him down the center of the sidewalk, even though a guard offered to call for a car. They declined but asked the guard to keep watch, because at some point along the way they expected him to throw up into the street and someone needed to cover it with dirt or litter or something to make it less offensive. When the guard said he would make sure it was cleaned up, Jax said, "No, just cover it. We'll make the prince clean up his own vomit in the morning."

I don't think the guard knew if it was all right to laugh or not.

Oz met us at the door, and once they had him up the stairs, she said she would make sure he was all right.

"I didn't hork," Drew said proudly.

Jax patted his shoulder. "Yeah, good job there. Sweetheart, if he vomits all over you, I'm sorry."

"Not gonna throw up," Drew insisted. "I have *plans*, you know."

"And I don't need to know about them."

Drew leaned toward Oz and whispered loudly, "It'll be like an amusement park." He held his hands several inches apart and added, "I must be this long to ride."

"Jesus. All right, I'm out. Good night." Jax headed up the stairs, but I could hear him laughing under his breath.

"Grab a bucket or trash can to keep by the bed," Will told Oz. He plucked me off his shoulder and set me on the floor. "Wick, stay with them. If Drew gets out of hand, come get me."

"He'll be fine," Oz said.

I don't know. He's already taking his clothes off.

He'd stepped into the apartment and pulled his shirt off and was already trying to unzip his jeans.

"Let him try to figure out why his pants get stuck at his feet. Don't remind him to take his shoes off," Will said.

She was impressed when he sat down on the floor and wrestled his jeans over his sneakers. Five minutes later, he was standing in the middle of the living room in nothing but socks and shoes, his fists on his hips, beaming. "Ta-da!"

I looked up at Oz.

I don't think you're gonna get to ride.

She steered him to the sofa and took off his shoes and socks. He watched, quietly, and when she tossed his socks onto the floor, he grabbed her hands and set them on his thighs.

"Whatcha want, birthday boy?" she snickered.

"Not that. Not yet. And maybe not *that* at all. I just want" —he sucked in a deep breath— "I want us to love each other in thirty years the way your mom and dad do. You know?"

"We will."

"My parents love each other, I know that, but I never really *see* it. I want our kids to see it. I don't want them to look at other people and wish we were like them or that they'd seen it all along."

She stretched up and kissed him, and then stood up. "They'll see it. I promise. But maybe not like this."

Keeping her eyes on his, she slowly began taking her clothes off, tossing them in a pile next to his shoes. I wanted to leave; this felt a lot like Will's birthday, when they were dropping their clothes on top of me. I left then because it was private and intimate, and I didn't think I should be there, but this time Will told me to stay.

It wasn't like I'd never been there, but there were times it felt like I shouldn't.

He watched every bit of clothing come off. The corners of his mouth turned up just a little and the light twinkled off the moisture in his eyes, and when she was completely naked, he sighed. Oz tilted her head as she looked at him, and then straddled him on the sofa.

"Just how much did you drink tonight?" she asked. "It's all right if you had too much. We can just cuddle."

"Just two drinks. Tea! Like, *really* freaking good tea. No worries. I can get it up."

"Not worried about it, Drew. If this is all we do tonight, I'll still be happy."

"I'm happy." He leaned his head against the back of the sofa. "When I left home, I thought I was happy. But I got here, and damn. I am so damned happy, Oz. You make me so, so fucking happy. Like I'm this weird Drew-shaped balloon, and I'm so damned happy I might pop, but if I do I'm just gonna blow little bits of happy confetti all over the place, and it's because of you."

"Hey, keep talking like that and I might have to marry you."

"I can't wait for that, you know. We could spend every night together from now 'til then, but I still can't wait for that. I want to be as weirdly, stupidly sweet as Will is."

"And how is Will weirdly, stupidly sweet?"

"Just look at him every time he talks about Aisha as his wife. He says those words and it's like he's fighting to keep from grinning. I want to be like that. I want to smile like a damned fool every time I mention my wife. It's like saying, look, losers, she could have chosen anyone, and she chose me. Me."

"Hey." She gave him a long kiss. "You chose me first, you know. When we were still just kids, talking like we would be taking over the world by now, you chose me."

"I wanted you to want me. When you asked me to come here and stay, you chose me."

"Just two more months, hot stuff."

He touched the scar on her chest, running a light finger over it. "I know you hate this. I hate how you got it. But goddamn, Oz, you are the strongest..." He swallowed hard. "You wanted to keep it so it would remind you, but you don't need it, Ozzy. You're never going to lose sight of what people need from you. I'll miss it, I really will, but if you hate it, you should get it removed."

"Why would you miss it?"

"Because I touch it, and it tells me I need to be more, you know? But I'll be more for you no matter what. I swear."

"I don't need you to be more, Drew. Just be you."

"We're gonna be amazing, Oz. Like, fucking amazing."

"You are *so* drunk," she said, laughing. "Tomorrow is going to hurt. Maybe you should take a quick shower and go to bed."

"Kinda want to do it right here on the sofa. Just like this. Then I'll take a shower."

His fingers moved away from the scar, tracing over her skin. He watched his fingers slide over the rise and swell of her curves, slipping over her hips and across her thighs. When a soft breath escaped her, he smiled.

"I could spend all night just kissing you, you know," he murmured.

"I had a few more things in mind. Oh, and hello. You were right. Not too drunk after all."

"Ah. Happy birthday to me."

*

Will banged on the door at eight the next morning, loud enough that it made me twist off the foot of the bed and run for the cat flap to see what was going on. He stood in the hallway, fist poised to knock again, loudly, and he laughed when I poked my head out.

They're asleep and I think they'd like to stay that way.

"I'm sure. How late were they up?"

Two or three. I lost track. I fell asleep a few times. Drew was yakking his head off.

"By yakking, I hope you mean talking and not vomiting."

Talking. Because he LOVES Oz and had to tell her every other minute how much and how beautiful she is and how amazing and there was something about perky boobs and pointy nipples, but I stopped listening somewhere around then.

He banged on the door again. "I thought you enjoyed boobs."

I do, but there's something creepy about looking at Oz's and thinking they're nice. Like it's inappropriate.

"Indeed. However, it's entirely appropriate if Drew does."

They like all of each other's stuff. Do you want me to go in and wake Drew up?

"No, I'm sure this will work." He pounded the door with his palm. The guard at the front door knew how drunk Drew had been and laughed out loud. I heard him shuffling behind me, so I pushed my way all the way through into the hall, lest he step on my tail. When the door creaked open, Will bellowed, "Good morning, Prince Andrew!"

Drew set his forehead against the edge of the door and groaned.

"Formal attire, I see." Will gestured to the towel around Drew's waist. "Come on, get dressed. We have errands to run this morning."

"God, no."

Will stepped past him. "God, yes. Go brush your teeth and get dressed. I'll feed you along the way, when it's less likely that you'll throw up on me."

"I can't."

"Still drunk?"

Drew tried to shake his head, but it hurt too much.

"Fine. We're running errands for the King, so get dressed. You weren't going to your morning classes anyway, were you?"

Somewhere in the fog that was slicing through his brain like soft cheese was the realization that Will would not let up.

Drew left the door open and went into the bedroom, shuffling like an old man.

This is mean.

"Of course, it is."

You could run errands yourself.

"I could."

You're enjoying his pain.

"Little bit, yeah."

Oz bounced out of the bedroom, dressed, running a comb through her hair. "I'll get someone to take notes for you," she called back to Drew, who was still groaning. To Will, she said, "Be nice to him. It's half your fault he's hung over."

"I did not pour the alcohol down his throat."

"He said he drank tea. What the hell kind of tea was it?"

"The kind with about five shots of alcohol. He'll be fine. And presumably, soon he'll learn to order his own beverages and drink at his own pace."

She stretched up on her toes to kiss his cheek. "Well, he was fun last night, so you get points for that."

She got to spin the teacups. Or maybe he did. But he made her laugh a lot.

"Good for them."

Drew's hair was a mess, and he didn't take the time to shave, but he remembered to grab my sweatshirt so that I would be comfortable while he followed Will around. We started at Union Square, even though there were people around who might see us slip into the portal.

"Don't think too hard," he told Drew. "Just 'follow Will.' I'd like to end up in the right place this time."

Drew grunted but didn't defend his early-summer mistake that landed us in Finn's simulator with the elves and wizards and my favorite dragon and giant cat. He did as he was told and walked right behind Will into the portal, and we stepped out into Will's birth When.

"First things first," he said before Drew could ask what we were doing there. He headed for the lab and scrambled down the stairs; the sound of his feet slapping on stone bounced all around us, which made Drew even more miserable.

Finn was waiting for us in the little kitchen area, and without saying hello, he picked a cup up from the table and held it out to Drew. "Drink this, you'll feel better. I promise."

"Dog hair?"

Finn looked puzzled.

"The hair of the dog that bit him," Will said. "No, Andrew, it's not more alcohol. But it will put an end to your pain." He told him to sit down and drink it, and in a few minutes he'd feel better. "But you don't tell Jax about this. He can suffer through his hangovers."

Drew tried to smile but couldn't. He started drinking, his face contorting as his mouth filled with thick, sticky, putrid-smelling goo, but he drained the cup and then set his head on the table while he waited for his headache to ease up.

"Keep doing this to him, and he'll never drink again," Finn said.

"That's fine. I intend on teaching him to drive. He can be our chauffeur while Jax and I bar-hop. You should come with us."

You and Eli. I want to see you both drunk.

"That would, indeed, be fun, Wick. Next time, we'll drag Dad and Eli along."

"Zed and Jay will feel left out," Drew said, his head still on the table. "I don't care what Mr. B thinks, if we do it we have to find something that doesn't involve a bar."

"Jax," Will reminded him. "Use his name."

"I really don't think I can."

"You don't have a problem calling me by name," Finn said. "I'm a hell of a lot older than Jax."

With a sigh, Drew finally sat upright. "Yeah, but I knew you when you were younger, and we thought you were my age. I don't look at you and see an old man. I see my friend, Finn."

"Flattery will get you everywhere." He dug into his pocket and pulled out a shiny metal card. "The only thing in the fridge is beer, put it there an hour or so ago."

"Did you ask Rod about the chocolate?"

"The store is still there, and the owners were among the people who stayed. They're expecting you, and he warned that they want to thank you properly, so be nice. Pay for the things Jax wanted, but if their thanks come as a gift, let them give you whatever it is they want."

"I don't understand. Thank me for what?"

"Their son relocated to your When," Finn explained. "Whoever took him through basically abandoned him without adequate resources. He found you, and you placed him in an apartment, made sure he had food, and found him a job. Rod brought him back a few months ago, and they've wanted to thank you personally since then."

Will didn't look happy, not one bit. "Dad, people here cannot know that I'm the Emperor."

"Don't panic, Dash. All the parents know is that William Blackshear made sure their son was safe. The few who know are not going to out you."

"What's wrong with anyone knowing?" Drew asked.

"Cult of the Emperor," Finn answered. "They want his babies."

That made Drew laugh, but Will was not placated. "How many people were placed in the same time frame that I was? And how many have returned?"

"I don't have the statistics for that, but I don't think you have anything to worry about. They're looking for a man long dead and have no way to get to him."

"I'll protect you, Will." Drew got up; he looked significantly better than he had just five minutes before, and he was grinning. "Whatever that was, it's amazing."

That's his new over-used word. Everything is amazing.

"I do not over-use it, Wick."

Your life is going to be amazing. Oz's boobs are amazing. Being able to twirl your di—

"You can stop talking now."

If I did, would it be amazing?

"Remind me why I was so excited to be able to understand him."

"You thought it would be amazing," Will said.

"You're both assholes. Where are we going?"

The first stop was a florist's kiosk at the edge of Chinatown, although here the neighborhood was more subdued. There were none of the brightly colored decorations that had captured Drew's amusement in 2016, and none of the cultural aesthetic of 2416. It was a long hill dotted with generic shops, and Will guided Drew to one near the Grant Street entry. We didn't go inside; instead, he touched the screen on the kiosk outside the shop and began flipping through a digital catalog. It contained every flower the shop had available for same-day delivery, and he scrolled, looking for the flowers that Jax had requested.

"You're skipping over a lot of nice things," Drew said. "What's all this for, anyway?"

"Jax's requests are specific and particular. He wants Aubrey's favorite flowers waiting for her, although the colors he wants are somewhat rare now."

What if you can't get them?

"He'll have me beheaded. Or he'll pout. I'll take my chances."

It took twenty minutes, but he found the ones he was looking for. Drew looked over his shoulder and asked, "Is that expensive? It looks expensive."

"It is indeed expensive. What I'm spending on roses here could buy you a car at home. Something we will not tell Jax."

"Yeah, but he's gonna pay Finn back, right? He'll have to know how much."

"If your great, great grandfather asked you to buy flowers or anything else for that matter, and you had the means to make the purchase without it hurting your bottom line, would you ask him to pay you back? Or would you brush it off and ask that he allow it to be your gift?"

"Fair enough. But still, it's a lot of money."

"Finn has a lot of money to spend," Will said simply. "Inheritances, investments, salary he never spent. He and my mother have led rather frugal lives."

"Still."

Will finished the purchase and pointed him down the street. "This brings him joy, Andrew. Finn has never forgotten being a scared, displaced young man in a city he didn't recognize, nor the people who helped him. Even if they weren't family, he would feel a connection. He would do this for Jax and Aubrey simply for that."

"Well, hell, I was nice to him, too."

"And when you turn fifty, he'll buy you flowers and chocolate, too."

"Well, then. Something to look forward to."

A high-speed whine shot down the street behind us and Drew turned abruptly, startled when a teenager in a flight pack screamed down the center divide, his feet a few inches overhead. Will didn't flinch and didn't bother looking, and he kept walking, knowing Drew would catch up.

He headed in the direction of the Embarcadero, down the street from the Ferry Building. Tucked into a shop along near Pier Seven was the chocolatier Will wanted to find; it had been in the city for nearly a hundred years, owned by one family. He'd never met them personally, having been inside the shop only once when he was a boy, which he thought explained why he hadn't recognized their son.

"Do you think he knew who you were?" Drew asked.

"If Mass is any indication, he did. Those who were left in the time frame of my life were sworn to leave me alone. Given his lack of options, I understand why he sought me out yet never mentioned where he was from."

"You didn't ask him personal questions?"

"I don't press when people are reluctant to answer. It would be the epitome of hypocrisy for me to attempt to wring personal information out of someone hesitant to share."

He also had no idea who the son was. He'd helped enough people over the years that most of them blended together, with only the remarkable standing out in his mind. From time to time he was stopped on the Square by people he'd helped who wanted to thank him; they'd done well and stayed in the city and wanted him to see the results of his efforts. He was always polite, but rarely remembered who they were, though he was good at pretending.

Outside the shop door, Drew wanted to know how he would handle the parents. "You're not a gift-getting kinda person. I think you get embarrassed when someone gives you something."

"I'm rarely comfortable," he admitted. "I prefer to be on the giving end."

You did okay when Oz and Zed gave you books when they were little.

"That's different, Wick. I was able to express my thanks with hugs and kisses. It's never been as easy with adults."

You can hug and kiss now.

"Sure, Will," Drew said. "If they give you something, kiss 'em."

He remembered the son once he caught a glimpse of him behind the counter. He was still young; Will remembered the teenager who had wandered into the shelter's office ten years earlier with nothing but the clothing he wore and a patchy beard that made him look especially young. Will took him at his word: he was eighteen and had no one to turn to and nowhere to go. He'd spent several nights in Golden Gate Park, until a custodian rousted him from his spot under a tree and gave him a ride to the office.

"Stefan." Will spoke as if he'd spotted a long-lost friend. "I had no idea—"

He still looked like a teenager. "Emperor! Rodrigo told us to expect you, but I didn't believe him. You really came home."

"For a bit." He gestured to Drew. "This is Prince Andrew."

Stefan nodded. "You're about to get married, aren't you? When I left, people were starting to talk about it. They're very excited."

"So am I." He reached over the counter and shook Stefan's hand. "Nice to meet you. Man, you haven't been home long, have you?"

"A month or so." He turned his head and yelled to the back of the store, "Mutter! Er ist hier! Komm heraus, sag Hallo."

An older woman sped from the back room, chattering in German, ignoring her son, who was either barking at her or warning that Will wasn't a toucher; it was hard to tell, and I had no idea what he was actually saying.

"He saved my son's life," she said to her son. "I need to thank him properly."

Will smiled warmly. "I would like that, very much."

She stomped right at him and pulled him into a tight hug, uttering, "Danke, danke, danke," before she grabbed his face and kissed his cheek, hard.

"Bitte," he said, softly. "Wirklich."

"Sprechen sie Deutsch?"

"Very limited," he said.

He can call you a dickhead in Scottish.

"Then I'll speak to you in English. Stefan told us how he was left without anything in your time and how you helped him. He wouldn't have done very well without you."

"I'd be dead," Stefan said.

"He had a happy life while he was there. I don't know how to thank you."

Will leaned over and kissed her cheek. "Frau Ruths, you just did. I only gave him a few tools. He did everything else on his own."

She had more to say; it was poised on the tip of her tongue, but then their shop cat wandered out from the back room and spotted me. His tail shot up, his fur puffed up and he hissed, standing on the very tips of his paws as if that was somehow impressive.

Chill, dude. I'm just here as a snoopervisor.

"Snookie!" Frau Ruths waged her pointy finger at him. "Be nice."

Snookie? Sorry, I'd hiss, too, if I was a dude named Snookie.

It was decided that Drew and I were better off waiting outside while Will paid for the order Rod had put in for him.

"Could Snookie understand you?" Drew asked.

I don't know. All he did was hiss so I don't know if I would have understood him, either.

"Do you? I mean, I've seen you with other cats on the Square. Can you speak with them?"

Speaking is the easy part.

"You know what I mean, furball."

He's a German kitty, you know. I didn't understand anything Stefan or his mom were saying. I probably wouldn't understand Snookie.

"Cat, I don't speak cat, and I understand you."

You have a thingy in your brain that does that for you.

"Then how do you know what we're saying?"

I have a thingy in my brain, too. But I understood Will before I got that, so who knows?

"You never answered my question. Can you—" He winced when a siren cut through the air. His hand reflexively covered my ears, even though he would have been happier sticking his fingers in his own. He looked around, trying to understand where it came from and what was happening, and I wanted to tell him to look up, but he wouldn't have heard me.

Will came out at the same time the siren-screaming vehicle shot overhead.

"Ambulance," he said, answering Drew before he could ask. "With that particular tone, it's likely a collision."

"Like, air car collision?"

Will nodded.

"Don't they have passive controls? Oz keeps promising me that I can't hit another car because it will sense them for me and stop me from wrecking. How can you not have that here?"

"The controls can be disabled, and teenagers often play chicken in the narrow alleys between buildings." He didn't let Drew dwell on that too long. "I assume you can eat by now? No longer queasy?"

"I can definitely eat. Whatever the hell that was Finn gave me, it's...well, it works great."

"Amazing?"

"Shut up."

We wound up at the Ferry Building, at a café on the water. We sat outside where we could see the bridge, and it was clear enough to see the island, too.

Drew stared at it, his mouth hanging open.

"You can never tell Zed about that," Will said. "Blackshear Academy. In my timeline, it's the pinnacle of his life's work. That and Alcatraz, the legacy he left."

Drew's face pinched.

"Your Zed is alive, Andrew."

"Yeah, but—" His breath caught. "I never think about this part of it, when we're all gone."

"I'll tell you the same thing I told Aisha. Think of them as different people. Because they are now. Truly. The Zed that built that school" —he pointed at the castle that loomed in the distance— "lived a life that I truly hope our Zed does not. If that never gets built, I will take it as a sign that he will live a far happier life."

"What happens?"

Will only knew what was in the history books he read, and some family gossip. "I won't give you details, but I will tell you that the man I read about did great things, and he did much of it alone."

"And you don't want our Zed to do those things?"

"I don't want him to be alone."

"You're going to change something, aren't you?"

"My continued existence may be enough to alter the path he's on, but I will ask something of you. If you find opportunities to encourage him to explore other work, to venture beyond crafting eulogies and speaking truths for the dead, take them. I don't think the Zed of this When looked beyond the work he already knew. Our Zed has so many possibilities."

Drew glanced at the castle and then nodded. "Why are you letting me see this, Will? You were pretty clear last night that we didn't need to know."

"Because I didn't want to say anything to Jax, and the future is not set in stone. While I understand that Zed's work gave comfort to many people, I also understand that as he aged, he took on some of Aubrey's attributes and bore the pain of those grieving. He buried his own pain beneath the weight of the grief of others. I want more for him. I want peace for him."

"And you think a different career path will do that?"

"I think it's one of two important pieces to the puzzle of his life."

"And the other?" He watched as Will picked up his cup and carefully sipped his coffee. There was no joy in Will's eyes, no twinkling that suggested he was tugging on Drew's leg. "You're going to do something. What are you changing, Will?"

"We'll see." He set the cup down, carefully turning it so that the café's logo faced Drew. "This is a lovely spot, though, don't you think? We're buffered from the breeze, yet we have a clear view of the bridge and the castle, and when there's no fog, we can see part of Alcatraz from here."

Z Island.

"Indeed, Wick. It's now known as Z Island."

"Yeah," Drew said, "it's nice. Kind of classy for a waterside café. The Mexican-Italian-American fusion menu is a little odd, though."

"It's been here for over one hundred fifty years. There's a very good chance you'll dine here with Oz one day. You could even be at the opening."

"I'll keep it in mind." He touched the logo on the cup. "Sof y Z. All right."

Will tapped on the center of the table to pull up the tab, and waved Finn's bank card in front of it. "All right, by the time we get back to the apartment, the florist should be just a few minutes behind. Let's get this set up."

*

He directed Drew to work in the master bedroom, plucking rose petals to spread across the bed and the floor. Drew gave him a pained look—like, "Seriously? Something this corny?" — but he grabbed an armful of flowers and headed back while Will sat down to order groceries.

You could have bought the roses pre-plucked, you know.

"For twice the cost. Why do you think I brought Drew along? I needed a minion."

You brought him because you want him to prod Zed into

doing something else. Even though Zed gets his castle if he sticks with what he does.

"That's only a small part of it." He stretched to look down the hall. "I want to give Drew reasons to get closer to Zed," he said, softly. "Ideally, I'd like them to be as close as Jax and I are."

Because Zed will need him someday?

"In case Zed does. I swear, Wick, I'll do everything in my power to change the worst parts of his life, but if I can't, Zed will need Oz and Drew in ways that the rest of us can't touch."

Drew's not stupid. He knows who the Sof from the café is. And the Z.

"I know."

He turned his attention to the grocery list, tapping away at the tablet Finn had left for him. He bought enough to stock the kitchen for a week and then turned his attention to making reservations at restaurants and renting a car. I heard Drew grumbling down the hall when he pricked his fingers on rose thorns, and Will chuckled to himself every time it happened.

Will was opening his When to everyone in a way he said he never would.

How does Sophia die?

"What?"

That's what you want to change. Zed marries her and they have kids but she dies, doesn't she? How did it happen? I won't tell anyone.

He set the tablet down, and patted the table, inviting me closer so that he could speak softly. "In my timeline, yes, he married her quite young, and they had children. What I know of them, they were quite happy together, and yes, she died far too soon. He never recovered from the loss. I want to prevent that."

What happened?

"Inattention and a speeding vehicle."

This isn't one of those things time is going to insist on, is it?

"I don't think so. Other things I've changed settled in fairly well. Oz lives. So do Jax and Drew."

Time doesn't want you to be back home. What happens when you have babies? Time isn't going to know what to do with them.

"Time wouldn't be that cruel, I hope. I believe our baby will be fine, and time will understand she's where she's supposed to be."

"A baby?" Drew asked. He was halfway down the hall, plucked stems in hand. "Are you—?"

"No. We're not."

"But...?"

I'm sorry. I knew it was private and I talked about it anyway.

"It's all right, Wick. We're discussing it, Drew. And this goes no further."

"Yeah, sure. All right. But are you discussing it, like, abstractly or discussing it, like, hell *yeah* let's do this?"

"You're nosy."

"So? Come on, Will. You'd be a *great* dad. Are you really thinking about it?"

Reluctantly, he nodded. "We'd like to have a child together, but understand, we don't know—" He sucked in a deep breath. "We're both still young enough, I know that, but we're also not *young*. And we're not sure if we want to go so far as to seek out medical intervention to assure that we conceive."

"But it would be a guarantee."

They want to have fun trying first.

"Well, yeah," Drew snorted.

"This would be a child that never existed in another timeline. Were I religious, I might worry about that."

"I doubt there's a limited number of souls to go around. Be a dad, Will. Have a couple of munchkins, maybe Oz and I will catch up, and they can grow up together."

"You need to focus on school." He grinned anyway. "I'd be happy with just one of my own. And I hope Jax understands when I pull back from my workload. If we do this, I fully intend to be there as much as possible."

"You get the same offer you made. Oz and I will babysit anytime you need."

"I appreciate that. And we'll undoubtedly take you up on it. But Jax still needs to allow me the same time I had when Oz and Zed were infants. Aisha is starting a new job soon, and if either of us gives something up, I want it to be me."

Jay will babysit, too. He wants to be a big brother.

"I know. And he'll be a wonderful brother." He turned the tablet off and set it down. "Come on. We have a good three hours before the groceries are delivered. Let's go borrow a couple of flight packs and have some fun."

*

They played until Will noticed the delivery van pull up. We waited on the Square while Drew took the flight packs back to the lab, allowing a woman who'd been flying nearby to stop and take a picture of me sitting on Will's shoulder because that was the cutest thing she'd ever seen, and then went upstairs to put things away. Once that was done, Will set out silver trays with the chocolates he'd bought, one in the living room and one on the bed.

"No," Will told Drew when he asked if everything would go bad before Aubrey's birthday. "I'll bring them back to this evening, show them where the apartment is, and then let them have the night here alone. Everything will be fresh."

"Where are you and Aisha going, then?"

There was a hotel near the Embarcadero that he wanted to take her to. "View of the bay with inclusive room service and Dad swears it's the perfect romantic place to take her. If he's wrong, I'm not paying him back for the room."

"Yeah, don't think he'd complain."

"One of my father's charms. He is, indeed, a generous soul." Will reached into the cupboard for glasses and filled them with ice, and then told Drew they were going up to the roof for a bit. When he grabbed a bottle from the cabinet by the fireplace, Drew hesitated, because he thought he'd had enough to drink the night before.

"Trust me," Will said. We followed him up the stairs, past apartment doors that looked out of place, to the rooftop garden. There was still a grass lawn, but it was smaller, and there were flowers and vines along the back wall.

They sat on the grass and Will poured from the bottle into the glasses, and when Drew hesitated, he repeated, "I promise, we're not getting drunk, but I miss this and I wanted to share it with you."

Drew sniffed at it. "That's not scotch."

"Chambrizi. It's a liqueur, more of a sipping beverage. My father and I shared it occasionally, right here on the roof. I wasn't even sixteen, but he wanted those moments with me."

He knew he only had a little time left with you.

"Indeed, Wick. But the time spent with him made this my favorite." He lifted his glass toward Drew. "Take it in very small amounts and let it breathe on your tongue." He took a tiny sip and then inhaled through barely parted lips. "Very smooth."

After another long sniff, Drew took a sip, imitating Will. "Damn. You aren't kidding. It even has a little cinnamon kick to it."

"That's why I knew you would like it." He took another sip and then set the glass down. "Last night was a one-off, Andrew. We won't intentionally get you that drunk again. But Jax and I would like to take a night every now and then and go out to have a drink or two with you."

Drew stared down into his glass and swirled the liquid a bit.

"What?" Will said. "Do you have a problem with that? The alcohol is not a requirement. We truly don't drink as much as you might assume."

Half-shrugging, he said, "I know alcohol isn't a requirement. But honestly?" He looked up. "Between you and me, and please don't tell him I said this, but he makes me a little nervous sometimes. I respect the hell out of him, but yeah, making small talk with Mr. B is kinda like socializing with the school principal. You like the guy, but in the back of your head you know he can make your life turn on a dime."

What's a dime?

"I dunno, Wick. It's just a saying."

"It's a coin. One-tenth of a dollar, pre-twenty-second century. And I do understand, Andrew. I feel that way about the old King. I love and respect him, but it's going to take some effort on my part to be comfortable socializing with him."

But you'll do it. Right?

"I'll do it, of course. He truly has been like a second father to me."

"I think that's half of it," Drew said. "Mr. B is like a dad, and I never hung out with mine. Like, does everyone become friends with their parents? I never saw that growing up. My grandfather was a dick, and my grandmother was dead before I was born. I barely saw my other grandparents, so I never saw them all being friends."

"I know."

"And hell, the time we could have spent hanging together, when school was out, they sent me here. I wouldn't trade that, but still. I just don't know how to get past that whole parental thing."

"Consider this. Until last year, about this time, you were still a bit afraid of me. We wouldn't have sat here on the roof, sipping my father's very expensive liqueur, and you wouldn't have been comfortable enough to confide in me. Nor I you. But here we are."

"True."

"You have no fear of Jax, only a social construct telling you there's supposed to be a divide between the adults in your life and yourself. You're an adult now, and he sees that. Let the divide fall away."

Sheepishly, Drew admitted, "I might be a little bit afraid of him."

"Andrew, I cannot count the times I saw you sprint across a conference room filled with dignitaries, squealing because he was there, and you always jumped right into his arms. You've never been afraid of him. When you were small, you climbed all over him, regardless of the circumstances. There are pictures of you on his shoulders, his hair in your fists, and your gleeful laughter shows in your smile. Before Oz became old enough to play with, he was your favorite Blackshear."

He wants to be friends, Drew. If you can talk to Will, you can talk to Jax.

"Indeed. Jax wants a relationship with his son-in-law, one not terribly dissimilar to the one he had with his father before his mother died. You've lived with him, you're marrying his daughter. Give it a chance."

"Of course, I'll give it a chance. I'm just kind of uncomfortable, that's all."

Will finished his drink and got up. "I promise you, that won't last. Now come on, we need to leave here before I return with Jax and Aubrey."

"You know how odd that sounds, right?" Drew asked as we headed down the stairs. "And yet, it makes sense in my head. We really could run into you on our way back. Wait. Has that ever happened?"

"I have met up with myself, but never unintentionally. Tread carefully if you ever do, Andrew."

"Well, we've already established that I won't explode if I touch myself."

Not like that, anyway.

Just before we went into the portal, he stopped. "This is a freaky weird thought, but say I did go forward a dozen years or so and caught up with Oz. If we hooked up, would that be cheating?"

"Why would you even think of that?"

He shrugged. "I think that any version of Oz would make me consider it."

"It's cheating. Stop considering it."

"I should consult with Oz. She might not think so."

How would you feel if she met old you and grabbed him by the—

"Wick." Will poked at me. "Stop it."

I'm just making him think about it. He probably wouldn't be happy about it. But Oz might like older Drew, since he would have had a few years of practice.

He didn't take the bait. "So would she. That's probably why I thought about it."

Will pushed him into the portal, but he was laughing. And probably thinking about the same thing.

15

Thanksgiving was loud. It was a cheerful loud, with enough people in the apartment that a second table was needed, and Will declared it the Official Kids' Table even though the youngest person at it was seventeen and in need of a good shave. Jo and Finn brought wine, which Will turned his nose up at because wine seems like alcohol that hasn't grown up yet, and Eli brought scotch, even though he only brought it out of his room. That counted, he said. Sophia brought homemade fudge, and she slapped Zed's hand to keep him out of it, even though she was laughing as he tried to grab it from her.

I did not jump on the counter to watch. It was loaded down with food, and people don't like to floss with cat hair, so I perched on a chair at the kids' table and waited for them to sneak bites of turkey to me.

"You don't like turkey," Drew said. "Yet here you are, begging for it."

I don't beg. Cats that beg don't get bites. I'm waiting patiently.

"Maybe it's just turkey cat food he hates," Zed said. "I mean, I like apples, but not apple flavored things. Not even applesauce."

See? Someone gets me.

They fed me turkey with dribbles of gravy until I'd had enough—I was actually full and not just tired of it—and when dinner was over, everyone at the kids' table got up and started parsing the extra food onto plates. Aubrey always made more than enough, and it usually went into the refrigerator in the guard's lounge downstairs, but this time she had made sure that there was enough for each guard on duty, every shift, to have two plates full, and there would still be leftovers in their fridge.

Will brought up a cart from the staff kitchen and they loaded it down with dozens of plates and pies and then Drew and Zed took it downstairs while Will and Jay started clearing the tables. When they had everything off the table, Jay practically shoved Will into the living room and told him they would finish cleaning up.

"I almost miss the whining," he said. "What happened to the days when they were forced into the kitchen with threats of no computer time or watching a video?"

When Zed and Drew returned, they headed into the kitchen to help, prompting Eli to wonder if they were human or if aliens had overtaken all the kids.

"They're not kids anymore, that's the problem," Jax said.

"You raised decent adults," Eli said. "That's the opposite of a problem."

"Mine has a mouth on him," Aisha said, "but yes, overall, I'll take that problem."

Jay told you he would work on that.

"He tries, Wick," Will said. "It's a hard habit to break, but he doesn't have any ill intentions regarding the words he uses."

"I should just set the word list on fire," Aubrey mused.

"Now that would be a fucking shame," Jax said, sliding out of the way of her pointy finger, which was aimed at his ribs. "No, really. Keep the list. Maybe our future grandkids will be better about it."

After listening to them for another hour—the not-kids-anymore joined them, so it got loud again and my head was hurting because of it—I went into Oz's room to take a nap on the window seat. I could still hear the chatter from the living room, but it was electric happiness that was easy to fall asleep to, and when I woke up it was dark outside. Lights were on down below at Union Square, and people were lining up to use the skating rink, which had only been open for a week.

The living room was quieter, but voices still rumbled from it. Oz and Drew were there with Jax and Aubrey, and I had no idea where everyone else was.

"We've been talking about it since Drew's birthday, basically," Oz said as I padded my way into the room. "With both of us in school and his work and all the meetings Dad drags me to, it makes sense. We could make the time to take care of an apartment that big, but—"

Aubrey cut her off. "Sweetheart, you don't need a reason other than this is what you both want."

"It is," Drew said. "I mean, we're here a lot, anyway. And I don't have a lot of stuff as it is. It's not like we'd be cramming an actual apartment's worth of things into one bedroom."

"You won't have to," Jax said. "I was serious. If living here is your choice, we'll move Zed into the next room and blow out the wall to give you more space."

Oz seemed skeptical. "Is that unfair to Zed? We're fine the way it is."

"The guest room is bigger than his, and he's not unreasonable."

Are we moving back up here?

"After the wedding," Drew answered. "Until I graduate, it just makes sense."

You mean until Aubrey isn't so fidgety about you guys leaving. When she won't cry every day because her babies are grown up.

"We'll still have Oz's room, Wick. The window seat isn't going anywhere. You'll still have it for naps anytime you want it."

Zed won't mind moving his room if you point out that your apartment will be vacant. He can use it for things.

"Is the idea upsetting Wick?" Aubrey asked.

"He's just trying to assure me he approves. He prefers the napping spots in Oz's room over the ones in my apartment."

You're a pretty quick thinker.

"You spend more time with Will, anyway, and his napping spots are about to greatly improve."

Where is he?

"They're all outside. Aisha is trying to talk Will into skating."

You have to take me there. I have to see that!

"What's so special about Will skating?" he asked.

"Because he stubbornly refuses," Jax said. "We tried for years to get him onto that rink until our being there was more intrusive than fun. He said it was undignified, as if vomiting up the booze we'd stolen from my dad was."

Please, let's go see if Aisha can win.

Oz and Drew got up and started putting their sweatshirts on, but Jax and Aubrey did not.

"Come on," Drew said. "You can get away with going down there and not causing a fuss. Just don't look so...I dunno, royal or something. Wear a hat."

"People will still recognize us, sweetheart," Aubrey said. "Our presence plus the guard would detract from their fun."

Oz shrugged. "So? We'll be down there, which means having guards all over the place, anyway. And most of those people won't go home and bitch because the King and Queen interrupted their evening. They'll go home and brag that they got to skate with the King and Queen, and it was awesome."

Amazing. Drew thinks it's amazing.

"Bite me, Wick. Oz is right. Come on. It's not like people in San Francisco aren't used to seeing you around. Passing the King while he's out jogging is common enough. No one even thinks about it."

"A lot of them were your students," Oz reminded them. "They see you as people. And if they don't, you'll have fun for an hour and then let them have the Square again."

They were still reluctant—worried mostly about ruining someone else's good time—but Jax admitted he would really like to go down there and give Will hell, and he wouldn't mind a few minutes on the ice with his favorite wife.

"Fine," Aubrey said as she got up. "But I'm telling your lesser wives and making them all jealous."

"As one would expect."

Will and Aisha were outside the rink, leaning against the rail as they watched Jay and Zara fumble their way around the ice. They were holding hands and moving in two-inch increments, and Jay swore at Zed every time he sped by with Sophia. Will looked amused by it all, even though he probably didn't skate any better than Jay.

Drew handed me off to him so that he and Oz could rent some skates. I perched on his shoulder, where I could see everyone. I could even see Eli if I turned around. He was at the corner bakery with a mug of something hot between his hands, and he flirted with a toddler who was speaking to him without seeming to take a breath.

See, Drew was right. No one cares if you're here.

"Why would anyone care if I was here?" Will asked.

Not you. Jax and Aubrey. They don't want to be the fun vampires.

"Ah. You're fine," he told Jax. "There was a bit of excitement over your father, but it was relegated to people wanting to wave and say hello, all at the same time. Since they like him more than you, they'll leave you alone."

"And you can kiss my ass," Jax grumbled.

He did it.

Will leaned over, and kissed Jax on the cheek.

"Oh my god, I wish we had video of that," Aubrey said, laughing.

Jax grumbled, "So do I. Then I'd have the proof I need to have him beheaded."

Old guard dude is trying to not laugh. He's biting his lip so hard it might come off.

The guard was leaning against the railing just behind Jax. He finally coughed once to get it out of his system, and then went back to watching all the people who might be watching the King.

"All right." Will reached for Aisha's hand. "I'll do this, but only if you swear to not make fun of me. I've never skated before."

She promised, but Jax couldn't wait to poke at Will. Aubrey tried to reason with him—he's finally doing it, be nice—but there was no changing his mind. He wanted to see Will shuffle and fall, slip and go splat, and he intended to mock every moment of it.

Will got the skates on, watched Oz and Drew for a moment, and then stepped out onto the ice, holding Aisha's hand. He wobbled once, then found his balance and they skated away.

"Hey!" Jax called after him. "You're supposed to suck."

You could go slower. I'm not happy up here.

He pulled me off his shoulder and tucked me into the pouch on his sweatshirt. "Better?"

Better. But don't fall.

It was fun, feeling the cold air rustle my whiskers, and he moved easily enough that I stopped worrying about him face-planting. Jax was still better and faster, and he pulled ahead of us, skating backward. "You're not half bad, Emperor," he said, waving to Aubrey to skate a little faster so he could hold her hand. "Just enough to make me think you're lying about never having done this before."

"I've had years of observation to fall back on, Jax."

"So why now? Why'd it take so long to get you out here?"

"Because I no longer care if I bump into someone. And now I get to hold the hand of the most beautiful woman in Pacifica while I try to not fall."

"He wants to hold your hand, angel," Jax said to Aubrey. He grabbed both of her hands and moved to the center of the ice, where he skated in a slow circle with her.

I heard a few people outside of the rink babbling excitedly— look who it is!—but everyone on the ice kept skating around them. When he leaned in to kiss her, I heard the click of pictures being taken along with a few giggles, and one of the gigglers was Zara. Jax showed off a bit, doing circles around Aubrey as she tried to skate away, and when she wagged her pointy finger at him, he glided backward, his hands to his chest as if she'd wounded him.

The giggles were louder then, and she caught up to him, kissed him, and then pushed him toward the exit.

Almost everyone followed them off the ice. We were still halfway across from the gate and moving slowly; the absence of a bunch of knife-footed people gave me a notion, and with the notion came an impulse, and then before I knew it, I'd jumped out of Will's sweatshirt onto the ice and was sliding away.

"Wick! Stop!" He let go of Aisha's hand and skated toward me. "You'll freeze."

My paws were cold, no doubt, and as I slid toward the rink wall my nether region became a curious kind of numb, but the impulse hadn't abated, and I wasn't done.

I tried to run, but I couldn't get any traction, not until I'd butted up against the wall. Then I sprang off the sideboard and leaped as far as I could, knowing that when I landed it would result in a cold, wet slide. Will braked hard and slipped onto his asterisk as he turned after me, barking that I needed to stop before someone ran me over.

No one was going to do that because the few people who were still in the rink stopped to watch him chase me around the ice. I jumped and slid; he turned to chase and fell. He skated after me for five minutes, ignoring the laughter around us—at some point, he just went along with it for their amusement, and Zed was recording it on his phone—until he stopped in the center of the ice and ordered me to slide to him before I wound up with frostbite.

"I'm serious, Wick. You could get hurt."

I ended up at Aisha's feet and didn't argue when she picked me up.

That was fun. Can we do it again tomorrow?

"What the hell were you thinking?" Will hissed as he shoved me into the sweatshirt pocket. He kept me there as he pulled his skates off and warned me against wiggling out. "No, really, what were you thinking?"

I wanted to skate, too.

"Your feet are far too exposed. You could have damaged your paws."

"Let him be, sweetheart," Aisha said. "You never told him he wasn't allowed on the ice."

"Fine. But you stay in my sweatshirt now, Wick. You need to warm up."

We joined Eli at his table near the café, and Aisha darted inside to get cups of hot chocolate for them all. Eli pulled a scarf from around his neck and handed it to Will, with the suggestion that he stuff it in the pouch to take the edge off the cold.

That feels nice, thanks. It has your warms on it.

While Aubrey slid her chair over to be closer to Jax, a boy who was about the size that Jay had been at the start of summer ran past and yelled out, "Hi, Mrs. Blackshear!"

"Oz might be right," Jax said. "The kids out here think of you as a teacher."

"Some of the adults think that of you, too," she said. "How many of these parents were your students once? To a lot of people, you're their old history teacher."

"Miss it?" Eli asked.

With a sigh, Jax nodded. "I wouldn't change anything, Dad, but I do miss it. The kids, at least. I don't miss dealing with parents who are so sure their little snowflakes can do no wrong."

"I have those snowflakes this year," Aisha said. "This semester can't end soon enough. I am so done with teaching surly high school students."

"They're only surly because you now know how badly they treated Jay," Will said. "Before then, they were just assholes."

That made her laugh. She looked over to the rink to find Jay; he was inching along the railing with Zara, their heads close together, and they were both laughing.

"He is so happy right now," she said, softly.

"Indeed. Remind me to thank James for letting him stay home tonight. That couldn't have been an easy decision."

"He knew Jay wanted to be with all the other kids," she said.

"At what point does Jay get to decide where he's sleeping on any given weekend?" Jax asked. "I mean, he's seventeen."

"The custody agreement goes through his eighteenth birthday, though I may encourage Jay to stick to it. It would be too easy for him to keep putting off going over to his dad's, and I honestly don't want that."

"I dunno. Dad's apartment might be party central," Jax teased.

That wasn't far from the truth. Aisha hoped he'd get it out of his system by the time Jay turned eighteen, but she wasn't holding her breath. "He's never done well with monogamy," she explained. "But right now? I think he's determined to sleep with every single person in the city."

"That sounds exhausting," Eli said.

"Says the man who hasn't looked at a woman in years," Jax said.

"That you know of."

"All right, that's fair." Jax raised a playful eyebrow. "So, who is she? Is she why you didn't want to come home?"

"You make it sound like it was just one woman, son. Look at me. How could I keep the ladies away from this?"

"Open your mouth, for starters," Jax said.

"You sound like they do," Eli sputtered. "I'm offended."

"Don't let him goad you, Eli," Aubrey said. "He enjoys poking the bear."

"I saw that display on the ice. He enjoys being the center of attention."

"Damn right." Jax sucked in a sharp breath and grimaced. Jay had fallen, and he took four people down with him. "New name. We'll call him 'Grace.'"

No one's crying. They're probably okay.

He had a hard time getting up. When everyone else popped up and skated off, he was still trying to get his feet underneath him. Zara was trying to help but was laughing too hard to be much good, so Zed stopped and picked him up by the back of his sweatshirt, and when Jay found his footing, Zed shoved him toward Zara.

I thought that was a bit mean because he might knock her over, but she slid backward until she hit the railing, pulling him with her. She was still laughing, and I think he was, too, but it was hard to tell from the angle, and then he kissed her, so no one was laughing then.

Well, no one except for Eli, who decided Jay had planned that.

"The boy has been going in circles for an hour, waiting for the right moment. Meanwhile, Zed has damn near licked that Lopez girl's lips right off her face." He sipped at his drink. "On the whole, I find Jay's approach to be much more considerate. He's a sweet boy."

"Give him time," Will said. "A few more months, he won't be as shy."

"That's a shame. There's something to be said for decorum."

Aubrey sighed. "Eli, if Zed has been inappropriate—"

He waved it off. "No, he's been fine. He's been far less obvious than his father ever was. I simply see something of myself in Jay. I appreciate that bit of hesitation, the uncertainty mixed with hope that the girl feels the same way."

"Asking cuts through the worry," Jax said. "You know, 'Hey, I really like you. And I'd *really* like to kiss you.'"

"That's not a question," Eli said. "And where's the fun in that? The chase?"

"It gets you to the kissing faster."

"Is that what he did, Aubrey? Marched up and told you he wanted to shove his tongue down your throat?"

"Jax had a few manners back then," she said.

"Barely," Will chuckled.

"I bought her coffee first, Dad. I'm not an animal."

"Our first kiss was sweet and mostly innocent, Eli," Aubrey said. "It was weeks before I had any inkling he had a sordid past."

"I wouldn't call it sordid," Jax grunted.

She reached over and rubbed his arm, laughing. "Jackson, you make Zed seem like a saint in comparison. And I'm not happy with the things he's apparently done."

"Girls are not things," Jax said.

"Good lord." Oz and Drew had come off the ice and were heading towards us. Aubrey nodded in their direction and said, "Now those two. In this entire family, they may have approached a relationship with the most maturity."

"Jax was mature with you," Will argued. "Isn't that what matters?"

"There might be other concerns, but yes, overall that's what matters."

Oz dragged a chair from a nearby table and nudged it close to Jax's. "Why were you guys staring at us?"

"You," Jax said as he leaned over to plant a kiss at her temple, "look very happy. That's all."

"Where did Zed disappear to?" Aubrey asked, glancing back to the rink.

"Changing out of his skates," Drew answered. He grabbed another chair and made Will scoot his over. "He and Jay are going to walk Sophia and Zara home. If Zed can pry Jay and Zara apart, anyway."

"Really?" Aisha stretched to see past Will. "Where are they?"

"Behind the kiosk. Don't worry, kissing is the only thing going on. His hands have stayed in plain sight."

"Good for him," Will murmured.

Aisha patted his arm. "Phfft. Good for her."

A few minutes later, after Jay and Zara finally came out from behind the kiosk, the noise level around the table tripled. They were talking over each other, and I stopped listening until Eli handed Zed his bank card and told him and Jay to go get hot chocolate for their girls. When they all went into the café, Oz and Drew with them, it felt like a blanket of quiet settled over the table.

"You didn't have to do that, Eli," Aubrey said. "But thank you."

"Eh, they all looked cold, and my grandsons are not letting their girls shiver."

"You might want to consult Jay's mother before you lay claim to him," Jax said.

He wasn't about to do that. "William is my son. Jay is his son. That makes him my grandson. Argue if you want, but I won't change my mind. And ask Zed what he thinks. He and Jay are brothers every bit as much as the two of you. I can see it already. When the rest of the world pushes against them, they'll stand together."

No one was going to argue that, but I don't think Aisha knew what to say.

When they came out of the café, Zed handed Eli his card and gave him an awkward side hug, then took off with Jay to walk Sophia and Zara home.

"Did you talk to Zed about the bedroom?" Aubrey asked as Oz and Drew sat back down.

Oz nodded. "He's actually happy about it. He wants the bigger room as an excuse to get a bigger desk and new computer."

"And why would he need bigger and newer?" Jax asked.

"The desk because of school work," Oz said. "And the computer because he needs a better system to run the software he'll need soon. He's changing his major. Well, declaring a major. I don't think he had yet."

"What's he declaring and why hasn't he talked to us about it?" Jax asked.

"Architecture, and hell if I know," Oz said.

Aubrey laughed lightly. "Architecture. He wants to learn how to design that castle."

"Hell, let him explore," Jax said. "What about you, Ozzy? Any thoughts on your major?"

She nodded. "Heavily leaning toward history and government."

"Dual majors?" Will asked.

"To avoid the pitfalls of not knowing enough of what came before," she said. "Besides, if I'm following in Dad's footsteps, I want to be able to actually fill the imprints, you know?"

"You want to teach?" Jax asked, sounding hopeful.

"I've had an inkling I wanted to teach for a while now. I get to kill two birds with one stone with this. I learn our history inside and out, and I get to pass that on to kids who don't know they really want to know it."

"Advice?" he asked.

She nodded.

"Concentrate on history. I'll make sure you understand government."

She got up and kissed him. "Best teacher yet." She kissed Aubrey, too. "Both of you."

Great. They're gonna cry now, aren't they? Jax is gonna cry and I can't even make fun of him.

16

"This is like a damned spaceship." Jax stopped in the center of the hospital hallway, and he didn't know where to look. Will took them through the portal near the operating rooms because he didn't want Aubrey startled by the abrupt noise and bigger crowds on Union Square, but he also wanted to see Jax's reaction to the brushed metal hallways with their bluish tint and what he would do when they passed a door that whooshed open.

Finn made sure that happened. He waited in Mass's office with the door closed all but an inch and listened for their approach. The door made a loud, airy noise as it slid open, and Jax grinned like a kid with a new toy.

"I want that at home. Someone needs to make that happen."

Doesn't Jax know about grocery stores? Their doors swoosh. You should take him grocery shopping.

Will took them on a short tour; he let Jax drool over the view of the launchpad from the cafeteria and warned Aubrey that sooner or later, Jax was going to want to try that. While they looked around, Finn took their bags to the apartment, so that Will and Aisha could take them out to begin the birthday celebrations.

"It's hardly the same city," Jax observed on the way to the restaurant. "Change in tastes, cyclical rejuvenation, or did something happen to force new growth?"

"Urban renewal, for the most part," Will said. "The twenty-first-century charm of our When no longer pulled tourists in. There are regrets, but people opted to rebuild to modern standards. It was partially the inability to retrofit older buildings to newer earthquake standards, but largely it was a tourism issue."

It made Aubrey a touch sad. "People could always go outside the city to experience metal and glass. One of the things I love so much about home is how we've held onto its history."

Even so, she thought it was beautiful. She had a sense of where we were headed because the street layout hadn't changed much even if the names had, and she grabbed Jax's hand to enjoy the walk. That was something she missed, wandering down the street holding hands with him without worrying about who might be following or who might feel like they were in the way.

No guards were trailing, and no one paid any attention to them.

If we keep heading this way they might see the castle.

"We've discussed this, Wick," Will said. "I'm not answering most of their questions, and they're not intentionally seeking information."

"We're just here to relax," Jax said to me. "Don't worry."

The restaurant Will picked was on a pier a few blocks from the café he'd taken Drew to. It had a patio with a canopy decorated in bright red paint with twinkling white holiday lights and plastic chili peppers hanging on thin wires—it was the opposite of regal and dignified. It reminded me of the cheap, sketchy places they used to go in the Haight and the Mission before they were old enough to drink in bars, when Aubrey was mostly opposed to spending money and Will just didn't have much to throw away.

It was perfect.

No one else was on the patio when we arrived, so that's where Will asked to be seated. It was chilly and fog swirled around the pier in thin wisps, but several heaters were blowing warm air around the patio, and they had enough alcohol that they didn't care. Jax was thrilled to have fajitas for the first time in almost twenty years, and Aubrey cheerfully embraced the idea that a giant margarita was not going to land her in the news.

"I almost feel guilty that I might be enjoying your birthday more than you," Jax said. "Only reason I don't is because when we go home, you get to have a birthday all over again."

"Two anniversaries, too," Will pointed out. "You have reservations at the Cliff House, which does not resemble the one you remember but is a wonderful place nonetheless. My father says it's classier and has a very romantic ambiance these days."

"You're celebrating with us," Aubrey said.

"No. You're going to be saddled with family on your anniversary at home. This one is yours alone. Twenty-five years. You should have the night to yourselves."

"What will you two be doing, then?" Jax asked.

Off somewhere else, bouncing.

Oh, take her back to Bounce.

"Somehow I think we'll find something that will keep us distracted from your absence."

"A couple of years ago," Jax said, "I would have presumed that meant you'd wander off to find a library or a bookstore, or even take the opportunity to get work done."

"More likely I would have taken time to play in my workshop. Which I miss. Thanks, Dad."

"You could get another workshop," Aubrey said lightly. "Build another motorcycle."

"I technically have a workshop, though Drew has taken most of the available space. And I now have other things to occupy my free time."

"Oh, thank you, I'm a thing now," Aisha said.

"Not *a* thing. *The* thing."

"Still, thing?"

Jax snorted, "Yeah, you just blew your night, Will."

"Groveling is not beneath me. And I apologize," he said to Aisha. "I was not comparing you to an object. I simply meant I would rather spend my free time with you. Tinkering in the workshop has nothing on—"

"If you say tinkering with me, you're getting a margarita bath."

"I am *so* glad you got married," Jax said. "This is much better than listening to your lectures on governmental responsibility and social programs. This is entertaining. Will getting bitched at. I've waited my entire life for this."

"Be nice," Will said. "I have dirt on you. Dirt that your children would find fascinating."

"Fountain of vomit?" Aisha teased.

"That would be a good starting point."

Jax's eyes narrowed. "You wouldn't."

Will didn't say one way or the other, but from the look on his face, there was a good chance that given the right impetus, he would.

They poked at each other for hours, sitting on the restaurant's patio, ignoring a table of women who arrived half an hour after we did, and who kept staring and then leaning close to each other to chatter, probably complaining because we were closer to the heater and they wanted it. It had been dark for a long time when Aubrey realized the staff was probably waiting for us to leave so that they could close. There was a car waiting for us—Finn had rented it and made sure it was parked where Will could find it—and Will drove home, ignoring Jax's questions about where he'd lived and in what part of the city.

The kids didn't tell him?

"Apparently not," Will answered. "I didn't expressly tell them not to. It wasn't intended to be a secret once they'd been there."

They had the same reaction that Aisha had—you lived in Finn's lab?—when he parked near Union Square. Jax thought he was kidding when he steered them toward the front door of the building until Will reminded him that he was their descendant and family homes were still a thing.

"The family's main apartment—your apartment—has a door now. My grandfather had to make some changes when the last of the guard was gone, and a few non-family members moved into the building." We went up in the elevator, and Will showed them how to unlock the door, but we didn't go in with them. Once the door was open, he wished Aubrey a happy birthday again and kissed her on the cheek, ignoring Jax when he asked who Will's grandfather was.

Instead, he handed Jax a phone that would work in this When and showed him how to access texting and calling, and we left them there to spend the night alone.

They might have liked the hotel better.

"Possibly, Wick. We've saved that for their anniversary."

"Twenty-five years," Aisha mused. "God, we were all so young."

"Well, except for Aubrey," Will said. "And I'll deny I ever said that."

*

The hotel room was everything Finn had promised; it was spacious, with an oversized bed decorated with fine linens and shiny fabrics that Will thought would be too slippery to sleep on, and the view of the bridge spanned to Treasure Island. The sky was bright with twinkling lights that ran along the bridge's support cables and towers, the reflections glittering on the water like fairy lights. There was no window seat because it opened to a small balcony with a tiny table and chairs with plush cushions, so Will dragged a comfy chair from the other side of the room and placed it near the door for me, in case I wanted to sleep with moonlight spilling over my furs.

In the corner near the balcony, there were crystal bowls, already filled with water and kibble, and a clean plate with three cans stacked next to it. There was a note on the plate that said, "Welcome, Mister Wick! Enjoy your stay!" It was the premium canned food, too, so I was pretty sure I would enjoy my stay there and was certain I would when I discovered the automatic litter box in another corner of the room. I hopped in and out of it, just to make it clean itself, and when I'd made enough noise to bother Will he told me to find something else to do, something that didn't hum and whirr and get on his nerves.

Fine. I was amusing myself, but whatever.

He wanted to amuse Aisha instead, but before he could get his shoes off, his phone pinged and made him laugh.

"Jax wants to know how the hell to fill the bathtub, and failing that, what the fuck is up with the humming shower that won't even drip?"

"The future is confusing," Aisha snorted.

He was nice and did not remind her that she'd yelled at the shower when she couldn't make it work the first time. She'd been stressed—they were in this When for Jay's surgery—and teasing her didn't seem fair.

After he got Jax sorted out, she asked Will why there was a massive bathtub in the room when there was a perfectly good one in the bathroom, and why was it already filled? That seemed like a waste of space and resources. Will flipped a switch on the wall, causing the water to bubble, and then tapped on a little screen near it.

"It's a hot tub. Very retro, and strictly for fun."

She peered down into it. "The bathtub does the same thing."

He started pulling his clothes off. "Deeper, wider, and I'm assuming more fun than a bath."

"Guessing?"

"I've never been in one. But I thought we might like to try it."

Once they were naked and submerged, and she was half sitting on his lap and half floating, I worked up the nerve to sit at the edge. I could feel heat pour off the water, and little droplets of steam settled on my whiskers.

You know a lot of other people have been in this thing.

Doing the same thing you're thinking about doing.

It's people soup.

"People soup, Wick?"

"He has a point," Aisha said. "There are probably five liters of bodily fluids simmering in this thing."

"I would assume they clean it regularly."

"But define 'regularly.' After every customer? Once a week? Think of all the semen clogging the filters."

"I'd rather not."

Isn't that heat just gonna kill off all your little swimmers?

"My what?"

I read a lot. You have swimmers and too much heat hurts them, so if you stay in there and cook things, you're gonna wind up with a three-headed baby. Or an omelet.

"What the hell have you been reading, Wick?"

Stuff on Drew's tablet. He doesn't have a password on it.

"Half an hour in a hot tub is not going to render me infertile."

Aisha got out of the tub. "That's all the reason I need, Bilbo. Between thinking about what might be floating in that water and our fertility? Besides, sex in water isn't exactly comfortable."

"Groping is."

She handed him a towel and told him he could dry her off. That was enough to make me think it was nap time, so I took advantage of the nicely placed chair and the moonlight and tried to not listen to the things going on behind me.

For a guy uncertain about religion and an afterlife, Will sure as hell begged God a lot and he was becoming really good friends with Jesus.

When I woke up, the room was dark, except for the light coming from outside. Will was leaning against the wall by the door, staring out at the water. I stood up and stretched, trying to see if there was something else out there, but it was just the water and lights glowing on the bridge.

Can't sleep?

"I did, for a bit," he said, whispering.

You could put some pants on, you know.

"I didn't realize my nudity offended you."

For Aisha's sake. It's cold by the window.

He laughed softly. "The effects aren't permanent."

I probably knew that once. Before Finn found me, I still had all my parts. They probably worked.

"Do you think you fathered kittens, Wick?"

Well, look at me. Do you think the ladies could have stayed away?

"I suppose not," he said, but he was laughing, so I didn't really believe him. "If I knew how to find you in the years before Finn brought you home, I'd find out for you. The only thing we know is that you remember the Palace of Fine Arts during one of its restorations in the nineteen sixties."

I remember being hungry. A lot.

"And that makes me hope that you remember that particular time because you were born then. Not because it's simply the furthest your memory will go."

It's okay. You won't let me be hungry again, not for real. And Drew and Oz and Aubrey will make sure, too.

He squatted so that our faces were close together. "I worry that you'll outlive me, Wick. I don't know what future generations would do for you. Or if anyone else will be able to converse with you."

Finn.

"Dad would do anything for you."

And he's still alive. So he'll probably still be alive the next time around. He doesn't understand what I say, but he knows what I need. He won't let me starve and he'll make sure I have a nice place to live.

"Remind me to have this discussion with him."

And you might live until then, too. You still have almost a hundred fifty years, unless something happens.

"I'm not sure I want to hope for that, Wick. I don't want to outlive everyone."

Aisha slipped out of bed and came over to him, bending over to kiss the top of his head. "I was eavesdropping, I'm sorry. Are you worried about leaving Wick behind?"

"We worked our way around to the topic." He stood up and pulled her close. "It's a thing I prefer to not contemplate often. But yes, I worry about providing for him after I'm gone."

"There's not a person in this family who wouldn't make sure he was cared for. None of us will raise our children to be anything but loving toward him."

"He thinks I'll still be alive when this When comes around again. Clearly, I have time."

"I hope so."

He pulled back a bit. "Why would you want me to live that long?"

"Because the world is better with you in it. Because I want to have your child, and I want you to be around for our grandbabies, and great grandbabies. Besides, you never know. I might live almost as long."

You can find out.

"I would like that," he said. "We can be creaky, cranky, wrinkled old people together."

You should find out.

I'm being serious here.

"Wick, you know I won't do that."

What if she needs to be saved? You're gonna do it for Sophia. You should see if you need to do it for her.

The idea made him twitch. He let go of her and went to sit on the edge of the bed.

"Will?"

There was just enough light coming in that I could see his eyes go wet. He blinked against it and sucked in a ragged breath; when he didn't answer her right away, she sat next to him, rubbing his back.

I didn't mean to make you sad. But being sad now might mean not being sad later. And that's a happy thing.

"He thinks I should look up the details of the end of your life," he said thickly. "I am generally opposed to creating expectations, but he's right. I need to know."

She placed a kiss on his shoulder. "But you won't be able to tell me anything."

"I shouldn't."

"All right. I'm not sure why you need to know, but look me up, find out all my sordid details. I'll pretend you're reading someone else's biography."

"In a way, I would be."

"Can you tell me why? Other than curiosity?"

"Because accidents happen, and I want to be old and wrinkled with you."

"That's a hell of a burden to place on yourself, Will. I'm willing to take life as it comes and be done when it's over."

Softly, he said, "But I'm not willing for it to end anytime soon. I just got you back, Enzo. If I can stop" —his voice broke— "Let me be selfish in this. Wick is right, I need to know. If there's a premature ending that I can change, I will."

"All right. But not tonight, okay? For now, I'd like it if you crawled back into bed with me. I'm getting cold, and I want to use your body to warm up."

"Was that in our vows? You get cold, I get used?"

"Would have been if we'd had vows," she said, scooting up the bed. "Come on, turn up the heat for me, Bilbo. Anything else can wait for tomorrow."

I think he was about to tell her that it was technically already tomorrow, but she'd grabbed onto things that made him go about six degrees of stupid. I curled up on the chair and waited for daylight while they found religion again.

*

We checked out of the hotel long before Will was ready to. He wanted a sleepy morning in bed and then coffee on the balcony, but Aisha mused that if Jax couldn't figure out the bathtub, there were probably a dozen other things they couldn't figure out and going back before one of them burned the building down might be a good idea. Will settled for a few unhurried kisses and then agreed: someone probably needed to rescue them.

They couldn't have been too worried; we walked the two miles back to the apartment, and it wasn't at Will's usual brisk pace. They held hands, and I worked hard at not falling off his shoulder because he was moving around a lot, swinging her arm like they were thirteen years old and touching was still new and weird.

They probably should have walked faster. When we got there, Jax was on the balcony, alone, so Will went out there while Aisha took their bag into the bedroom.

"The future needs some fucking instructions," he grumbled before Will even said hello. "Do you know how long it took me to figure out how to flush the damned toilet? Or turn the lights off in the bedroom? Aubrey is still in the kitchen trying to figure out how to make coffee. We're not even sure which appliance might *be* a damned coffee maker."

Aisha was one step onto the balcony, heard that, and turned around to go inside to help.

"Voice command on the lights, though there is a switch—"

"Yeah, I figured the lights when I barked, 'how the hell do I turn the fucking lights off?' And Aubrey was not amused when I snapped, 'Flush, motherfucker,' and the toilet flushed."

"Again," Will said, laughing, "there's a rocker switch on the top—"

"Instructions would have helped. Just saying."

Will said he was sorry, even though he wasn't. "Aisha figured it out easily enough. I assumed you would, as well."

"Liar. You had to show her, didn't you?"

She almost cried.

"You survived. I hope other than those frustrations, the rest of Aubrey's birthday was pleasant."

Jax didn't answer; he just grinned.

"Had breakfast yet?"

"I was waiting for the damned coffee."

Will laughed again and got up. There was a café down the street with patio dining, and it wasn't far from a launch site where younger kids were taught to use flight packs. There was a good chance we'd see terrified six and seven-year-old kids hurtling through the air, screaming in terror while being chased by their instructors.

Breakfast theater.

The tables were clustered under a canopy of trees, which made Jax a bit leery of what they might wind up with all over their food and in their hair, but Will assured him it was less of an issue than he might suppose.

"Look around," he said. "Wick, you, too. What's missing that you are generally not thrilled with?"

He was right. There wasn't a pigeon in sight.

Someone finally banned them?

"There are fewer birds overall, but these days the pigeons tend to flock to the central piers, where more tourists congregate. Locals don't feed them, the tourists do."

Will showed them how to tap the table top to get a menu to appear, and how to order food. "If there's a slight indentation in the center of the table, the menu will appear. If there isn't one, then the restaurant has wait staff." He pointed to a shiny piece of glass near the menu indentation. "Pay by touching a cash card here. That will be the same even somewhere with servers. But no tipping. There isn't a function that will allow it."

"No tipping," Aubrey repeated. "People have talked about doing away with that for hundreds of years. How did it finally fall out of favor?"

"Foodservice is a career. Restaurant staff is well paid, and there's no need for it." He looked at Jax. "It works. This is why you keep getting petitions for a mandatory living wage for restaurant workers."

"I get petitions for higher wages for every possible job out there. The basic income entitlements should cover living expenses."

"Unless you're a waiter," Will said. "With few exceptions, they aren't paid in addition to the BIE. Tips are the difference between just paying for needs and being able to afford a life. Two or three cheap bastards who refuse to tip can kill a day's wages."

"If I institute a mandatory wage for one group of workers, I have to do it for all. Are you suggesting that someone who sits in a kiosk all day just to keep an eye on a bridge with no traffic should be paid as much as one of the highly trained kids who guards my children?"

"I'm suggesting that there needs to be a hardline minimum wage, and it needs to be separate from the BIE. Anyone willing to work should earn enough to be able to turn around and pour money back into the economy. The BIE was never intended to be more than enough to keep people fed and housed. It doesn't allow for clothing, education, transportation, or any sort of recreation."

"I've heard the debate before, Will. You've never had an opinion one way or the other."

"I've had the opinion. I've never felt able to give voice to it. It's going to happen sooner or later, and Pacifica will benefit greatly if it's done now rather than a hundred years from now."

"And you've run the numbers?"

Will nodded.

"Show me later."

There are people looking at us.

"What people, Wick?"

On the other side of the street. Those ladies. One pointed and giggled. Now they're talking really fast at each other.

He glanced but made a point to not be obvious. "It probably has nothing to do with us. They have no idea who we are."

"People you went to school with?" Aisha mused.

"Possibly. I would have thought no one would recognize me now, but when we were here for Jay's surgery, both Peter Lucas and Kathleen Rosy knew who I was on sight."

"They seem happy to see you," Aubrey said. "If you're what they're talking about."

They wandered off while we ate, and I almost forgot about them until Will was paying for breakfast. They came back and had two more women with them.

It's definitely you.

He didn't turn but asked me what they were doing.

Just looking. And talking.

"They could be discussing how this couple looks a lot like pictures of a king and a queen they learned about in school."

"No," Aisha said, "they're focused on you."

They all have a thing on their wrists. I think it's a tattoo. All the same.

Aisha's hand went to his arm. "Will..."

"It's a coincidence," he said. "There's zero chance that any of those groups know I'm here."

He explained the Cult of the Emperor to Aubrey and Jax. They wouldn't look for him here; they were concentrated on finding a way through a portal to meet him in his new When. Another group thought he was immortal and living in the Pacific Northwest, but they would be looking for a very old man.

"They want to have his babies," Aisha said, amused.

Jax snorted. "Well, who wouldn't?"

Will pulled his phone from his pocket—Finn's phone—and said he would call for the car, just in case.

"Didn't you rent a car?" Jax asked. "Why call for another?"

"I'm calling the rental. It will drive over here and park itself as close to my location as it can. Then we can avoid Wick's admirers." He scratched behind my ears. "They're clearly here for you, Mister Wick."

I had nothing to say to that. He was probably right.

Just to be an ass, Will drove to Ocean Beach, lined up to get onto the coastal thoroughfare, and then told them to hold on. He asked Aisha to make sure I was clipped in securely, and when the light turned green, he hit the throttle and we took off like a shot. Jax was in the front seat with Will, and when he spoke his voice went up an octave as he clutched at his restraint.

"What the actual hell, Will! Slow down!" There was another car a few hundred feet ahead of us, and Jax was sure we were about to plow into its back end. "I don't give a damn about passive controls, back the hell off!"

"Fine, Grandpa." Will's fingers glided over the control panel as smoothly as Zed's did over piano keys, and the car began to both hiss and hum, but it didn't slow down. He'd activated the underbody jets, and the car lifted, shooting into the air at twice the speed it had been hovering over the road.

We were almost over L.A. before he turned around, and when he did, he switched to the sky lane over the ocean, giving them a view of the coastline as he headed back to San Francisco.

"How fast will this go?" Jax asked, finally relaxing.

"Fifteen minutes to San Diego once airborne, if the central sky lane is clear," Will said.

He banked left, drifting further away from land, and began a wide turn to take them over the Golden Gate Bridge. He slowed so they could see the city without it being a glassy blur, and then continued over the Bay Bridge. He finally landed in SOMA, not far from where his old apartment was.

"I admit, I'm lost," Aubrey said as she got out of the car.

"We're near Yerba Buena Gardens," Will said. "Just 'the Garden' now." He pointed to a building half a block down. "Modern SF Art Museum, not to be confused with the SF Modern Art Museum." He pointed at that one, too, which was a block in the other direction. "The MSFAM displays works by prominent local artists of the last two hundred fifty years. I thought you might like a peek at what's to come."

It was loud inside. Unlike the museums that Zed complained

about when he was younger because he was only allowed to whisper, people were talking over each other. There were dozens of school-aged kids scurrying from one exhibit to the next, and the volume of their chatter made my ears go flat.

Will offered no sympathy for my distress. "Excitement over creativity is encouraged. Each of those kids knows their artistic efforts could be displayed here someday, in their lifetime." He gestured to a large sculpture in the lobby. "This was created by MacCallum Stewart, just fifty years ago."

We edged closer, peeking over the heads of small kids. It was a giant garden gnome, although not at all chubby and absent the hat. He had a short, clipped beard and his head was thrown back in glee, hands on hips. Aubrey was fascinated by the details: the folds in the clothing, how each hair appeared separate from the next, and how utterly human he looked.

When Jax was able to get close, after the kids moved on, he said the subject seemed familiar, and then barked out a laugh when he realized who it was.

"Read the description," he told Aubrey.

I stretched to see it.

'King Eli the Second.'

"He's remembered for his mirth," Will said. "His sense of humor is mentioned in every grade-school history book, and he's been raised to almost mythical levels as far as his laughter goes. I don't recall learning anything about his temper, though some texts touched on his grief."

Aubrey was curious about how history treated Eli's relationship with the Emperor. "When his grief was discussed, did it include how he must have felt when the Emperor died?"

That gave Will pause. He'd learned about them long before he knew who he would become and had avoided making the mental connection. "He spoke of the Emperor's death as a national tragedy and an absence that could not be replaced. Little was known about their personal relationship, and I'm sure that was intentional."

He said you had a stick up your ass. I remember that. 'The Emperor lived with a massive stick up his ass, but his death is a personal and national tragedy, and his absence leaves a hole in Pacifica that can never be filled.' That was in one of the history books Jo taught you from. I may be paraphrasing.

"There was not a textbook claiming I had a stick up my ass," Will sputtered.

There were several pieces of art depicting the royal family, from King Norval onward. There was a massive painting of him on a white horse, crown perched sloppily on his head, and he was galloping down the center of the Golden Gate Bridge, a sword raised in hand. Jax snorted at that; Norval was a quiet man who avoided public displays of attention-seeking behavior, and he would have been horrified at the thought of blazing down the bridge like that.

We spent hours wandering among the exhibit rooms. Aubrey found a piece made of delicate blown glass created by one of her former students, which excited her. While she told Aisha about him, Jax excused himself to go find a men's room, and when he returned, he grabbed Will by the arm and pulled him aside, whispering to him.

Will scowled and went out to see the problem. He came back looking like he was both pleased and concerned and told Jax to make sure that we turned left leaving that room and not right.

I want to see.

"Fine," Will whispered to me, "but you can't tell Drew about it, all right? Run to the next exhibit room and read the info tile next to the entry, then come right back."

I ran.

James Okuda, Jr.

I peeked in; the walls were covered in paintings and drawings done with bright colors, some framed, some displayed behind glass. The largest was a painting of a woman with soft brown skin holding the hand of a very small child as they walked on the beach. She was older, but there was no mistaking who it was.

I ran back.

There's a painting of Aisha!

Will wanted to see the exhibit for himself, but there was no easy way to do that without Aubrey and Aisha following.

Take them to the café for coffee or something. Then say you'll be back in a minute because you have to pee, and it would be rude to do it right there.

"I'll come back another day," he said.

Jax managed to steer them away from Jay's display and then outside. Will directed them to head down the sidewalk toward a restaurant he knew of, and he walked with Jax, trailing behind Aubrey and Aisha.

"Did you have any clue?" Jax asked him.

"None. I've likely seen that room before, but I have no clear memory of it. I've seen him sketch when he's supposed to be studying, but I've never heard him mention an acute interest. I thought he was using doodling as a method of distraction."

What I saw was really good.

"It would have to be good to be in that museum," he said. "I hope my continued existence and marriage to his mother hasn't changed that for him."

"You'll make sure he has a good life," Jax asserted.

He knew that; I knew he was going to look Jay up at the same time he checked on the details of Aisha's life because now that he had an idea about Jay, there was no way he could resist the temptation.

*

Over the next few days, Will took them to the places they had frequented when they were younger. We hiked through the woods near the Presidio because Jax wanted to see for himself that it was still there, that the fights he and Will had once had with the council over preservation of woodlands hadn't been a waste of time and breath. Will was able to point out spots long grown over, where he and Jax had hidden with beer smuggled from the staff kitchen, and he still knew the spot where they'd sat on fallen logs, when he told Jax that the next time he came, he'd be staying for good.

"I remember that," Jax murmured. "I was happy for myself and broken for you. Jesus."

"You can tell them I broke down and cried like a three-year-old," Will said, amused. "Aisha knows already."

"So does Aubrey," Jax said.

"He wasn't making fun of you," she told Will. "He was trying to understand. He had no idea where your family was and why you were leaving, and he wanted to know why you felt like you had to stay."

I thought that was going to make Will sad, but he snickered and asked Jax how many years it took him to realize that he was aging so much faster in comparison.

"Shut up."

We went to Golden Gate Park, Crissy Fields, and we explored as much of the city as we could. By the fourth day, Jax and Aubrey were sure they could find their way around if they had to, and on the fifth, we took a picnic to Dolores Park and sat on the hill where they used to pretend they were studying.

"We need blocks of ice," Jax declared. "This is still a good place for ice sliding."

"You would need a compliment of guards, as well," Will said. "I never thought you would get them to ride down the hill with you."

"Come on, I had young guards. Half of what we got into, they wanted to do, too."

"Tip?" Aubrey asked, laughing. "Oh, lord, I'm surprised we didn't get that poor boy fired."

"Hey, he knew damn well there was no such thing as the Royal Taster of Beer and Liquor," Jax said. "He also knew damn well I couldn't give him orders. It's not my fault he went along with it."

"His poor liver."

"Whatever happened to him?" Aisha asked.

"He's in charge of training the kids' guards," Will said. "New selectees get the lecture: 'I was King Jackson's guard when he was a teenager, and I know you've heard stories about him. They're all true. You will *not* allow his children the same leeway I gave him.' They all know about the drinking and especially about his ride down California."

"And the girls?" Aubrey prompted.

"No. Honestly."

Aisha wanted to know what leeway guards had when it came to the kids' romantic lives. "I never thought about it when you two were dating. But now that Jay has guards and apparently a girlfriend?"

"Not allowed to interfere," Jax said. "Not unless they're in a dangerous situation or causing one."

"Causing one."

"If one of Jay's guards feels as if he's being pushed into something he doesn't want to do, or if he's pushing himself on someone else, then they'll interfere."

"If Zara ever utters, 'no' and Jay doesn't seem to be listening," Will said, "one of his guards will yank him away from her without hesitation."

"He wouldn't."

"Of course not. But the guard has leeway when it comes to that. If Jay says no to someone and they refuse to listen, the guard will just as easily remove them from the situation. If there's even a modicum of uncertainty, the guard will step in, take him aside, and inquire, regardless of the level of embarrassment he might endure."

"Would we be informed?" she asked.

Will nodded.

"I wonder if he realizes."

"I have had this discussion with him. He understands what the guards will do and when, and what they will tell us."

"What they tell *you*," Jax huffed.

"Indeed. And so far, none of the kids has done anything worth bothering you over."

"Not even Zed?"

"Zed is remarkably well behaved, despite his dalliances."

"But—"

"I've asked, Jax. There's never been a question regarding consent. His head guard has never given inappropriate personal details but assures me that Zed is considerate and never pushy. Does that help?"

"It helps. I worry. He's a good kid, but I remember being his age, and everything I got away with."

Aubrey leaned over and kissed him on the cheek. "With respect to Eli, you've been more hands-on with Zed. He didn't have to figure things out on his own."

Those ladies are back. Just down the hill. Five of them.

They weren't the exact same ladies, but they all had splotches on their wrists. I couldn't tell what it was from that distance, but I could see a sameness in them and was sure it was a tattoo. Will tried to blow it off as coincidence, but Jax wasn't as willing to dismiss their presence and declared that the picnic was over. He'd spotted a shop at the edge of Union Square where the bakery used to be and thought it might be a good place to get coffee and watch people flying around.

"It's not," Will said. "You can get maps of the city and tourist-trap trinkets, but not much else."

Jax shrugged "Fine."

Take them to the place you took Drew. See if they get the name.

"Indeed, Wick. We can get coffee there and enjoy a view of the bay."

We sat inside this time, toward the back where they could still look out the window. It took Aubrey fewer than five seconds to spot the castle looming on Treasure Island, and she asked if Zed had finally gotten it. Will responded, "Sure. He saved his allowance and half his pay over the years to build a castle that cost somewhere around eight hundred and fifty million dollars."

"Don't mock me," she said, even though she didn't mind.

"It's a school," he told her. "San Francisco's population shot up, and the education system needed to spread out in order to meet demand."

"*That's* a school?" Jax was incredulous. "Damn."

"Private school, but yes."

Technically, he didn't lie.

"All right, Will, speaking of education. Tomorrow I want to learn to not kill myself with one of those jet packs. Is it even possible?"

"Indeed. We can either start from Union Square, or if you prefer we can use a commuter launch pad."

"Which is more fun?"

"There's a keener sense of danger taking off from a launch pad, owing to the steep fall from the roof of a building. But once you're in flight, there's no difference. It won't take much to get you both up in the air."

Aubrey shook her head. "Oh, no. Not me. You three can fly around all you want, but I have no desire to throw myself through the air."

"It's fun," Will said. Then, to goad her, he added, "Aisha tried it when we brought the kids here."

"But I don't need to do it again," Aisha said. "We'll go window shop or something while you two pretend to be fifteen again."

Will tilted his head as he looked at her. "Window shopping? That's rather stereotypical of you. Not something I would expect."

"Be nice, or I'll take your dad's card and do some actual shopping." Aisha looked to Aubrey. "Let's see how long it takes to drain his account."

She was only kidding, but Will shrugged it off and told her it would take more than the two of them could possibly carry. "If you want to shop, shop. I'll pay Dad back."

"Uh huh. And in which direction is the most upscale jewelry store?"

"You can't bait me with this," he said. "In fact, if you're really going to do it, then actually buy yourself something. Hell, buy *me* something. There's a liquor store on Market that sells Chambrizi. Get a bottle. I want to take it home."

Swipe Finn's and take it home.

"I don't think there's much left in that bottle, Wick. Actually, buy two bottles. I owe my Dad one."

"You want me to buy your dad a bottle of booze, using his money."

Will beamed. "Exactly."

"My head is going to explode when we settle up with Finn, isn't it?" Jax asked. "I haven't seen a damned price on anything here, but I'm willing to bet it's not cheap."

"Food is not expensive," Will said, stretching the truth. "Overall, this entire week isn't going to cost any more than sending Oz and Drew to Disneyland."

"All right, not bad at all. Sure, go shopping," he said to Aubrey. "I want a t-shirt that says, 'San Francisco Twenty-Six-Sixteen.' People will think I'm being obnoxious when I wear it."

"People think you're obnoxious without the shirt," Will said.

He glanced out the window; people were being seated on the patio, and he noticed the same thing I did: all women, all under forty, and they all had that same tattoo. He didn't say anything, but he made sure that when we left, we exited through the street side of the café, and went straight to the car.

*

I slept on the window seat in Will's childhood bedroom, wishing it was still Oz's because hers was more comfortable and less cold seeped through her window. It was still a good place to avoid all the bouncy things that happened on the other side of the room, though on this night they were quiet, and it was more like they wanted to be gentle and sweet with each other than enthusiastically horny.

After Aisha was asleep—Will made sure she had been asleep for a while—he slipped out of bed and sat at the window with me, reading on Finn's tablet. I knew what he was doing and knew he wanted to concentrate, so I left him alone while he searched public records for information about Aisha's life without him. His main intention was to find the date and cause of her death, but he started chasing one of Drew's rabbits and wound up down a hole he was in no hurry to climb out of.

He poked around online for hours. It was still dark when he set the tablet aside and folded his arms across his belly. I wanted to ask what he'd found, but if it was sad news, I also didn't want to know.

After a while, he whispered, "One hundred thirty-four years, Wick. She lived to one-thirty-four and died in her sleep. She never remarried after James, and she went on to have a lengthy career as a teacher and then as a theorist. From everything I could find, she was happy."

What about Jay?

He pulled me closer before he answered so that he could whisper even softer. "He lived a very long time, too, and found his success as an artist when he was relatively young."

Sticky people?

"I found no mention of children. But remember, the Jay of this When had to wait until he was an adult for multiple surgeries and likely wasn't fertile. I found a brief mention of a wife, but no name. I admit, I didn't dig too deeply. I'm afraid if I know too much, I'll try to influence him."

He's gonna be okay no matter what. You made sure he got to be himself. Everything else is like getting shrimp with the steak.

He hesitated when Aisha rolled over. "Aisha and James made sure of that. They have been extraordinary parents to him."

James, too?

"James loves Jay without reserve, Wick. I respect the hell out of him for the father that he's been. They've both been exactly what that boy needed."

So you know Aisha is gonna be a good mom for your kid.

"I think part of why I want a child so badly is knowing that she will be its mother."

You want more than one?

"I'll be content with one. If she wants more, I'm certainly open to that. And if we don't have any, I'll be fine. But I admit, with each day, I want one with her more than anything."

Boy or girl?

"Healthy. That's all I care about."

You fell in love with Oz right after she was born, when you got to hold her.

"Indeed, I did. When Jax placed her in my arms, I felt like my heart exploded. I can't imagine how he felt or how I'll feel."

So you won't really be okay if you don't have a baby.

"I will truly be fine if we don't have a child, Wick. I will admit to disappointment. My desire to be a father increases daily and exponentially, I'd be lying if I said otherwise."

"We'll have a baby, Bilbo." Aisha's voice sounded sleepy as she sat up in bed. "If it doesn't happen on our own soon, we'll go see Mass."

"Sure, and you'll have the good doctor knock you up," he said lightly.

"I don't know about the *good* doctor, but Mass swore he could do it." She patted the bed next to her. "Come back to bed. And bring Wick. He's been by that window all night and is probably cold."

I would not mind the warmth of the bed.

Will placed me on the bed next to her and slid under the sheet carefully. "How long were you listening?"

She didn't hear anything about Jay. Just about how awesome a mom she is.

"Are you ratting me out, Wick?" She rubbed a finger under my chin. "I haven't been spying on you, sweetheart. I'm barely awake as it is."

"But you heard enough."

She leaned over me to kiss him. "Just enough. And thank you. Especially for understanding that in spite of himself, James is a good father."

"He is. He's a good man, Aisha."

"Except for the way he's screwing his way through the city, sure."

"He's single," he reminded her. "And he's working through his divorce. He's allowed to let go while he attempts to regain his footing."

"He doesn't handle monogamy well, Will. He cheated on me, he cheated on George, and if he's ever in another relationship, he'll cheat again. That's a major character flaw, especially when he needs to be an example for his son."

"Jay knows how much James loves him. And we know he doesn't approve of the parade of men and women in James's apartment. It may not be the example you wanted, but it has certainly driven the point home."

You can be his example.

You'll never cheat.

"No, Wick, I'll never cheat." He gave her a quick kiss. "And I know you won't. That's not you."

"If I had stayed married to James? Eventually, I think I would have. We're human, Will. We have limits."

"I will never give you cause," he said.

"If we'd spoken actual vows at our wedding, that would have been part of it. I promise to not fuck my way across Pacifica. No matter what."

"And I promise to not even make my way across the city."

"You can't quite say it, can you?" she said. "I've heard you say 'fuck' before, Bilbo."

"As an expletive. But I refuse to equate anything I do with you with...that."

"Give it time. I'm still waiting for that afternoon when we both come home from work and just go at it. You'll barely get your jeans down around your hips, I'll have my underwear wrapped around an ankle, and it'll be over in about five minutes. We will just *fuck* at some point, sweetheart."

"And I look forward to that," he said. "But I still can't reduce it to fucking. Just...a quickie."

Do I need to go back to the window? This usually means bouncing.

"I think you're fine, Wick," Will said. "We really should try to sleep."

"You sure about that?"

"I don't think the little emperor would cooperate much right now. You've pretty much worn him out for the night."

"All right. But Wick, would you mind crawling on top of Will for a bit? I'd like to snuggle up against him."

I can go to the window again.

Will patted his chest. "You're cold. Curl up here." He rolled onto his back, and I hopped up, leaving room for Aisha to cuddle against him. They were quiet for a long time, and when Aisha's breathing started to shallow, he whispered, "Wick, I am a happy man."

*

At six in the morning they were still wrapped around each other and Will was sleeping soundly, so I carefully slid off his chest and made my way into the living room. The coffee maker was gurgling, which meant Aubrey had finally figured it out and she hadn't started a fire, so I started looking for them. The bed was still unmade, but it wasn't warm anymore, and they weren't in the kitchen.

They were on the balcony, cuddling under a blanket, waiting for the city to wake up. It was the least regal I'd ever seen Aubrey outside of the bedroom; her hair was messed up, like she'd only run her fingers through it, and sleep still swirled around her.

Jax had a heavy early-morning whisker-fest going on, and his hair was sticking straight up.

You guys sleep at all?

I jumped onto Aubrey's lap, and she took a corner of the blanket and tucked it around me, declaring that it was too chilly for someone as small as I was. She set her hand on top of the blanket for extra warmth and told Jax they needed to keep an eye on me. If I shivered, they were going inside.

"He knows how to find the warmest spots inside, Aubrey," he said.

"He'll also sit with us until he's miserable if he thinks we need him."

Jax tapped me on the head. "We don't need-need you right now, furball. Go inside if you get cold."

I know. I will.

"If *you* get cold," he said to Aubrey, "tell me. We'll go back to bed."

"Ah, I see. You're hoping I start shivering."

"I'd be happy to go inside and make breakfast for you instead."

"Sweetheart...you might burn the building down. I'm not sure either of us knows how to turn the stove on."

"Seriously. I'm grateful Finn lent us the place, but it takes an engineering degree to take a damned shower."

She set her head on his shoulder. "But it has been a lovely week here, Jax. I didn't realize how much I missed being able to just walk the streets without guards trailing me and people scrambling out of my way. Being able to stroll down the Embarcadero holding your hand has been so soothing. We might have to beg Will to do this again sometime."

"Time off like this might be the only way to keep me on the throne. I'm starting to understand why Dad bailed so young."

"Having second thoughts about never abdicating?"

"No. As long as we have this to run to every now and then, I'll hang on. Hell, Oz might be the better ruler, but I don't want this for her."

"She might not want it for you, either."

"Good thing I'm in control, then. I don't hate it. And I know I'm good at it. But I want more for Oz, even though I'm tired."

"I know."

"But not too tired. Anniversary tomorrow. Twenty-five years, angel. I'm still surprised you put up with me."

"So am I." She laughed and lifted her head. "Apparently I'm putting up with you for at least thirty-five more years. Will went to your eightieth birthday."

"I kissed him on the lips," Jax snorted. "I wish I could have seen that."

"There's still time. But I want someone recording it. All of Pacifica wants to see that."

"Maybe when I'm eighty."

They both twitched and sat forward a bit, startled. I poked my head out from under the blanket to see what had happened; they were watching a ship streak into the sky, heading for space.

"Did we just see a launch?" Aubrey asked.

"I think so. That was close. Marin County, I think." They watched, waiting for it to disappear. It tracked slowly to the left, a bright blue dot streaking away from Earth. "Heading for Elysium."

"Do you think it will be finished in our lifetime?"

"If Drew and Will get their way, it will be. I never would have thought that the little boy throwing his toys at our daughter would grow up to have so many huge ideas spinning around in his head. My gut feeling is that we'll be able to power it up before he's thirty."

Twenty-five. Before then.

"My father thought it was evil," she said, softly. "Men playing where only God should exist. As if heaven was actually in outer space."

"Where would hell be, then?"

"Florida."

That made him laugh. And then, as softly as she had spoken, he said, "Our remains are here. Downstairs. Us, the kids, even Will. I think you're going to get your ultimate wish. Even when we're gone, our entire family will be in this building. As long as it exists, in whatever form, we'll be together."

That earned him a kiss.

"Any regrets?" she asked him. "I'm feeling a little bit selfish, having asked you to get the vasectomy before coming here. Ever since then, the thought has pricked at the back of my head that you waited so long because you were hoping I would change my mind."

He had no idea how she might think he'd have even a single regret. "I went to Jacobsen years ago to get this done. He led me to believe you'd confided in him that you might want another baby. So, I waited. I'm content with our family, Aubrey, but I would have had as many kids as you wanted."

There was a flash of anger in her eyes that left as quickly as it had come. "I never told him I wanted more kids. We never discussed it. What the hell is wrong with that man?"

He had no answer. "Still. Did you ever want more?"

She sighed. "If we'd had them soon after Zed? I think I might have wanted at least two more. But then it didn't happen, and right around the time I considered we should do something, Eli began grumbling about retiring."

"I'm sorry. I—"

"No. No apologies. You know I believe in God and have a deep sense of faith."

"I do, and I appreciate that."

"I prayed about it often, Jackson. For a long time, I thought those were unanswered prayers, but eventually I accepted that the answer was no. And I was fine with it when I came to the realization that we had the children we were meant to have. When I've prayed about a larger family, the thought has always come to me that we're going to have grandchildren someday, and we have William and Aisha and Jay now. That's the family we're meant to have. That was the answer. Love those who already surround you and wait for those still to come."

"We create some awesome kids together, angel. If there's any part of you—"

"I want grandchildren, and for Oz and Zed to be truly happy in their lives, that's all. I want William and Aisha to live upstairs from us until we're impossibly old, and I want Jay to come to love us enough to stay, too. No more babies for us, sweetheart, no doctors or medical intervention. I just want to love the people we already have."

"God, you're amazing."

"And don't you forget it." She rubbed a thumb over his jawline. "I have no regrets. Except, perhaps, last year's chicken casserole that everyone swore they enjoyed but Wick refused to sample. I might try to make it again, just to see how many of you run from the table."

"That was nasty," he said, trying not to laugh. "But those kids will sit there and choke it down and not say a word, you know it."

The door squeaked behind them, but they didn't hear.

"Is that a dare I hear?"

"Damn right."

"Who is daring whom to do what?" Will pulled a chair up.

"Feed that chicken casserole to the kids again," Jax said. "Whoever spits it out does the dishes for the next month."

"Are we required to consume any?"

"Not a chance."

"You're hurting my feelings," Aubrey said. "I slaved for days on that chicken."

"That was the problem. It tasted like it had been sitting out for days." Jax leaned away from her, just in case she took a swing.

"Make it for Eli," Will suggested. "He'll either eat it without saying a word, or we'll all learn colorful new ways to swear."

"In Gaelic, no less," Jax said.

"No swearing at the table. William, are you going to go see your grandparents while we're here?"

"Briefly," he answered. "They're both in the middle of rejuvenation, so they won't know I'm there, but I promised my mother I would check in."

"Rejuvenation," Jax repeated.

"The clock is being turned back, so to speak. It gives them back the years they lost when they followed me."

"Will you need that someday?"

"No. They spent a few years waiting for me on the other side, and Mass is essentially returning those years to them. And regardless, I'm not sure I would want to do it even if there was even a moderate need."

"Why the hell wouldn't you?" Jax asked.

"Why the hell would I? If Aisha dies before I do, I can't imagine wanting to live much longer. If we get to be old and wrinkled together, that'll be enough."

"Until Jay has children," Aubrey said. "Your tune will change."

"I hope that his children will be grown and old themselves before that happens. I'm looking forward to having sunset years. I don't need anything beyond that."

"Yeah, we know Aisha," Jax said. "There's not gonna be anything sunset about it. She'll be on you until the very last day."

17

"You're him."

We weren't five steps out the door when a woman with red hair, wearing a red shirt, and obnoxiously tall red high-heeled shoes marched up to Will. She didn't say hello, didn't so much as glance at Aisha or Jax or Aubrey. She sort-of looked at me, but only because I was perched on his shoulder and had my tail wrapped around his neck.

He stepped in front of Aisha. "Excuse me?"

"I know it's you. Wait, I have a picture—" she began patting her purse and then started digging into it.

"I think you're mistaking me for someone else," he said, trying to be polite. "Now, if you don't mind?"

He started to turn.

"Wait. No, I have it on my phablet. Look. It's you."

He ground his teeth together for a second or two. "Ma'am, I am not the person you're looking for. I promise you that."

"No, I have—"

Jax was behind us, laughing under his breath and I heard Aubrey poke him. Will heaved a tired sigh, trying to beg off.

When he started to step away, she grabbed his arm. "Please, look. You're the Emperor."

Will glared at her hand, surprised anyone had the nerve to grab him. Aisha, on the other hand, wasn't shocked at all and stepped out from behind him, using the back of his shirt to pull him to the side. "Bitch, get your hands off my husband, or I swear to God I'll tie your tits in a knot and use them to fling you across Union Square." When she was too stunned to move, Aisha growled, "Move! Now."

The woman let go of Will and took a few cautious steps backward, mouth hanging open as Aisha yanked the car door open.

"I'm glad I don't have tits," Jax whispered loudly to Aubrey. "That sounded painful."

"Careful," Will said as he pulled the car away from the curb and headed for breakfast. "You have other things she'd stretch out and knot."

Aisha was not amused. "Will, how the hell did they know you were here?"

He didn't think it was a conspiracy. They'd both read enough about the cult to know that their center was in San Francisco, and he assumed they were always looking. She wanted to know who else had known he'd be here; he made a mental list—Finn, Rod, the owners of the chocolate store, and Mass. He didn't think any of them would talk.

"They've memorized a few photographs, that's all," he told her. "And what are they going to do? Grab me and start ripping my clothes off in the middle of the street?"

"Well, if having your progeny is their goal," Jax snorted.

"It's fine," Will said. "Another couple of days and they'll be losing their damned minds trying to find someone who went back where he belongs."

*

The only thing Will cautioned Aisha against buying were books. He knew she would be tempted to get him something he couldn't get at home, but it was an exorbitant extravagance. "Buying a printed book in this When is the same as buying your apartment and my old apartment. Printed books are exceedingly rare and are generally only purchased as an investment."

He gave her Finn's phone and created a conversion chart for her, so she'd know what she was spending, and then he and Jax disappeared into Finn's lab.

I rode on Aisha's shoulder, mostly because Aubrey wasn't used to carrying me and she would fret about dropping me, which would ruin her fun. There was nothing specific they wanted to shop for, though Aubrey wanted to find cupcakes. "I rarely make them, and he knows better than to send someone to the bakery as often as he'd like. I don't think I could pick up anything else that would make him as happy."

"Think Will would eat one?" Aisha asked me.

I head bonked her. That could have been yes, it could have been no, but it made her happy.

Without noticing that's where we were heading, we wound up near the intersection where Aisha and Jay used to live. There was still a park on the corner, but where her building should have been there were five giant round towers connected by enclosed walkways on three separate levels. In between, on the ground, were paths that gently curved, lined with flowering ivy, and I could smell it from where we were at the park entry.

They decided to cut through the park and were over the little hill when Aisha sighed and said, "Dammit to hell."

Aubrey stopped, trying to find what had upset her.

Aisha gestured to the playground. Sitting on a bench near the sandbox was George, and he'd spotted them. We could have turned around and gone back the other way, but he stood when he noticed us, and she decided to not be rude.

As we neared, he glanced at a boy playing in the sandbox, but when she was close enough, he took several steps to meet us, and he smiled at Aisha.

"Never in a thousand years would I think I'd run into you here," he said. He said hello to Aubrey, but he had no idea what to call her.

"Jax and Aubrey needed a vacation," Aisha said. "Coming here seemed easier than trying to get away at home with all the guards and nonsense that follows them around."

"Makes sense." He had more—he wanted to ask about Jay—but the little boy hopped out of the sandbox and ran over, brushing the sand off his hands onto his pants. When he grabbed George's leg, George said, "This is my cousin, Darren. Dar, you remember when I told you about Jay? This is his mom, Aisha."

Darren was five or six years old, and not as shy as I expected. "How'd you get here? Jay lives a long time away."

"She has her ways," George said. "I don't suppose he's with you?"

Aisha shook her head. "This was just the grownups. And no matter what he thinks, he's not."

Darren looked up at Aubrey. "Who're you?"

"That's a little rude," George said.

Aubrey was not offended. "I'm Aisha's friend, Aubrey."

"You're Zed's mom. George told me about you, too." He held his dirty, sand-encrusted hand out to her. "I know all about Jay and Zed. George says I would like them."

"I think you would, too." Aubrey shook his hand without flinching at the grime.

George tapped him on the head and told him to go back to the sandbox, and he would be there in a minute. "He only knows about Jay as Jay. I've never mentioned Jaime to him."

"How much family do you have here?" she asked him.

"More than I realized. Finn found cousins I'd never known about and an uncle who's still alive. They've been accepting and accommodating, helping me get on my feet again."

"Then you're doing all right?"

"I'm surviving." With another glance at his cousin, he said, "Good kid, but he eats sand. I need to get back to him. But, please, tell Jay I said hello. I miss the hell out of him, but...well, don't tell him that."

George went back to the bench, where he could keep an eye on his little cousin, and we turned back around.

"He seems amiable now," Aubrey said.

"Don't let him fool you. He's always been able to make people think he's a nice, normal person, but that's still the man who tried to get Jay to run, and he's still the little sociopath who tried to kill Will."

"No bitterness there, then," Aubrey said lightly.

"Oh, hon, there's a huge part of me that wishes he'd taken another swing at Jax and given Will a reason to break his damned neck. I hate it, but it's the truth."

"You had the chance, didn't you?"

"I did, but it hardly seemed fair. He was broken and nearly dead. But at least I got one good kick in, and I'm pretty sure his balls lodged themselves somewhere near his liver."

I'm not sure he had any to begin with.

She reached up to pet me. "That's right, Wick. You got your licks in, too. Poor baby was spitting chunks of George out of his mouth for an hour."

I can still taste him. Something dead and delicious would help.

"Sweetie, we're not sure what you need," Aubrey said, "but if we go near something you want, let us know."

"Wonderful. He'll bite me on the ear. That's how he's gotten Will's attention before."

"No biting," Aubrey said. "Lick her if you must, but no biting."

That seemed fair. I wrapped my tail around her neck and kept an eye out for the first place that looked like it might have food.

*

Three hours later, we went back to Union Square to wait for Jax and Will, but they were already there, just outside the lab entry.

"We're retiring here," Jax said before Aubrey was even fifty feet away. "We flew to Golden Gate Park, buzzed a flock of geese, and got yelled at by a cop."

"Then, you did things you would yell at your kids for."

"They're not here," he beamed. "Seriously, it was so much damned fun. Why the hell can't these be a reality for us *now*?"

"Because no one would let you play with one," Will said. "Everyone else would get to have fun while you watched from the balcony, whining about it."

"Couldn't just let me have this for ten minutes, could you?"

"Why would I do that?" He leaned toward Aisha to get a kiss. "No bags. What happened to shopping?"

"We're total failures. Except for getting Wick something to eat."

"Not even cupcakes," Aubrey added. "Sorry, sweetheart. I was going to bring you a box, but we never found anything that looked like a bakery."

"Well, damn. I didn't know I wanted any until you said that."

"I'll make some next week," she promised. "I won't even complain when you sneak a few for breakfast."

"Yes, you will."

There are some other ladies over by the statue. They're looking at you.

"Same ones, Wick?" Will asked.

I'm not sure, but they have blob-thingies on their wrists, too.

This time, he looked angry. He turned his back to them, which didn't help because he spotted George coming from the other direction and decided a great day had just turned to shit.

George shoved his hands into his pockets, looking a little sheepish. "I know, exactly not the person you wanted to see. But I didn't know how long you'd be here, so I took a chance."

"Um, we ran into him a while ago," Aisha told Will.

"All right." Will's hands went into his pockets, nearly mirroring George. "What's up?"

"I had a letter—" He stopped and looked over Will's shoulder at the women who were approaching. "Looks like you have a fan club."

"Dammit," Will said under his breath. He turned so he could see them; the woman in red was toward the back, a fake, nervous smile stretched across her face. She caught Aisha's eye and then took a step back, not willing to risk making her mad again.

The woman who spoke to him had a tablet in hand, one with his picture on it. It looked like it was taken within the last year, on Union Square. He was wearing a faded gray sweatshirt and still had his beard, and it was definitely him.

"This is you," the woman said. "We're certain of it."

Will glanced. "No, I don't think so."

"The image is very old, but there's no mistaking it. You're him. You're the Emperor."

"The Emperor of San Francisco?" Will asked. "He's been dead for two centuries."

She shook her head. "We all know better. He's alive, and he's right here in front of me." She flicked her finger across the screen. "My sister took this picture of you recently. It's the same man. You're him." She had the photo of me sitting on Will's shoulder, taken when he'd brought Drew here. "It's you."

George moved to her side and took the tablet from her, flicking to the older picture. "Not him, Cherry."

"What, you know her?" Aisha asked.

"Neighbor." He handed the tablet back. "It might be an old relative, but it's not him." When she started to object, he added, "Cherry, I've known him since I was four years old. We went to school together. We took karate lessons together."

"Karate," she repeated, unbelieving.

"Kicked my ass a dozen times. Look, I know he resembles this man" —he gestured to the tablet— "but I guarantee, he hasn't been hanging around here for the last two hundred years."

The women started talking amongst themselves, but the one holding the tablet wasn't willing to let it go.

"Look," George said, "he's my son's stepfather. I don't like the guy, not at all. I have nothing to gain by protecting him. But he's not the man you're looking for. Maybe that's his great, great, great grandfather or something, but *this* man isn't a couple centuries old. He's forty-three, same as me."

When she still didn't budge, Aisha sighed. "Hon, if you want to keep staring at him, do it from over there. And ask Red there what I promised to do if she laid another hand on him. That goes for all of you."

They finally backed off but didn't apologize for bothering him.

"That's a lot of tits to tie up," Jax said.

"Thank you," Will said to George. "You didn't have to do that."

He gave a light shrug. "You think I'm unhinged? Try having a conversation with one of them. I'll seem like the most level-headed person you've ever met. Besides, why the hell would I help them? They want another one of you."

Aisha put her arms around Will's waist and gave him a quick hug. "I'd still like to know how they plan on making that happen. It's not like you'd cooperate."

"They don't need his cooperation," George said. "They just need his DNA. But, if you want details, I can find out and leave them with his father. Cherry's a drinker, it wouldn't take much to get her to talk."

Will said it wasn't necessary at the same time Aisha said, "Hell, yes."

Let George get the neighbor drunk. It might be the only fun he has.

"Just don't tell them who he really is," Aisha stressed.

"You said you had a letter?" Will asked George.

He reached into his back pocket for a hand-sized tablet. "This is old tech, I built it to store notes. He won't think anything of it. James, I mean. The letter is for him."

"You sure that's a good idea?" Aisha asked.

He handed it to Will. "You know James. He'll self-medicate the pain I left him with, and that's not good for Jay. I'm hoping an explanation will take some of the sting out of the way things ended."

"He can't know where you are," Jax said.

"There are no details about that. You can read it," he told Will. "Decide for yourself. I just—I want to give him some peace. And I selfishly want him to know that I still love him, and I always will. And that I was wrong."

He swallowed hard and turned to Aisha. "I've had a lot of sleepless nights to think about it. I love Jay, I've loved him from the moment James introduced him to me. I come back to the same thought every time. If James had said, 'hey, this is my son,' I would have loved him just as much. It shouldn't have mattered."

"But it did, George."

"I know. And it comes from an archaic school of thought, but it's how I was brought up and not something easily shaken." He took a deep breath. "Did they tell you about my sister?"

She nodded.

"I was raised, from the time she was born, with the certainty that girls are to be cherished and protected, at all costs. I feel that in my soul. I failed my sister. I wasn't going to fail Jaime. I was going to be the person who made sure she had a chance to grow up and have a say in her own life, and I was terrified that by letting her transition so young she would be robbed of that. I refused to believe that she was *always* Jay. Believing meant not protecting her. But I was wrong, and I want James to know that."

Aisha didn't know what to say.

Will did. "If James reads this letter and wants to see you, are you willing?"

Hope and fear crashed head first on George's face. "How would that even be possible? He can't come here. And I've changed physically. I can't explain that."

"You would have to go back. You wouldn't be permitted to stay, but a visit can be arranged."

"My face," George said thinly. "My skin. I look so much younger."

"He would have no trouble believing you were vain enough to get cosmetic surgery."

"I can't believe you're willing to do this."

"It's up to James. If this" —he held the tablet up— "will give him enough peace to want to see you, I'll make the arrangements."

"Thank you."

"Still think I'm a freak?"

"I could lie and say no. You scare the hell out of me, Will. You have for almost forty years. Hell, sixty." His hands went back into his pockets. "I don't hate you, but yes, the whole mind-reading thing whispers 'freak' to me. And I'm aware, that's my problem, not yours."

"George, you tried to kill him," Aisha said.

"I know. And not that it matters, but it's not something I would wish on him now." He looked to Will. "James is probably going through his own personal hell and isn't the greatest example for Jay. Regardless of how I feel about you, I know you'll be there for him. I don't like you, and you'll always scare the hell out of me, but I grudgingly admit...I respect you. I know you'll give that boy everything he deserves."

He turned and left before Will could say anything else.

"He's drunk," Aisha murmured. "He has to be."

"Gonna read that?" Jax asked.

"Hell, yes. I'm not taking the chance that there's anything other than a simple letter on this tablet."

"George Denton," Aisha breathed. "The gift that keeps on giving. Will, don't let him suck you in. He can be friendly as hell when it gets him what he wants."

"I am aware. Now might be the time he learns that no matter how well he behaves, it won't necessarily work out the way he hopes."

Aisha wasn't as sure about that; Jay wanted nothing to do with George, yet he'd still needed to see him. James might think he was done with his marriage, but once he saw George again, it would take very little for him to open up. And if he intended on bringing George back for good, they were going to have a problem.

"I won't," he said.

"George is banned from Pacifica," Jax reminded her. "Permanently. I won't yield on that."

She wasn't convinced, but let it go because a teenager zooming overhead lost control and bounced off the net around the statue, and even though he landed on his feet, she was right next to Aubrey, running to make sure he was all right.

*

Jax wanted to know how much trouble Will had gone through to make the arrangements for their anniversary dinner at the Cliff House. We were at the café near the Bay Bridge, waiting while Aubrey and Aisha wandered down to the pier to get a better view of the bay. It was cold, but Jax wanted to sit outside where they could still see Aisha and Aubrey—not because he was worried about them, but because he didn't think there was anything better than watching his wife enjoying herself.

"It was no trouble," Will said.

"If it's all the same to you, as nice as it sounds, we'd rather spend the evening with you two. We still have our anniversary coming up at home, and we'll celebrate loudly and long into the night with the family, but tonight we just want to hang out with our best friends. One more night before we head back home and to reality."

"Is this what Aubrey wants, too?"

"Without a doubt. She wants to get a little drunk and laugh until she damn near wets herself. I want what she wants. Without the peeing."

It wasn't a problem. Will fished the phone from his pocket and tapped away at it, then proclaimed all reservations canceled and Finn's money refunded.

Did you really get Finn's money back or are you just saying so?

"Yes, Wick, I did." He reached over to scratch by my ears. "You're getting very suspicious in your old age."

Ask Jax something for me?

He stopped rubbing my head to listen.

Why doesn't he celebrate his birthday? Today is his birthday, too.

"Indeed, it is. Wick is curious why you no longer celebrate your birthday."

"He remembers?"

Of course, I remember.

"I don't celebrate it often because I value my anniversary more, Wick," he said. "My birth was my parents' doing. Marrying Aubrey was our doing, and the day was my choice."

We celebrated Aubrey's birthday.

"Because it was a milestone birthday," Will said. "Surely you've noticed none of us tend to do much on birthdays unless Aubrey instigates it."

The kids do.

"Kids deserve a celebration every year," Jax said. "We make a big deal about that because having them made our lives better and we want to make them happy. I suspect as they get older, they'll opt to do less and will celebrate quietly."

"Unless Aubrey has a say in it," Will chuckled.

Aubrey and Aisha were on their way back, and I waited until they'd sat down to make my point.

You're forty-five today. That seems like a milestone.

"It's less of a milestone than fifty," Jax said. When Aubrey asked, he explained, "Wick remembered that we married on my birthday and is questioning my choice to rarely celebrate. We tried explaining milestone birthdays, and he thinks forty-five counts."

"It should," she said. "You always do something for mine. Sometimes it bothers me that you don't want to bother with yours."

He raised an eyebrow. "You can offer me a birthday bl—" His face twisted, and he grunted, "Ow."

"Tonight, we'll celebrate your birthday and not our anniversary," she said. "Next week, we'll have the anniversary."

And then comes Christmas without Santa Claus.

"Wick, you're just a grouchy mess today, aren't you?" Will asked.

I'm not grouchy. But this is Aubrey's favorite time of year. Why don't we do Santa anymore?

"Because the kids are grown," Will said.

But you people don't even give each other presents. There used to be presents and wrapping paper that got balled up and thrown for me to chase, and ribbons that you teased me with.

"We have so much, Wick," Aubrey said. "It stopped being special. It was Oz and Zed's choice, and to be truthful, it lifted a lot of weight off the holiday. We focus on it being a family day and spend it together."

"I'll get you a gift this year," Will told me. "You don't have to miss out on anything."

I didn't care about getting a gift, but I wasn't going to say no to some fresh-off-the-boat real live fresh dead shrimp. I cared about missing the kids' excitement and watching them open presents.

"Someday we'll have grandkids, sweetheart," Aubrey said. "The insanity will start all over." She looked at Will. "I hope this year your parents will come for dinner. I understand why they didn't last year."

"Last year was new for all of us," he said. "I'll extend the invitation, and I'm sure they'll want to come." He turned to Aisha. "We haven't discussed how you want to handle the holidays. What do you and Jay usually do?"

"We've always spent Christmas Eve together, and then he headed upstairs to his dad's around noon Christmas Day. But I'm sure James will be willing to switch as long as he gets to spend time with Jay."

Will pointed at Aubrey. "No. We will not be inviting James."

What about tonight? What are we doing for Jax's birthday?

"Well?" Will asked Jax. "Your birthday, your choice."

"Know of any really sketchy dive bars?"

"Jax, I left home when I was seventeen. I know where a few bars are, but the ambiance is something with which I have no experience."

"Fine. Then I want fajitas again. And after that, drinks on the balcony with my favorite people that Aubrey did not give birth to."

"I'm telling your father you said that," Will said.

"I'm telling yours you used his bank card for gambling and hookers."

Will shrugged it off. If anything, that would only impress Finn, and his only curiosity would be which one of them the hookers were for.

*

By the time dinner was over, Aubrey was drunk. She wasn't pleasantly tipsy, she was drunk, a level of drunk she hadn't been since Jax was eighteen and had no idea what to do with a woman who was so far from being able to consent but was still offering him a blatant invitation to do whatever he wanted to.

They were still in the early days of dating, before he'd even gotten his hands under her shirt, much less seen her naked. She pinned him to the wall of a bank on Market Street and pressed against him, whispering into his ear, trying to talk dirty but failing miserably.

She reminded him of that on the walk back from the restaurant, and I don't think she cared if Will or Aisha knew. "I didn't have a clue," she said, laughing louder than regular-drunk Aubrey would have. "He was terrified."

"I think it was 'I'll lick your ear and make you scream' that got me," he said. "I was thinking that's not what I wanted you to lick, but there was no way I could show you, not as drunk as you were."

"First time you ever said no to anyone," she snorted. "I should be honored."

"If it helps, you were the first to shove a tongue into my ear," he said.

"Who the hell was second?" Will asked.

"Wick."

It was gross.

Aubrey cackled, grabbed Aisha's arm, and they dashed ahead. When they were far enough ahead, Will said, "I don't think you're getting the birthday blowjob. A hundred bucks says she's vomiting by ten o'clock."

"I'll take that bet. As long as we don't let her drink anything else, she'll be fine. And this time around, I sure as hell won't tell her no."

"She's in no shape to consent, Jax," Will said. "I don't care how long you've been married."

"Well, you're a fucking killjoy."

Aubrey said once you had blanket consent. I remember that.

"She said that," he agreed. "That doesn't mean I'll take advantage. If she doesn't sober up a little, the anniversary shenanigans will wait until we're home."

"Aubrey gave you open consent?"

"It's not like I can throw her down on the bed and just do her without seriously pissing her off," Jax said. "I'd never consider it. But she knows when she gets a little tipsy she gets seriously handsy, and that's when her offer of consent comes into play. As long as I make her toes curl, she's open to it. But you're right, this level of drunk is not covered under any agreements we made about iffy situations."

She and Aisha had their arms linked, mostly to keep Aubrey from wandering into the street. They were both laughing, but Aubrey was practically howling, and it made Jax laugh, too.

"Hell, maybe Aisha's gonna be the lucky one tonight."

"Would not be the first time," Will said under his breath.

Jax heard it anyway. "You're shitting me."

"We have not had an in-depth discussion of her previous partners, but she was upfront that there is at least one woman in her past."

"And you haven't *asked* her about that? What the hell, Will. I'd want details."

"Her sexual history is none of my business."

"Bullshit. She knows yours."

"Very funny. I know you haven't told Aubrey about everyone."

"No one in specific. She doesn't want confirmation that I was a total slut. But we did talk about potential offspring I might not be aware of."

That made Will pause. "You were careful."

"As careful as you can be with only condoms in your arsenal. I told her I seriously doubted there were any, but honestly? I have no way of knowing."

"Do you want to know?"

They started walking again. "No, I really don't. Don't go looking, Will. If someone ever comes forward claiming to be my son or daughter, we'll go straight to DNA and then I'll deal with it. But I don't want to invite trouble."

You just jinxed yourself.

"He did not jinx himself," Will said. "Well, unless the jinx comes in the form of a failed vasectomy."

"Shut the fuck up," Jax said. "I just let your wrinkled old friend handle my balls, and it was not pleasant. That better not have been for nothing."

"He did tell you it takes ten weeks to be effective, didn't he?"

For a split second, Jax believed him. "I am so fucking taking you out of my will."

Will. Will. Will.

There's someone behind us. I hear footsteps getting faster. Little feet. Short stride.

Will cocked his head and listened. He heard shoes slapping the pavement, not quite running but not walking, either.

Instinctively, he nudged Jax ahead of himself and then turned sharply, blocking the path between whomever it was and his King.

"Son of a bitch," he grumbled.

It was the lady with red hair. She stopped when he turned, but she was close enough that if he'd been unaware, she could have lunged and touched him. She wasn't expecting him to confront her, and whatever she'd wanted to say got stuck in her mouth.

"Really," Will said tightly, "*what* do you want?"

Aisha and Aubrey turned around.

The Woman fumbled a bit, trying to pull something out of her pocket, and he lifted his arms, trying to protect everyone behind him. "You just—" she held her gloved hand out to him "—you dropped this."

"No, I did not."

"It's your cash card, you dropped it—"

That's not Finn's name on it and it has sharp edges, Will. That card will bite.

"I absolutely did not. Now tell me what it is you're after or leave."

Aisha tried to push past Will, but he got hold of her arm. "What did I tell you before?" she seethed.

Jax didn't react quickly enough to stop Aubrey. She stomped past Will and marched up to the redhead, jabbing her pointy finger at the woman's chest with each word she spit out. "Get. The. Hell. Away. Come another step closer to him, and we'll turn Aisha loose, and bitch, she will definitely tie your tits in a knot, and I'll be the one who holds you down so she can get them nice and tight."

"It's just that you're here," the woman said, looking at Will over Aubrey's shoulder. "We may never have another chance—"

"I'm not who you want me to be," Will said.

"But—"

"Run," Aubrey growled. "Run before I lose my temper and tie your damned red hair into a noose."

The woman took a few steps back, and realizing that Aubrey just might mean it, turned around and scurried in the other direction. Jax reached for her, slipping his arms around her shoulders, and said, "You are *so* drunk, angel. We need to get you back and pour some coffee down your throat."

They got a few steps ahead, but not far enough to keep us from hearing when she leaned close to him and said, "All the coffee you want, but I'm still blowing you so hard you pop."

"Your King and Queen, ladies and gentlemen," Will whispered to Aisha.

Aubrey's hand slipped from his waist, and she squeezed his ass.

Aisha laughed. "Surely the people realize their King and Queen get naked together every now and then."

"Yes, but it's dignified coitus done only in a missionary position, and only on Saturday night after the weekly royal bath."

"Cat bath," Aisha snorted. "She licks that man from his toes to his head."

Gross.

"Speaking of..."

"Ah, Bilbo wants a bath."

"No, Bilbo wants to start at Enzo's toes and work his way up, until she's begging him to not stop."

"And if Enzo had the same thing in mind, nibbling on Bilbo's toes, then his knees, onward and upward?"

"Ladies first."

"Or." She grabbed his hand and stepped ahead, turning to look at him. "We approach this with math. Then we both get our way."

"Go on."

"I think it's time Will was introduced to the number sixty-nine."

He stopped walking, and yanked her back toward him, pulling her close.

"Problem?" she asked.

"Um."

"Which number is tripping you up? The six or the nine?"

"Holy hell, Enzo, just the notion of that gave me a raging erection and there's no hiding it from those two."

Her hand slipped between them. "Just checking for myself. That's as hard as hard gets, handsome."

She started to unzip his pants.

"Jesus, Aisha, no."

"Just flipping it around for you. Tuck it under your waistband. It'll be less noticeable."

"You keep touching me like that and we're both going to wind up sticky."

"Problem solved, then."

Jax and Aubrey stopped and are watching you and they know what Aisha is doing, and she's laughing so hard I think she might throw up.

"Good," Will said. "If she vomits, I win the bet."

*

She refused the coffee but agreed to a freakishly large mug of hot chocolate. She and Jax waited on the balcony while Will made it, and when he and Aisha brought it out Jax took one look and wanted to know who the hell needed a mug big enough to swim in?

"My mother bought the set when I was a little boy," Will said, settling into his chair. "I was—her words—not much bigger than a piece of spaghetti and she thought I would consume a greater number of calories if I drank from a cup as big as my face. Mom logic."

"Did it work?"

He nodded. "I loved these. She could get me to eat almost anything as long as I had one of these."

"Wick could sit in one of these," Jax mused.

"Wick *has* sat in one of these."

Jax spit his hot chocolate back into the mug. "Goddammit."

I did not sit in Jax's mug.

"I'm just giving him a hard time, Wick."

I sat in yours.

Aubrey took a long sip and then sighed. "I threatened to hang someone by their own hair, didn't I?"

"My bad ass Queen," Jax laughed.

"How badly did I abuse the list?"

"Bitch," Will said.

"Hell. Not so bad," Jax added.

"Don't forget the tits," Aisha said.

"Oh, lord. I am so glad we're here and not home. Can you imagine?"

"Angel, that would never happen at home. You'd have had guards between you and her, and you never would have had that much to drink. She's stalking Will. She deserved it."

"Still."

Aisha agreed, she deserved it. "What the hell do those women realistically think you'll do, Will? Whip it out right there on the sidewalk and masturbate into a cup so they can spin off a hundred little samples to create their little emperor army?"

"There's a visual," Jax said. "Does he drop his pants to his ankles, or just enough to get the job done?"

"Why are you even picturing it?" Will asked.

"What do those who launch cults usually want?" Aubrey mused. "The answer is there."

"Money," Will said. "Power. Neither of which can be achieved by having my offspring."

"Inheritances?" Jax asked.

Will shook his head. "By now, anything I left would be dispersed amongst Oz and Zed's children and grandchildren. Some would have gone to my parents. There would be nothing left of the Emperor's estate."

"You provided for our kids?" Aubrey asked, her voice squeaky.

"I have invested on their behalf," Will said. "Some of my own funds, some of which Jax trusted me with."

"Oh, sweetie." She stretched over to kiss his cheek and missed. "You're so thoughtful."

"She's still drunk," Will said to Jax.

"Sober up, Woman," Jax said to her. "I can't take advantage of you like this."

"I am in full possession of my faculties, Jackson. You have consent, and two witnesses to my saying so. It's your birthday and our anniversary! I don't care how drunk I am, we're getting laid."

"Does that pass the consent law?" Jax asked Will.

"One would assume."

"All right then." He set his mug down and got up, reaching for her hand. "You two might want to put some music on. It's gonna get loud."

As she got up, Aubrey glanced down at the Square. "There's a coven of w'bitches down there, William. Make sure you lock the door."

He peeked over the railing. "A coven. There are three people, and two of them are teenagers. The other is a police officer."

"I'm stealing w'bitches from her."

"Wibbitches. Yes, you should steal that."

She took his mug and set it next to Jax's, and then reached over to rub his leg. "Didn't I promise you a math lesson?"

"Indeed." He pulled his shirt out from his waistband, and the little emperor flopped out. "See what you did to me? I've been sitting here with my waistband choking him off. I think he's numb."

You could have fixed that while you were making the hot chocolate.

"Then we need to go inside so I can breathe life into the little fellow."

He got up. "Little?"

"Sweetheart, it's cold out here."

"All right. We'll go with that. It's cold."

*

I sat on the window seat and watched the people on Union Square. Awkwardness was happening behind me that I didn't want to see, and I wasn't sleepy enough to take a nap. I could hear them, but I was more interested in the people down below. The police officer had lapped the Square a few times, followed by a hovering robosniffer that stopped at trash cans, peeked under benches, and circled the plants and statue, looking for things that didn't belong.

I had a vague memory of being chased by one and could feel the panic of trying to get away from it and across the street without being run over bubble in my chest. And I remembered listening as eight-year-old Will was lectured by a cop for letting me use a corner planter as a litter box.

More people were wandering about than I expected for the middle of the night. After the cop left and the sniffer moved on, a younger man with a hoverboard began riding the perimeter, occasionally getting brave enough to speed toward the center of the Square where he attempted to loop over his own head. He'd get his feet a third of the way up, and then chicken out, jumping down before he could be tossed off. He'd snatch the board out of the air and start over.

"All right," Aisha said sleepily from the other side of the room, "we now know something you're not exactly a fan of."

"It may be an acquired skill," Will said. "I prefer to be able to concentrate on what I'm doing."

"You concentrated just fine."

"My brain was disengaged. For all your jokes about choking, I kept worrying I would move wrong and that's exactly what would have happened."

"It wouldn't have, but that's all right. And now I know something I can drive you nuts with."

"Hm."

"Your ass is sensitive as hell, Bilbo. A couple of fingers run lightly over your skin? Now that you liked. You quiver and get even harder."

Hoverboard boy started riding in wide circles, leaning back, his arms extended. It was graceful, and with his eyes closed, he appeared to be lost in the moment. He didn't notice the two women who had come onto the Square and stopped to watch him, enjoying his solitary ballet.

"We should figure Christmas out soon," Will said. His voice sounded surprisingly sleepy, like he was fighting to stay awake. "Aubrey's plans are not mandatory."

"Spending the day with extended family? I've never had that, Will, neither has Jay. I'm looking forward to it."

"We stopped exchanging gifts a few years ago. It was a relief to me because I am not a receiving sort of person, but I do enjoy giving them."

"We've always made Jay the focus of Christmas. We don't go overboard, but we do gifts."

"Then we'll do gifts. If James will switch with you, when Jay gets home in the morning, before we head upstairs. Downstairs. Hm. We'll have moved by then."

"Let's set limits, Will. You and me, one small thing each. And you're not getting Jay anything like a car."

"Aubrey and Jax had a three-gift rule when Oz and Zed were little. Jesus got three things, they got three things. It kept them from inundating them with toys they'd lose interest in."

"That's roughly what Jay's always gotten, although doubled since he essentially gets two holidays every year."

"We'll win Christmas."

"It's not a competition."

"Uh huh."

"All right, fine, once in a while it ends up that way. Go to sleep, Bilbo. You're damn near drooling on your pillow."

The kid on the hoverboard abandoned his circles and was riding over the steps, heading down, turning gently, then going back up. The women moved to a bench, still watching, though I wasn't sure he was aware of them there or not. He seemed to be lost in himself, but he could have been showing off.

Will's breathing slowed, and Aisha slipped out of bed to sit at the window with me. She moved quietly and sat close to me, reaching out to stroke my fur.

This is a first. You sitting here with me while he sleeps.

"You've been looking out the window for a long time, Wick," she whispered.

Hoverboard boy went back to doing circles.

"It's like ice dancing," she said. "He's very elegant."

I wanted to tell her she missed his attempts at loops, but I didn't want to wake Will. The women waiting on the bench had gotten up, too, and I wanted to see if they were going to knock the kid off his board and take it, or if they wanted to tell him he was talented.

They didn't approach him. Instead, they headed for a man who was coming toward them, stopping near the steps on this side of the Square. One of the women had her arm extended before he was close enough to touch, but it wasn't to shake his hand. She wanted something from him.

"Goddamn," Aisha breathed. "What the hell is he doing?"

George.

*

She wasn't letting Will out of her sight. When he crawled out of bed at six in the morning to go see his grandparents, she insisted on going with him. He warned her that they were unconscious and floating in tanks and there would be no conversation, but she wasn't letting him out the door alone.

"I'm only going so that I can tell my parents, yes, I visited them. But it's wholly unnecessary."

He told me to stay in the apartment where it was warm because outside was cold and he didn't have a coat with him that I could snuggle into. They were going straight there and straight back, so I wasn't going to miss anything. He turned the fireplace on for me—it was nothing more than a pretty holographic display with a heated blower in it, which was a bit of a letdown—and I was still curled up on the hearth when they came back an hour later.

"I don't trust them, and I would have hated myself if something had happened and I wasn't there," she told him before he could get the door open all the way. "Sue me."

"What would you have done? Realistically?"

"That's not the point, Will!"

He was amused, which made her more upset than she already was. "If George is right, the only thing they want from me is DNA. Those women aren't going to whisk me away to some underground harem where they'll take turns having their way with me. They'll grab a handful of hair and run."

"Or they'll find a way to draw blood."

He nodded. "That's a possibility. And moot. We're going home after breakfast."

Aisha folded her arms, defiant. "I know I sound like I'm stuck on this, but no one is having your babies but me, mister."

Jax coughed from the hallway and came into the living room sheepishly. "Sorry. Coffee. I'll get out of your hair before conception commences."

"We're out," Will told him. "I'd only planned through yesterday morning. You weren't supposed to be here right now. You were supposed to be yelling at a random appliance in a hotel room, begging it to ooze coffee and cream."

Coffee could be procured at breakfast. Will had planned on returning home using the portal near the Plaza and thought that the café would be a good place to go. Aisha headed into the bedroom to pack their things, which Will intended on leaving in the living room. Finn would bring everything back in a day or two, and they could walk to the café without looking like tourists departing on the next ferry.

"Are you?" Jax asked him when Aisha was in the bedroom.

"Am I what?"

"Having a baby."

"Yes, Jax, I'm currently six months along and quite proud that I've kept my figure."

"Shut up." He laughed and dropped onto the sofa. "You know damn well what I mean."

"She's not pregnant," Will said as he sat down, and he looked over his shoulder to make sure she wasn't in earshot. "Between you and me, no further."

Jax nodded.

"We're certainly not doing anything to prevent it from happening."

Jax pretended to consider it and then asked, "So, how many would it take to constitute an army of little emperors?"

He doesn't know that's what you call your junk.

That makes it even funnier.

"One. Just one." He turned his head at the sound of footsteps, but it was Aubrey at the end of the hall, and she groaned, "Oh my god."

"Royal hangover," Jax said. "Literally."

Her hands were on her head as she shuffled out, and she nudged Jax aside and sat down between them, hard.

"Who wins the bet?" Will asked.

"I'll pay up when we get home," Jax sighed. "There are things worse than fingers to stick down a person's throat when they're drunk."

"Jax," she hissed.

Will got up. "Aubrey, you were quite clear on what you intended to do with him. That's not his fault."

She slumped against Jax and pulled her legs up onto the sofa, curling up. "I am never drinking again."

Five minutes later Will came back with a glass filled with the same thing Finn had given Drew. She tossed it back without questioning him, grimaced, and then set her head on Jax's shoulder. "I will nipple twist the next person to talk," she said, closing her eyes.

Aisha picked a bad time to finish packing.

18

"I might be slightly disappointed that your nipples remain unmolested," Will said to Aisha just before we went through the portal. "It would have been a memorable end to an enjoyable week."

"There's still a chance tonight, if we get her drunk at her birthday party."

Jax and Aubrey were through the portal already. When we stepped through, the first thing Will said was, "Aisha wants to get you drunk again, Aubrey."

"You're uninvited to dinner."

"Will just wants to see you do unspeakable things to my nipples, that's all."

Jax looked at Will, a little too hopefully. Aubrey noticed and poked him in the ribs, but before we left the alley behind the old Hyatt, she pinned him to the hotel's wall and demanded one last, really good, really nasty kiss. Once they left the alley, there would be guards, and there would be people, and they would have to behave themselves.

Will and Aisha gave them privacy, making their way to the alley entry. I looked back; he was groping her boob and she had her hand on his crotch.

I don't think Jax will be able to walk for a few minutes.

Aisha laughed when Will repeated it. "We definitely need to do this more often. I can't imagine the Queen giving the King a hand job in an alley, but I can believe Aubrey giving him a good squeeze."

"I don't think she's going to finish him off with us standing here."

"No, but she'll make him wish she would."

"Projection, much?"

"Sweetie, the difference between Aubrey and me is that if we were the ones at the back of the alley, I just might finish you."

You can come back later.

Leave me at home, though. I've seen your junk enough for a while.

"Enzo, I have a feeling that sooner or later, you're going to get us arrested."

"Life goals." She reached for his hand to tug him along because Aubrey and Jax were done pawing at each other. "Make sure Jay knows how to get the bail money."

*

They weren't done with the groping and bouncing things. Jax and Aubrey went upstairs, and I was pretty sure she intended to finish what she started in the alley, and since Jay wasn't in the apartment, Aisha pushed Will down the hall and told him she wanted a do-over for last night. He didn't seem to have enough fun, and she owed him.

He was not going to refuse that.

I went into Drew's apartment, hoping that there was someone home who wasn't naked, wasn't groping or touching themselves, and someone who wouldn't mind lending me the use of his thumbs to open a can. I'd gotten bites of Will's eggs at breakfast, and a few nibbles on some bacon, but I was hungry, and a snack wasn't going to cut it.

The apartment was quiet, but Drew's giant feet were on the arm of the sofa. He was stretched out, reading, and thankfully he had pants on.

I would like a whim catered to.

He peered over the top of his tablet. "Back already?"

It's been a week. And I'm hungry.

"Hungry or peckish?"

Hungry. Did you miss me?

"Wick, I saw you, like, half an hour ago." He set the tablet aside and got up. "But sure, I missed you. Was it fun?"

Aubrey got super drunk and called some woman a bitch last night. And she threatened to turn her hair into a noose.

"No way. Seriously?"

Before that, Aisha yelled at a lady and said she was going to tie her tits into a knot. She wasn't even drunk.

"Damn, I wish I'd been there." He spooned the food out onto a plate and set it on the floor. "Sounds fun. And funny."

They want to do it again, so I think everyone had fun. And I don't think they were done having fun, either, because as soon as we got home, everyone went to bed, but I don't think anyone is sleeping.

"Good."

Where's Oz?

"She went to Sophia's to work on a paper. I should be studying, too." He went back to the living room while I finished eating, but he didn't pick his tablet back up. "When you're done, I'll take you out to get a new bow tie for your collar. Something classy for Mrs. B's birthday."

Study.

"All right. This afternoon, then. I'll read for a couple more hours, and then we can go."

I'll take a nap.

"What'd they do for her birthday?"

Drank a lot. I'm gonna go nap in Oz's room because if I don't you're gonna keep talking and then you'll fail, and everyone will blame me.

"Fine. Use me for my thumbs and just leave me."

Yep.

"Come back in an hour or two. I'll wait for you."

Wait.

I used the litterbox before I left and made sure he'd know it.

Greetings from twenty-six-sixteen. Don't say I never bring you anything.

*

We went to see Mr. Kovlov for my new collar; not because it was the only place to get a tie worthy of the Queen's 50th birthday, but because Jay tried one of his suits on and the legs were several inches too short, and the jacket was tight in the shoulders. Drew let me ride in his sweatshirt and Zed came along so that they could get matching shirts and ties.

That's kind of girly. Matching?

"When did you get so sexist? Besides, Mrs. B will love it," Drew said.

What about Oz? What's she gonna wear?

"Clothes," he grunted.

No need to get snippy.

Will and Aisha took me to the restaurant; I had a beautiful new black collar with a matching bow tie that tickled my chin and made me twitch my whiskers a lot. It was too big, but it was sparkly and meant for Aubrey, not me. I told Will I could suck it up for the night, but he thought I would only need to wear it long enough to make her smile. Once dinner was underway, if it still made me twitch, he promised to take it off.

Guards were already in place at the entry to Kaluto's, and two lingered by the dining room inside. There were four other customers in the main dining room; they glanced up but didn't seem any kind of impressed, which told me they were either tourists and didn't know who Will was, or they were locals who saw him often. The bartender looked up, laughed, and gave Will a wave when we went inside.

"What did you do?" Aisha asked him in a loud whisper.

"You'll see."

Jax and Aubrey were already there, waiting in the dining room. We walked in mid-kiss, and even though they knew we were there, they didn't stop.

"You know, I can have one of the guards drag a hose in here to separate you two," Will said.

I'll pee on them if that will help.

"We will not pee on the Queen tonight." Will pulled a chair out and set me on it. "Well, we won't. There's no telling what Jax might do."

Jax demonstrated what he might do with his middle finger, just as the bartender came in with three glasses of scotch and a margarita so big I could have bathed in it.

"You're an ass, William," Aubrey said.

"Note that she didn't refuse it," he said.

She might have thrown it at him, but then Finn and Jo arrived, and if she missed she might have hit them.

Ten minutes later, the kids showed up. They came into the dining room in a line; Drew and Zed and Jay wore black suits with black ties, and Oz was in black slacks and a black shirt. As soon as they walked in Aubrey popped up and squealed about how adorable they were, and she had to hug and kiss each of them. By the time she was done, Eli was there, and everyone was talking too loud for me to be heard.

After dinner, Finn quietly asked Will and Jax to join him in the bar. The bartender laid a cloth on the bar so that I didn't have to sit on Will's shoulder, and they each pulled up a stool because Finn said he needed to talk to Will and didn't want people to overhear.

"You're breaking up with me, aren't you?" Will joked as he sat.

"Worse." Finn scooted as close to Will as he could get without jamming his knee into his crotch. "I was in the other lab early this morning, before sunrise. It was still dark when I left, and I thought the Square was empty—"

"Cut to the chase, Dad."

Finn had just started through, with only part of his leg in the portal, when a woman lunged to grab him. He tumbled forward with her arms wrapped around him and pulled her into this When. "By the time I understood what had happened, she was running away. I barely got a glimpse of her."

Will said a few things from the bad word list under his breath.

"Hair color?" Jax asked. "Clothing? Anything, Finn. She's out of her element here, we should be able to find her."

Finn hadn't seen much more than the back of her legs as he rolled over to get up. "Maybe about Oz's height, wearing dark colored pants and brown shoes. Waist length, dark jacket. That's it."

Will pressed fingers to his forehead, trying to hold the anger in.

"Dash, I had no idea what to do or who to call. I don't know who here has been told about the portals, and you weren't back yet."

"Dad, you could have turned around and gotten me. I was right there in your apartment. I could have come home and timed it to be there on the Square when you fell through."

"No, you were there a couple weeks ago, Dash. You took them backward, not in a static line."

Will exhaled hard, but Finn was right. He hadn't lined up the dates so that none of the things he and Drew left out would spoil.

"You could still go wait for her," Jax said.

"Changes leave ripples," Will said. "Not knowing what she's done since getting here, nor whom she might have interacted with, I'd be reluctant to interfere now."

Look for the tattoo. It's probably one of those ladies.

"Did you get a good look at the tattoo?" he asked me.

"The cult?" Finn asked. "The only sect I know of that stayed in San Francisco marks themselves with a small lotus flower, but they don't consider them to be members of the main Cult of the Emperor."

"What else do you know about them?"

"They're a tiny group, fewer than twenty people. All related, I think. I'd heard gossip that they've recently taken to wandering the city looking for the Emperor, but I dismissed it as just that. Gossip."

"They think I'm immortal," he explained to Jax.

Finn knew little else about them. He'd never bothered to examine their activities too closely because there was no chance they would find Will and it seemed harmless enough. The group never seemed to grow, always a small number of people searching the city, and they weren't intrusive or violent. They'd simply followed an old belief about a man who'd given his life to save a world he would never see, and then along the way decided he'd somehow survived, either by portal hopping or good luck.

"Why do they want my DNA?" Will asked. "Aisha read about a sect that was intent on spawning my progeny, but there seemed to be no reason behind it."

"Damned if I know. These women don't seem to be organized. I'd be surprised if it's the same group."

Jax was less concerned than either of them. "We'll get the guard on it, but she can't survive here very long. Sooner or later she's going to get very ill and wind up in an emergency room, or she's going to come begging Finn to help her get home."

"She got here without asking," Will said. "If she returns the same way? She'll know who I am."

"People know who you are there," Jax said.

"People who won't talk."

"Not intentionally, but people talk, Will. They don't want you dead, they just want your offspring. Relax. Enjoy the rest of the night, and we'll talk to Myers and Soto in the morning."

"I know who Myers is," Finn said. "Who's the other one?"

"T'Neeka Soto, the guard's second in command," Will said. "In charge of those who guard family and the few who know about the portals."

Jax wanted to get back to the others and suggested they not mention the woman. He wanted Aubrey to enjoy her birthday, even if it was the second one in a week.

Will picked me up and set me on his shoulder. "Dad, it's time to think about closing the portal on the Square and opening one in the lab itself. People here will begin to notice."

Finn said he would think about it, but I don't think he meant it. He agreed because he wanted to keep Will from being madder than he already was, and to push his focus away from the idea that a woman was running around out there who wanted his DNA and who knows what she would do to get it.

*

Half an hour after we got home, the kids scattered and left the parents sitting in the living room to have one more drink.

They claimed they were going downstairs to study, which usually meant snacks and a video, with a lot of talking and not much reading. I was torn; I wanted to be where the snacks were, but if they were really studying it was going to be boring.

It was boring upstairs, too, but at least there was a fire and the hearth to curl up on. They were talking about the new apartment upstairs; Will grumbled about needing to go furniture shopping and Aisha grumbled about the actual move, but only because it meant packing up her things again so soon, so I drifted off and let them whine without my input.

They didn't really mean it. The apartment was twice as big and a lot brighter than Will's place. He'd made sure that their bedroom overlooked Union Square and it had a nice, wide, comfortable window seat, one I could stretch out on, and they could sit together and not fall off. Aisha thought the kitchen was a waste because it was so big and beautiful and she couldn't cook to save her life, but Will could. And Jay's room was both huge and far enough from theirs to make him happy.

He was looking forward to moving upstairs more than anyone else, because Will had asked the designer for a media wall, which meant a massive inset monitor, and there would be enough seating for him to invite friends over for movies and games. The office Will and Aisha planned on sharing was at the back of the apartment, away from any noise Jay and his friends might make.

There were two extra bedrooms; Jay had hinted that he could make use of one of them, but they told him he had more space than he needed in his bedroom and one of those rooms needed to become a guest room. Neither of them mentioned what they hoped the remaining one would become, though they'd already decided where they would put a crib and a chair for Aisha to sit in when she nursed, and the colors they wanted to paint the room.

There was even a space for me, a nook near the living room where Will planned on putting a me-sized bed, and the bathroom right across the hall was my own, though he said I needed to share it with guests, which was fine. For once my litter box wasn't wedged into a corner but had a room of its own inside the bathroom, with a linen closet on top of it. It was tall and spacious and had a self-cleaning litter box, which meant I never had to bug someone about scooping.

They could whine all they wanted but moving into that apartment was going to be awesome.

By the time I woke up, they had moved to the dining room table. I got up and stretched because they were close to the food, and if someone noticed me there was a chance I'd get a snack. I jumped up onto the empty chair at the foot of the table, ready to use my charms to convince Will to feed me, but realized I'd better not even open my mouth.

Aisha was upset, and Will sat back in his chair, arms folded across his chest. Aubrey looked uncomfortable, and Jax had his king-face on, so it was hard to tell what he was feeling.

"I have never had guards," Will said. "I don't need guards. I am perfectly capable of defending myself."

"Until we find this woman it might not be the worst idea," Jax said.

Thinly, choking on tears she refused to give in to, Aisha said, "Bend on this, Will."

"Find me the guards who can fight better than I can, and I'll consider it," he said to Jax. "Otherwise, it's a pointless waste of manpower."

The chances of there being someone within the royal guard who could beat Will were slim, and Jax knew it. "You're never armed, and they are," he said. "Consider them backup."

"Assign a guard to me, and my life becomes that much more complicated. It's one more person I have to keep track of, and dammit, Jax, you know as well as I do that I'd wind up babysitting the damned guard, not the other way around."

"Your safety trumps your ego," Aisha said.

Will sighed and leaned forward, his hands on the table. "It's not ego."

Aubrey reached out and touched the back of his hand. "You're going to accept a guard, William." Her fingers lingered, inviting him to listen to the thought she most wanted him to hear. "Sometimes you don't get a say. Sometimes Jax gets the final word."

The final word was that he was getting a guard. "We'll talk to Soto in the morning. She'll get you the least obtrusive and most skilled guards."

Oh, he pulled rank. How pissed are you?

He must have been a least a little because he ignored me. He accepted that he wasn't getting his way, and got up, taking Aisha's hand as they left the room.

When they were down the stairs, Jax asked, "What did you tell him?"

"I reminded him that the guards do anything he tells them to and giving in on this is for Aisha's peace of mind, not his."

"So, he gets a guard who basically does nothing, because that's what Will's going to order."

"Sweetheart, he's right. He can defend himself better than anyone. This is to make Aisha feel better. She's worried, and he needs to learn to not be so stubborn sometimes."

"Yeah, well, we'll take care of it tomorrow. There's not a snowball's chance in hell that woman is getting into the building tonight."

"Good." She got up and held her hand out to him. "It's still my birthday, and I would like it very much if my King would join me in the bathtub to soak for a while, and then see what comes up."

I knew what would come up.

I went downstairs instead. Oz and Drew might be studying, but there would still be food there, and he could understand me.

*

They weren't studying.

Oz and Drew weren't even there.

I crawled in through the cat flap, expecting them to all be at Drew's table, but the only people in the apartment were Zed and Sophia, and they were on the sofa with their lips mashed together in a horribly uncomfortable looking smooch. I sat on the floor in front of them—*come on, Zed, come up for air*—until he noticed me, hoping he would take the hint and feed me.

"Drew's outside," he said. Instead of getting up to find food for me, he picked up his phone and tapped at it. "Go wait by the desk guard. Drew will come get you in a minute, all right?"

Fine.

Check the front of her bra, it might unhook there.

I went down the short staircase and hopped up on the desk to wait, which startled the guard and made him a little bit uncomfortable. He wanted to pet me—he started to reach out but wasn't sure I would allow it—so I stuck my head under his hand to give him a little thrill and let him stroke my fur until Drew came inside.

"Zed said you were lonely," Drew said as he picked me up. "No one amusing you tonight?"

Jax and Aubrey are taking a bath. Will and Aisha are having an argument. No one else will feed me.

"We're having scones at the bakery. You can have a bite."

The girl inside will give you a slice of bacon for me.

He didn't even argue; he left me with Oz and went into the bakery, and when he came out he had a freshly cooked slice wrapped in a napkin to soak up the grease. "You're well known, Wick. She didn't even charge me for it because it was for you."

Did you thank her?

"Of course, I thanked her." He crumbled it for me. "I have *some* sense of manners."

"Aw, you didn't pound your fist on the counter and yell, 'bitch, you better have bacon for Wick'?"

"Wanted to," he snorted.

Where's Jay?

Drew gestured to the skating rink. "Out there trying to not fall down."

"Come on," Oz said, "he really just wanted to have an excuse to hold Zara's hand."

He stretched up to see. "Nah, they're just skating. Her dad is here somewhere, watching. Jay doesn't want to piss him off."

"You know, I get why he's protective, but damn, she's eighteen. He should trust her enough to deal with teenage boys on her own."

"He *was* a teenaged boy, Oz. He knows what's swirling around in Jay's mind, like, *all* the time."

"And I *am* a teenaged girl, Drew. She's thinking about the same things he is, and she's old enough to decide if she wants to act on those thoughts."

"Think he's clued into the fact that she's hanging around with someone who has her own apartment and is probably willing to let Zara and Jay use it?"

Oz snorted. "I wouldn't be surprised if he shows up randomly and bangs on the door to make sure nothing is going on."

Sophia has a safe room. Jay can hide in there.

"Seriously, Wick? She has a damned safe room?"

Behind the bookcase. Jay could jump in there, and Zara's dad would never know. You should tell him that.

"Should we help corrupt them?" Drew asked.

"Why the hell not? You're helping my little brother get laid even as we speak. He's doing unspeakable things to Sophia while we're sitting out here freezing our asses off, watching poor Jay inch his way around the ice with no hope of getting so much as a kiss."

"Eh. Tonight, I don't care. We shouldn't be the only ones not getting any. Your parents are going at it. Will and Aisha are probably banging out makeup sex right now, and Zed is doing God knows what in my living room."

"We *know* what he's doing," she said. "And stop feeling sorry for yourself. I'll make it up to you later."

"If we ever get my apartment back. It's freaking cold out here. Why did we agree to this?"

"Because," she said, scooting closer to him, "if they go to her place, he'll wind up spending the night, and then the shit will hit the fan. This way, they get a couple hours together, she goes home, and our parents are spared having his sex life shoved in their faces."

"He could always tell them he's working."

"And that would be the one night someone from Alcatraz calls looking for Zed to fill a shift or pick up a body. Come on, he doesn't ask you every day."

"I'm still surprised you're in favor of this."

"He loves her, Drew. This isn't Zed using some poor girl to get off with. My gut says they'll be together a long time."

Poor Jay didn't even get a kiss.

Drew looked up; Jay was walking toward us. Zara left with her dad, and he didn't even try to kiss her first.

"You are one patient son of a bitch," Drew said when he sat down.

"Yeah, well, from what I hear, so were you."

"Fair enough. So have you two worked out what it is you're doing? Officially dating or not?"

He shrugged. "I dunno. I'm still dragging my ass on how much I should tell her."

"What's to tell?" Oz asked.

"Come on. It's big. If I don't tell her early enough, when it comes out later it might blow up in my face. And don't tell me it won't come out. Shit like that always comes out."

"You have no surgical scars," Oz pointed out. "You don't have to take hormones. I've never seen you naked, but I'm guessing there's not a single thing about your body that would even suggest you transitioned."

"The detachable balls might be a hint," he said dryly. "And if Zed tells her I actually *sat* on them?"

The memory of that made Drew snort. "None of us are going to tell her, Jay. Don't get in your own way."

"Not gonna use her, either. It's not as big a deal as you think. I'm not ready to go even half as far as you guys and Zed have. I'm just not."

Then don't tell him about the safe room.

"That's fine," Oz said. "I didn't mean to suggest you grab her and go for it. I suppose it sounded like it."

"I know." He started to get up, mumbling about reading for a while before going to bed.

"Yeah, you might want to hang out here for a bit," Drew said. "According to Wick, Will and your mom were having an argument, which means right about now they're, you know, apologizing."

He got up anyway. "So, like nearly every other night, then. I have headphones and music. If they get too loud, I'll yell at them."

"Sure."

"Yep. When they get going, and it's too much, I stand in the hall and bellow 'finish her!' That usually does the trick."

"Oh, god, I wish that was true," Oz said as he walked away. "Come on, it's cold, I'm shivering. I want to go inside."

"And then what? Sit in the hallway while your brother screws half the night away in my apartment?"

She told him they could go upstairs and cuddle on the couch, and text Zed to let him know where they were. But even sitting in the hall would be better than freezing half to death.

I thought they should sit on the stairs and stare at the guard until he cried or called for backup, but they didn't think that was as funny as I did.

No one ever does.

*

Instead of going upstairs with them, I went into Will's apartment. It was late enough that with Jay going into his room, it would be quiet, and I could sleep on the sofa. There was also a good chance that he would head right for the kitchen to get a snack, and he was getting pretty good about feeding me because he felt guilty eating without sharing.

Will wasn't in bed, though. He was on the sofa with his head leaned back, fingers pressed to the bridge of his nose, and he had a drink in his other hand. Jay stood a few feet inside, and when I popped through the cat flap Will was telling him that nothing was wrong.

"We're not fighting. I have a headache, and your mother is taking a bath."

Jay didn't buy it, but he wasn't going to argue with Will. He headed for his bedroom and closed the door quietly, and I jumped onto the hearth.

"Don't tell them when Aisha and I argue," he said without looking at me. "It's none of their business, and Jay doesn't need to worry."

I didn't tell them what it was about.

"And you won't, understand?"

You're kinda grouchy for a guy who's probably getting make-up sex in a little while.

"I'm not—" His hand fell away from his face and he looked up. "Perhaps."

You're gonna get a guard, right?

"I apparently have no choice. And yet, I feel as if I'm more in danger with one than without."

Pretend he's not there. That's what the kids do.

"The kids don't have to worry about their guards' safety, Wick. I'll always have it in the back of my head that if something happens, that's one more person I need to protect."

That's backward. It's also bullshit.

That caught his attention. "Since when do you swear?"

When you're being a dillhole. You have people around you all the time, and you don't have any problem with keeping an eye on them and protecting them. If you can protect me and Aisha and the kids at the same time, a guard isn't a problem.

"Knowing where he is at all times—"

You're making trouble where there doesn't need to be, Will. You have a stalker. Make Aisha feel better and shut up about the guard.

"You're a mouthy little shit tonight."

If you want to shut me up, feed me.

"You ate tonight, Wick. More than you should have." Jay came back out, heading for the kitchen and Will said, "Whatever Wick tries to tell you, he's had enough to eat tonight."

He set the drink on the end table and went to the back of the apartment. I waited until the bedroom door closed and went into the kitchen because no matter what Will told him, if I stared at Jay just right, he would give me something.

*

T'Neeka Soto was shorter than Jay, had muscles like Oz, and refused to take any of the Emperor's attitude. She listened to

Jax's explanation and Aisha's insistence that Will have a guard, and before he could open his mouth, she jabbed her pointy finger in his direction and told him to stop talking.

"You'll have a guard team. Until we find this woman, alive or dead or some inexplicable state in between, you'll have four."

"I don't—"

"Emperor, you've made the point yourself that she's put herself into a situation she can't survive. Sooner or later she'll either surface trying to contact you, or an emergency tech will have picked up her body."

"If you find her alive?" Aisha asked. "What happens then?"

"We can't send her back," Jax said. "Will's pretty clear on not wanting the masses at home to know who he is here."

"If she stays here, she dies," Will said. "I think my birth-home anonymity is over with. Find her and I'll take her back."

"And then what?"

He shrugged. "I come home, and then never return to that When. They can continue to wait for my supposedly immortal self to surface."

But your grandparents moved there.

"I know, Wick. Finn will make sure they're able to visit. Or Eli. He can bring them through."

"You could all just stop using those damned portals," T'Neeka said. "It's a goddamned nightmare for Oz's guards and the day will come when someone mentions the existence of them to the wrong person."

"Is she abusing use of the portals?" Jax asked.

Before T'Neeka could look it up, Will said, "She and Andrew sometimes use one to get away for a few hours, mostly on nights she can't sleep. They aren't going off to spy on you nor to engage with other people. They simply find a quiet spot to sit and watch the ferries come and go, without being bothered by people who would recognize them. Once she's relaxed, they come home."

"You're missing my point," T'Neeka said. "Oz will do whatever the hell she wants. But the portals will eventually become a problem. Your guards, her guards, Andrew's guards. Each shift head knows about them and where each portal is located. It was a manageable secret when you were a boy, your Majesty, but as time goes on, the number of guards who know increases significantly. And as they age? Grumpy old people talk."

"Duly noted," Jax said.

Half an hour later, it was just Will and T'Neeka in the room. He repeated his objection but agreed to a guard for no reason other than it would pacify Aisha. Whoever she assigned needed to be aware that guarding him would be more frustrating than guarding the kids and they needed to be able to cover the city on foot, quickly. He walked and ran everywhere, and he wasn't slowing down for someone unprepared to match his stride.

"Get your panties out of a wad, Emperor. You'll have two guards, one day, one night." She handed him a computer tablet. "These are the currently available guards. Pick four. We both know that you have more control over these kids than I do. They'll provide protection however you ask them to."

He didn't look at the list. "Sav Ng and Eva Young for the first shift. Blue Remington and Tash Ventura for the second."

"You want four female guards."

"I want guards who will do more than follow me around. I want guards who have the potential to draw this woman out. If she notices them, she may assume they have an objective similar to hers, and she may approach them."

"It's a stretch, but I'll buy it."

"There's also Wick to consider."

She glanced at me. "Why Wick?"

"They'll consider him if there's a physical altercation. I have no problem defending myself, T'Neeka. I know it, you know it, and they know it. These women have no ego where fighting is concerned. They'll let me handle my own battle unless it's clear I can't, and they'll protect Wick."

"Then it's true. You actually need him as more than a pet."

Will nodded. "He's something this woman doesn't have. Without an anchor, she will die."

"Damnedest thing I've ever heard. All right, I'll pull them from their current assignments, but you get to explain to your wife why you selected the four most attractive people from the guard pool. I'm sure as hell not doing it."

*

Will sat on the planter that ran the length of the church across the street from Aisha's school and waited for her to come out of the building. She wasn't expecting him, but he worried that she was still upset and wanted to smooth it over before Jay got home. I sat next to him because the planter was in the sun and it was giving off more warms than his shoulder.

The downside was that when he stood up, my only real view was of his ass. I had to move to be sure that if he sat back down, I wasn't going to become a fluffy little splotch on the landscape.

He sent her a text as soon as he spotted her. She looked annoyed at first—like who was bugging her this late in the day when all she wanted was to leave the hormonal monsters behind and get home—but she softened when she saw who it was from.

I don't think she's mad anymore.

"I hope not."

You didn't get make up sex last night, did you?

"I did not."

This morning?

"No."

She's stubborn, isn't she?

"Indeed."

So are you. The next ninety years are gonna be fifty-seven kinds of fun.

"And you'll be poking the bear the entire time, won't you?"

I didn't get a chance to answer. Aisha crossed the street, and before he could say anything, she grabbed the front of his shirt and pulled him in for a kiss. It was a good one, too; he grabbed her face and held on, ignoring the kids across the street who were cheering her on.

"I'm sorry," he said when she finally let him breathe. "It was a stupid thing to dig my heels in over. I shouldn't have argued over something that gives you a little peace."

This is where you tell her your guards are ladies.

"I don't care if I'm being unreasonable, Will. I—"

"I know."

Don't forget to say that they're super-hot, too.

"What's Wick want?"

"He seems to think the gender of my guards matters."

"Ah." She picked me and kissed the top of my head before setting me on Will's shoulder. "I don't care. As long as they're armed and willing to take down little Hillary Homewrecker, it doesn't matter."

Tell her they're hot.

He held her hand, and they started walking, but he was ignoring me. I reached over with a paw to touch Aisha's face to get her attention.

He's not telling you they're hot.

"What's up, Wick?" she asked.

Tell her. If you don't, I'll tell Drew to tell her.

With a heavy sigh, Will said, "Apparently they're attractive, and he thinks that also merits mention."

"*Apparently* they're attractive," she repeated. "Just apparently?"

"I have no interest in whether or not my guards are aesthetically pleasing."

"Uh huh. And did you choose these women yourself or was it a random assignment?"

"Does it matter?"

She laughed and leaned into him. "I can't complain, Bilbo. I wanted guards on you, I don't get to bitch if you decided you want to be followed around by pretty women."

"I won't see them, really, unless something does go wrong."

"You don't need to make excuses. I don't care where your horny ideas generate as long as you bring them home."

He stopped. "I think you'd care if one of those ideas actually involved one of my guards. I'm not...bringing that home."

"Just one?" She raised an eyebrow. "Sure I wouldn't enjoy that?"

I wish I could laugh because right now you look like you want to wet yourself.

"Have you? Ever?"

She tugged his arm to get him moving again. "You said you didn't want to talk about my past."

"Yes, but…"

You liked that idea a little too much, didn't you? Is William sporting a semi?

"What the hell, Wick? How do you even know what a semi is?"

I would have answered him, but Aisha was laughing too hard, and I didn't want to.

*

Because they weren't sure they had argued enough, they went furniture shopping. Will pointed out that they had an entire apartment to fill and they needed to just get it over with, because the things in his apartment belonged to the state, and Eli would need it anyway.

Besides, it was all old and he thought it would look horrible upstairs.

"I have furniture in storage," she pointed out.

"Furniture purchased for you by your ex-husband, without your input, before you'd even left Las Vegas."

Several hours later, after they'd looked at sofas and chairs and tables and beds, and not fought over anything—mostly because he didn't care what she picked out as long as she picked something—Will declared it was food o'clock and told her to text Jay. They could meet at the diner with the server who always had meaty bites for me, and then decide if they wanted to keep shopping.

He dropped onto a showroom sofa to wait while she texted him, which was a mistake because he really liked it and she scowled when she saw the price tag.

"That's a big sofa, Will."

"It's a big living room."

"It's red."

"It's comfortable." He patted the cushion and told her to try it. "Snuggling would be quite nice on this. It's long and wide."

"Hey, appealing to my libido is not fair." She sat there for a minute and then sighed, "Dammit."

"Nothing wrong with red."

"It's expensive, Will. Really expensive."

"And?"

"If we get this, we'll wind up getting the matching chairs. And then we'll have to decorate around it. That's a hell of a lot of money."

"We have a hell of a lot of money. Spend some. Get great furniture that will last until we're so old that Jay has to replace it all."

She laughed. "That's mean." She glanced at her phone and added, "And he's not joining us for dinner. He and Zed are studying, and Aubrey fed him already."

"All right." He stood and then reached down to help her up. "Let's buy this and the chairs that match, and the coffee table, too. And then let's go somewhere we can talk."

"About?"

"Your social life," he said. "I think I finally want to know."

*

We didn't go to the diner. I sucked up the disappointment of no special meaty things so that they could go to Fuzzy's and sit in a private booth, way too close to each other, and talk. I decided to be mature about it and not complain because sometimes the dead delicious things have to wait.

And sometimes, when a cat is mature about it, a person makes sure they have even better dead delicious things.

Will ordered a small steak for me and promised he would cut it into tiny bites, which proved that sucking it up just plain works. He also ordered the tea that Drew liked for both of them, and when she asked if he was trying to get her drunk, he sucked down half and said, "I think I might want to have a buzz for this."

"I'm not sure exactly what you want to know. The numbers? The relationships?"

He nodded.

"And why now?"

He had to think about it. "Because I no longer worry about what I bring to the table, so to speak. And the longer we're together, the more curious I am about your curiosities."

"Ah, you want to know about women."

"You did hint that you'd been in at least one relationship with another woman."

"Not a relationship, Bilbo. Just...a fling, I suppose. One and done. I met someone I liked, and it felt like there was a connection. She was clear on where she wanted things to go. So I gave it a try."

"I take it the connection wasn't there?"

"Emotionally? We clicked. I cared, a lot. But I learned that there are some things I don't enjoy as much as others, and it makes me appreciate that those are things you obviously love doing. I mean, I didn't hate it, but it did nothing for me."

He had no idea what she was talking about.

"Sweetheart. It's just that when I'm on the giving end, I damn well want a dick in my mouth."

"Oh."

"And the implied threesome? No, I never have. And I sure as hell never will now. I'm not sharing you, mister."

"I can barely keep up with you. What the hell would I do with someone else in bed?"

She leaned into him. "Good boy. You didn't assume the imaginary third person was female."

Yes, he did.

"All right," she went on, "what else did you want to know? You met Scotty, you know the story behind that. I was not scarred by my first love. I loved him, we parted as friends, and the memories are all good."

"When you moved to Vegas?"

It was her turn to drain half her drink. "I kind of hated myself for a while, Will. I was hurt and angry, and yes, I made some monumental mistakes with men in those first few years. I chose poorly, I let myself get used, and I am not proud of how many there were."

"But you met James along the way."

"There was another stellar choice. I knew he preferred men, he never lied about that. I went into that relationship with my eyes open, but it *was* a relationship and not some itch I wanted to scratch." When he didn't say anything, she went on. "Between leaving here and marrying him, I think there were fifteen different men. But I was faithful to James, even if he wasn't. I prefer monogamy."

"I don't mean to imply judgment, Enzo," Will said, softly. "Nor that you should feel there was anything improper about your love life. You're outgoing and affectionate. You like sex. I can't imagine you not acting on that."

"Oh, it was improper. I may have broken the definition of improper. But it *did* teach me what I wanted and sleeping around wasn't it."

"And after James?"

"Well, there was that fling *with* James. But it was a couple of years before I even considered dating again. And when I did, I was pickier, and I made sure I had feelings that went beyond being horny. They were nice guys, Will. A lot of casual dating, but always monogamous. The longest relationship lasted about six months, but it never got as serious as things did the moment I walked into your birthday party."

"My happiest birthday ever."

"Every man I dated had an impossible standard to meet, sweetheart. If you need the numbers, over twenty-three years, it's somewhere around forty-five, maybe fifty. I've loved only three men, ever, and you've met the other two."

"I'm sorry to be one of the two who hurt you."

"I'm not. You said it yourself. Without that pain, there would be no Jay."

"And I wouldn't trade him for anything."

"You're a little disappointed that there was no real relationship with a woman to tell you about, aren't you?"

"My imagination may have taken a slight hit."

"I'll make something up later. Remind me tonight. I'll tell you all about my fling with Troy and his girlfriend, Martha. By the time I'm done, you'll know exactly what you'd do with two women at once."

He blinked rapidly, but he refused to let the image settle in his head. "I don't need to know. I only need to know one thing."

"Anything."

"Were you happy? After the dust settled with James, were you happy?"

"Bilbo." It came out like breath. She touched a finger to his chin to make sure he was looking at her, and said, "I was happy. If my life had gone on just like it was, I'd think it couldn't get much better. But now? So much happier."

"Good."

"And I don't need to ask you. I saw so much of your life unfold on the news. The stories that popped up now and then with the kids hanging off you? Pure joy."

"I was fortunate," he said. "Jax and Aubrey made sure I had family. I love those kids like—"

"Your own, I know."

"The most difficult part was pulling away from them when they reached the age where I could no longer touch them. But still, I knew I would die happy. I was all right with that."

Aisha's eyes filled, and it caught her by surprise. "Don't be all right with it anymore."

"I have too much to look forward to. I will fight for that, Enzo. No matter what the woman who tumbled through the portal with Finn wants, know that. I will fight for every moment we're owed."

That earned him a kiss that went on even though the food had arrived. The server chuckled under his breath and set the plates down, making sure I could reach mine—half the steak was already cut up—and he backed away quietly.

19

A few days after Will caved and agreed to the guards, and finally let Aisha tell him about life between their youth and now, Will scooped me up so that we could meet her at the bakery for bacon and coffee.

I had bacon. They had coffee.

She was showing Will the exam she'd written—intended to do maximum damage to the egos and souls of thirty pre-calculus students—when Drew came across the Square by himself. He waved when he spotted us, and I think he intended to just go home, but Will called him over and told him to sit. Oz had gone to Sophia's to help her study for a test on Pacifica's government; he wasn't needed and Oz thought he might be a distraction, so she encouraged him to go home and find something fun to do.

"They kicked Zed out, too, so it wasn't personal," he snorted. "He went back to school to give Jay and Zara a ride home."

"Why doesn't he just take my car?" Will asked Aisha. "He has blanket permission to use it."

The garage was a mile in the wrong direction, and he wouldn't be able to pick Zara up nor take her home. She lived in the part of the city that restricted use of cars and trucks, and if he couldn't pick her up, he didn't see the point. Half of what peeled him out of bed every morning was the idea of walking to her apartment and then catching public transit to school together.

"I can't blame him for that," Will said. "I used to run across the city in order to ride a bus with a beautiful co-ed. How angry will James be if we get Jay an air bike? He can legally operate a bike downtown."

"He opposed getting Jay a car," she reminded him.

"This would be considerably less expensive. And not his financial undertaking."

"Not for Christmas, Will. We've already paid for his gift."

"Zed has been talking about selling his and getting a new one," Drew said. "Front Zed money toward the new bike and then let Jay buy his old one. Dad can't argue that can he?"

Aisha snickered, "With my luck, I'd give Zed the money and then Jay wouldn't want the bike."

"Tell Zed ahead of time what you're doing. If Jay doesn't want the bike, Zed won't take your money."

"I'm not in favor of deceptions," Will said, even though the idea appealed to his immature impulse to win the parenting game. "If Zed is selling his bike, I have no problem buying it outright and giving it to Jay."

If you buy it for yourself, James can't say anything if you let Jay use it every single day.

"And the day he turns eighteen, sell it to him for a buck," Aisha said. "Why the hell not, Will? He really doesn't want a car, but I know he'd use the bike."

"You're comfortable with doing an end run around James?"

"It's not an end run if we buy it for us and just let Jay use it ninety percent of the time. We'd be getting a family toy. I wouldn't mind taking a few rides with you, you know."

Will wiggled his eyebrows, which made Drew snort and Aisha sigh. She was spared their immaturity after that; a little boy was playing nearby, squealing with delight over the toy robot he was commanding. She pointed him out because he was adorable and they were bubbling with parental hopes and expectations, but Drew was most taken in by the boy's toy.

It was a metallic pink and purple robot designed to look like a teddy bear. He was operating it with a remote, making it walk in circles around his mother's legs, occasionally bumping into her. It was cute, but I didn't understand Drew's fascination, not until the boy tossed a handful of small blocks on the ground and set the bear to gliding to each one, where it bent over and picked them up, then stacked them in a neat pile.

When the last block was in place, robo-bear kicked it over, scattered them, and started over again.

Drew was so focused on watching the bear that he didn't notice that Will and Aisha had stopped talking and were watching him. She leaned close to Will and whispered, "What is so riveting about a toy bear?"

"Don't distract him," Will whispered in return. "His brain has engaged."

We sat in silence for half an hour, until the boy's mother made him pick up all his toys and turn the robot off. Drew's gazed was fixed on the spot where the little boy had been playing, barely blinking, eyes darting back and forth as he watched the pictures inside his own head.

When he finally took a loud breath and his eyes closed for just a bit longer than a blink, Will tapped his finger on the table and said, "Before the thought retreats, tell me. What did you just see?"

"Elysium," Drew said. "How to expedite using the array despite the cooling issues. If we could come up with a human-sized version of that bear, one with humanoid features, that has flexibility and dexterity..."

Aisha glanced at Will and said, "That pretty much exists—"

He shook his head very slightly. He knew what she was thinking about, the 'bots that had been created for personal gratification, but he didn't want Drew distracted by the implications of a glorified sex toy. "Tell me what you mean," he said to Drew.

Drew's brain finally settled on the image he'd had spinning inside his head. The major issue with keeping Elysium's computers cool enough to function was partially owed to room temperature. The existing systems would have worked if the rooms in which they were stored were held at near-arctic temperatures. The protective gear people needed to wear to survive those low temperatures was clunky and uncomfortable and relegated them to shifts too short to be practical. It also robbed them of the dexterity necessary for the delicate tasks necessary to work with tiny parts.

Will pointed out that people had been working in the Arctic for centuries; it was not an insurmountable task.

"But they can't stay outside long. With all the protective layers and heated clothing, they're still limited to working for a short time. They also don't deal with the super delicate tasks of maintaining the type of machinery and computers that Elysium needs."

"What's the issue of rotating through short shifts?" Aisha asked.

"It wears a person down," Drew said. "And tasks that require multiple uninterrupted hours are impossible. That's why all the initial equipment tests were done in landside facilities kept at temperatures humans wearing cold gear can withstand for eight hours at a time. And that's also why so many systems went up in flames. It wasn't just the holographic computers they were setting on fire, it was the operating systems for all of Elysium."

"You theorized once before that the problem could be solved by utilizing off-site computing," Will said.

"That's part of it. The kink is that people would still need to maintain those systems, which means the temperatures would have to be above the ideal for operations. But if we had robots, like, android-type robots, manning the equipment instead?"

"Robotic drones?"

"Not drones. I think autonomy is necessary. Fractions of a second matter sometimes, and a walking, thinking computer can make necessary decisions faster than a human brain."

"Artificial intelligence," Will said.

"Close to it."

"Development of A.I. has been at a standstill for three hundred years, by design. The statistical probability of sentient artificial life is significant, and every theoretical model considered came to the same conclusion. After some time, A.I. could, and likely would, end human life."

Those restrictions had been made based on twenty-first and twenty-second-century technology, Drew argued. Programming would have to be tightly controlled and continuously monitored, but if the robot of his mind existed, he could give Jax what he needed to resume work on Elysium within a year.

"Tethered satellites containing most of the computers necessary to run life support and operations, staffed by robots. If something goes wrong, the tether is released, and the satellite is either left to burn in the atmosphere, or destroyed."

"Destroyed," Will said. "We wouldn't risk incomplete combustion."

"Am I on the right track or not?"

Wil nodded. "You're on the right track. The only thing in your way are laws on the development of artificial intelligence."

"Are there ever any exemptions?" Aisha asked.

"Rare, but a few exemptions have been granted. The development would be tightly controlled, and we would be subject to government oversight. It would mean allowing General Myers access to our data."

Drew shrugged. "It's just an idea at this point. Toy teddy-bear robots are one thing. We need a humanoid with working fingers and a sense of touch."

Aisha chuckled under her breath, prompting Drew to ask why.

Will sighed, because he knew what she was thinking about.

"Sweetie, how do you feel about buying Drew a sex 'bot?"

20

The two weeks before Christmas were made of noise. While Will and Aisha's furniture was delivered, Zed moved bedrooms. While stuff left Will's apartment—Jay's entire bedroom had to be moved—stuff from the guest room in Jax and Aubrey's apartment went downstairs. And in the middle of all the moving, most of the wall between Oz and Zed's old room was torn out, leaving a wide archway to connect the spaces.

I spent as much of that time as I could curled up on Jax and Aubrey's bed with the door closed. No one had to ask me to stay out of the way; I knew they were worried I'd get stepped on by an inattentive delivery person or squished by chunks of wall coming down, and I didn't want to be around the chaos. The noise made me nervous, enough that Aubrey sensed my upset and turned music on to help drown it out.

Three days before Christmas Drew called me out of the bedroom; I'd been cooped up too long, I needed fresh air, and he was taking me with him to run errands. I didn't want to go and had turned around to head back to bed when he said the magic words: "I'll buy you some shrimp for lunch."

All right, then.

The first stop was the Kovlov's. He met Zed and Jay there for one last fitting for their wedding clothes, but this time Oz wasn't there to make him uncomfortable about being mostly naked in front of everyone. He was in the measuring jar and out in under fifteen minutes, and when he told Mrs. Kovlov that he would be back later to pick up his suit she wagged her pointy finger and said, "No. Not today. You see suit on wedding day. Now go home."

No one was allowed to take their clothes home. When we stepped outside, Zed groaned, "What the hell did Oz pick out? If we wind up in pink puffy shirts, I'm gonna be pissed."

"If Oz wants you in a pink puffy shirt, you'll wear the damned pink puffy shirt and be nice about it," Drew said. "She gets what she wants, every single thing, this one day."

"It's your wedding, too," Jay said. "What about what you want?"

"I'm getting what I want. A wedding that's not on the beach, grinding sand into my ass."

Drew settled me into the pouch on his sweatshirt, and we headed toward the Wharf because there was a shop on the pier he wanted to go to. Zed wanted to tag along, so Jay just shrugged and started following. The only thing to do at home was unpack, and he was tired of it.

What about studying? Don't you guys have to study?

"The semester is over," Drew answered. "We're done until the middle of January. I'd like to get into the workshop to tinker around a little bit, but Will changed the passcode to keep me out."

"Now isn't the time to turn into Finn and get lost in shit," Zed said. "He's just keeping Oz from changing her mind about you."

You met old Oz. You know she doesn't change her mind.

He wasn't taking chances. He figured his job over the next ten days was to do what he was told, and when she didn't have things for him to do, he could stretch out on his bed and read for fun. Since school started, he hadn't read more than a few chapters here and there, and he was looking forward to having a couple hours every night to just read.

"Oz found a treasure trove of early twenty-first-century science fiction and downloaded a bunch of it for me. I started this series by Hugh—"

"God, you're exciting," Zed snorted.

He didn't need to be exciting. He just needed to get through Christmas and most of the week following it. New Year's Eve would be *amazing*.

We wound up in a toy store. It was crammed full of too many things, and I felt like I wanted to run away, because if he turned the wrong way my head was going to smash into something. It even smelled funny, and Jay noticed it too. He crinkled his nose and asked Drew what the hell we were doing there.

"They specialize in old toys. I spotted a car in here a while back, and they're holding it for me."

"Learn to drive, and you can borrow Will's," Zed said.

"It's for Oz. For Christmas."

"All right, now you're just cheap."

Drew called him a name plucked right off the bad word list. "You know I used to throw things at her, right? Well, half the time it was because she did something to piss me off. When we were little, I think I was around six, she spent all day getting me into trouble, and we almost didn't get to walk down to the Ferry Building to watch the boats come and go."

Aubrey frequently took them to see the ferries docking and departing. She told them it was because Oz loved to watch them glide through the water, but the truth was that it was an hour she could take without them fighting in the apartment, when Shazia was off doing royal things with Jax. One afternoon, when she was frustrated enough that dangling them over the side of the balcony by their ankles while downing a bottle of wine seemed like a great idea, she took them just to get out of the house, hoping the fresh air would inspire deep, silent naps later.

Drew shoved a toy car into his pocket before leaving the apartment. He almost always had a small car or truck with him, but he'd learned that chucking one at Oz would get him into more trouble than it was worth. It wouldn't even have to hit her; all it had to do was land near her and she would scream and cry, then he'd get yelled at because that could have really hurt her, and he was older so he should know better.

Most of the time, she wound up playing with his cars, even when he didn't feel like sharing.

"We'd been sitting on the pier for a while, playing nicely, when she decided she wanted a turn with my car. She even asked me nicely. But I was feeling like a little dick, and I knew if I said no she would cry and Mrs. B would get upset, and I just plain didn't want to share my car. So, I threw it into the bay, for no reason other than to keep her from having it."

"I'd call you an idiot, but even I remember how Oz could be back then."

"They have a car that looks just like the one I threw away. So I'm getting it and giving it to her, even though it's fifteen years too late. Just so she knows, she can play with any of my toys."

"That's so sweet I might barf," Jay said.

"Oz isn't exactly sentimental," Zed warned him.

"She is, more than you realize." Drew handed me to Zed and pushed through the stacks of old toys to find someone to help him.

"Why the hell was he shopping in a toy store in the first place?" Jay wondered.

"Knowing Drew? He's had the idea and has been looking for that car for years. Any idea what you're getting Zara?"

"I've been making stuff," Jay said. "Can I borrow your computer and printer later?"

"Something on actual paper? Yeah, sure. You know the rest of us don't really do gifts? I know your family does but you don't need to worry about the rest of us."

Drew came back with a tiny bag in hand and took me from Zed. The next stop was a jewelry store down the Embarcadero, and when Zed raised an eyebrow Drew said, "You didn't think I was only getting her the toy car, did you?"

I think they did.

The store clerk wouldn't let me in; he didn't care that Zed and Drew were royalty. I was a cat and cats shed, and he worried I would leave furry little reminders for allergy sufferers. Jay waited outside with me, tucking me into his jacket to keep me warm.

We sat on the sidewalk because he didn't know how long it would take them. He left the jacket unzipped enough that I could see out and watch people walking past, and he kept his hands pressed against me to make sure I wasn't shivering.

I'm still glad we kept you.

"Can't understand you, cat. I wish I could, but to me it just sounds like a kitten begging for lunch."

That's all right. You're pretty good at figuring out what I want.

"You wanna know something I haven't told anyone else?"

I head bumped his chin; it wasn't so much that I wanted to hear his gossip, but that he needed to tell someone. Listening wouldn't hurt.

"I almost told Zara about me last night. We were talking about how everything changed from junior high to high school, except for me, and I came super close to telling her."

Almost isn't telling.

"Even when I didn't hit puberty like everyone else, she was hoping I would ask her out. Years ago. Like, when we were fourteen, freshman year."

Yeah, that's a lot of years. A whole three.

"The entire time we were talking, I just wanted to blurt it out. I mean, we talked about a couple other kids in school who were openly trans, and she was cool with it. But then I heard Will's voice in the back of my head...I can't tell her. I can't ever tell anyone. The difference between those other kids and me? I'll be able to *have* kids."

They will, too, just not the way Will and Aisha are going at it.

"There's no way to explain that. I still feel like not telling is a lie. But then Zed is right, I was never a girl. Not really. But it's major, you know, like Zara has a right to know if we ever actually hook up."

Maybe not. It's not a big deal.

Wait, I don't mean it like that. I know it's a big deal to you.

"Anyway, I finally worked up the nerve to ask her if she thought we were dating or just friends because I really wanted us to be dating. And she says, why not both? Fucking hell, Wick. I've only been me for like six months, and I have a girlfriend."

You've always been you, dude.

I headbutted his chin again because I didn't know any other way to let him know I was happy for him.

"Her dad is even okay with it. She's never dated before because he's so damned strict, but he likes me enough to loosen up. He likes that I have guards, and he likes that my stepdad is the Emperor. And man, I still want to find something else to call him. Like, step isn't enough, you know?"

Call him Bob.

"I'd fucking call him Dad if it wouldn't hurt my actual dad."

Pop. Lots of people call their fathers Pop.

"I suppose I could ask my Dad what he thinks."

He's gonna tell you that Will's new name should be Bob.

"All right, people are looking. Like they don't talk to their cats at home. But you're a good listener, Wick."

Good listeners get real live fresh dead shrimp, you know.

Drew remembered he'd promised shrimp. We were right there on the Embarcadero where the shrimp lived, so he grabbed food for everyone, and we sat at a picnic table on the pier, one that looked out over the bay. The seagulls wanted some, too, so they saved some bites, which upset some tourists who wanted to sit on the bench next to us without being molested by feathery rats.

When I was done eating I jumped into Drew's lap.

I had a good time today, thank you. Now can I borrow some money and go shopping, too?

"How much money? And what is it you want to get?"

I don't know how much I need. But I want to get Jay a present. I want him to know that we really, really like him and want to keep him even when he's grown up.

He agreed to take me shopping without Zed and Jay, warning me that we might not be able to find what I wanted, not exactly, but he had the rest of the day. If it was in the city, we would get it.

*

It was dark by the time we were done; we were both tired and hungry and wanted to find food, but Oz called Drew and told him to meet everyone on the Square. He grumbled a little bit because he just wanted to go home and eat everything in his kitchen, but Jax and Aubrey wanted to sit at the bakery with hot chocolate and watch little kids losing their damned minds over Christmas. Will and Aisha were tired of moving stuff around the apartment, and there was a chance Will might eat something with sugar, so he said he would suck it up and be there.

They'll give you bacon at the bakery if you ask nice enough.

"They also have donuts and as hungry as I am, if I eat a dozen no one better make fun of me."

There are a lot of other things about you to make fun of.

He took the packages to his apartment and offered me the chance to stay inside where it was warm, but I wasn't passing up the chance that I could get bacon. I was warm enough inside the sweatshirt, but I made him promise that I wouldn't have to go out on the ice with him.

I trusted Will not to fall; I wasn't as sure about Drew.

"It's fricking cold, and you guys want to sit outside?" he grumbled as he sat next to Oz. "We could all go inside and sit on the floor and you could just stare at us if that's your objective tonight."

"Who peed in your hot chocolate?" Will asked.

Aubrey was the one who most wanted to be outside. "I love this time of year, Andrew. I wanted to come out and enjoy the lights and the tree, and all the excited children. We skipped most of it last year, so this year, we're enjoying it."

"Sorry. I'm just tired and hungry."

Oz got up, kissed the top of his head, and said she would get him a sandwich. He didn't ask her to get the donuts instead, even though I know he wanted to.

"You weren't in the workshop, were you?" Will asked.

"Shopping."

"Well, nothing like waiting until the last minute."

He was helping me. I wanted to buy something.

"Let me guess. Steak or shrimp."

Drew bought me some shrimp for lunch. It was delicious. I think I even remembered to thank him.

"He never thanks me," Will said to Drew. "What the hell?"

"You provide for him. It's your job. I'm his minion, it's not mine."

He was a lot less cranky after he'd eaten. Well, there was a mid-meal cranky moment when he set the sandwich down on his plate and I took a bite. That got both him and Will excited, but not in a happy way. In my defense, there was a nice chunk of roast beef hanging out the back end that I was going to get anyway; I just saved him some time and effort. There was no need to tell me taking a bite was rude and that I needed to wait until he offered it to me.

What if he forgot? He'd feel bad and I'd still be hungry.

"Has he ever done that?" Aubrey asked.

"There were a few times when I was a boy," Will said. "Every now and then we'd see his paw reach over the edge of the table, and he'd snag the closest thing he could get. He stopped when Dad started watching and sliding plates covered with water under his paw."

"It's not that big a deal," Drew said.

Will leaned toward me. "It is a big deal. Drew doesn't need your germs on his food, understand? Next time ask him to pull a piece off for you."

I said I would, but Drew and I both knew that if I had a chance, I'd do it again.

Oz came to my rescue. "Hey, remember when you guys were showing us pictures last year? There was one of you with Will in front of the Christmas tree here. I want to recreate it."

Aubrey studied the picture on her phone to make sure they stood in the same places, and Will shoved me into his jacket because part of my head was sticking up in the original. Drew took the picture, but he wanted another just to be sure, and that was when Will decided it needed to be updated. When they were younger, there was space between them. This time he got in the middle and put his arms around them, and when Drew said, "just one more," Will kissed Jax right on his temple.

"The picture that should have been," he said. "The one I truly wanted."

We spent the next hour taking pictures, because the existing 150,000 images on the hard drive weren't enough family photos, and Will especially wanted some with him and Aisha and Jay. The one I liked the most, though, was a picture Drew took when no one else was paying attention. Jax and Will went to the ice rink to watch the kids skate, and Drew went to the far side of the rink to get the picture. They were shoulder to shoulder, laughing, holiday lights twinkling behind them, and we could really see how much they both looked like Eli and why the rest of the world had always been sure that Will was his son.

That's gonna be you and Zed and Jay someday. I mean, you won't look like each other, but you're gonna stand there and watch your kids, and people looking at you will see the same thing you see right now.

"I could do worse. I don't think I'll ever be that close with my own brother."

You never see him.

He's coming for your wedding?

"No. He didn't think he would miss it, but the army has other plans."

Jax didn't call someone and say he had to be allowed to come?

"He probably would have, if we'd asked. Carter doesn't want special favors because of who he is. When Oz and I are getting married, he'll be in Africa. But I get it. It's all right."

No, it's not.

"It wasn't his choice, Wick. And it really is okay. It's not like I'll have a lot of time for him."

Getting excited?

"You have no idea."

I had an idea. Will was that excited before he got married, even though he tried to be all mature about it. It was like marital Christmas, but Santa wasn't the one coming.

*

On Christmas Eve, I went into Will's old apartment without thinking. Eli was watching the news, and he looked up, surprised to see me, but perhaps not as surprised as I was to see him. It would have been rude to turn around and leave, so I jumped up onto the sofa, and after I was sure he wanted me to, I climbed into his lap.

"Checking up on me, Wick?" he asked as he scratched under my chin. "You can tell William that I'm fine. I had a drink or three with Jackson, chastised Andrew for wanting Oz to spend the night with him, ate everything Aubrey put in front of me, and I'll be heading to bed soon. He doesn't need to worry about how the holidays are bearing down on me. I'm fine."

I bet you miss your friends, though.

He'd gone to see them once, right after they were pulled from the tanks. Finn snuck him into the hospital—they didn't tell Will or Jax they were going for a visit until after they returned— and he spent a few days helping them get settled into the future's version of his own apartment. He was amazed at how young they looked now; Henry was old for this When, but at home she was barely more than middle-aged, and she now looked it.

What stumped him was how Finn and Will and Jo managed to hold onto their youth, when Craig and Henry, especially Henry, had not.

"Their lives were shadowed by the idea that they would lose their grandson." Finn guessed. "Sure, they understood Jo and I would be here eventually, but there's something very wrong about losing the young."

Donna had not been much older than Jax was now when she died. A decade, maybe a little more. Eli understood that ache, and the burden it placed on a person's soul. When he saw them again, full of light and energy, he was grateful that Will had dragged them off and guilted him into coming home.

Here, he had an easy way to go see them. And it wouldn't keep him from traveling again if he wanted. Craig could come back and go with him, and nothing was stopping him from stepping forward and seeing the world in two hundred years.

"Shouldn't you go upstairs and go to sleep, Mister Wick?" he asked me. "You've been a good boy. I'm sure Santa is bringing you something."

He knew I didn't like being called a good boy.

I jumped off his lap onto the floor and stared at him.

He wagged his pointy finger at me. "You're still my junior. You're a good boy the way Jax and Will are. You're my boys."

Fine.

He turned the video monitor off. "All right, Wick. I'm going to bed. Be sure to tell Will I enjoyed tonight and I am looking forward to tomorrow, and if they don't all stop worrying about me, I'm going back to Glasgow."

No, you're not.

"They'll know it's an empty threat. Besides, I think Jax suspended my travel visa. If he can't keep me home one way, he'll do it another."

I don't think he did, but okay.

My hover cart was upstairs, which made me think a couple things off the bad word list. It meant I had to walk up to the fifth floor, and I had gotten used to riding around the building. Will warned me it would make me soft and out of breath if I used it too much, but it was fun and I was old, and I wanted it.

I paused when I reached the family apartment and peeked into the living room. Oz and Drew were on the sofa exchanging a disturbing amount of spit and didn't notice me there. Zed was probably in his room talking to Sophia on a video chat, and Jax and Aubrey were probably in bed, so I headed up another flight.

Will and Aisha were already in bed, too, but their bedroom door was open and I could hear them talking. Jay was at his dad's, so there was still a chance they were doing bouncy things, but I took a chance and went in. They cuddled together on the window seat, watching the last of the skaters on the rink below. They both had clothes on, so I jumped up on the other end and sat down to give Will Eli's report.

"Eli wanted me to know he's fine tonight," he told Aisha. "He spent the evening with Jax and Aubrey, poked at Drew, and has gone to bed."

Why didn't you go have drinks with them?

"Because this is our first Christmas together, and we wanted to enjoy it alone."

But you still have clothes on.

"We can enjoy each other without taking our clothes off, you know."

"Give us a bit," Aisha said, snickering. "I'll get those jeans off you soon."

Eli said we have to go to sleep so that Santa will come.

"That's why I want to get the jeans off him," she said.

The last skaters were off the ice, and the entry gate was being locked up. We sat and watched as the lights went off one by one until only the holiday lights hanging from lampposts and the Christmas tree were on. That meant it was midnight, and now it was Christmas.

You should kiss now. It's Christmas. I'm pretty sure that's what the baby Jesus would want.

Aisha leaned her head back so he could kiss her, and it was a really good one that was probably going to mean his jeans really would come off, but then the front door creaked open and Will froze, listening.

The footsteps were soft and squeaky, size twelve sneakers on a newly polished cement floor.

It's just Jay.

They got up because he wasn't supposed to be home until almost noon. He had gone into the kitchen and was digging through the refrigerator, and he didn't hear them coming. When Will called out his name, he startled and almost dropped the milk.

"Holy fuck, Will."

"Please tell me you didn't come home because your dad had friends over," Aisha said, taking the milk from him.

Jay laughed. "I know what you mean by friends, Mom. Did he have a fuck buddy or two over? No. It was just us."

"Then?"

"We had a good time, stop worrying. But he knew I wanted to come home and sleep in my own bed and said that he got it. New apartment, first Christmas with a big family. First with Will. He thought that was more important than me sleeping there and then scrambling to get back in the morning."

The milk changed hands again. Will took it and started making hot chocolate while Jay and Aisha sat at the table.

Did someone buy stock in the hot chocolate factory? That's all anyone drinks anymore.

"Are you sure he was all right?" she asked him.

"Honestly, I think he wanted to stay up all night to play video games, and just didn't want me to feel like I had to stay up, too. And he meant it, he wanted me to have a first Christmas here."

"God, I hope he's not alone tomorrow," she said, half under her breath.

"He's having dinner with a group of friends. He's okay, Mom. A little lonely sometimes but he's okay."

Does that bother you? That she worries about James?

He mouthed the word 'no,' after making sure she wasn't looking at him.

"He wants to talk to you guys after Oz's wedding," Jay went on. "He finally read George's letter, and he wants to see him. But he said there was no hurry. He knows the wedding comes first and it won't hurt to make George stew a little longer."

"I can arrange that," Will said. "Does he want to speak with both of us or just me?"

"Both, I think. He admitted he still misses George, even if he was an asshat."

"I hope he understands George can't come back to stay," Aisha said.

Jay shrugged. "I dunno. I'm not sure that's what he's thinking about at all. He's still pretty pissed off. I mean, if I mention George and the surgery, he gets really upset and goes off on a rant about him being willing to let me wait until it would have been seriously painful and all."

"It's possible for someone to get past being horribly hurt," Will said.

Aisha started to protest; there was no getting past that, but Will set a mug of hot chocolate in front of her and said, "You forgave me."

"That's hardly the same thing."

"Mom, they were married for a long time," Jay said. "If you could still love Will over a couple decades, Dad can love George over this."

"But—" She looked to Will for help. "Will didn't hurt my son."

Jay shrugged that off. "You did still love Will the whole time, didn't you? It explains a lot if you did."

"I always did," she said, softly.

"Kinda figured. I mean, I know you dated when I was growing up, but man, only meeting one person in, like, a dozen years? And that was by accident. It's like you knew nothing else was going to stick."

"I suppose not."

"Can I give you your Christmas present now? It's after midnight." He was out of his seat before they could say it was all right, and he picked a package from under the tree and brought it over. "It's for both of you."

Aisha peeled the wrapping paper off carefully, and when she saw it, she started crying. There was no warning, just sudden, great big tears spilling over her cheeks. "You drew this?"

He nodded. "Mrs. B got me the original picture."

Will swallowed against the lump in his throat. I jumped onto the table so I could see it, too, because they weren't letting go of it.

It was a framed drawing of the two of them when they were young and not-dating. He'd drawn it from a picture of them sitting in the parklet; Will was playing his guitar and singing, and her head was thrown back in wild laughter, and every detail was colorful and exacting. I remembered the original; it was taken back when they weren't touching but were wrapped around each other anyway.

"This is incredible." Will's words caught in his throat. "I can feel that moment. I can remember what I was thinking, even."

"I know what you were both thinking," Jay said. "I saw in in the original. Your eyes—even from that side view, what I see? You're thinking, like, goddamn I love her. And she's thinking she wants that to go on forever."

"I knew you had talent," Will said, almost whispering. "This is so far beyond what I assumed."

"How? Jay asked. "I never show anyone—"

"You've left your tablet on the table," Will said. "Often it's open to sketches you're working on. I didn't mention it because I didn't want to intrude. But I've been aware of your talent." He got up. "Come on, if we get our gift, you get yours."

Aisha was still crying, but she nodded and followed him. They led Jay to the closed bedroom door one down from his, the one they'd told him would be for some of Will's books. She told Jay to open it, and they stepped back so that he could take it all in.

"What the hell?" He went in, turning several times to take it in. "This is, like, a fucking art studio."

"It *is* a fucking art studio," Will said.

There were shelves with paper and stacks of blank canvases and containers of paint brushes and pens and pencils. On one wall there was a desk with a long, skinny light fixture where he could sit and draw, on another wall, there was an easel, and the last wall had a shining, tilting black table with wires that went to a computer.

"That's a graphics table," he breathed out. "Like, a real one."

"We wanted you to have options, sweetheart," Aisha said. "Will knew you enjoyed sketching, but we weren't sure what else you wanted to explore."

Whispering, he said, "I want to do it all."

"Everything is moveable," Will said. "You can arrange things to suit your needs. And the walls are white to serve as a blank canvas if you choose."

He wasn't sure what to look at first.

"Wait, what about your books? This was supposed to be a library."

The bookshelves were being moved to the staff kitchen, and all the books were coming out of Drew's apartment and out of storage. "With a few exceptions, the books will be available to everyone. Keeping them behind a closed door is beginning to feel like a selfish waste. Drew enjoys them, and I hope you will, too."

"God, this is all—" He hugged them both, hard. "Thank you. I didn't even know I wanted this, but damn, I think it's the best present I've ever gotten."

"Should have gotten him the car," Aisha teased. "That might have made him happy."

"I don't need a car," Jay said. "But this? You have no idea."

After they went back to the table—the hot chocolate was now cold chocolate and no one wanted it even though they all liked chocolate milk—I asked Will if I could give Jay his present, too.

"Is that what you took Drew shopping for?"

Yes, and since you're doing presents now, I want to give Jay what I got him, but I can't pick it up. It's under the tree toward the back. Drew put it there for me.

Will retrieved it and handed it to Jay as I jumped back onto the table. "Wick got you something. And trust me, I'm as curious as you are."

Jay looked a little confused, but he laughed as he took the small frame out of the box. "Scissors, Wick?"

They're black.

Will was confused, too, until he got a better look. "Those are shears," he said.

Because we like Jay and want to keep him, and now he's one of us. I wanted to get him something to remind him of that. He's us.

Will repeated what I said. Jay thought about it and then ran his fingers over the glass of the frame.

"Black shears," he said.

"Long way to go for a pun," Will said to me.

Expensive, too. You owe Drew around two hundred bucks for this.

Jay set the frame on the table and asked me to come to him for a hug. "I'm hanging it by my bedroom door, Wick. That way I'll see it every time I leave my room. It'll remind me who I want to be."

You're an Okuda and *a Blackshear now.*

I really didn't mean to make anyone cry, but Aisha's waterworks started up again.

"I'm not surprised you get it, Wick," Jay said. "Like, I have brothers and a sister now, and Mr. and Mrs. B are like an uncle and an aunt, and you know what I think about Will. I really did want to be a part of this family. Like, from the day Will told me he wasn't stringing along a bunch of women. He only wanted mom. I wanted it then."

"So did I, Jay," Will said.

"I can't, like, change my name or anything—"

"I would never ask you to. I would never want you to. Your father is a good man, and he gave you his name for a reason. But you can be both. You are my first-born heir."

Aisha picked up the mugs and put them in the sink and told Will that while I was in the room with them watching the lights on the square wink off, Santa came, and I might want to see what he brought me.

Will went over to the fireplace and turned it on; it was bigger than the one downstairs, and the flames danced higher. It was very pretty, but I didn't think Santa had anything to do with that.

"Come here," he said.

I jumped down and padded over there, curious. When I rounded the sofa, he gestured to the floor, and said, "Santa knew you wanted a new one."

It was a rug.

A new, unspoiled rug.

I stretched out on it, and it was soft and warm, and no one—I made Will promise—was going to bounce on it, ever.

21

By royal proclamation—because the Queen said so—Drew was not allowed to see Oz before the wedding. She eliminated any chance that it might happen; she made reservations for herself and Oz and twenty guards at the Marks Hotel across the street from the Cathedral and told Jax he was responsible for getting the groom and man-of-honor there on time. Wedding attire would be delivered at noon, and she wanted everyone showered and shaved and ready to leave by one, even though the ceremony wasn't starting until almost three.

I peeked out the window in Oz's bedroom; three shiny black limousines were hovering on the street, and each was surrounded by guards decked out in their formal uniforms. Even from the window, I could tell that their pants had been pressed with a crease sharp enough to cut a kitty open, and enough shiny things were dangling from shoulders and chests to make a lot of noise.

These men and women had earned their way into the guard the hard way: they were soldiers once, some tested in battle, some proven in dedicated service. They were the guards who were trusted with secrets, who knew about the portals, who knew the family secrets, and who would die before they'd talk.

Some of the guards were young and inexperienced, and those were the ones who sat at the front door, bored, waiting for their turn to be trusted with more. A few would get their chance on this day; they'd been selected to the King's Honor Guard and would watch over the wedding and the reception. Drew thought they wanted something to happen—to prove themselves—but also dreaded that it might because their loyalties were firmly rooted in favor of the safety of the family.

I thought they wanted to be there for the free food.

Several guards were posted on Union Square, keeping an eye on people who might not realize they weren't allowed walk down the steps near the royal house. The Square hadn't been closed off, and the skating rink was still open, but no one was getting down the stairs on the side closest to the royal house, and no one was walking on the street.

People were gathering, regardless. They wanted to watch as their royal family left the house to get into the cars.

They're worried you're gonna trip.

Or hoping. I dunno. There are some sick freaks out there.

"No one wants us to trip," Drew said.

He'd been pacing since he woke up, first in the hall, then the living room, and now he was wearing a path in Oz's room, shuffling between it and the newly opened space that used to be Zed's room.

Are you nervous? Did you change your mind?

"No, I didn't change my mind. Why would I change my mind? I just want it to get here, that's all." He stopped near the foot of the bed. "I'm sweating. I should shower again. I have time for another shower, don't I?"

No. I hear the elevator. I think your clothes are here.

"I can't believe we had to wait until the last minute for them. Like, what if there had been a problem? There's no time to fix it if something is screwed up. And if something is screwed up, Oz will be upset, and I don't want anything upsetting her today, not when—"

"Take a breath, Andrew," Will called from the living room.

The elevator dinged, and a guard pushed a rolling rack out and into the living room. Five black bags were hanging from it, each with a name tag. Drew darted from the bedroom and got to the cart at the same time Zed and Jay did, but none of them reached for their suits.

Why is no one wearing pants?

They were all in shorts and t-shirts as if this weren't a special day.

"Do we really want to know what Oz finally picked out?" Zed asked. "I swear, if the shirts are pink and puffy..."

"I'm thinking they're each a different color," Jay said. "One of us in yellow, one in blue, one in green, and one in orange. And they're super bright neon colors."

"Oz has a red tux," Drew said absently. "She planned on putting all of us in red."

"No suit for you, Dad?" Zed asked.

Oz wanted Jax to wear his official uniform, minus the crown. Will wasn't worried about what she'd chosen because he wasn't about to refuse her choices. He was the first to reach for his bag, and he turned it away from them as he unzipped it.

"Oh," he murmured. "I will look horrible in purple."

"No!" Zed grabbed for the bag and then spun it on the rack so they could all see. "Jesus, you're an ass."

Will peeled the bag off the suit. It was a dark blue jacket with tails, gray pinstriped slacks, and there was a dark blue vest with white shirt and tie. "It's a morning suit," he said. "Very old, very traditional wedding garb."

"Classy as hell," Eli said. "I'm glad I didn't insist on a suit I already owned."

Zed and Jay opened their bags; their suits were identical to Will's, which made Zed whistle and mutter, "Damn. These are sweet. And *not* red."

"Drew?" Jax prodded.

He still hadn't opened his bag. "I think I want to wait for my parents," he said.

Will nodded, then slipped the bag off the rack and took it into Oz's room.

"They're on their way," Jax told Drew. "They should be on the roof in about ten minutes."

"Why are they waiting until the last minute?" Jay asked.

"They were in France," Jax answered. "It was a trip that couldn't be avoided."

Drew didn't mind. "They'll be here, that's all that matters."

I think Jay was going to say something else about it because he didn't quite understand, but Zed looked at him and said, "If Drew's mom hadn't taken the meeting, Dad would have. And no one would risk the bride's father missing this."

Only because he's the King.

"It's part of being us," Drew said. "There will be times Will winds up missing some of your stuff, or he'll barely make it back on time. It sucks, but you learn to not take it personally. And France's president was super cool about it. He pushed his own schedule around to make sure they would make it in time."

"You know, sometimes you guys talk about world leaders like they're no big deal."

"When you've seen most of them drunk, they kind of become no big deal," Zed snorted.

"You may get that chance," Will told Jay. "There will be quite a few at the wedding and the reception."

"Robert Lopez," Jax said. "Zed—best behavior. Don't make him regret sending his daughter here for school."

"He knows we're dating, Dad."

"I know. Just...be respectful."

"No, Dad, we were planning on dry humping right there on the dance floor with the Japanese Prime Minister on one side and Red Munson on the other."

"That would certainly be educational for the Munson children," Will mused.

"How'd you guys get from small, personal wedding to inviting half the world?" Zed asked Drew.

He shrugged. Will said that once it was made public, there were inquiries, which led to invitations simply to be accommodating. The guest list exploded from thirty friends and family to over 600 people, because when it got right down to it, Oz didn't want to hurt anyone's feelings, and she especially didn't want to slam down a political wedge between Pacifica and another country.

She and Drew planned on pretending it was just their family and friends. The first few pews were reserved for the people closest to them, and the rest they hoped would fade into the background. They weren't going to have a traditional reception line because no one wanted to stand there for four hours while people waited to say hello, and if there were a line, people would feel obligated.

They wanted a party. The invitations were clear on that: after the vows have been said and the bride and groom leave the church, go home or back to your hotel room and change into comfortable clothes, then come back hungry. The bride and groom would return in slacks and sneakers, and they wanted everyone prepared to have fun.

The fun was hours away, though. Drew was anxious, circling the living room in shorts and a t-shirt, waiting for his parents. He twitched when the elevator pinged, and he was ready to spring at his mother, but the door slid open and she wasn't there.

Carter was.

He was dressed in his formal military uniform, everything neatly pressed, his hair cropped close, and there wasn't a hint of whiskers on his face. Colored braids dangled from his shoulders, and he had several new medals pinned to his chest.

Drew's surprise rooted him in place.

"Thanks for dressing to see me," Carter said as he came into the living room. "Royalty, my ass."

"You couldn't come," Drew managed to spit out.

"Yeah, I traded a shitload of shifts, and I'll probably have to leave before the reception is over, but I wasn't missing this, ya hoser." He pulled Drew into a hard hug. "Mom and Dad are right behind me. She's still on the roof yelling at her pilot for cutting into the lawn and knocking down a bunch of lights."

When Richard and Shazia finally arrived, Drew practically jumped at them. It was like seeing a six-foot-tall five-year-old grabbing onto mom because she was ten minutes late picking him up from the babysitter, and he'd been there *so* long and he missed her *so* much. His dad got a hug, but it wasn't as long or hard as the one Shazia got.

After all the niceties that people go through when they see each other for the first time in a while, Drew's family went into the bedroom. He wanted to show them the view and how the wall had been blown out, and I wanted to help, but Will scooped me up and said, "Give them privacy, Wick."

Why? They're not gonna bounce or anything.

"I'm sure Shazia and Richard have things they want to say to their sons, and it's none of our business. They haven't had time together as a family for a very long time...just give them this."

Richard knows that Drew doesn't need the talk, right? Or is that a secret?

"If Richard feels it's necessary, Drew will humor him."

I snoopervised while everyone else changed into their new suits, mostly because they didn't bother hiding in bedrooms. Zed and Jay dropped their shorts right there in the living room and started to get dressed, and since there were no girls other than Drew's mom, Will shrugged and changed there, too. Only Jax went to his room because his suit was hanging in the closet.

After three false starts with his tie, Jay asked Will for help. Will stood behind him because it was the only way he knew to do it, and when he was almost done Aisha came out of the elevator carrying a box of flowers. She stopped in the entryway to watch them, smiling when Will pressed a kiss onto Jay's temple after he smoothed out the tie.

Eli leaned close to her and whispered, "Don't worry, I'm getting pictures."

"Damn, we clean up nice," Zed said once they were all done.

Aisha set the box on the end of the sofa to open it and started pulling flowers out, handing them over one by one. "Boutonnieres," she said, handing one to Jay. "Pin it to your lapel."

It was a tiny red rose with a bit of baby's breath. The color stood out against the blue jacket, prompting Zed to say, "Damn, all we need now are top hats. We're classy as hell."

"We're also getting short on time." Will knocked on the bedroom door and called out, "Time to get dressed, Andrew. We need to leave soon."

Wasn't I supposed to get a new tie?

Will reached into the stand by the door and pulled out a tiny red bow tie for me. "Remember," he said as he clipped it onto my collar, "until Jax enters the church you need to stay very close to me. Then run to the front pew and wait with Aubrey, all right?"

"It's also going to be noisy, Wick," Zed warned. "More people than you're used to, even outside."

I can ride on your shoulder?

Will nodded. "I'll carry a cloth for you to sit on. Before the ceremony starts, I'll hand it to Aubrey. Make sure you sit on it with her, as well. She won't want her dress covered in cat hair."

Will people get mad that I'm there? Aisha brushed me, but I can't help it if I shed. It's going to get on someone.

"It doesn't matter if people are upset by your presence," Will said. "Oz and Drew want you there, and that's all that matters."

"Seriously," Zed added. "Asking Wick to stay home would be like Drew banning his best friend from the most important day of his life."

The bedroom door creaked open. Richard and Carter came out first, followed by Shazia. She had clearly been crying, but it seemed like happy tears, so I wasn't worried that she was trying to talk Drew out of getting married. Will had warned me, people were going to cry. Aubrey would for sure, and he gave Jax a fifty-fifty chance.

His eyes reddened a little bit when Drew came out. His suit was cut like the everyone else's, a jacket with tails and a nice vest, but it was all white, even the shoes.

It was the first time since I'd known him, since he was a baby, that he looked like a real prince.

"Damn, dude," Zed said. "Slick."

Drew laughed nervously. "And it's not red."

"Disappointed?" Aisha asked.

"Maybe a little. I hoped Oz and I would match." He tugged on the jacket to straighten out wrinkles that weren't even there. "No. It's perfect. And you all look—"

"Amazing," they said together.

"Oh, bite me."

Aisha handed the last red rose to Shazia so that she could pin it to Drew's lapel. When she was done, Will covered his shoulder and picked me up, and we headed down in the elevator. There were two guards just inside the front door who snapped to attention and another outside who pulled it open. Union Square was packed with people, and when we stepped out, it was as if they all started yelling at once.

"Remember," Will said, "it's going to be loud. Try not to startle."

All along the street, there were guards in dress uniforms, and they snapped to attention at the same time. Only two didn't because they needed to be able to open the car doors for us. Eli got into the first one with Zed, Jay, and Aisha, and we rode with Drew's family. Jax rode alone, on the back seat of his car, flanked by General Myers and Guard Colonel Tiptich.

All the way up Powell Street, people lined the sidewalks, and when we turned onto California, the lines became a giant wad of multicolored fleshy blobs choking the intersections. I wanted to ask Will why they were there when they wouldn't really be able to see Drew and for sure wouldn't be able to talk to him, but I couldn't remember if Shazia and Richard knew he could understand me and I didn't want to put him on the spot.

Guards and police kept people away from the Cathedral. It was safe enough to linger outside the car for a few minutes before going in, and Shazia reminded Drew that he needed to acknowledge everyone. She prompted Zed to wave, too, because he was their prince and they were just as happy to see him as they were the groom. We walked up the first set of steps, and they turned around and waved, which made everyone cheer.

Eli wiggled his fingers at a little girl who was on her father's shoulders across the street, and we could hear her squeal over the noise.

I was glad to get inside, where the only noise was quiet conversation among the few guests that were already there. People turned to see Drew come in, but they left him alone. Eli and Jay were pulled aside by a woman wearing bright red and blue robes, and she made them stand near the entryway as if they were guards on duty.

That seemed a bit beneath them, and I complained to Will.

"They're serving as ushers," he said, quietly. "As guests arrive, Jay and Eli will escort them to their seats. It's perfectly acceptable."

Isn't Eli a little old for that?

"He volunteered."

They were already taking Drew's parents to the front pew. Eli held his arm out for Shazia and Jay walked alongside Richard and Carter, but he didn't offer them his arm or even try to hold their hands.

Zed nodded toward the door. "How the hell is Oz going to get across the street? The hotel doors are blocked by a ton of people."

"She and Aubrey have been here for two hours now." Aisha gestured toward the small chapel to her left, which was usually used for quiet prayer and reflection, but today was closed off. "She's expecting you soon."

As Oz's man-of-honor, Zed was supposed to help her get dressed, but Aubrey was going to handle it if Oz couldn't get her tux jacket on by herself. Zed would probably get to help with her bow tie. She wanted him there before the ceremony started; the same way Drew had a few minutes alone with his family, she wanted a few with hers. He muttered, "Sweet," and then knocked on the door, waiting to be let in.

"All right, best man." Aisha gave Will a kiss and patted his chest. "I'll see you up there."

Where's she going?

"Jay is going to escort her to her seat."

Without you?

"I won't be seated. I'm standing with Drew."

Like he did for you.

"Exactly."

I stood with you, too. Shouldn't I stand with Drew?

"As you've pointed out many times, you felt as if you were marrying Aisha, too. You only get one pretend wife, Wick. Drew needs you next to Aubrey."

There was a little alcove off to the side for us to wait. It didn't have much, but there were a couple of chairs and a teenager who rushed to cover one for Drew, so he didn't get anything on his white suit. Once we were as comfortable as we could get, he left us alone.

Gonna cry today?

Drew snickered. "Why not? Will did."

"Indeed, I did. I told you, Wick, people are going to cry. It is entirely acceptable to shed happy tears."

It's acceptable to cry when someone kicks you in the balls, too. What's your point?

He ignored me.

"The church looks really nice," Drew said. "Oz did a—" He tilted his head, listening. There was a sudden whine coming from outside, followed by a crowd of voices laughing. "What the hell?"

They both got up and went to the window. Guards at each corner of the Cathedral, halfway up the steps, were pointing hoses into the air and sending streams of bubbles over the crowd, as guests' cars pulled up and people got out.

"Oz," Drew snorted. "She wanted butterflies, but it's cold, and she thought it would be a little mean to the butterflies. This is way funnier."

"Indeed. People will talk about this for quite a while."

People would be happier if you shot candy out of the cannons. People like candy.

Drew grunted. "You might be right. We could have pelted them with jawbreakers. Not a thing dangerous about that."

Gummy bears, dude. Soft candy. I'm not an idiot.

When the last of the guests arrived, the hoses were put away, and other guards rolled out giant screens and blocked the front door. "They'll be able to watch the ceremony," Will explained. "It's being broadcast, as well."

You're gonna be on a worldwide live feed. No pressure there, Drew.

"I didn't see any cameras," he said.

"Four near the front, four to the outside center, four will be to the back. Others are located behind the altar and at the center aisle, in the ceiling. Once you and Oz are in place, another will be at the back of the aisle. They're unobtrusive so they won't take any focus away from the ceremony."

"Manned cameras?"

"Some, yes."

Drew laughed under his breath. "Long way from the tiny, rooftop wedding we originally talked about."

"You'll appreciate it later, I promise."

"Oh, I appreciate it now, Will. This is what I wanted. I mean,

Oz hates the idea of using taxpayer money on personal things, but she's worth this, you know?"

"I don't think she fully embraced the idea that this was paid for long before she was born. By design, Pacifica's monarchy has been paid little, but part of that design was assuring some perks and some dignities. This is one of the dignities provided for as far back as the first king."

"Pretty spiffy dignity, I think. What about your wedding?"

"I paid for it."

Yeah, but you shit money.

"Wick, what the hell has gotten into you lately?"

"He's been hanging around Jay a lot," Drew said. "Hell, same can be said for Zed and me. I—"

Jay stuck his head in. "You ready?"

He was ready enough that Will had to hold him back. He set me on the floor and told me to follow him closely, but we wouldn't start walking until the music started. Will held Drew's elbow, and when the first notes were plunked out on an organ that I couldn't see, he let go and nudged him forward.

I did as I was told and walked right behind him. I heard a few titters and one grumpy person grumbled, "Hell, they brought the damned cat," but I refused to let it upset me. I kept my eyes on Will's ankle, and I held my tail high as we walked the length of the center aisle. We stopped in front of the altar, where the lady in the robes waited.

A minute later, the door at the little side chapel opened, and Zed stepped out. He looked at Drew and grinned, glanced into the chapel again, and then gave Drew a thumb's up. A few seconds later Aubrey came out and slipped her hand into the crook of Zed's arm so he could walk her to the front pew. Once she was sitting next to Aisha, he stepped up to the other side of the altar, still grinning widely.

Drew sucked in a deep, shaky breath. He was fixed on the door of that chapel, waiting for the first sight of his bride. The doors to the Cathedral opened first, and several of the guard streamed in, standing at attention on either side of the little chapel's door, and at the head of the aisle.

I could barely see. Will hadn't told me it was time to sit with Aubrey, so I moved to the middle, between Zed and Drew, where I could see right down the aisle. Zed laughed and Will hissed at me, but I had the best view and I wasn't going to move.

"He's fine," Drew whispered loudly.

The guards by the little chapel each took three steps forward, and Jax came out. He waited there, his hand pressed to his chest as he gazed into that small room and smiled so hard that it hurt, until both guards dropped to one knee and the music began to swell. It was then I was glad I moved because everyone stood up and turned. Even Drew and Will and Zed moved a little closer to center, and when Oz stepped out, I heard Drew draw in a sharp breath.

Oz took a few slow steps to Jax, pausing so that he could kiss her, and when they turned to head down the aisle, I looked over my shoulder at Drew. He had both hands clasped over his mouth and tears were streaming down his face, his breath hitching. When the processional music changed, and she began walking toward him, Will had to grab him by the elbow to keep him from hitting his knees.

She forgot her red tux.

Someone needs to run and find her red tux.

Oz was in a trim-fitting white satin dress with delicate lace down the arms, and it trailed behind her so far that before the guards stood up, they reached for the back and smoothed it out so that it flowed behind her. I wasn't sure what was holding it up because it didn't have straps and her boobs weren't big enough to grab it and hold on. Her scar peeked above it; she'd done nothing to hide it.

She clutched a bouquet filled with tiny red and white flowers that matched the ones Drew and Zed wore on their suits, and she was wearing a necklace I had never seen before. It was simple and shiny, and as she neared, I realized that hanging on it were two tiny charms. One was a dragon, the other was a cat.

Dude, you gave her that for Christmas, didn't you?

"Wick," Will hissed. He nodded toward Aubrey; she already had the cloth I was supposed to sit on, so I jumped up onto the pew and sat on it next to her as Jax kissed Oz again and placed her hands in Drew's.

No one sat down until he did.

Stand up again. See if they follow.

As the woman standing at the altar began speaking, the church went quiet. This was the part that Oz said was disturbingly ancient, but she would go along with it because it seemed to matter to her parents, when the minister asked who was giving the bride away. Jax stood again—no one else did—and said, loud enough for all to hear, "Her mother and I do."

I thought it should be Drew's parents giving him away. He was going to live in Pacifica, in the royal house, and he was taking Oz's name. If anyone was being given away, it was him.

The view from the front pew was better than the one on the floor by Will's feet, but I was still looking at Oz's backside for the most part, and I wanted to see her smile. Drew's hands were shaking and she squeezed them a few times, and I was sure she was grinning as much as he was.

I risked it.

I jumped down and sat in the center aisle, just ahead of the two front pews, where I could see everything. Will's jaw set as he glanced at me, but there wasn't a whole lot he could do about it. Jax hissed, but I pretended I couldn't hear it over the laughter that bubbled outside the church.

Drew glanced at me, too, but he didn't look upset at all. His shoulders shook a little from trying to not laugh, and he gave a tiny nod of his head so that Oz would see where I was. And I was right, she was smiling, but it was all for Drew.

They half-listened as the minister droned on about love and loyalty and the sacrament of marriage. Drew bounced on his toes every now and then, too excited to stay still. Will stood with his hands clasped behind his back, which I thought was risky, because what if Drew fainted? Someone needed to be able to grab him before he smacked into the floor with his face.

That might ruin everyone's day.

Zed held the bouquet; if Oz fainted he could still catch her, but she was getting a face full of roses while he did it.

Drew brightened when it was time for the vows. They promised to love and care for each other—but not obey because Oz was not obeying anyone and Drew thought it was bizarre that it was ever part of anyone's wedding vows—and to be faithful, forsaking everyone else (which I am pretty sure means that if other people come on to them, they get to kick 'em in the junk) and only batting their eyes at each other. Drew's hand was still shaking a little bit when Will handed him the ring—a plain gold band because that's what Oz wanted—and he had a hard time getting it all the way onto her finger.

Zed gave Drew's ring to Oz, but she wasn't trembling, and she slid it onto his finger without any trouble at all. This was the part I was waiting for, when it was official and nothing could stop it, and they were married. The minister told Oz she could kiss the groom, which made her laugh because it was usually the other way around.

The kiss went on for a long time, and right when I was sure they were going to stop, it was time for me to move. If I stayed where I was, I would block the aisle, and if Oz tripped over me, Drew would not be forgiving about that. I ran over to him and climbed up his leg and then his back so that I could be on his shoulder to give Oz a kiss of my own before they pulled too far apart.

Will had other plans. I was halfway up Drew's back when he snatched me off and stuck me on his shoulder. He didn't even care that everyone laughed at me, mocking my disappointment at not getting to kiss the bride.

"You will not move from here," he said under his breath. "Understand?"

I understood.

I wasn't happy about it, but I understood.

The minister raised her hands in the air and said loudly, "Ladies and gentlemen, Princess Australia and Prince Andrew Blackshear."

Ozoo!

We followed them down the aisle to the church doors, and when the guards opened them, the giant screens slid out of the way and Oz and Drew stepped outside, standing there so people could take pictures and cheer.

"There's going to be a loud boom," Will said. "Two, actually. Don't panic, and don't leave my shoulder."

Drew reached for Oz to give her a kiss, and when he did the loud booms happened, and tiny shreds of paper filled the air. Most of it was aimed at the crowd, but Oz wound up picking some off Drew's face before deciding she hadn't kissed him enough.

There were more cameras outside, and at least two photographers. Instead of getting in cars and driving away, we stood outside while a few hundred official pictures were taken. I was handed from person to person because Will had to be in a lot of them, and at one point Eli was holding me, but he wouldn't put me on his shoulder where I would be more comfortable.

"Don't let them yell at you today," he murmured, holding me close where I could hear him. "You had the best seat in the house, and it made Andrew happy."

I still haven't gotten to kiss Oz.

I want to kiss the bride!

Drew heard me and reached out to take me from Eli. He set me on his shoulder, risking that I would shed all over his nice white suit, and when the next picture was taken, he whispered that this was my chance. I stretched out as he said her name just loud enough to make her turn her head, and I licked the tip of her nose.

There. Now you've been kissed.

"It's official now," he told her. "You've been blessed by Saint Wick."

22

Foot traffic around Union Square was blocked off even after the wedding. The family went home to change clothes and then pretend to not notice that it took Oz and Drew a lot longer than anyone else. After that, we headed for the Westin Hotel, half a block away. People were still clustered on sidewalks and in the street, hoping to shout things at Oz and Drew, so the police and the guard kept the path clear.

Because the streets were closed until the party was over, those barriers were going to be up until morning. Guards would wait along the street and on rooftops around the Square until after the King and Queen were home safely. Oz and Drew planned on sneaking out—as far as the world was concerned, they were staying in the hotel all night, engaging in unspeakable acts of newlyweddedness—but they didn't know exactly when. Will reminded them that it was entirely up to them. They could stay until the last guest left, or they could leave after everyone was drunk and dancing and wouldn't notice their absence. It was their party, and they got to make the rules.

Zed fed me while everyone else went to change clothes, and while he was scooping the food out, he apologized that I couldn't take my hover cart because it might get lost. He was sure he could grab one in service as it floated past and rig it the way he had at the reception for the First Minister of Florida. It was important that I have one because it made people laugh, and the one thing Oz and Drew really wanted was for their reception to be a party.

"You're gonna make the news tonight, you know that, right?" he asked as he put my plate down. "I know Will was pissed off, but you totally made Drew's day. He freaking loved it when you jumped down to get a better view."

Will will get over it.

He went to change while I finished. People started coming out of bedrooms, and they congregated around the table while musing that it would be really funny to stand outside Oz's bedroom door and applaud.

They would have if Aubrey hadn't sighed dramatically and asked them to be mature about all of this.

Everyone was dressed in black. The kids were wearing the same clothes they'd worn to Aubrey's birthday, which didn't seem like comfy clothes but since I'd never had pants on I couldn't be sure, and Will, Jax, and Eli had dressed to match them. Even Aisha and Aubrey had changed into black dresses.

Was this planned? A 'We are the Blackshears' kind of thing?

"We look bad ass in black," Drew said. "You have a black collar, right?"

I don't think so. At least not one without a giant bow tie clipped to it.

"Well, you do now." He pulled one out of his pocket and changed my collar. It wasn't as pretty as the red tie, but it was soft and fuzzy, and very comfortable. He picked me up, pretending to check how tight it was, but he whispered to me. "Thank you for making me laugh today. I was really nervous with all those people watching us, and you gave them something else to see."

I just wanted to sit where I could see your faces.

"I know. But I still loved it."

Oz came over, and he set me on the table—Jax sighed, but he didn't say anything—and she put her arms around him. "I see how it's going to be. Secrets with Wick, a boys' club I can't join."

"It's an exclusive club. We even have a secret handshake."

I'll show it to her after you show it to me.

She didn't want the handshake. She wanted a kiss.

You're going to be doing that all night, aren't you?

"Get a room!" Carter bellowed from the living room, cackling like it was an original idea.

"No, don't," Aubrey said. "We need to get going. Most of the guests went straight from the church to the reception."

"Hey, we told them to go change and get comfortable," Oz said. "This isn't going to be stuffy, they know that."

"Pacifica's informal prom," Zed said. "What's the theme? Under the sea? Starry night? A night to remember?"

"Holiday leftovers," Drew said. "Heavy on the New Year's Eve. We even have a ball to drop."

Only one?

Will clipped a leash to my collar. "Based on your behavior earlier, you're not having free rein until I'm sure you won't jump onto the buffet table."

I wouldn't have.

He told me to not pester Drew for things because his attention should be on Oz. If I needed anything, I was to ask him and failing that, Zed or Jay would figure out what I wanted. I didn't tell him Zed had already figured out what I would want the most, but I promised to stay in the ballroom, and if I needed to go out, I'd find him.

Pretty sure I could find a potted plant to go on, but okay.

The noise outside hurt my ears. People were pressed up against the barriers, waving and shouting, and when we reached the corner, two younger teenaged boys were holding up signs. One said KISS HER in giant block letters, and the other said WE WANT TO SEE THE FIRST DANCE. Oz ran over to them and kissed each one on the cheek and told them there was no music, but if they could find something quick, she and Drew would do it.

Almost on cue, music exploded from speakers on the Square. Oz ran back to Drew, grabbed his hand, and pulled him to the middle of the street. They gave the people their first dance as a married couple, and the second one, too, even though they knew Jax and Aubrey wanted to get them out of the way in case someone out there wanted to do something stupid.

They ended the dance with a long kiss and then ran along the line of people shaking as many hands as they could. It looked more like they were slapping peoples' hands, but it seemed to make everyone happy, and Jax gave up trying to get them to move. They were having fun and trusted people more than he did, and it didn't help that while they were trying to make people happy Carter grabbed Zed and made him dance for a minute, too.

"I am not kissing him!" Zed yelled to the crowd when Carter let go.

Aisha leaned toward Will and said, "They would have the reception right here if they could."

In a way, they were. The music would continue, inviting everyone to celebrate with them. Food vendors had set up on the other side of the Square in the street, and once we were inside, there would be an announcement telling everyone where other party spots were.

There was music playing at Herman Plaza and the Ferry Building, at Civic Center, and along the Wharf. People could spread out and enjoy the party, and at midnight, when the year flipped over from 2416 to 2417, there would be fireworks.

There were fireworks every year, but these were promised to be spectacular.

It took almost an hour to get Oz and Drew to go inside. Everyone's cheeks were red from the cold and I thought they wanted to stop and hug each other warm, but there were lines of people inside, too. Hotel staff wanted to greet them—it wasn't planned, Aubrey promised Oz that—so they shook a bunch of hands there, too. By the time they made it to their own reception, the guests had been there for two hours, probably wondering if they were at the wrong place.

A massive squealing erupted from Oz's friends as she and Drew entered. They darted to the center of the room, surrounded by the kids who used to spend their summers on the roof, along with Drew's friends from home. Anyone over twenty-five wasn't getting near them for a long time; the party had started, and these people were with the ones they most wanted to party with.

That left the mingling to the parents. Jax muttered, "Divide and conquer," before he and Aubrey headed for one side of the room while Shazia and Richard went to the other. Someone needed to play nice with the dignitaries. Will and Aisha headed straight for the bar. He reasoned that they weren't required to rub elbows with the self-proclaimed important people yet, and he wanted to be off his feet for a while.

I went with them, mostly because Will still had a death grip on the leash and didn't leave me any choice. Still, he let me sit on top of the table, where I could see everything going on.

"I remember having that kind of energy," Aisha said. "What the hell happened to it?"

"You gave birth to Jay. That first breath is the transfer of boundless energy, leaving you with only enough to navigate parenthood."

Next one is gonna kill her.

"Next one will sap my energy instead, Wick."

You better be the one pulling it out, then. If you're not right there, it might go after her.

"Let's get to conception and gestation before we worry about delivery."

Maybe your little swimmers are broken.

"My—" He sighed heavily. "Change the topic, all right?"

Just saying. You guys do it all the time. There's nothing wrong with her, so it's gotta be you.

"Is it crass if the I tell the cat to fuck off during a wedding reception?" he asked Aisha.

"Only if Aubrey hears you."

Not far from the bar was the buffet table. It stretched down most of this side of the ballroom and was loaded down with nearly every dead delicious thing I could think of. Servers were standing behind it, ready to cut chunks off hams and turkeys and a giant hunk of meat that might have once been a cow, and there were trays filled with little shrimps and cracked lobster claws. Will saw me looking and promised he would get me something soon, but he wanted to sit and sip his beer for a little bit.

I can wait. Drew is gonna be pissed when he sees all that.

"Why? He knows the guests expect to be fed."

Okay, he's gonna be pissed if it doesn't all get eaten. That's a lot of dead animals. He'll think it's disrespectful to not eat it all.

"It won't go to waste, Wick. The guards and hotel staff will be fed tonight. The real dilemma will be if there's not enough."

"Drew will still be disturbed by the sheer volume of meat," Aisha said. "Wick's not wrong."

"He eats meat. He doesn't have a strong moral leg to stand on."

Drew and Oz were dancing, but it didn't look like they were dancing with each other so much as they were dancing with all their friends. They stopped to kiss a lot, though, and they were never more than a foot or two apart.

You two should dance.

"We will later. Leave the floor to the kids for now."

Fine. Then maybe you want to talk to the guard over there. She keeps glancing at you.

He looked past Aisha. T'Neeka Soto was at the end of the bar, surveying the room. When she looked Will's way again and realized she'd caught his eye, she made her way over, acknowledging them with a formal, "Sir. Ma'am."

"Last week you said I was an ass." He pointed to the chair across the table. "Sit."

It sounded like an order, so she sat.

"Here to guard the kids or guard the guard?"

"Supervising," she answered. "We have more people here than usual. I'm not taking any chances tonight."

"Any problems from the kids deciding to greet people on the street?"

She shook her head. "We anticipated the possibility. The King appeared somewhat anxious, as expected."

"I can hardly blame him. He would have been happier if there were underground tunnels to shuffle the kids around in."

"That would make my job exponentially easier."

"Any word on Will's stalker?" Aisha asked. "Though he doesn't seem to mind his guards as much as he said he would."

"No signs of anyone following him or word that she's asking people on the street for information. No unidentified body in the morgue. She might not have stayed in the city."

"Or she wasn't here for me at all," Will said.

T'Neeka didn't care. "She made it through that portal by assaulting your father. If we find her, that's a minimum of two charges against her, simple assault and entering Pacifica without a visa. Whether she's here for you or not, she's a fugitive."

"That seems rather harsh."

"She could have hurt Finn," Aisha said.

"A crime that has not yet been committed," he reminded them.

T'Neeka got up, promising she would keep him apprised, and went back to her spot by the bar. Before Aisha could get upset, he told her that they could worry about the woman later. Finn was clearly all right—he was walking across the ballroom with Jo, holding her hand as they headed for the buffet—and if the woman he pulled through wasn't dead, she was surely feeling ill by now.

Unless she has an anchor here.

"I'll feel better once we know." She gave him a kiss, her fingers trailing across his cheek, which made him sigh. "Tired, aren't you?"

"I could use a day or two with nothing but lounging in bed or on the sofa with you. Between the holidays and moving and pointless meetings, yes, I'm tired. Even more tired knowing that we promised we'd go to Disneyland with the kids."

"We don't have to be with them every minute of the day. Zed and Jay are going to go off on their own a lot, and Oz and Drew are probably going to hide in their room more than they think they are."

"We could trust Jay and Zed to go without us. They're old enough."

"We could. I know the guards will keep an eye on them."

"But you want to go." He smiled and kissed her back. "All right. But I reserve the right to spend more time sitting on benches than I do walking around."

Make a baby while you're there.

"Are you sure about that, Wick? Because you're going, too, and you'll be in our room."

Like you stop when I'm in the room.

"He wants us to conceive at Disneyland."

Her hand slid across his arm, reaching for his hand. "Timing might be right."

If it's a boy, you can name him Mickey. Or Goofy.
Oh! Pluto!

"We are not naming our child Pluto."

Can I ask a question?

"If it's about conception, no. Anything else, yes."

How come Goofy has pants and Pluto doesn't?

"I don't know, Wick. Why are we even discussing this?"

Donald Duck doesn't have pants, either. But when he gets out of the bath, he wraps a towel around his waist.

"Wick—"

Winnie the Pooh doesn't wear pants. Neither do Chip and Dale. What's with the half-naked characters? If they get a shirt, they should get pants.

"They don't need pants."

They don't need shirts, either, but here we are.

He got up. "I'm getting you food. If you have something in your mouth, you won't be able to talk."

"You shouldn't tease him tonight, Wick. He's tired, and he'll be up very late."

Hey, he's the one who brought up Disneyland.

"Sweetie, listen to me." She unclipped the leash from my collar, and then pulled me closer. "Everyone is exhausted, except maybe for the kids. We need you to be on your best behavior, all right?"

I'm always well behaved. But I'll be good.

I meant it, too.

But then I spotted the fly.

It darted behind Aisha and then zipped over my head, a fur's width out of my reach. She let go when I squirmed to swat at it—I was not letting a wayward fly ruin a perfectly good reception—and when it landed on the very edge of the table, I scrunched down to get a good look at it rubbing its filthy little legs together. There may have been some butt wiggling; that's not something I can control, and I began counting. One, two, three—

—I pounced a split second too late. It wasn't going to escape. I could not allow that, not at the only wedding party Oz and Drew would ever have.

It stayed in my line of sight as I leaped to the floor. Will apparently wanted it for himself because I heard him hiss,

"Goddammit, Wick, no," but he wasn't fast enough to catch it. That left it up to me.

It zipped into the ballroom, darting between guests. Every time someone tried to swat it away from their face, it changed direction, which made tracking it more difficult, but I could hear that annoying buzz slice through the chatter of voices and shrill notes of the music and kept it on my radar.

I was not going to allow it to get anywhere near the food, nor near Oz and Drew. Part of my job as the family cat was to keep pests at bay, and there had never been a time when it was more important.

You're gonna die, fly. Will and I are both coming for you.

Will ran behind me, hissing, "Wick, don't you fucking dare!" I still didn't think he could catch it, but if he could get to it first, more power to him.

I zigzagged my way between moving feet, twisting to the left and then the right, its fuzzy foulness never leaving my sight line. It buzzed over Governor Lopez's head, circled Red Munson and his wife, and then it stopped to rest on Jax's shoulder. There it would die a miserable, toothy death.

Claws out and ready, I jumped onto the back of Jax's leg and scrambled up, clamping my paw down hard, and as I rounded his shoulder, I pulled it into my mouth and bit down.

It tasted awful.

I wasn't eating that.

I flicked my tongue out, sending the little black corpse on a death spiral to the floor, where England's Prime Minister stepped on it.

You're welcome.

Jax grabbed me, and not gently, and thrust me at Will, who was at least three kinds of upset that he didn't get to the fly first and asked what the hell was the matter with me.

There was a fly.

"He was chasing a fly," Will said. "I apologize, it won't happen again."

"Did you get it?" Jax asked me.

"He spit something out," the Prime Minister said. "Good job, Wick."

See? I'm useful.

"Do I need to take you home?" Will asked as he carried me back to the table. "You've been a complete little shit today. I don't understand why you can't sit quietly and stay out of trouble."

That's not fun.

And I'm leaving Oz and Drew alone so they can play with their friends.

"Did he get it?" Aisha asked as he set me down. She was laughing, which didn't amuse him.

"Got it and spit it out at the Prime Minister's feet. I should be grateful it went in that direction and not toward the food."

I wouldn't have stepped on the food. I was protecting the food.

"I'm irrationally irritated, aren't I?" he asked her. "We can't expect him to sit on a table all night. I'd let him roam, but there are so many people. I should have asked for a guard specifically for him tonight."

"Feel like dancing? He can ride on your shoulder."

Zed said he would grab a hover cart for me to ride on.

"We're not serving on carts tonight, Wick."

But carts are fun. We should have had carts.

"Using servers assures that people derive income from tonight. Oz and Drew wanted this to be an opportunity for others, and the pay for tonight is not insignificant." He asked Aisha to watch me and went over to the bar. I thought he was getting something stronger than beer to soothe his disappointment at not getting to the fly first, but he spoke to the bartender briefly and then left the room.

I bet he had to pee.

You want to dance with me? We can slow dance, and I won't dig my claws in. I promise.

"I need a translator, sweetie. All I hear is 'meow, meowmeowmeow.' Sometimes I think I know what you're saying, but not tonight."

Okay. But you're really missing out. I'm an awesome dancer and I don't even grope.

We watched the bride and groom and their friends dance while we waited for Will. None of the older adults were out there with them; they rimmed the room and talked to each other, grabbing drinks from servers that wandered around, but it was like two separate parties were going on. One looked fun, the other looked like a political reception, and I knew that's not what Oz wanted.

There were holiday lights and shiny streamers, and it was supposed to make everyone feel like having fun. She hadn't noticed yet, but I was afraid that when she did it would make her feel bad.

You need to go out there and dance, I told Will when he came back. *The old people aren't cooperating, and they're sucking the fun out of Oz and Drew's party.*

"We will," he said. As he turned, a hover cart floated past him and stopped. "All set up for you. I want you to stay with us at first, all right? And then follow the rules."

I know. Stay inside. Keep off the food table. Find you if I need to pee.

"All right. Come on, then."

We went over to the stage where the band was playing; he said something to a lady standing near one of the big speakers, and then grabbed Aisha's hand, and we went onto the floor. Within seconds, the song that was blaring faded and a slower one started, something gentle, so they could move with their arms wrapped around each other. It probably disappointed all of Oz's friends, who were counting on him to jump up and down and wave his arms, but he hadn't had enough to drink to do that.

Some of the kids left the floor, but Oz and Drew stayed right in the middle. They had their arms looped around each other and barely moved, whispering to each other and stealing kisses. Slowly, as that song faded and another began, everyone moved off the floor, even Will and Aisha, and it was just the two of them, dancing in a spotlight. I don't think they even noticed.

Toward the end of the song, a deep voice dripped from a speaker overhead, "Ladies and gentlemen, Mr. and Mrs. Andrew Blackshear," which spurred everyone into clapping and made Andrew grin. When the next song started, I thought other people would go back, but the dripping voice wasn't done.

"His royal majesty, King Jackson, her royal majesty Queen Aubrey, and parents of the groom, Richard and Shazia Van Hoff."

Can I dance with them yet?

"Not yet," Will said. "When they're done, Jax will dance with Oz and Shazia will dance with Drew. Then you can go."

I waited patiently, floating in a tiny circle. Zed was on the other side of the room with Sophia, and he looked like he wanted to be out there, too.

There should be a family-only dance. I'd even dance with Carter so he wouldn't be alone.

"I'm sure he would appreciate that," Will said.

Oz and Drew parted; they had the same idea I did, running to grab Zed and Jay, then Will and Aisha. Finn and Jo came when beckoned, but Eli didn't because he didn't have anyone to dance with and he didn't want to dance with Carter.

I floated over to him and bounced off his chest until he understood what I wanted.

"All right, cat. I'll go out there and embarrass myself with you."

Carter found a girl to dance with, one of Oz's friends, so he didn't feel left out. Eli danced with me for a minute, and then I floated between everyone, making sure to bump into Will several times because he was already annoyed, so why not? When the song ended, Jax loudly announced that it was time for everyone to stop mingling and start having fun, and the old people finally joined in.

Aubrey shoved Oz and Drew toward a table and told them they needed to sit down and eat something. Oz had barely touched her breakfast, and she didn't think Drew had been able to eat, either. "The nerves are gone, now go eat."

"Did you have anything yet?" Drew asked me, nudging my hover cart so that I would go in his direction.

A fly. But it was gross, so I spit it out.

He fed me from his plate, dropping bites onto the cart. He and Oz sat so close that they kept banging their elbows into each other, which made them laugh hard even though there wasn't much funny about it. There was also a lot of kissing mid-chew, which was almost as gross as the fly, and on the third or fourth kiss I started to say something, but Carter dropped into the chair across from them.

"What's up with Zed and Sophia?" he asked.

"True love." Drew chuckled and then asked, "Why?"

"Eh, I was hoping to hook up with her again before I have to take off. Fun girl."

"Again?" Oz asked.

"Hey, bored, horny teenagers stuck at stuffy receptions," he said with a bit of a shrug. "There were always places to hide."

"So you're bored now?" Drew was not happy. "Come on, this has been a shit ton of fun."

"Not bored. You throw a hell of a party. I just figured she's here, I'm here, why the hell not get reacquainted?"

Oz poked her finger in his direction. "You won't say a word to Zed about whatever creepy things you've been doing with her. Got it?"

He held both of his hands up. "I got it. No hurting the little prince's littler feelings."

"Jesus, you're still a dick," Drew sighed.

"Half-mast prick," Carter said. "A year ago, I wouldn't have given a shit about Zed's feelings. Hell, a year ago I would have tried to get one of your very hot friends to wander off for a while."

"I wouldn't bitch about that. Much. They're all capable of making up their minds about you."

Drew leaned his shoulder into Oz's. "Ah, Carter *likes* Sophia. He was hoping for more than banging in a men's room stall."

Carter snorted like it was absurd. "How the hell did she and Zed get together, anyway? He's a little young for her."

Drew told him about the reception for Levi Munson, when Zed apologized to her for being a pain in the ass when he was younger. She was in a good mood, made him dance with her, and he had a sudden, hard crush on her. "Once we got back from Chicago" —he said it like it had been a vacation and not pulling Oz out of Munson's clutches— "she called him to make sure he was all right. It just snowballed from there."

Oz laughed. "Yeah, she didn't ask about the rest of us, just worried about poor Zed."

"If she had any idea..." Carter was suddenly serious, his temple twitching as he worked his jaw together. "You were so fucked up. Red and I stood over that son of a bitch while we waited for backup, and he gave serious weight to the idea of killing his own father. When he knew he couldn't, he hinted that if I wanted to stomp a boot into his head, he wouldn't stop me."

Oz looked up, searching the room for her uncle. "Seriously?"

"He was dead serious, Oz. And I wanted to, I really did. But I had that tickle in the back of my brain telling me if Drew hadn't blown the bastard off the face of the earth and the Emperor didn't rip his head off with his bare hands, then it wasn't up to me."

Drew mused that Red was probably worried about his soul, not wanting to risk bringing down the wrath of God if he killed Levi.

"What'd the Emperor say to stop you?" Carter asked him.

"He asked me to consider the kind of man I wanted to be."

Carter got that. He nodded and was quiet for a moment, then looked at Oz. "How are you, really?"

"Dealing with it. I have moments, but life is good, and I'm happy."

"Good." He got up "You drinking yet, bro?"

"He loves cinnamon whiskey," Oz said, laughing.

Carter went to the bar and asked for a bottle and three glasses, and then poured them each a tall shot. "My first drink with my baby brother," he said as he lifted his glass. "To the best damn couple I think I'll ever know. An incredible brother and now a wonderful sister. Here's to a hundred years together."

After they slugged the drinks back, Carter got up again and kissed Drew on the cheek. "You know, when I grow up, I want to be you. Seriously. I love you, bro."

"So maybe he's only a quarter-mast dick," Oz said as Carter made his way back onto the dance floor, where he grabbed Shazia away from Richard.

"I still can't believe he made it."

"Year-ago-Carter wouldn't have made an effort. He keeps this up, and when we have kids, I might even let him babysit."

They were going to start smooching again, so I floated back to where Will and Aisha were moving in a slow, tight circle and then decided to greet the other guests. Most of them saw me coming and said hello, and a few even petted me. I zipped past the band and thought I would go say hello to Finn and Jo, but then the Prime Minister's wife screamed as I went past her face. Will grabbed the edge of the cart and stopped me, but he didn't yell because there were too many people watching.

"Just go get Oz and Drew. It's almost midnight."

I did as I was told and sped back to the bar to get them.

Only one person squealed as I zoomed by, and another ducked even though I wasn't all that close.

Drew. Drew. Drew. Drew. The ball's gonna drop in a minute. Then you'll have two. You might need them later.

"Jesus, Wick."

They slugged another shot of the whiskey and then followed me out, just in time for the countdown. Will made me stay close to him while everyone shouted out numbers, and he kept a grip on the cart when a roar of HAPPY NEW YEAR went up. He even held it while Aisha kissed him, as if he couldn't trust me to stay still for ten seconds.

When she was done kissing him, she scooped me up and planted one on my head, too, because it was still midnight and I needed a happy new year kiss, too.

"Put him on my shoulder," Will said. "People will start leaving soon, and I don't want him flying out the door."

Oz and Drew had one more dance and then pulled Will off to the side. They were ready to leave; Jax and Aubrey already knew they planned on sneaking out to avoid any fuss, and they wanted to be able to go without an announcement being made. We were going to sneak down to the garage, where Will's car had been parked, and he was going to drive away with them hiding in the back seat.

"A limo will leave before we do," he told them as we made our way down a hall. "Two guards somewhat resemble you will speed away and hopefully draw any reporters and curious people away from the exit."

I sat on Aisha's lap while Will drove. We waited while the limousine left; there was a guard at the exit who would wave Will on when it was clear.

"All right, Wick," Will said. "What the hell have you been up to today? You have never misbehaved this much."

I didn't misbehave. I was just energetic.

"You didn't listen."

Are you tired?

"Yes, I'm exhausted, you little shit."

Did you still have a good time?

Drew was laughing, and Oz elbowed him in the ribs. "I had a wonderful time," Will said.

And do you want to do this again when Zed or Jay get married even if you're this tired?

"Of course I do."

Then congratulations. You're ready for parenthood.

23

Behaving at Disneyland was easy; I didn't go. I did go with Will and Aisha when they took Oz and Drew to spend a couple of days in his birth When. Will wanted to stay in the city while they were tucked away inside the park, but he didn't want to wander around where strange women were after his DNA. He checked Oz and Drew in, lingered long enough outside the entrance to their private oasis to hear Drew utter, "Holy shit, Oz, this is amazing!" and then turned around and rented one for us.

"Changed your mind about the hotel?" Aisha asked as we made our way to a door three down from Oz and Drew. "I'm not complaining, but you seemed intent on getting a room overlooking the bay and spending two days in bed."

Will tapped my front paw. "Wick has never been in here. I asked for feline-friendly entertainment and enough dead delicious things to make him happy."

You're very thoughtful sometimes. Maybe Aisha will keep you, after all.

He pulled me off his shoulder. "I was limited in what I could get, Wick. Shrimp is prohibitively expensive here, and they ask that fish be reserved for human consumption. But there will be plenty of chicken and pork, and they have the canned food you liked when I was younger."

Do I get a minion to open the cans for me?

"Indeed, you do. His name is William, and I suggest you tip him well at the end of your stay."

Tipping isn't allowed in this When. It must suck to be him.

He set me down and opened the door, and then waved me in first.

If I were human, my jaw would have dropped and I would have squealed.

That's the Tree of Life! I know it is, I've seen pictures. But it has leaves of every color on it. And they look like they have lights in them. And the lights have lights.

This is like if a Christmas tree had lights instead of needles!

The light shifted as he closed the door, which faded into the backdrop. Except for the bright lights glowing around each leaf of the tree, the room was dark and quiet, so quiet I could hear the hiss of air with each breath Will and Aisha took, and just behind that was the beating of their hearts. His thumped slowly, the same *lub-dub* he had when he was still, but when she smiled at him it sped up.

Aisha tilted her head back to take in all of the tree, her face washed in bright yellow and blue and red. Her voice rode on breath as she said, "This is beautiful, Will."

He slid his hand along the wall until he found a control panel and flipped a few switches, and the air swelled with delicate chirps of birds and nattering of small bugs. He asked Aisha what she wanted, a sunny day or starry night, and when she asked for stars and hints of the northern lights, the sky went dark, and thousands of pinpoints of lights appeared.

Where will you sleep?

"Under the tree. It's comfortable. Look for a spot where the color of the grass is a bit darker than the rest. It's a bed."

It's not cold like night.

"It will remain twenty-four degrees in here unless we change it."

He showed me where my food was, what to use instead of a litterbox, and then told me to explore. It felt like being in the simulator, with real grass that wasn't real under my paws, and all the smells and tastes of a spring night. No matter how far it felt like I wandered, I was never more than a hundred feet from them.

At the far edge of the park was the beach. I worried about seagulls and water lapping onto the grass until Will promised me that it wouldn't. I could step right to the water's edge and not get my paws wet, so I ran toward it. Real or not, if I jumped up high and landed hard, I could make nice divots in the sand, and no one would get upset with me for getting dirty.

The room had plans of its own. I was halfway there when a frog leaped out of the grass at me, striking my nose with its slimy webbed foot.

I was just attacked by a frog.

It punched me. Right in the nose.

The chase was on.

It hopped away, and I pounced after it. It would not, I promised, get near the spot where Will and Aisha were going to sleep.

Do I have to eat it if I catch it?

"Do you want to eat it?"

No.

"Then don't. Just play, Wick. You haven't had the chance to play in so many years, I'm afraid you've forgotten how."

This is about the fly, isn't it?

"A bit. Go look around. If you lose the frog, there are other things you can chase."

I don't want to hurt anything.

"You won't. They're simulated. It's fine."

"Are Oz and Drew getting the northern lights?" Aisha asked him as I searched for the frog.

"Northern lights, fireworks, and a campfire tomorrow night. They may never want to leave."

There was the potential that I wouldn't want to, either. They spent most of their time under the tree, bathed in the light glowing from the multi-colored leaves, time in the ocean, and more time talking than bouncing. Will slept deeply, which no longer worried Aisha, and I chased frogs and fireflies and even made friends with a tiny bunny that hopped out from behind the tree.

The bunny was bigger than I was; chasing it was not an option.

I wanted to stay, but at the same time, when Will said it was time to meet Oz and Drew, I was ready to go home. Will thought it might be hard to drag Drew away, but Disneyland awaited and he was just as excited about that.

"He's twenty-one going on twelve," Aisha snickered.

When we got home, timed to be two hours after we'd left, Zed and Jay were waiting near the Ghirardelli Square portal with an air van, and I asked Will to have a guard take me home. He didn't need me, and if I went home, he could go on rides and enjoy the park without worrying about what might happen if they lost track of me. He asked me four times if I was sure, and then called Aubrey to let her know I was coming home.

She needed me more than Will. The apartment was a level of quiet that hurt her, and she wanted my advice about rearranging Oz's room to accommodate Drew. We snoopervised as Jax and Finn painted the walls a deep red with white trim and as they moved the bed and her desk into Zed's old space, and later I watched from the window seat as Aubrey power cleaned the floor. She took me shopping and let me help pick out a sofa and two chairs, and even gave me the final say between two different coffee tables. She wanted them to feel like they had their own little apartment, and when she was done it looked more spacious than Drew's apartment downstairs, and a whole lot cleaner.

The only thing we didn't buy was art for the walls. She thought that was too personal, and Oz had tastes closer to Drew's than her own.

When we weren't taking care of the room, I sat with her while she read, and in the evening we indulged Jax and watched ancient space shows while they cuddled on the sofa.

She tried fussing over Eli, but he would only allow it at dinner time. He spent his days either playing with Finn or taking long walks. He was on a mission to see the things he didn't get to see much of when he was King—all the museums, the tourist shops on the Pier, and he even took a few ferry rides. He made sure he was home in time for dinner, but only because he knew she missed her kids.

She also worried that Oz and Drew wouldn't like what she'd done with their room. The day they were supposed to come home she sat on the window seat of their new living room, watching for them out the window, willing them to get back early.

You need school to start again so you have sticky people to worry about.

I thought she would be excited when they came home, but she was nervous. When the elevator pinged, she jumped up and left the bedroom, waiting near the stairs for the doors to open. Oz was the first out, and she did exactly what Aubrey needed, practically jumping at her for a hug.

Zed slithered past, grunting, "Yeah, hi," as he headed for his bedroom.

"He hasn't slept much in the last couple days," Oz said. "He and Jay are just about punch drunk."

Aubrey forgave him for being rude because she wanted to show them what she'd done yet at the same time she didn't. "All right," she said after she'd hugged Drew, "if this is out of line, I'm sorry, but I wanted you to have your own space, and I didn't want it to feel like a bedroom."

She gestured to the door. "We can change anything you don't like."

Based on the squeal, Oz liked it. Drew dropped his bag on the floor and said, "Hot damn," which made Aubrey happy and relieved.

"This is exactly what we were talking about doing," Oz said.

"Well, a sofa," Drew added. "This is better. Like, a thousand times better. Thank you."

She reminded them it was only temporary. They could live there as long as they wanted, but Drew's apartment was on the remodeling schedule, and it would be bigger and nicer, with three bedrooms and two bathrooms. Drew shrugged; because they'd taken over Zed's room, they had two bathrooms and two huge closets anyway, and this place had a view.

It's too grown up for you.

And clean. You're not this clean.

"And you can bite me," Drew said after Aubrey left. He sat on the window seat and patted the cushion so that Oz would sit with him. "This really does look like an apartment. Our first place together."

"Lots of firsts might happen here. I can finally get you naked and do things to you in here."

Is that gonna happen now? If it is, I'm leaving.

Oz thought they should keep their clothes on and spend time with Aubrey. She'd worked hard to make sure their wedding was perfect, and then she created a wonderful home within a home for them; they wanted to take her to the bakery and have donuts or scones and be all adult while they told her about Disneyland.

I got bacon, that's the important part.

24

Even though Oz and Drew had specifically asked that no one get them wedding presents, Will had a gift for Drew only a few days after they came back from Disneyland.

"Anthony Myers was absurdly excited about this." Will held the door until Drew and Aisha were all the way into the workshop. "He asked that we not question too deeply about how he came to acquire it, nor how he signed off on its licensing, but it's ours to do with as we see fit."

"Were we wrong about him?" Drew asked. "He said he wasn't going to confiscate our research, and now this. Maybe he was being honest."

"I am leaning in that direction."

Jax was, too. When Will told him about Drew's idea of using robotic technology to man and maintain the computing infrastructure for Elysium—an idea considered in its developmental stages but discarded because of the laws limiting the development of artificial intelligence, as well as the limits of the temperatures drones could work in—he set up an informal meeting with the general to discuss the possibilities.

Anthony Myers showed up in civilian clothing, leaving his literal and metaphorical general pants at home. He was as excited about the ideas Will outlined as Drew was about books, and after an hour Will had the notion that Myers was an older version of Drew, stuffed into a military uniform. He spewed forth bits and pieces of things he had once read, the possibilities threaded through books he'd read as a teenager, and the mental picture of Anthony Myers became quite a bit clearer for Will. His interest in Drew's work was personal; he'd been disappointed over the years to be standing on the fringe of seeing his dreams become a reality, only to have them snuffed out by technological roadblocks and archaic laws.

"We met at Fuzzy's," Will said. "Two drinks in, the general was more animated than I have ever seen him. He wants this to become a reality in his lifetime, Drew. His dream is to one day step foot onto a fully functional Elysium."

"Did you tell him that if this works, it'll only be a few years?"

"I did. That was the point Jax told me to shut up, because he's afraid that given the opportunity, Anthony will retire and join whatever security force is placed on the station." He unlocked the cabinet that the drone had been delivered in. "The General declared that wouldn't happen. He told Jax that if he has anything to offer this project, he'll resign outright and come work for us."

"Was he serious?"

"He was slightly intoxicated and enthused about what we're doing, but I think he realizes he's a greater benefit to this endeavor from where he currently sits."

The cabinet creaked as he pulled the door open. Inside was a shiny, metallic blob with arms and legs and a head. It didn't look human, something Drew envisioned, but it had fingers and that's what he had been concerned about.

"This device is genderless—" Will looked pointedly at Aisha "—and functions only as a drone, but we can replace its primary computer and operating system."

"Genderless," Aisha sighed. "What a shame. We could have had so much fun."

"I believe the scenario you're pondering would be beyond my current skill set."

Drew groaned, but then took a step back. "Wait. Drones with gender are a thing? Like, uh, useable gender? I thought you were joking."

"Sex 'bots are a thing," Aisha said. "Everything looks real, feels real, and the 'bot does everything you ask it to."

"Male or female?"

She nodded.

"And it *all* feels real?"

"Focus, Andrew," Will said.

Aisha patted him on the arm. "Oh, stop being stuffy. He's just curious."

"Well, yeah," Drew sputtered. "I mean, like, why isn't this better known? You know how many kids wouldn't be hooking up in high school bathroom stalls and in the Presidio woods if they knew about this?"

Or in Will's car?

"There's an entire field of science dedicated to the research of human sexuality," Will said. "Studies showed that providing a fully functioning 'bot to an adolescent can foster unrealistic expectations in actual relationships, and the history of primitive personal robots has shown a decisive disconnect between owners and other people."

"Kids who fuck 'bots become antisocial," Aisha said. "Simple as that."

"That's what I said," Will grunted.

"Of course you did, sweetheart."

"Well, I did. And not just kids."

"They're insanely expensive," Aisha told Drew. "It's not something the average teenager can afford."

"Yeah, okay. But is it, um, you know, worth it?"

Will sighed. "He's going to beat his way around the bush endeavoring to inquire about your personal experience without actually asking. I presume to avoid embarrassing you."

She wasn't embarrassed. "I've never used one," she said, as much to Will as to Drew. "I dated a guy who owned two, though. Male and female. They were powered down, but I got the chance to check them out." When Will raised an eyebrow, she went on, "Seriously, I've never had sex with anyone's 'bot. I just looked. Closely. Touching might have been involved."

"But you thought about it, right?" Drew snorted.

"Enough," Will said.

"Maybe a little," Aisha said, ignoring Will's awkwardness. "I did ask him if he'd ever powered them up at the same time and instructed them to do each other. He said it was the most boring porn a person could think of."

Drew cackled, and Will sucked in a deep breath. "Now you're messing with me."

"Oh, sweetie, sometimes it's so much fun to make you squirm." She gave him a little kiss. "But no. I really did ask him, and he swears he'd done it and hated the result. Apparently, robot-on-robot sex is, well, robotic."

"And I'll never know," Will said. He reached into the cabinet for the controller and flicked a switch, powering the drone. "This model has the dexterity required but is currently absent of programming beyond a few basic commands."

He brought it out and sent it shuffling across the room, where it picked up one of my nip toys. It turned around and shuffled back, placing it at my feet.

It could be my minion.

"What's the power source?" Drew asked.

"Stacked niconium batteries. It requires a recharge every seven to ten days under normal workload. Exposing it to the levels of cold you propose might cut that in half."

That was something Drew thought he could work with. The drone weighed a bit more than a person of the same relative size, but it moved like a human and was as flexible as one needed to be to work in the confined spaces he envisioned. The key to making it as valuable to Elysium as he hoped was a replacement motherboard, one that could function in extreme cold, and a revamped operating system.

Those weren't insurmountable hurdles.

He pulled up a rough sketch on his tablet, something he'd scratched out while looking at the schematics General Myers had provided. The external design wasn't exactly what he'd had in mind, but he was sure he knew what he needed to get it working.

"This cannot interfere with your studies," Will said.

"I know," Drew sighed. "School first, then work."

"No, for you it's wife first. I will shut this down before you can get three words out if I think you're placing work before Oz."

"You're kinda mean."

"Little bit, yeah."

"No worries. But I might need some help getting through

my math courses this semester." He looked at Aisha and grimaced a little. "Calc four and linear algebra. I'm okay with the computer science classes I'm taking, but those are gonna kick my ass."

"Why on earth are you taking them together? Take one this semester and save the other for next."

"I wanted to get math out of the way. If I survive this semester, then next I'm concentrating on practical and computer sciences. If I juggle things just right, I'll finish with my master's."

"In?" Will prompted.

"Engineering and computer science. I considered a minor in physics because I think I'll need it someday, but I'm counting on you and Finn to fill in those gaps. I have a plan, Will. I know it seems like I'm making this up as I go along, but I have a pretty clear direction."

Will trusted his instincts.

"All right," Aisha said. "You can count on me to help when you need it. You understand I'm the only one teaching advanced calculus this semester, right? You're at my mercy either way."

"I'll sit front and center, and I'll pay attention," he promised. "I'll be confused and lost half the time, but totally paying attention."

The door creaked open, and Oz came in. She dropped her gym bag near the stairwell door and came over, tilting her head as she looked at the drone.

"You have a new toy. I suppose this means I don't have a workout partner today?"

"I'm still yours to kick and throw and yell mean things at." He looked at Will. "Seriously, if I can work on this during the rest of the semester break and afternoons after class, I think I can have a basic working model by summer."

Will directed the drone back into the cabinet. "All right. I won't keep you locked out of the workshop. But you don't spend all day in here, understand?"

"Oz won't let me."

"Damn right," she snickered.

"What comes after that," Aisha asked. "Working model, then what?"

"We'll need a deep freezer," Drew said. "And I had an idea about the substance the nanobots can work in without freezing up, something to insulate the casings with, and I kind of know how it should be made, but someone better versed in chemistry would help."

Will was certain he could borrow someone from Finn; he had a feeling they would need to work closely soon, and Finn would be open to the exchange of ideas and personnel. Once the cabinet was closed and locked, Will told Drew to let it rest for the moment and to go upstairs and let Oz beat the snot out of him.

When the door behind them clicked shut, Will said quietly, "And here we go. With this, if Drew really does have a viable solution to the first nanogel prototype, he can operate the robots at sub-freezing temperatures, Ozoo Enterprises becomes a legitimate business. Andrew Blackshear takes his first step onto what will become an extremely crowded platform."

"Crowded by what?"

"By the thousands of ideas that will pour out of that cluttered brain. He's years ahead of schedule. Finn will appreciate that."

"Finn."

"The last version of him didn't solve his transporter woes until Drew spelled out the obvious to him. According to data stored in the old Mint, Drew is the one who solved Finn's biggest problem."

Aisha picked me up and settled me into the pouch in Will's sweatshirt. "All right. What does that mean for your plan to create a personal transporter?"

"It might not mean anything," he said as we left the building. "Finn managed to invent the system that became the infrastructure for object transport, but living things were an area he never ventured into."

"Because of the ethical dilemma?"

"When you've inverted an embarrassing number of bowling balls, human trials are staggeringly unappealing."

"But you think you know how."

"Enzo," he said as we crossed the street, "*he* knows how. He's done it. He's transported *himself* through space without involving any time parameters. He just hasn't connected the dots. And I admit, once Drew points him in the right direction, I might connect those dots for him. Doing this was never really about creating the technology before he could. It was simply something for us to work on while establishing the company. And Drew's already pushing it to fruition."

"The nanogel will launch you, won't it?"

"He'll have a few false starts, but it's coming, and it will change everything."

25

Sitting at a table outside the bakery became Will and Aisha's afternoon routine. He made sure he had either finished work or could take a break by three o'clock, and she came straight from school to meet him there. They had coffee or tea, and every day there was a bite or two of bacon for me, though one afternoon they were out of it and the girl at the counter chopped up a bit of ham, which was almost as good.

Late in January, Will finished a meeting with General Myers half an hour sooner than he'd expected and instead of going home he headed straight for the bakery. It was sunny and a little warm, so he let me stretch out on the pavement instead making me sit in a chair, and I rolled onto my back to give my useless nipples some sunshine.

I dozed, but not deeply enough that anyone could have snuck up on me. I heard Jay approach—he had a particular foot strike; I didn't have to look up to know it was him—and didn't move because he was harmless enough. I trusted Jay.

Jay betrayed my trust and touched my tummy.

Asshole.

"Where's Mom?" He pulled out a chair and sat down, patting his lap to invite me onto it.

I declined.

You poked my tummy. You're dead to me now.

"I'm here early. Shouldn't you be in a class right now?"

Look at you, getting all Dad on him.

"Canceled. Hell, all but one of my classes was canceled today. I got a shit ton of studying done while I waited to not go to class. Boring as hell."

"I can find things for you to do if you're bored."

Jay snorted. "Yeah, not falling for that. Zara and I are checking out an artists' fair on the Plaza, and then I have a project to work on."

"Very convenient."

"Almost like I planned it that way."

They started talking about Jay's mid-term art project, so I drifted off. I'd already heard about it—he was taking an introductory drawing class—and I'd seen the initial sketches. They didn't need my input. I thought his taking an introductory class was a lot like Zed taking beginner's piano, but they both swore they were learning new things. Jay said he was learning more about depth and composition and Zed realized that he played more by ear and needed to stop treating the keyboard like it was a delicate flower.

Jay's drawing was improving; Zed still sounded like Zed.

Aisha was happier now that she wasn't dealing with disinterested students. She was excited about teaching again; she had students who could challenge her abilities, who were interested in math and not taking the class simply because they needed it to graduate.

Finn was excited because among her students were several science majors, older students with interests in physics and engineering. Where she saw young adults working toward graduate degrees; he saw potential interns and employees. She didn't tell him that Will had first crack at the ones she thought had the most potential, but she promised to keep an eye open for him.

I opened one eye just a little bit because I heard unfamiliar footsteps coming from the stairs and they were headed toward us. It was coming from the wrong direction to be Aisha. Those were giant man feet in my field of vision, so I rolled over and decided it was time to accept Jay's lap invitation, just in case.

All right. You've risen from the dead.

It was Scotty, Aisha's old boyfriend. He went straight for Will and didn't bother saying hello. Instead, he gestured behind himself with his thumb and told Will that Luca Barnes was looking for him, so if he wanted to avoid the inevitable, it would be a good time to run.

Will shrugged it off. "I'm summoned often," he said. "The court process server isn't someone I avoid."

"Hell, Emperor, I'm a damned lawyer, and I avoid him." He looked at Jay. "You're Aisha's boy, aren't you?"

"Jay," Will said. "This is Scott, a friend of your mother's."

Jay held his hand out, but he didn't get up. "Hi."

"Nice to meet you." To Will, he said, "Just wanted to warn you. Luca's such a twitchy little bitch, and he seems to enjoy upsetting people for no good reason."

"What's a process server?" Jay asked as Scotty sped off.

"He has the joyous task of serving court summonses. Luca tracks me down several times a year to serve me notice that I'm expected to testify in matters regarding the shelter or some of its clients."

"People come to you for help and then screw it up?"

"The shelter's legal issues tend to cluster around the mundane. Sometimes it's as simple as unauthorized tenants in shelter-provided residences, or clients exceeding pet limits and refusing to relocate. It's rarely an urgent matter."

A few minutes later, a short, wiry man came up the steps and headed for Will. He had paper in one hand, and as he approached Will he apologized. "Sorry to be the bearer of bad news. But you've been served."

He's not really sorry.

Will took the folded paper handed to him. "You enjoy saying that, don't you?"

"Centuries' old traditions should come with a bit of fun."

He turned around and left the way he came. Will set the paper on the table, not bothering to check it, because Aisha was halfway across the Square and he presumed it was just another unimportant matter.

Jay looked at it. He stretched to see across the table, reading the upside-down letters printed near one of the folds. "Fucking hell, Will. You're being sued for paternity."

That startled him enough that he didn't stand up when Aisha reached the table. Instead, he grabbed the paper and opened it, reading furiously.

Aisha bent over to kiss his cheek and asked what the problem was.

"Fucking paternity suit, that's what," Jay spat.

"What?" She took the summons from Will as she sat down. "Who?"

Before he could answer—he had no idea—Jay abruptly set me on the table and stood up, hard enough to knock his chair back. "You *promised* me, Will. You swore she was the only one you were seeing. I fucking told you I was okay with it as long as you weren't stringing her along, and you *swore.*"

"I wasn't—"

Aisha handed the summons back to Will. "Jay, don't."

"Don't what? Call him on it?" Jay's face flushed red. "I *trusted* you."

"And you still can," Aisha insisted.

He held his hands up and took a step back. "No. I'm going to Dad's."

"Jay, wait." Will started to get up, but Jay shook his head.

"No, fucking *don't.*"

"Jay, stop," Aisha hissed. "Sit down and listen."

"Like hell." He stomped off, walking quickly at first, and then he sprinted across the Square as fast as he could.

She wanted to go after him, but Will set a hand on her arm and suggested she let him be angry for a while. She called James to warn him that Jay was on his way and that he was upset, and while she talked to him Will read the summons.

You know who it is.

"I know."

How?

He didn't know. He didn't care, either, because the details were less important than the outcome.

"He'll calm down," Aisha said. "I don't know why he wouldn't listen, but once he thinks about it, he'll calm down. A paternity test—"

"I have to avoid that, Aisha. This woman may very well be carrying a child with my DNA profile. I am not the father, but—"

"But you might be."

The sadness in her voice nearly broke him. He swallowed hard, and when he said, "I'm sorry," his voice wavered.

"We both know what this is, Will. You didn't cheat on me. Yes, I'm upset, but not because of anything you did."

"I don't want this child to *be*," he said. "I'm angry that Jay is hurt, I'm angry that no matter what, you're hurt, and I don't want this child to exist in any way, shape, or form."

"I'm not happy, either." She got up, reaching for his hand. "Come on. Find Jax, talk to him. Talk to the lawyer. We have to come up with a plan."

"Can that plan be to shove her through a portal the same way you did George?"

"There would still be a baby involved," she said, picking me up. "Don't throw it out with the bathwater."

*

At the same time Aubrey asked, "How is she even still alive?" Jax spat out, "How the hell is that even possible?"

Will had no answer for Aubrey. If it was the same woman—and it had to be—she should not have lived this long without an anchor, not well enough to file a lawsuit. But he could tell Jax how: with the right equipment and a few hairs, some spit, or some blood—even trace amounts—his DNA could be extracted and combined with an ovum and then placed in either someone's uterus or an artificial womb. "It's entirely possible that I have never laid eyes on this woman, and yet the child she carries is genetically my offspring."

"There won't be a way to avoid a paternity test," Jax said. "How many days did they give you to respond?"

She had been given an expedited date for a hearing. Ready or not, Will had to be in court in three days; while Jax sputtered, Will reminded him there was legal precedent for speeding paternity matters through the court. There was little arguing in those cases; there was typically only a court-ordered, on-the-spot blood test. He would be allowed to testify, and if he could prove that prior to any encounter there was an agreement that consent specifically excluded post-conception support, he would be able to walk away with no judgment made against him.

"Since I can't do that, it will be incumbent upon me to prove that the child was conceived through means other than coitus."

"So how the hell?"

"If she conceived in this When it might be possible to find the facility and recover the records. Still, even if we had time to subpoena any records, I suspect the matter was accomplished before she tackled Finn into the portal."

Maybe the baby is her anchor.

He allowed for the possibility. Maternal instinct might outweigh a long-term pre-existing attachment. He thought it was more likely that she came to this When knowing she had someone, someone who had left home when Finn was transporting people to safety.

"Wouldn't they have an anchor of their own?"

"George managed to replace one anchor with another. It's a matter of attachment. If she arrived knowing a parent or sibling was here, someone to whom she had been very close, that could be all she needs."

"What if it's a bluff?" Aubrey asked. "What if there is no child, and she's using the claim to get close enough to you to do... whatever those people need from you?"

There had to be a child, Jax said. The case wouldn't have been allowed to move forward without proof. "The real question is still why."

"Indeed." Will sounded defeated. "Why?"

*

"I understood what Jay truly wanted when he asked that I not hurt you." He was speaking into the dark, lying flat on his back in bed while Aisha sat on the window seat. She was half-watching outside, hoping to see Jay slink across the Square, mortified at his own behavior, but she was giving Will her full attention regardless. "He'd known me for so long, and I was changing everything about our arms-length relationship. He was asking me to protect his feelings as well as yours."

"You've done a wonderful job of that."

"Until now."

"You didn't do this, Bilbo. And he didn't give either of us a chance to explain. He's not letting James get two words out. He just locked himself in his room, turned up the music, and won't open the door."

James called twice to keep her updated, but there wasn't much he could say. He offered to unlock the door from the outside and drag him home, but Will especially didn't want that.

"He needs time to process."

"Without having the details?"

"We could talk to him, explain every little thing, but if he's not listening, he won't hear."

"Tomorrow," she said. "I'm going over there tomorrow, and he'll listen to me one way or the other." She slid off the bench seat and came to bed, stretching out close to him, laying across his chest to give him a long kiss. "You know that no matter what, I'm right here with you."

"It could become complicated, Aisha. The moment the court orders the test, I'm responsible for a child I never agreed to and everything that comes with it. That woman is in my life for at least eighteen years. I could make arrangements to provide for him or her and never see—"

"Your flesh and blood. I know. That's not you and I would never expect it."

"And Jay..."

They were going to worry until Jay pulled his head out of his ass, which could take forever if they left him alone. I left their bedroom and went through the cat flap to find Oz and Drew because Drew had a giant high horse and wouldn't be afraid to ride it right into Jay's bedroom at his dad's place.

They were awake, snuggling together on the new sofa, watching a video. I jumped onto the coffee table, right in their line of sight, and made them listen.

Will might be about to become an unwilling father, but he damn well wasn't going to lose the son he'd just gotten.

*

Zed was the one who told Jay he had five seconds to open the door or he was kicking it in. James happily let us into the apartment, probably because the music blasting from Jay's room was so loud it made the floors vibrate, and he knew we could stop it. Jay made it to the count of four before he yanked the door open, but he wasn't happy to see us and all he did was glare at Zed.

Oz pushed past them and turned the music off, then shoved Jay in the general direction of the living room.

"What the hell is wrong with you?" she hissed.

Instead of answering, he dropped onto the sofa and folded his arms, and scowled.

"Did it ever occur to you that Will's being sued for something he didn't do?" Drew asked. "That someone is trying to ruin his reputation, and nothing more?"

He sneered. "Did it occur to you that Will might have been fucking his way across San Francisco?"

"No."

"You know him better than that," Zed snapped.

Stop growling. No one listens when there's growling.

Oz was the one who softened first. She sat on the sofa and asked, gently, what the real problem was.

"Math," he said. "I'm not the reddest apple in the barrel, but I can fucking add. Mom and Will hooked up late last May at the earliest. So that means that he knocked up this woman *after* that. The only way it happened is if he cheated on her."

"God, you're a moron," Zed groaned. "He didn't cheat on her. It's not his kid."

"Then why the hell sue him? Just take a fucking test and be done with it."

Zed was pissed. "You didn't even give him the chance to suggest that. It sounded to me like you saw the summons and threw a fucking temper tantrum without letting him get a word out."

"He *said* that?"

"No," Drew said, "but Wick was there. You read the summons, freaked out, and ran off."

"Fine."

"So, he takes the test and you have to eat shit for being such a little prick," Zed said. "It's not his fucking kid."

"Back up," Oz said. "He didn't cheat on Aisha, but it still might be his."

Zed flinched. "How?"

James sighed and sat next to Jay. "Fetal cloning. Jay, people often go to great lengths to hurt or get close to people in power. Will is the Emperor and the King's only brother. There are a lot of people who would like a piece of him, even if they have to resort to unprincipled means to get it. Like it or not, he's a target."

Jay's jaw set, and he wouldn't look at anyone.

"How's that work?" Zed asked. "You can't just clone someone. You need their cooperation."

"You need their DNA," Drew said. "Nothing more."

Jay huffed and grumbled, "Bullshit."

"Seriously, *what* is your problem?" Zed asked.

"He *promised* me—"

James set his hand on Jay's leg. "Look at me. It doesn't matter whether Will is being used or if he actually is this baby's father. You don't get to throw a temper tantrum about your mother's marriage. If she trusts him and she stands by him, you owe it to *her* to not make a fuss."

"No, I really don't."

"You need to go home, apologize, and listen to what Will has to say."

"Like hell." He got up and headed for his room. "I wanted one goddamn thing from him, and he made it sound like I'd get that. Just one fucking thing, for once I'd have a family that wasn't built on rage and lies, where cheating wasn't fucking *normal*, and that wasn't about to implode on itself."

He slammed the door again and the lock clicked, but he didn't turn the music on.

"That was my fault," James said. "I'll talk to him again in the morning. Will shouldn't bear the blame for how badly I keep screwing up."

*

I got Will up when we got home—he wasn't asleep, so I didn't have to wake him—because Oz and Drew wanted to tell him what we'd done. He slid out of bed and closed the bedroom door most of the way so that Aisha would stay asleep, and trudged out into the living room to let them in.

Before he could close the front door all the way, I needed to take the fall for making it worse. Getting Drew into trouble wasn't what I'd intended.

It was my fault. I thought Jay would listen to Drew, but his feelings are so hurt that he couldn't even listen to his music when we were done.

"Slow down. What happened?"

"We went to see Jay," Drew said. "Wick filled us in, and he thought we could talk some sense into him, but the only thing that happened was him kicking his dad in the emotional junk, and then locking himself in his room again. He's not listening to reason. I don't think he wants to."

You should go put clothes on. Oz doesn't need to see your useless nipples.

She didn't seem to have a problem when he dropped onto the sofa with a grunt, running his hands through his hair as if that would help anything.

"He's not ready to hear anyone else," Will said. "Let him be angry for a bit. He feels like I lied to him and that everything I promised is about to explode in his face."

Oz told him what Jay had said, about thinking he finally had a family that didn't feel like it was about to implode. "We could have talked him down from that if he had stayed put. I mean, seriously, it's not like he'd lose any of us over this."

"He takes being a member of this family quite seriously."

He's just scared.

"I know, Wick. That's what makes me the angriest. Not that I'm being dragged into court and will undoubtedly lose. He shouldn't bear the brunt of someone else's mistake. He shouldn't, and Aisha shouldn't."

"She believes you, right?" Drew asked.

"Never a doubt."

What if Jay doesn't, not ever?

"He will," Drew said. "He has to."

"I will not allow the quirks of my life to come between Aisha and Jay," Will said.

"Don't you dare." Her voice was soft, laced with tears. She stood just outside the bedroom wrapped in Will's t-shirt, holding it tight against herself. "Jay will get over being angry. And he damn well better apologize, because this is unacceptable."

"I don't need an apology," Will said. "I just need him home."

Drew told Will to call if they could do anything else and closed the door behind them quietly. He stayed on the sofa, but held his arms out to her, because she was about to crack and he needed a hug. Any other night I would have expected groping and kissing things to start, but they held on for a few minutes and then went back to bed.

Sleep wasn't happening; I heard their voices rumble from the bedroom and decided they needed to be left alone. I had nothing for them. No words that would take the sting out of Jay's bad behavior. Nothing funny to lighten their mood. I was at least three kinds of upset, trying to figure out how I could fix even a tiny part of things. I curled up on the sofa to think and spotted Will's phone on the coffee table.

I knew the passcode.

I knew how to make it light up.

I jumped over and touched my nose to the spot that made the screen light up, and then the little picture of Jay's face.

Is Wick. U awake.

It took a few minutes before he answered. "I'm not that stupid, Will."

It took me a long time to type. Mistakes were made.

Ur waring red shirt tnight.

Ur also not red apple. Not in barel.

"Fine. Okay. It's you. What do you want?"

We R keeping U.

Right?

We luv you. I do.

I waited. It took him ten minutes to answer, and I was starting to think he had turned his phone off.

"Wick, I love you, too, but I have a right to be pissed off."

No.

Will not cheated.

Didnt.

"He wouldn't tell anyone if he did. Men lie. They fuck around, and they lie about it."

Ask Oz.

She can see lies.

U can't lie 2Oz.

Wills not like ur dad.

No cheating.

Ask Oz.

I waited. Ten minutes, then fifteen, and nothing.

Will luvs you.

Ur not step.

Ur son.

He would die4U.

"He made promises, you know."

He would die4U.

If I made U allergyc he wood give me t0 Drew t0 live there.

U first.

Ur hisson.

Come home.

Plz.

"Tomorrow. I'm still pissed off, though."

Ok.

"Still there?"

Ys.

"Love you, buddy. I mean it."

Luv U2. U luv Will.>?

"Yeah, but I'm not gonna change my mind about being mad."

Ok. Go sleep.

"You're a pushy little fucker, you know that?"

Ys. Bed now.

*

Something that would have been nice to know: text messages don't go away when you turn the phone off. When I was done talking to Jay I poked the power button and thought that was it—Will would never know I had used his phone. But then I woke up to the sound of eggs being scrambled, and Will's voice coming from the kitchen.

"Look at the time stamps. It took him over an hour to type all of that out. I can't be mad at him. I should be, but..."

"Well, Jay is right. He's a pushy little fucker."

I peeked over the back of the sofa. The apartment was mostly open space, and I could see straight into the kitchen. Will was at the breakfast bar—still no shirt—phone in hand, poking through the texts.

Staying right where I was seemed like a good idea.

"Jay can remain as upset as he needs to be, as long as he comes home."

Aisha pushed eggs out of the pan onto his plate, and they didn't bounce, which was impressive. Also, there was bacon, which made me consider being officially awake. "It didn't take long for that, did it? For this to be home, and his dad's place is just that—his dad's place."

"Let's see how he feels about that in two days. When the judge orders—"

"Nope, we're not talking about that. Jay will have to listen to reason and accept the facts. And whatever decision you make about how involved you'll be in that child's life, he doesn't get a say. He accepts it and moves on."

"I don't want to be involved at all. I had nothing to do with its creation."

"Will." She leaned across the breakfast bar and kissed the tip of his nose. "We're talking about a baby. A human life. I don't expect you to have anything to do with his mother, but a child deserves a father. Like it or not, it's your DNA."

"I *don't* like it. And I don't think I will ever be able to consider it my child."

"Not it. Him. Or her. And the moment you lay eyes on him, you'll melt."

"I'll melt the moment our child is born." He took a deep breath as the idea dipped into his mind, and asked, "Do you still want to have a baby?"

"Of course, I do. Though maybe not right this second. Jay might walk in, and I see tiny little cat ears and eyes peeking over the sofa, watching us."

He didn't look. "Wick. Come in here."

I don't want to.

"Now."

I really don't want to.

"There's bacon," Aisha said. "Come on. I won't let him bite you."

I sat at the far end of the breakfast bar, just in case.

"You used my phone without permission," he said, waving the phone at me. "You also interfered in my relationship with Jay. That could have ended quite badly, do you understand that?"

Jay likes me.

"Yes, I know. He's very fond of you. But he's angry with me, and he needs to deal with me. Pushing back at him could have easily made him shut down and refuse to discuss this at all."

You're mad at me.

"No, I'm not mad, Wick. Well, I'm not happy with your spelling and grammar. I know you know better."

It takes me too long to spell and it hurts my nose. I just wanted to talk to him.

"Ask me next time, all right?"

You would have said no. Better to say I'm sorry than to take a chance.

"Then you're really not sorry, are you?"

Aubrey says saying you're sorry is important because it makes other people feel better. I don't want anyone to be mad.

"Everyone was upset last night, sweetie," Aisha said. "Upset enough that we might have let you text him."

"You've never done that with anyone else," Will said. "I think he knows that."

Don't tell Drew. He might feel left out. Or Zed. I don't think Oz would care.

He didn't think any of them would care, but he promised to keep my secret. I promised to stay home with Aisha and wait for Jay. He hadn't said what time he'd come back; Will wanted to wait, but he had an appointment with the lawyer and it didn't seem like a good idea to postpone it.

She wanted time alone with Jay, anyhow.

That was something he should have been more afraid of than Will being home and upset. She sat at the kitchen table after Will left and let her anger simmer. I watched, silently, as she tapped her fingers on the table, then as she ground her teeth together. She glared at the door, willing it open while praying that it wouldn't.

I heard his feet on the stairs; he was stepping softly, trying to be quiet. He hadn't taken the elevator because it would have announced his arrival with an annoying ping, and he wanted to slip in without being seen.

The door creaked open, and he started for his bedroom and twitched when she told him to come into the kitchen and sit down.

"Let me take a shower first. I'm still wearing yesterday's underwear, and I feel gross."

He turned as if he expected her to just let him go. When she spoke again, her voice was low and as close to a growl as I thought a person could get. "James Jordan, get in here and *sit your ass down*. I won't tell you again."

Jay did as he was told, but he did it with as much irritated flair as he could muster. There was an audible *thunk* as he dropped into the chair, and he folded his arms with an exaggerated sigh. "What?"

"You damn well know what."

"You knew where I was. I know you talked to Dad, you know that I went exactly where I said I would. And I stayed there."

Dude.

"I have never been this angry with you before, Jay. You didn't give anyone a chance to explain, and you flung Will's promise in his face. You hurt him, and you had no right."

He shrugged. "Will's a big boy. He'll get over it."

Aisha clenched her jaw to keep from erupting. She waited, staring at him, trying to make him squirm. Then, "There is a zero percent chance that Will fathered that baby."

"And you know that because he, what, told you?"

"I know because that's not the kind of man he is. I don't have to ask."

Jay huffed through his nose. "Yeah, and I bet you never thought Dad was that kind of man, but he cheated on you anyway, didn't he? Nice guy, means well, but he can't keep it in his pants."

"Don't you dare."

"Why not? It's the truth. You loved Dad, he loved you, but he fucked anyone he could and thought he was hiding it. But he *sucks* at hiding it, and you knew when it was happening. What makes you think it's not happening now?"

Evenly, trying to keep her temper in check, she asked, "What makes you think it is?"

"Because a goddammed pregnant woman is suing him to get him to admit he's the father! You don't do that unless you know for fucking sure who that is!"

"If you had stuck around and asked him, Will could have explained."

"Lied, you mean."

"Stop. You don't get to be judge and jury here. And don't lump Will in with men who lie and cheat. It's not a gender flaw, Jay. Not all men cheat."

"From where I sit?"

"One man. You know *one* man who has a problem with infidelity. And I'm sorry that it's the most important man in your life, but he's not a shining example of how men should treat the people they love. He knows that, too, Jay. It's the thing he hates about himself."

He softened, just a bit.

"How'd you stay friends with him? Hell, how come we lived so close to him? I've seen how he is, Mom. Like, he loved George, but it was one person after another, and George fucking *knew*."

It took her a few minutes to find a way to explain. When she met him, it was clear that he preferred men and that he was never with someone more than a week or two. But they became friends, and they fell in love. He believed he could change and he believed he could be faithful. He said he wanted that and she assumed he had been for the first few months. Even then, she thought he could figure it out, what mattered more to him: his family or his impulsive, wandering eye.

"He loved me, Jay. He truly did. He still does. Once we split, we still had you, and we knew we had to parent together...we realized we were much better as friends than we were as a couple. And after that, he became George's problem."

Jay snorted. "You know, *George* was faithful. Say what you want about him, but he never cheated."

"Even serial killers have their shining moments, sweetheart."

"I hope you're not wrong about Will, Mom. But what the hell will you do when the judge orders a paternity test and if it comes back as his?"

"Jay, we fully expect that it will."

He flinched.

"That doesn't mean he cheated on me."

"Oz said something about fetal cloning. I was only half listening because I thought it was bullshit. You believe that?"

She explained about the cult and the offshoot that was actively trying to find him. "Finn inadvertently pulled a woman through a portal, and she took off before he could get his wits about him. We think it's the same woman, and that she managed to get a good enough sample of his DNA to conceive."

"Mom, that's freaking expensive. Why? Why would someone spend that kind of money just to have *his* kid?"

"That's one of the things we don't know. We kept joking that they wanted to raise a bunch of tiny emperors to form their own army, but the truth is that we have no idea what the motive might be. We only know they've been trying to find him for years, stuck in his old When, and now they may have found a way."

"What happens if the test says it's his kid? He can't tell the court or a judge about time travel and portals, or even the cult."

She shook her head. "I don't know."

"He's on the hook for a kid that's his but also isn't?" He said it as if he didn't expect an answer. "Wait. Does he have any other kids? I mean, like, from an old relationship?"

"No."

"You sure?"

"He would have told me, Jay. He wouldn't hide a child, and he wouldn't ignore his own."

"So he would help raise it."

She blinked and sent tears down her cheeks. "He doesn't want a baby this way, Jay. Not like this. I don't, either. But once he works through the anger, I don't see him turning his back. He truly isn't that kind of man. He'll see himself in that baby—"

I ran across the table to purr for her. Jay thought about it, saw how it ripped at her, and the realization settled with him. "You're trying to have a kid together, aren't you? He *wants* a baby. He just wants it to be yours."

She took her time answering. "Whatever happens in that courtroom, it doesn't change what Will and I want together and for each other."

"Fuck it. She's from the future. Shove her ass back through a portal and be done with it."

She didn't say anything, but the light in her eyes flashed, and we all knew what she was thinking.

*

"It would be helpful if we could depose Wick," Will mused. "Though, even if we could, it would be hearsay."

"Give him a tablet, he can testify," Jay said.

Aisha wasn't sure he was serious, but she quickly told him that wasn't happening. "Even if it was a closed hearing, Wick's abilities are a family secret. Keep it that way."

Will asked me to jump onto his lap so he could show me a picture. I'd noticed more of the women who stalked him than anyone else; they had one photo of the woman who had filed the suit, taken from a security camera in the city clerk's office. It was full faced and clear, but he didn't recognize her.

It wasn't the red-haired lady, and it wasn't George's neighbor, Cherry.

She resembled one of the women who had stood by quietly but was significantly younger. I thought she might be someone's granddaughter or a niece, but I didn't think she was one of them.

"You have a name and address, right?" Jay asked. "Go knock her fucking door down and make her talk. And then drag her ass through a portal."

"I have a name, which may not be her true name. The address used is from a mail drop. And don't tempt me."

"Really, why not? She's from somewhen else, just send her home."

"Because we have no proof that she's the same woman who tumbled through the portal. Finn never got a good look at her."

That didn't matter much to Jay. He was still in favor of dragging her into a different When. He'd seen Aisha do it to George; it was a viable option as far as he was concerned. "What if you just don't show up? They can't arrest you."

"They can most certainly arrest me," Will said. "I am not above the law."

"Mr. B is, though. Can't he put a stop to all of this?"

Aisha twitched when he said that; she would never ask, but she knew it was possible. Jax could make it all go away. Including the woman.

"How would that look, if he did?" Will asked. "The case is a matter of public record. It's already been in the news. If Jax steps in and orders the court to not proceed, it taints his authority, as well as making me look guilty and petty."

"I just don't want Mom to have to go through this."

"Neither do I."

"I can handle this," she insisted. "Don't waste time worrying about me."

"Enzo, I have to worry about you. You might leap over the rail and twist her head off her neck."

She didn't deny it and even grinned a tiny bit.

*

"What's the game plan?" Drew asked. We waited for Will's lawyer on the courthouse steps, ignoring the reporters who bellowed questions from the sidewalk. It was a public hearing, but they weren't being allowed to get near any member of the royal family. There was a brief protest until Oz stated loud enough for them to hear, "We've always tried to be accommodating, but there's nothing to tell you. When there *is* something, we'll say so. Please, just give us a break right now."

They gave us a break.

Aisha and Jay followed Oz and Zed inside. Will had asked Jax and Aubrey to stay home—their presence might be intimidating—but Jax insisted on being there before the hearing began. He'd allowed the others to come because they were adamant that he have support, even if they weren't allowed to speak on his behalf.

"Plausible deniability," Will said to Drew. "The plaintiff hasn't asked for a paternity test yet, and we'd like to keep it that way. I have to make the judge believe that there's not a chance this woman knows me."

"Everyone in the city knows you, Will."

They did, but not like that.

Why are we outside?

"Just waiting for the lawyer."

He'll find you inside.

"Something about being out here that bothers you?"

She might show up. And then I might have to eat her face. I don't like the taste of people.

Drew thought I was melodramatic, but Will knew better. He'd seen what I did to George as Aisha hauled his asterisk through the portal. He decided to err on the side of keeping me out of the news and went inside to wait with her.

She wanted to be strong, to be the steely-eyed wife staring down the bitch who was picking on her husband, but when he reached out to put his arm around her, she fell into him. They stood like that, holding onto each other, and no one said a word until the click of guards' heels on the slick marble floor caught their attention. Jax, dressed in a new black suit that had been tailored to show off muscles he wished he had, arrived with his personal guards. He told them to stand down—which meant they could step to the side but not that they could relax—and he went to Will.

A police officer was waiting outside the courtroom who stayed mostly at attention, too afraid to move.

"She here?" he asked.

Will shook his head. "I don't think so. Not unless she arrived ahead of time and is already in the courtroom."

The only one Will was concerned about was his lawyer. There were only ten minutes until they had to be seated, and he hadn't heard anything from him. He pulled his phone out and was about to call when the door banged open, and he came running down the hall.

The lawyer barely acknowledged the King's presence. "Sorry. Had to take a call. Your accuser only secured counsel last night, and he's straight out of law school. Use that to your advantage."

Aisha finally let go. "How?"

"This is his first case. From a five-minute phone call, I'm pretty sure he's both cocky as hell and terrified enough to wet himself if pushed too hard." He looked right at Will. "This is a hearing, not a trial. You'll be able to direct questions from the stand. You're the Emperor. *Be* the Emperor. Don't be William Blackshear."

Duh.

Lawyer dude—Vincent—gestured to the courtroom and told everyone to head in. They went in one by one, until the cop stopped Drew and told him I wasn't allowed inside. "No pets. Sorry."

Jax reached for me and then set me on Will's shoulder. "Really, son? You're turning my cat away?"

"But—"

"I wouldn't recommend it."

Instead of turning around and heading down the hall with the guard falling in line behind him, leaving the cop with his mouth hanging open, Jax went into the courtroom. Will watched him go in, and he was momentarily perplexed because Jax was supposed to leave. He wasn't supposed to stay.

Jax never plays his royalty card.

"Assuring me one victory today," Will whispered. "I want your word today, Wick. You'll sit with Aisha or Drew. You will not try to get a better view, you will not speak, and you will not set your feet on the floor. Understand?"

What if someone asks me a question?

"Answer if it's a question from Drew or from me. But I need your absolute best behavior. We can't afford a repeat of the wedding."

I was fun at the wedding. Drew said so.

He apparently didn't agree because he refused to comment on it. Instead, he tucked me under his arm, took a deep breath, and went in. Jax had moved to the other side of the railing, the one that separated the audience from the court, and he spoke with Vincent as a bailiff dragged another chair over for him.

Will set me on Aisha's lap; she took the aisle seat, where she could see the judge and the seat Will would testify from, and if she turned her head she could give the woman suing him her best death glare. Aisha gave her a stern, wilting look when she arrived with only a minute to spare, scurrying after her own lawyer, but she didn't stand up and yell at her, which is what I wanted to do.

I'd promised to be quiet.

The courtroom didn't look a thing like it did on the news or on entertainment shows. This was just a badly painted, stuffy, oversized office with a bunch of desks, a couple of them taller than the others. In one corner there was a flag on a pole that tilted a little bit to the right, and we were in padded chairs behind a wood railing. It was all very old and worn.

Will sat with his lawyer just in front of us; Jax took the seat that put him closest to the woman and her lawyer, and he stared straight ahead. Will glanced at the other table once, but then refused to allow his curiosity to win. He was calm and collected, and unlike the lady at the other table, he didn't startle when the bailiff yelled for everyone to stand up because the judge was coming in.

He wouldn't look at her, but I did. I stared. She didn't have a tattoo, not one that I could see. She was young; she appeared younger than Oz but could have been a year or two older than Drew, if accounting for how slow Will aged compared to Jax. She also didn't look pregnant, not at all. I squinted to see if maybe I was looking at her from the wrong angle, because her shirt was tight and it should show, but even when she turned to check on a woman that had accompanied her—her mother or aunt, someone older and starting to wrinkle—there was no bump that said, *hey, someone knocked me up.*

The only one of the kids who looked at her for more than a second or two was Jay.

Everyone got to their feet, except for Jax. He sat quietly, watching as the judge entered, and he didn't react when the woman suing Will hissed, "Jesus, get up, it's the judge. You have to stand."

After the judge took his place and gestured for everyone else to sit down, he stood back up. "Your majesty." He was polite but clearly not happy. "We're honored to have you present."

Jax nodded, which the judge took as permission to sit back down. "I'm here to offer moral support to my brother, nothing more. I will not speak again unless you personally direct an inquiry to me."

The judge gave a short nod and then asked for a reading of the case. A woman seated near him stared down at a computer screen as she announced the case of Dallas Engle versus the Emperor of San Francisco in the matter of paternity regarding unborn baby Engle. Ms. Engle was seeking a judgment of paternity and sufficient support to carry the pregnancy to term, and then sufficient support post-birth to assure her ability to properly care for the child.

The lawyers immediately began griping at each other, fighting to be heard over the sound of the judge's boredom. He reminded them that while this was a hearing and not a formal trial, he wasn't putting up with anyone's ego and that they'd damn well better follow protocol.

Jay shifted in his seat and stared at the woman with strawberry blonde hair. She noticed and kept glancing his way, willing him to stop, but he glared until the lawyers quit picking at every word the other said and Will was called to the stand.

He'd barely gotten his mouth open to be sworn in when Dallas Engle's lawyer objected. They were suing the Emperor of San Francisco, not William Blackshear.

The judge sighed audibly, and Will simply said, "Indeed."

I couldn't see Vincent's face—Will's lawyer—but I was pretty sure he was trying not to laugh. He sat while Will was sworn in, promising to tell the truth, but when that was over he stood up and pointedly asked, "Mr. Blackshear, do you know the complainant?"

He glanced at her. "No, I do not."

"Have you ever met her?"

"I meet a substantial number of people on a weekly basis. I cannot say with one hundred percent certainty that in forty-three years we have never met."

"Does her name, Dallas Engle, seem familiar?"

"No."

"Have you ever engaged in relations of any sort with Dallas Engle?"

"No."

Her lawyer stood up with a half-hearted objection. "Come on. You meet women all the time. How can you be sure?"

"I am positive," Will said, trying to sound disinterested.

"You'll get your chance, counselor," the judge said. "Sit down."

Vincent didn't have many other questions. He opened a single door—do you know her, have you ever met her, have you ever spoken to her—and let Will step through it. When he was done, he nodded to the other lawyer and then sat down.

"All right," newby lawyer said as he got up. "You're a prominent fixture in San Francisco and a pretty powerful guy. Right?"

"One might make that argument. One might also assume that by now someone in your position would know the name of someone in mine."

"I'm not a native Pacifican. I've only heard you referred to as the Emperor."

"All right."

"Name aside—you're powerful and face it, you're an attractive guy who commands a lot of attention from women."

"I'll take your word for that."

"Do you honestly expect the court to believe that you remember every single woman you've been with?"

"Indeed, I do."

"You're under oath, Emperor. You're saying there's no possibility that you met Dallas Engle and had a one-night stand and have simply forgotten."

"That's exactly what I'm saying."

"Hard to believe, you know."

"Your level of difficulty with the truth should not be an issue in these proceedings," Will said.

"A powerful person such as yourself, who is routinely surrounded by women, who likely can—by his reputation alone—get pretty much anything he wants? I'm sure I'm not the only one who believes that you have a history long enough that the names have basically blurred together."

Will's lawyer jumped up, ready to object, but Will leaned forward just a touch, and calmly said, "I can name every woman I've been with, counselor. Is that what you're fishing for? A list so that you can determine whether or not I truly do remember, hoping that I falter?"

"Jesus, no," Jay whispered.

The lawyer shrugged. "Not exactly what I was after, but sure. Give us the names in your little black book, so to speak."

He looked to Aisha, silently asking permission. She gave a short nod, and her hands tightened around me.

"Aisha Blackshear."

The lawyer waited, then screwed up his face, confused. "I'm sorry. Were you waiting for me to write the names down?

The court reporter will catch them all."

"No. I've given you the list, as requested."

"One name."

"Indeed. I think it's safe to say, had there been someone else, I would remember."

"Seriously? *Just* your wife?"

"Counselor," the judge barked.

He turned to Dallas and whispered harshly. "What the hell did you get me into?"

"He's lying," she hissed back.

Ten minutes into the cross-examination, Will had had enough and demanded his right to question his accuser. The judge asked him if he was sure, and when Will said he was, the lawyer was told to sit down and only speak if he needed to confer with his client.

"Your insistence that I am your child's father lends itself to a presumption of familiarity," he started. Her eyebrows knotted, and she gave a little shrug, not sure what he meant. "If you were intimate with me, you surely would have noticed a few things about me. If you would, then, tell the court, what about my body is unusual?"

She immediately began whispering to her lawyer. I looked up at Aisha to make sure she was all right; she was trying not to smile. Jay was looking right at Will, but I couldn't tell what he was thinking. His eyebrows made me think he was angry, but his eyes seemed sad.

"I don't get it," the woman finally said.

"It's simple enough. What stands out, regarding my body? Do I have any unusual birthmarks, scars, tattoos, or piercings? Am I circumcised or not? Average? Small? One nipple out of proportion to the other in a noticeable manner? Tell me about our alleged encounter and what you saw."

"It was dark. I don't know."

"Dark or not, surely you would know if I were average or not, or if I were circumcised or intact."

She leaned toward her lawyer and whispered just loud enough for me to hear, "I don't even know what that means."

"Jesus, you're fucking kidding me," Jay said under his breath. Jax didn't turn to look, but his shoulders twitched the way he did when he laughed, and I heard Zed snort lightly.

"Ms. Engle, I don't know you. I can't say for certain we've never crossed paths, but I do know that I have engaged in physical relations with only one woman, ever, and it was not you."

More whispering from her lawyer and it went on long enough that the judge ordered them to move forward or admit defeat.

Dallas Engle stood up, looked right at Will, and said, "Fine. I demand a paternity test."

*

The judge directed the courtroom to be cleared, except for the lawyers, Will, and Dallas Engle. He couldn't order Jax to leave, but he did suggest that everyone wait until the King had made his way to the door before getting up. When Jax stood, the judge did, too, and gave a sort of half-bow, because he wasn't sure what the protocol was when the King decides to play courtroom spectator.

We waited in the corridor while Will's blood was taken and while samples were acquired from Dallas and the fetus—he insisted on being present for that, because he didn't trust that there would be a clean sample otherwise—and then he came out, rubbing the spot where they had stabbed him to get his blood.

Jay sat on a bench away from everyone else, elbows on knees and chin resting on his hands. He wanted to be alone after leaving the courtroom, which confused Zed because as far as he was concerned, everything said in there was enough to put any of Jay's doubts to rest. Drew tried to tell him Jay was processing it all, but I don't think he completely understood, either.

Will did. He held a finger up to Aisha—he would be there in a minute—and he went straight to Jay.

Let me down. He's upset. I might need to purr for him.

Drew set me on the floor and watched as I ran over and jumped onto the bench.

"Are you all right?" Will asked him. "Be honest. I can handle any anger or confusion you may have."

"I hate that I have to ask, Will. I wanted to ask Oz what she saw, but—"

"I was telling the truth."

"Seriously? Only Mom? Like, ever?"

Will leaned back and slid his arm on the bench behind Jay. "I spent most of my life thinking I couldn't touch anyone. Being with someone would have involved contact."

"Yeah, I knew that, but I assumed…I dunno. Maybe it was an exaggeration? I just thought you'd had other girlfriends. Like, maybe along the way you risked it. You said you'd learned to control it." He sucked in a hard, confused breath. "Fuck it, Will, I mean I knew, but I didn't *know*. You know?"

"I have loved only one woman, Jay. If along the way I had learned that I had a modicum of control when I touch someone, she would have been the first person I looked for. When your mother came back into my life, I'd only been working on that control for a few months. And still, she was the one who inhabited most of my thoughts when I considered the possibilities."

"All those years."

He nodded. "I loved her all those years."

"You had crushes, right? I mean, there had to be a few women you were interested in. That's just normal."

"I certainly notice women who are warm and personable and women who are attractive. I always will, I hope. But I've never been interested in pursuing an emotional relationship with anyone else, and I've always known that a relationship would be a personal requirement preceding any intimacies. That she was the only one occupying that space within me is not an exaggeration. I never made room for anyone else."

"I'm sorry. I mean, not that you waited for her. I get that. But all of this. It's not fair."

"It's more unfair to your mother. This is not what she signed up for." His hand slid forward, and he rubbed Jay's back. "It's not what you signed up for, either, but this is something you need to come to terms with. There will be people who will try to take advantage of your place as a member of the Blackshear family, simply to see what they can get from you. This could have just as easily been someone who filed a suit against me, whose only intention was to have my lawyer offer a settlement without a paternity test, just to see the amount offered. People assume things about those in public positions, and money is one of them. A high number of acquaintances is another, and they hope you'll assume you simply don't remember them and offer a payout to quiet them."

"What that dickhead said, about you not remembering all the women you'd slept with. I was thinking that, Will. When you said you'd name them all, I was ready to freak out and leave the room, and I was pissed that you'd make Mom hear it. I didn't want her to have to go through that in court."

"I'm sure anyone within earshot thought the same thing. I understand I fall outside the norm."

Jay sighed and got up. "Well, I'm also sorry you felt like you had to admit that in public."

That seemed to surprise him. "I'm not ashamed of my inexperience, Jay. It might raise an eyebrow or two, but it was never a secret, and I truly do not care if people know. Anyone paying attention over the years shouldn't be surprised." Will picked me up, and we went back to the others. Aisha gave him a hard hug and a quick kiss just as three of the royal guard and a police officer marched in, stomping past us and into the courtroom.

"What the hell?" Oz sputtered.

"Those samples are not leaving here without guards," Will said. "The results will be ready tomorrow afternoon. For now, we go home and wait."

"What?" Drew said. "They could have the results in five minutes."

"If I trusted her lawyer and used the lab he pre-selected, it would be. I wanted an independent lab for this, regardless of the expected outcome."

We started to leave, but then Dallas came out of the courtroom, escorting the woman who had sat there quietly through the entire thing. She leaned heavily on Dallas, shuffling in tiny increments toward the door, and as they passed she looked at Will, her eyes red and watery, her head twitching, and she breathed out, "I'm so sorry."

The skin on her arms was not half as wrinkled as her face, and I recognized that twitch. George twitched the same way, just before Aisha grabbed him and pulled him into the portal.

Will, look at her wrist. Look.

Look!

He looked at her over Drew's shoulder and saw the same thing I did. A tiny, misshapen lotus tattoo, faded but still utterly recognizable.

Time is eating her alive.

Will wanted to care, but he didn't. All he wanted to know was why.

*

Vincent Jayne had been the head of the King's legal team for five years. He knew personal details of the royal family's lives, but he was not aware of the portals, nor where Will had come from. He dealt with the facts of their entanglements: when he started at the bottom of the legal team, Will was a teenager known only as the Emperor, and King Eli insisted the matter not be pursued. While he never openly said so, Jax and Will both suspected Vincent shared the world's assumption that Will was Eli's bastard son, a belief supported by his formal adoption at age forty-two. That Will's parents were also named as legal members of the House of Blackshear did nothing to shake that suspicion. He presumed they had been around, somewhere, and had no idea that Will had gone twenty-five years without seeing them.

It was not information Will wanted to share.

"You're certain the results won't be in your favor?" Vincent asked.

We were at the corner bakery. Jax rode in the car with us, and the lawyer met us there. Oz and Drew knew better than to hang around, and after a few minutes, Aisha asked Jay and Zed to give them privacy.

"I was truthful on the stand," Will said. "But we have reason to believe my DNA was co-opted and used to conceive that child."

"Not something one does at home, stretched out on the kitchen table," he mused. "There's evidence somewhere. I suggest we start with the lab she wanted to use to process the paternity test."

"The kitchen table?" Jax said. "Really?"

"You'd be surprised. Turkey baster, fresh specimen. It happens."

The idea made Jax laugh. "Bullshit."

"Eh, you never know. But I think we can safely rule it out. I'll subpoena the lab records as soon as we leave court tomorrow and I'll appeal whatever the judge orders as far as monetary support."

"I'm not worried about the money," Will said.

"Scare the hell out of her," Aisha said. "When the results come in, announce that you're seeking custody. Full custody, with no financial support for the mother."

"That's cold," Jax snorted.

Will scowled. "It could also backfire. I don't want custody, and I'm not certain about any form of visitation." His voice started to go up in volume. "I had no part in the creation of this child and feel no connection. I can't—"

She set her hand on his arm. "Will. It's all right. That's not something you even need to think about right now. I should have known better. I know how horrible the timing of this is."

"Something happen?" Jax asked.

Aisha's finger tapped on his hand, and he listened—it's all right, tell him.

"You need anything else?" Jax asked Vincent, who understood he was dismissed.

"We've gone past—" Will sucked in a deep breath. "We've been trying, that's all. We've moved past simply thinking about it to actively trying."

Jax perked up. "That's *all?* That's major!"

"So you can understand why I am less than enthused about the possibility of someone else bearing a child using my DNA."

"A baby with Aisha would still be your first child, Will. This—whatever the hell this is—doesn't count, not like that."

"A child counts, Jax," Aisha said. "He shouldn't bear the consequences of his mother's actions."

Will withered a tiny bit. "This child would be in our lives, Aisha. If you want me to count him as mine, he would be in our lives, expecting my love, and I'm not sure I have that in me."

*

Late that night, while I sat on the window seat and watched another cat stalking tiny prey on Union Square, Will laid flat on his back in bed with his arms folded behind his head. He wasn't sleeping; his breathing hadn't slowed, and every now and then he made a noise that was a cross between a sigh and a grunt, a sure sign that his brain was stabbing him right in the feelings.

Aisha wasn't sleeping either. I heard her roll over, and then the sound of her hand sliding across his bare chest. There was a kiss—one set of lips, probably kissing his shoulder the way she often did—and then she lifted onto her elbow.

"How horrible is it of me?" he asked. "Were this happening to someone else, my concerns would be for the child. Yet I feel nothing but anger and can't imagine that changing."

She waited a beat before answering. Her breath went in deep and came out in a rush. "You're having a child against your wishes, sweetheart. You're allowed to feel conflicted."

"The only conflict is the thought that I should feel differently."

"All right. Let's change the scenario. Suppose you'd had a relationship with a woman who swore to you that she was on contraceptives or had been sterilized. You were very clear up front that you did not, would not, not ever, want a child. A few months later, she says, 'Surprise! I'm pregnant!' What would you do, in spite of your anger?"

"I honestly do not know."

"Bilbo...I think you do. You'd be mad as hell, you'd rail against the intrusion into your life and the obligation forced on you, but then you'd meet that baby and fall in love. You could relinquish parental rights and have nothing to do with him, but I think the moment you saw yourself in that tiny face, you'd accept the inevitable."

"A child under those circumstances would exist because of my own actions. In that scenario, I might reach eventual acceptance because I fathered him, regardless of want and intention. And in that scenario, I would willingly offer financial support."

"I'm just trying to frame this."

"I know. I also know that I can petition the court to sever my obligations. It's my first impulse."

"And yet—?"

"It speaks to who I am. No matter what I do, I'm not quite in the right. My head says I should step up because this child bears my DNA and is absent of any blame. My heart thinks it would break me. And selfishly, I am somewhat concerned about the outcome of the test damaging my credibility, especially if I turn my back on this baby."

"I'd still like to know why they're doing this. What's the end game?"

Union Square kitty pounced on a tiny rodent. I knew what came next: let it go, chase, pounce again. He would trap that mouse as many times as he needed until he was either bored or the mouse was too tired to fight. It was cruel, but I had done the same thing before.

I wasn't even hungry. The mouse was there. I hunted. It gave up and I bit down, and my mouth was filled with regret.

I let my mouse go. I didn't need the food, and I didn't like hurting it.

Union Square kitty had no choice and was preparing dinner.

That was the ultimate end game. Survival.

"My mind is also wrapped around that. Why? What do Dallas Engle and her apparently apologetic companion have to gain? Why me? What was the point of coming here with no way home, while still attempting to fulfill the objective of a scattered sect that won't form for well over a hundred years?"

"You're loaded, sweetheart."

"And you're currently the only one aware of my financial portfolio. The Emperor of her history left his money and property to members of the royal family, and it was diluted to very little by the time she was born. He was half of a chapter in high school history texts, and a footnote in higher education sociology classes."

There were books about you. Finn read them to you. The Emperor in those books was kind of your hero.

I heard him sit up. "What was that, Wick?"

When you were little, Finn read stories to you from books about the Emperor. I turned around. *They were your favorites. You loved the story about the Emperor saving the Prince, that's why you went to watch it happen.*

"But most of the stories he read to me were simply inventions, based on wishes and little else."

But someone wrote those books, and kids in your When grew up on them. Some of them might not understand reality-based fiction. They think all of it is real.

"People have believed stranger things, Will," Aisha said. "Think of how many cults have popped up waiting for alien life to arrive and take them home. How many routinely spring up to worship infants they believe will be the world's savior. There's a cult in Wyoming centered around a damned tree that grew shaped like T-rex, and they think when it dies, so will humanity. It's not a stretch that there are people who believe those stories are built around more truths than not and think you're still alive. Statistically, you could be."

Finn's stories always made you sound like a hero. Maybe those people need that.

"Then explain the baby, Wick. Help me figure that out. Having a child here does the members of that sect no good."

You could find out, you know.

"All right. How?"

Ask. That's the one thing you haven't done. Ask her.

*

Finn called at seven in the morning: meet me by the lab. Will hadn't slept at all and was in no mood to socialize or cater to his father's whims, but Aisha prodded him out of bed. He combed his hair but didn't shave, and then dressed in jeans and a t-shirt he picked up from the floor. Aisha scooped me up on the way out because I was pawing at her legs as she walked behind him toward the door. He grumbled when he realized I was tagging along, but he didn't tell her to put me down.

I recognized his fog. It usually began wrapping around him when he had gone days without sleeping and was especially upset. His temper was at its breaking point, and I didn't think Aisha had ever seen that happen. If it did, I wanted to be the one he got mad at. I understood the fog, and I wasn't sure she would.

He took the elevator. That might have been a clue for her.

"He knows you have court today," she said as we exited the building. "He wouldn't have called if it wasn't important."

He answered with a grunt.

Don't be a dick. None of this is her fault.

"Am I being a dick?" he asked without saying which one of us he was asking.

"A dick? No. Grumpy? A bit. It's all right."

Finn was on his knees by the portal, bent over Dallas Engle's companion. She was out cold and barely breathing; he was checking for a pulse, and when Will was close he looked up but didn't move otherwise.

Finn now knew who she was. Dallas Engle's mother.

"She's been here for five years, Will. She split from her anchor three or four months ago. I'm guessing she has an hour at best. Do I take her home, or leave her for her daughter to deal with?"

"Goddammit, Dad." His words were breath that caught in his throat. "How the hell—?"

She'd tried to get into the lab before dawn, pounding on the passcode keypad when the elevator door wouldn't open. The security system counted her fist banging on the keys as entry attempts and set off an alarm that brought three of techs up from the lower levels. They found her in a heap on the elevator floor, curled in a tight ball and moaning in agony.

"They knew the symptoms and called me instead of an ambulance."

"So you called me? For what? What is it you expect me to do?"

"It's your life she's helping someone else turn inside out. By all rights, I could simply call an ambulance and let her die because there's nothing they can do for her. Or I can take her home and give her a chance. What do you want me to do?"

He erupted. "Why the hell are you asking me, Dad? Why put this at my feet? What possible reason could you have for bothering me at all?"

"Sweetheart." Aisha rubbed his back, trying to calm him. "He's giving you control over this. You haven't had it in any of this, until now."

"Son of a bitch. Dad. This isn't fair. Y'know I can no' leave her here to die. Y'goddamn *know* it."

Aisha handed me to Will and helped Finn get her off the ground so that Will wouldn't have to touch her. She watched as Finn took her through, but Will turned away and marched over to the bakery and set me on a table, barking for me to sit there and not move so much as a whisker while he went in to get coffee.

He's turning Scottish again.

"Let him throw a temper tantrum, it's all right." She used both hands to scratch under my chin and my neck before planting a kiss on my head. "He's dreading today, and he's angry. We can let him have a little tantrum."

That wasn't a tantrum. That was his panties wadding up.

"It's fine. None of this is fair. And you know what? I would really like to grab that little bitch by her strawberry blonde ponytail and drag her into Finn's simulator, and then introduce her to Jeff right at breakfast time."

"Wibbitch." Will set a cup of coffee on the table for her. "And don't think that notion hasn't crossed my mind. I could literally drag her to another time where she would have no bearing on my life."

"But?"

"She has no anchor. I would be condemning her to death. As well as her child."

"So wait until he's born."

The idea pained him. His face pinched, and then he shook his head slightly, almost the way he did when he was warning one of the kids but didn't want to be obvious about it. "That leaves the child to me. No."

You want a baby. It's a baby.

"No, Wick. I want a baby with Aisha. No one else. That detail matters to me, very much."

"Will."

"Don't ask me, please. And even if I come to terms with this, and learn to accept him, I would never ask you—"

"Bilbo. Sweetheart." She reached for his hand. "Just accept *this*—I will love any child that exists as part of you. I may want to break his mother into tiny pieces, but if I can coexist with George, I can coexist with anyone. You'll never have to ask me to accept him. I already do."

*

Will waited on the same courthouse bench that he had sat on with Jay, but this time he was by himself and Aisha made everyone leave him alone. I sat on Drew's shoulder, trying to keep an eye on Will; he was quiet, sitting with his elbows on his knees, fingers laced together while pressed into his forehead, holding his head up.

He looked like he was praying. If his eyes had been closed, I'd have thought he was embracing the things Aubrey had shown him when she wanted the kids to pray before bedtime on the nights when he was the one making sure they were fed and bathed and tucked in.

"He's crawling out of his skin," Aisha said, softly so that her voice wouldn't carry. "Nothing I've said has made a difference.

He's angry and can't quite keep it buried, and I honestly don't know what to do for him."

He was usually good at controlling his anger; the surprise this time was that he allowed us to see his struggle. "He runs when he feels twitchy," Oz said. "This might be a hard run to the Golden Gate kind of thing. He'll run until he can't."

"I'll go with him," Drew said. "Once he gets me puking, he'll feel better."

Aisha wanted to laugh at that but could barely work up a smile.

"This is seriously fucked up, you all know that, right?" Jay said. "No one should be able to do this to someone else. He's on the hook—"

"Sweetheart, I know." Aisha slipped her arm around his shoulders and tugged him closer. "Will appreciates that we're all upset for him, but he doesn't need to hear it right now, all right? Just be here for him, and when the judge reads the test results, don't react. Don't give her the satisfaction of seeing his family rattled."

"What happens next?" Oz asked. "He leaves court today with the judgment against him, but then what? Is he obligated to her for anything other than support?"

"Let the lawyers handle it after this," Drew said.

"He's not sure—" She stopped when the courthouse door opened, and Dallas came in with her lawyer. She stared straight ahead, refusing to meet Aisha's gaze, and she barely glanced at Will when he stood up.

"Just tell me why," he said. "One good reason. That's all I need. One."

She hesitated for only a moment. Her lawyer grabbed her by the elbow and guided her into the courtroom, whispering in her ear.

Vincent arrived shortly after that. He didn't have much to say but reminded Will that he'd asked that the King not be present today. The potential for the post-hearing atmosphere to be a spectacle was high, with reporters and photographers waiting outside for a chance to get the first word with the Emperor; adding Jax to the mix seemed like a bad idea.

"I don't think the judge was happy that he stayed for the hearing," Vincent said. "Let's not irritate him before we can file an appeal."

Will went inside and sat at the table, stiffly, refusing to look at Dallas. She craned forward to look past her lawyer several times, but Will didn't budge. He stared ahead, his hands clasped together on the table, but he listened to Aisha as she spoke from her seat behind him.

"No matter what, Bilbo. We're in this together. I promise."

The judge didn't ask for anyone to speak before he demanded the report. The tablet it was contained on was brought in by a royal guard and a police officer, accompanied by the doctor who ran the test. The guard handed it directly to the judge, who asked the officer if this was, indeed, the correct tablet, and when he nodded and said yes, the judge turned it on.

His eyebrows knotted as he read, and his jaw twitched from his teeth being ground together. He read quietly, taking his time, and the longer he read, the tenser Will became. I could see one of his hands gripping the edge of the table, his fingernails turning red, his fingers white.

When the judge finally looked up from the report, he turned to the doctor, who waited by the bailiff.

"You personally conducted this test?"

"I did."

The judge ordered the doctor to the stand and swore him in.

"Did you personally conduct this test?" the judge asked him again. When he said yes, the judge went on, "Were these results cross-checked for potential errors?"

"Yes. I ran the test five separate times. There are sixteen markers we look for, and if ten match we can be certain of the results. On each run of the test, the results were identical."

"How many markers did Ms. Engle match?"

"Thirteen."

"How many markers did the Emperor match?"

"Zero," the doctor answered.

"What the hell?" Dallas sputtered. "That's not possible!"

The judge ignored her. "Based on the DNA collected from both parties and the results of the test, is Emperor William Blackshear the father of this fetus?"

"No."

"Liar! You fixed this!" she spat, looking at Will. "It can't be anyone else!"

Dallas's lawyer tugged on her arm and told her to be quiet at the same time the judge warned her against another outburst. He ordered her and Will to stand, and then issued another warning when she insisted the tests were wrong.

"It is the ruling of this court that the petition to name Emperor William Blackshear as the father of this infant is denied." He looked directly at Dallas and said, "You may file an appeal, but the results are not likely to change."

"There *is* no one else!" she shouted.

With a tired sigh, the judge said, "The Emperor is not your baby's father, no matter how much you wish it so."

Her voice cracked when she demanded, "Then who the hell is?"

The judge flipped through the report and asked the doctor if he was certain of the answer. When he nodded, the judge looked up and said three words that shut Dallas up but made Jay suck in a sharp breath.

"George Matthew Denton."

26

It was Jay's blurting of "Holy fucking shit!" that started a buzz rippling through the courtroom. The judge raised an eyebrow but otherwise didn't look up from the report, and Will covered his mouth with his hand, trying to not seem as amused as Drew and Zed, who laughed out loud. Aisha lunged across Zed's lap, trying to silence Jay, and rather than be squished by her chest, I jumped onto the railing that separated the audience from the court.

Drew hissed at me through his teeth—I knew I was supposed to stay on Aisha's lap, but this was self-preservation; death by lunging boobs was not the way I wanted to go—and tapped his leg with his fingers, ordering me to sit on him. I went to him, but not because he said so. He was more comfortable than the railing and I wasn't sure Aisha wouldn't have to make another grab at Jay.

"Ms. Engle," the judge went on, still not looking up, "how far along are you with this pregnancy?"

Her lawyer answered for her. "Nearly three months, your Honor."

Now the judge looked up. "According to records, the biological father has been deceased for five. Would someone care to explain this?"

Will leaned toward his lawyer to whisper to him, then stood up. "If I may?"

The judge nodded.

"This is a state matter, your Honor. It is not for public consumption."

He sighed audibly and then ordered the bailiff to clear the courtroom. I wasn't about to get shoved out into the hall with everyone else; I leaped from Drew's lap onto the railing, and from there onto Will's shoulder.

I'm not leaving you. I don't trust her lawyer.

He nodded to Drew. When the room was cleared of everyone except the lawyers and Will and the doors were closed, the judge asked Will for an explanation. "And it had better be good."

"George Denton is alive, your Honor," he said. "He was banned from Pacifica for an attack on members of the royal family and removed for both his and their protection. The King and a select few know of his whereabouts, but by his own request, to add a layer of security to his husband's and son's lives, he was officially declared dead."

The judge leaned back, scowling. "Why was he relocated? Acts of treason against the King are the only violations for which we have a death penalty."

"The King allowed him to live as a favor to me," Will explained. "George Denton was married to my stepson's father, and his execution would have come with a personal cost. Regardless of his actions, my son loves him, and I didn't want anything Denton did to permanently scar my son. The King agreed to spare his life and allowed him to be removed from Pacifica."

"Well, apparently he's back. Someone might want to get on that." The judge turned to Dallas's lawyer. "Your client committed perjury here, counselor. Give me one good reason not to issue a warrant."

"The baby," he said, hands splayed helplessly. "The child shouldn't endure punishment for mistakes made by its mother."

Will made the first concession. "George Denton may not have returned to Pacifica, your Honor. It's quite likely that Ms. Engle is from wherever he was placed. I would like the opportunity to speak with her, privately, to reach an understanding about why she did this and how deeply he's involved. I have no issue with her returning home, if that is, indeed, the case."

Vincent added, "We're reasonably certain that she's only been in San Francisco for a couple of months. Her mother has been in residence for five years. If she came to Pacifica with the intent to commit fraud against the Emperor, I would like to reserve the right to file suit at a later date."

"Nothing is easy with you people is it?" the judge asked absently. "Emperor, are you in agreement to waive issuing a warrant today in lieu of the right to file a personal case later?"

"If she will agree to speak with me, yes."

"So ordered. Counselor, you'll make sure your client meets with the Emperor at a time of his choosing or risk being in contempt of this court." He stood, scooping up the tablet, and sighed heavily when he said, "Dismissed."

*

Will waited in the courtroom as the lawyers stomped their way out. He didn't want to speak to Dallas yet but directed them to meet with her in the room the bailiff had sent her to while Will spoke to the judge. He wasn't ready to step outside and face reporters or photographers; he didn't want to answer questions, no matter how much in the right he was.

You're making Aisha worry, you know.

"For all she knows I'm still talking to the judge."

Not without your lawyer, you're not. And you know she saw him leave.

He wanted a moment to himself, to take a deep breath, but he also knew I was right and didn't want to upset her. After a second of hesitation, he yanked the door open, ready to be slapped with camera flashes and stupid questions, but the only people waiting in the hall were family and several of the guard.

Standing off to the side, keeping a close eye on everyone, was T'Neeka Soto. She wasn't standing at attention, but she was stiff and there to work, not to talk.

Will went straight to Aisha and lifted her in a giant hug. When he finally let go, she took a step back and asked, "*Now* can I yank her by that strawberry blonde hair and send her back where she came from?"

"After I get some answers from her, perhaps." He handed me to Drew. "I don't want him lost in the shuffle outside. Shield him from any cameras if you can."

T'Neeka stepped forward. "Not today, Emperor. You're leaving via the judge's tunnel." She turned to Oz. "Give us five minutes, then head outside. They're expecting him to follow you out with the guard."

"I doubt—" Will started.

"You won, Emperor. They expect you to stand on the courthouse steps and gloat. If that's what you want, I won't stop you, but I presumed you'd want to protect your wife and son's privacy. The boy should leave with you."

He had no desire to go outside and speak to anyone about his personal life. He also didn't want Oz and Drew to be surrounded by reporters.

"We'll be fine," Oz said. "They know better than to be anything but nice to me. I won't directly answer questions, but I can make it look like we're waiting for you, at least until the car pulls up."

He could have taken me, too, but with me on Drew's shoulder, they would expect him to come outside shortly after that.

They were disappointed.

Oz told them nothing, other than the outcome was exactly what she expected. When the car pulled up, and the guard opened the door for us, she turned and waved, and somehow resisted the urge to flip them off.

*

There was no celebration. Will directed the driver to take him straight home, hoping to beat the one or two reporters who would grasp that when Oz stepped out of the courthouse first, it meant that he had ducked out the back way. When we arrived home, a few journalists were waiting, but the guard blocked them from getting too close and Drew carried me inside before Oz even got out of the car.

She and Zed planned on just smiling and waving before running inside; Zed knew better than to answer any questions and Oz—if stopped—would only say that she couldn't speak for the Emperor. Call the official publicist, maybe you can get an appointment. But it would be rude for her to speculate on anything he was thinking or feeling.

Once Drew set me down, I ran up the stairs, not waiting to see if anyone followed. I bolted through the cat flap, expecting them to be drinking something to celebrate, but Will was in the bathroom and Aisha and Jay were in the kitchen, standing close so that they could speak quietly.

I jumped onto the counter to hear them better.

"He didn't say much on the way home," Jay said. "I can't tell if he's happy or pissed off."

"A little of both."

"And fucking *George?* How the hell? *Why* the hell?"

She wanted the answer to that, too. "I don't think we'll know anything until Will can talk to that...woman."

"Should I go to Dad's?" Jay asked. "Or even go spend the night with Zed? Just to get out of your hair, in case he's, like, furious or something."

"No," Will said as he came into the kitchen. "I'm not furious, Jay. I'm conflicted. That's no reason for you to go anywhere."

"Yeah, but—"

"I would very much like to have a nice, quiet dinner with my family. If the rest of this afternoon could be as normal as possible, I would appreciate it."

"All right." Jay pushed away from the counter. "I'll go change and then spend some time drawing. If anyone needs me, I'll be abusing Mrs. B's list under my breath while I try to sketch a realistic hand."

"A hand," Aisha said.

"Hands are fucking hard. They either wind up looking like a first grader drew a turkey, or someone has fat knuckles with tiny stick fingers."

Both Will and Aisha held their hands out and stared at them.

"I suppose all the tiny creases and veins make it difficult," Will mused, even though Jay didn't stick around to watch them ponder their own hands.

Aisha didn't think about it as much as he did. "All right, Bilbo. What do you want for dinner? I think I have everything to make meatloaf."

He blinked rapidly and stopped thinking about his hands. "Ah…"

Her hands went to her hips. "Fine. You can cook. I'm going to start taking this personally, you know."

"Enzo, I love you, but—" His phone pinged and he snatched it up. "Aubrey."

"Go ahead, answer it, save your sorry little ass." She wasn't upset; she snickered as she spoke. "See if I offer again."

His asterisk was saved twice; once by answering the phone and the next by Aubrey's insistence that they come downstairs for dinner. She assumed that neither of them felt like cooking, and since she had been banned from court, she wanted a recount of everything that happened.

"Well," Aisha said when he ended the call, "you wanted dinner with family. You're just getting a lot more of them than you expected."

I'll laugh if she makes meatloaf. No one likes Aubrey's meatloaf.

"My dad does," Will said. "It's how Aubrey decided she liked him. He liked her meatloaf. But then he was also only thirty and still had a cast iron stomach."

Oh. Then he should try her chicken casserole.

"No one should try that, Wick. Never again."

"I'm starting to feel better about my cooking," Aisha said as she tickled my chin.

We watched her disappear into the bedroom, and Will bent over to whisper. "That was helpful, thank you."

Don't thank me until you see what Aubrey's making. If it's meatloaf, I'll be very, very sorry.

*

"And that," Jax said as he sat in his comfy chair, "is why we like having them live here, and why we're taking custody of any grandkids. Someone else does the dishes."

"Jackson, tell me the last time you washed dishes." Aubrey tilted her head as she looked at him. "Go on. We'll wait."

"When was Oz finally tall enough to reach the sink?"

Oz and Drew were in the kitchen washing everything while Jay and Zed cleared the table. No one talked about the court case during dinner. It was parents poking kids for details on what they were all up to, and one stern warning to Drew from Jax to not finger fuck his dessert.

Once the dishes were done, after Zed and Jay went upstairs to watch a video and Oz and Drew disappeared into their room—domestic bliss, Jax snorted. They could count on not seeing either of them for an hour or two after dinner every night—Jax brought out the scotch and plied Will for details.

"I'll meet with her tomorrow," Will said. "I want to know why, simply that."

"Why, why here, why now, what the hell does that cult really want, and how is George involved?" Aisha said.

"I'm not sure I'm letting this one anywhere near her," Will said. "There might be bloodshed."

"No, there might be the dragging of that little bitch through a portal to take her home, but that's all."

They all looked at her like they didn't believe her.

"All right, maybe a little blood."

"What happens then, Will?" Jax pressed. "She's not from now, and she's carrying a baby from someone who hasn't been born yet."

"I'm not sure that's up to me."

"She's in Pacifica illegally. She brought a fraudulent case against you. It might be up to the court."

That was a can of worms Will didn't want opened. He thought they'd been lucky so far—no one had ever questioned the sudden appearance of his parents, and those who had been brought here from the future had done well at keeping quiet—but giving Dallas Engle any freedom in this When was offering exposure, no matter how unbelievable.

"If she remains here and begins talking, there will be those who will examine my history and will pay particular attention to the photograph taken the day I plucked you off the bridge.

No one has seriously examined the details of that time and the difference in our ages, nor has anyone made a formal, public inquiry as to my whereabouts before then. Give her any sort of latitude, and she might invite curiosity."

"Then she goes back."

Will nodded. "Once I have my answers, she goes back. She can pursue George or not, I don't care."

"I want answers from George," Aisha said. "What the hell?"

The bedroom door creaked open, and Oz came out. She headed for the kitchen, trying to be as unobtrusive as possible, but Will stopped her.

"Were you looking at Dallas when the judge read the report?" he asked. "I'm curious. Was she truthful in her surprise and claim that it couldn't have been anyone else?"

"I didn't see anything around her change," Oz said. "She was pretty much a mass of swirling confusion the entire time. Someone who wanted desperately to be believed. The only time I saw anything different was when she claimed she had actually been with you in the dark. She was openly lying then, but..."

"But?"

"She wanted it to be true. That's the sense I got. She's scared to death of you, but she really wanted it to be true."

*

Dallas's lawyer argued against Will speaking to her without him sitting next to her, fielding questions. She seemed resigned to it and didn't answer when he asked her to back him up on this, and when Vincent reminded him that this was the price for her not being brought up on charges, he reluctantly went to the far side of the room. There were two hard metal chairs in the corner, and they each took one.

She sat alone on one side of the table, Will and Aisha on the other. He allowed me to sit near his elbow but reminded me to make sure I was never within her reach.

She couldn't make herself look up at him. She kept her arms folded on top of the table and stared down, a fifteen-year-old student to Will's pissed-off school principal. Aisha, despite her want of spinning Dallas around the room by her hair, allowed the teacher in her to surface. She spoke first, and she was gentle.

"Just give us the truth," she said. "We're past being angry. We simply need to know why you did this, and why here and now?"

"It wasn't supposed to be here," she said. "Here was an accident. I never meant to come here."

Will folded his arms. "You tackled my father through a portal."

"I was trying to stop him. I knew he was heading through, but I needed to talk to him. Badly enough that I was willing to knock him over to get him to stay and listen. I didn't think I could get pulled through."

"Were you already pregnant?" Aisha asked.

Dallas nodded. "That's why I wanted to talk to Dr. Blackshear. I had my doubts—" She sucked in a deep breath and finally looked up. "We know who you are. Some of us, anyway. We've never betrayed that, we kept that secret."

"You kept secret the identity of a man centuries dead." Will looked dubious. "Would anyone two hundred years from now have cared?"

"Your father would have," she said. "And the old man would have. He insisted on it. He warned us about the end of time but thought that Dr. Blackshear would be able to save the world. He was the one who knew who you were and wanted your identity protected."

She says that like you know what she's talking about.

"Humor me." Will leaned forward. "Start at the beginning. What is the purpose of the Cult of the Emperor?"

She screwed her face up. "Those lunatics? Who knows?"

"You're not a sect of the cult?"

"God, no. Half of those nut jobs want to literally resurrect you. And I mean in a risen-from-the-grave way. The other half thinks you're still alive and that you're standing between the world and the second coming of Christ. They want you dead."

"All right. And you. Your people. What's your purpose?"

"Humoring the old man as far as I can tell. My family—they

do pretty much whatever he wants. My mother came here, to this time, in the last wave of emigrants. I think it was five or six years before the meteor was supposed to hit. He wanted her here if Dr. Blackshear succeeded. She was supposed to get close to you, get a good sample of your DNA, and then find a way back. But then people began coming home and she wasn't one of them, but you'd been spotted in the city."

Her hands went to her still-flat belly. "It wasn't supposed to happen like this. It was just supposed to happen in a lab, back home, in an incubating womb. But then my aunt said her neighbor knew you, and she could talk him into getting a real sample for us. It all happened so fast, and the incubator wasn't ready. They chose me, but I didn't want—" she sucked in a deep breath "—I had my doubts. The old man spent decades planning this, with my family's help, but when I saw Dr. Blackshear, some of the pieces kind of fell together. I just wanted to talk to him, to ask if he was who I thought he was."

"And that was?" Will prompted.

"It sounds insane to say it out loud. But the old man—"

"Who's the old man?" Aisha asked.

"My great grandmother's best friend, Liam Finnegan. She started working for him when she was my age, and they just kind of became close friends. He pretty much supports the family. He writes—"

"—stories about the Emperor," Will finished for her. "I was raised on those. And they were, largely, just stories. There was little fact in most of them. He built a mythos around the life of someone who was, truly, just a blip in time."

"Will." Aisha covered her hand with his. "Liam Finnegan?"

"I know."

"What did you want to ask my father about?" Will asked again.

"If he knew about the old man. If he knew who he was."

Will nodded. "You suspected they were the same person."

"Well, yeah. He kinda hinted he was, and I wanted to make sure. I mean, I'm carrying this kid, and he's the one who wanted it. I never meant to come here with your father. Honestly."

"But you ran," Aisha said. "The moment you were through, you ran."

"My mother," she said, voice trembling. "I was pretty sure about where I landed, and I didn't think I would get to see her if I waited around to explain. And it was a mistake, if I'd stayed home she would have come back..." She shook her head slowly. "She didn't come back sooner because she changed her mind. She didn't want anything to do with this. And then I showed up right after her boyfriend left, and she got sick. I'm not even sure where she is now. She was so sick, and I went through with the damned suit even though she asked me not to because I have no way to survive here and I figured you could support this kid... but now I can't find her. She left her apartment after the first day in court, and I haven't seen her since." Her breath hiccupped as she softly added, "I'd change it all if she would come back. I just want my mother."

"She went home." Will spoke kindly, something I wasn't sure she deserved. "She found my father, and he took her home before it was too late."

"Too late for what?"

"She was dying. I'm guessing her boyfriend left a month or two, just before she fell ill?"

"I think so. That sounds about right."

"Tucker Lee?"

Dallas nodded. "You know him?"

"Peripherally. He was her anchor, the person who made it possible to stay in this When. I'm also guessing she was yours, and without her, you'll need to go back soon."

"Go home and what? Tell them I'm carrying my aunt's crazy neighbor's kid? I'm not even sure why she trusted him. She told him why she wanted to get close to you and it was like, fine, I can get you that sample, I know the guy, he's married to my husband's ex-wife." She frowned, hard. "Why am I just now thinking about that? It's not like he could walk up and ask you for spit or skin or hair. You sure as hell wouldn't give him what he had. Why would he do this to us, even so?"

"He hates me," Will said. "He knows that I now occasionally return to my birth When. What better way to get back at me than to thrust at me a child I never intended."

"Get back to that," Aisha said. "Why does the old man want you to have William's baby?"

"Not just his baby," she said. "His clone. He's determined to bring his son back to life, and this was our shot at giving him what he wanted." She looked Will in the eye. "He didn't want your offspring. He wanted you."

27

There was nothing that Dallas Engle wanted to retrieve from her mother's apartment. She gave the address and passcode to Vincent—dispose of everything to anyone who needs it—and she promised Will that the moment she stepped through the portal, she would contact her aunt and get him access to George.

We waited on a bench near the lab while she called, and the silence that followed was filled with humming from people flying overhead and the clicking of cars in the street. She could have run; Will didn't ask her to stay after she'd called, but she sat on the edge of the bench as far from them as she could get without falling off and waited.

Fifteen minutes later, her grandmother and aunt skittered across the Square, with George strolling behind them. Dallas jumped up, but pushed past her family and went straight for George, slamming into his chest with both hands, screaming that he'd ruined her life.

He let her yell until she was out of breath, and he never tried to stop the barrage of open-handed strikes to his chest. He stumbled back once or twice, but then recovered and allowed her to continue until she could do no more than cry. He ignored the confusion on her grandmother's face and the irritation on her aunt's, and when Dallas had hit him for the last time, he said, "You don't get to be angry about this. What you wanted was wrong, and you damn well know it." Her grandmother started coming toward him, but he jabbed his pointy finger in her direction and barked, "No. I saved your granddaughter from something much worse than having this baby. You *know* that if you'd gotten what you wanted, and if he decided to challenge paternity *here*, she'd land in prison. It's a damned felony. You *knew* it and did it anyway. She's your *granddaughter*."

Dallas's words were tangled up in breath that hiccupped as she tried to calm herself. I couldn't understand what she said, but George half-shrugged and said, "No one will force you to have the baby. But I hope you do. I'm more than willing to raise that child."

She walked away without answering him.

He didn't watch any of them leave. "I'd say this is a pleasant surprise, but once I heard she'd disappeared, I expected you. Took longer than I thought, though."

"George." Aisha's hands went to her hips. "What the hell did you do?"

"Cherry was overly excited that I knew Will," he said. "She refused to believe it when I said that he's not the Emperor, and she didn't want to hear that our acquaintance didn't extend to friendship. I don't know the woman well, but I did know that she wasn't going to stop badgering me until I agreed to get her what she wanted."

"You had no hope of getting that close to me," Will said.

"I could have. One more contrived chance run-in here before you went home. A cup of coffee while we discussed Jay and the things he's been up to. All I needed was for you to leave your cup behind. It would have been simple, really."

"Then why?" Aisha asked.

"Why would I give them that? It's creepy as hell."

"To hurt me," Will said.

"Huh, I didn't think of it like that," George said. "Look, when I realized Cherry had some serious tunnel vision about the whole thing, I agreed just to shut her up. There was no way in hell I was going to go through with it. The lady is fucking insane. She actually thought I could waltz into your apartment like we were friends and steal hair from a comb or walk out with your toothbrush."

"But you let her think you could."

"Yeah, sure, why the hell not? She wasn't going to let up, so I stepped it up a notch. She wanted DNA, she got it. Used condom, supposedly fresh from your bathroom trash can. She never questioned it."

"You're fucking insane, George," Aisha hissed.

A spark of anger flashed in his eyes. "I wasn't about to let them do that, not any of it, just in case."

"In case of what?" Will pressed.

"Jay. And I swear to God, if I'd known she would rip through that goddamned portal to find you, I would have handled it differently. Jay is legally your first born, isn't he? You named him as your heir? Why the *fuck* would I let someone else take that from him? He has the protection of the royal family now. His life got exponentially easier."

"Another child doesn't take that from him," Aisha said.

"Maybe not if it's yours. But I know Jay. If Will had an unintentional kid floating around out there and he knew about it? It wouldn't matter what century that kid lived, it would matter to Jay. But if the little bastard turned out to be mine? That's just George being a narcissistic fuck up again. He'd get over it."

"The chances are high we would have never known about it," Will said.

George shook his head. "You keep coming back. You'll keep coming back, and you'll bring Jay with you. Sooner or later—they'd never leave you alone, Emperor. And while I don't have a problem with *your* life being a little difficult, I have major issues with Jay being drawn into it."

"I don't know whether to thank you or kick you in the nuts again," Aisha said.

"I'm not a nice person," George reminded her. "I did a fucked-up thing, and I know it. I had a decision to make, and I went with my gut. I'll do anything for Jay, you have to know that by now."

"Really." She huffed through her nose. "Anything?"

"Maybe not on your timetable, but *anything*." He considered it for a moment. "Ask James to set you up with our lawyer and find the rider to Jay's trust. It's very specific and will erase any doubts."

"George, don't make—"

"I didn't want him to have surgery, Aisha, we all know that. I felt like I was protecting Jaime, and I didn't want him to make that big a decision so young. But if he still wanted it on his twenty-fifth birthday? It was paid for. All of it. I didn't understand it, I will never completely understand it, but I was only standing in the way until I was positive. He couldn't undo it there, Aisha. If he'd gone through it early and then realized he was wrong? And if I'd known he could come here—?"

"He could change his mind here," Will said. "You would have allowed it because it could have been undone."

George's voice cracked. "I was protecting my daughter. But I would have loved my son every bit as much. I wanted him to have genuine options."

"Why didn't you ever say anything?" Aisha asked.

"James knew I wanted Jay to wait. He knew I would bend once he was old enough. I couldn't tell you about here and the possibilities. And there was no way to bring him here, even if I could have told you."

Aisha's voice was tinged with anger. "James knew your true intentions."

"He knew. He argued against it because making Jay wait meant additional surgeries. He was afraid the results wouldn't be as good. But goddamn, Aisha, you had Brian Massimo. Jay's results would have been perfect, even if he'd waited. Maybe he couldn't have had kids the usual way, but he would have had options." He gestured in the direction Dallas had gone. "All he would have needed is a healthy donor ovum and his own spit."

She sighed, and briefly closed her eyes. "I will never understand you."

"You don't need to."

"And now there's a baby at stake. What if she keeps it?"

"I went into this realizing that was the outcome. I was serious. I'll raise that baby if she doesn't want it. And if she does, I'll still fight for joint custody. It's my clone, for god's sake. It's not like she'll be able to tell the courts how that child came to be, not if she wants to stay out of jail."

He was never going home, he accepted that. He would trade everything to be able to go back and have a life with James, but he knew better. A child here tethered him to this When and gave him a purpose. "I'll do better this time."

"And if your child winds up with differences?" Will asked. "If you discover you fathered a—" he nearly choked on the word "—freak?"

"I'll deal with it." He started to leave but hesitated. "When you forced me through that portal, my life was rolled back a good twenty to thirty years. I'm not stupid, I see the gift in that. No matter how much I miss James and my life, I refuse to waste it being...me."

*

Old Finn looked a lot like younger Finn. He had less hair and what was left was nearly translucent, but he wasn't hunched over with age and his voice was still strong and clear. There was a cane propped up against his desk, but after a few minutes, I was sure he only had it so that he could hit people with it, not because he needed it.

Finn had taken us to see him, but he didn't stick around to make introductions. "You think I want to see that crusty old bastard? Why?"

"All those stories you read to me when I was small," Will said. "He wrote them."

Finn's face pinched. "Well. Fuck me sideways. I'm going to turn into a manipulative little prick, aren't I?"

I don't think he's bendy enough for anyone to do that.

Liam Finnegan's office, where he spent his afternoons making up stories about the son he'd left to the ages, was tucked into space between two storefronts not far from the Square. It was on Maiden Lane in our When, a street long closed off to traffic—even before the rest of downtown became a pedestrian paradise—a short stretch that had once been a hub of hookers that eventually became a space for small boutiques and coffee shops.

Aisha lamented the loss of its charm. It was sterile, the once brick walls now made of metal and acrylic; the old, carved wooden doors had become slick and shiny, and they opened with a bare touch of a finger. San Francisco had remained intentionally static for so long, holding onto the charm of its heyday, and seeing that it had become like every other city made her mentally itchy.

Old Finn's office was like stepping back in time. Once through the door, we were immersed in the early twentieth century, with dark wood-covered walls and shelves that went from the floor to the ceiling. His desk took up a large space toward the back, and he sat in a dark leather chair that seemed as if it wanted to swallow him whole.

He was tapping away at his computer when we entered, and it took a moment for him to look up. When he did, he was irritated at the intrusion, and it didn't matter that he knew without asking who Will was.

"What?"

Well, hello to you, too.

"I want an explanation," Will said. He made no introductions; Old Finn's gaze drifted to Aisha for a moment, but there was no curiosity in it. He looked at me and seemed to soften, but not enough to make me feel welcome.

"Everybody wants something," he said. "People typically leave here unsatisfied. I'm busy. Get to the point."

Will was already upset. He grabbed chairs from one side of the room and dragged them in front of the desk, and as he gestured to one for Aisha, he said, "Enough. Tell me why you want my clone. What possible reason could you have? I've been dead for two hundred years."

"Has it been that long? I'm not sure. But the science has come along enough for it to be possible. Cloning is a simple matter now."

"Stop it. Just tell me why."

"Why not?"

"You know what?" Aisha said, leaning forward to tap on his desk with her middle finger. "In my head, you're not Finn. *You're* not my father-in-law. I would have no problem leaping over that desk and giving you a few good reasons to stop dicking around with Will and answer his goddamn questions."

That startled him. "Finn is your what?" He looked at Will. "The Emperor never married."

"But William Blackshear did," he said.

Instead of softening, he grew irritated. "I knew Finn had done it. He moved the meteor. But William still died. The timeline would have demanded it. You're going to die. Look at you, it can't be that far off."

Will shook his head. "We didn't send Wick through as the test. Long story short, I never lost my anchor, I didn't die." He tilted his head a bit, considering, and then added, "I turn forty-four in just a few months."

Old Finn stood up sharply, grabbing at his cane. He smacked it against the floor sharply, and then spat, "No. This isn't possible!" As he rounded the desk, Will stood, and Finn jabbed at his chest with the handle of the cane. "I watched you die. I saw you wither and crumble until you were barely more than dust. And I turned away, I—"

"I'm sorry," Will said. "I know what it cost you. And I know why you couldn't be there in the end for him. You had a war to end, and his death wasn't going to change that. I promise you, he understood."

"You're not my son." He reached with his free hand and ran fingers over Will's jaw, feeling the stubble of whiskers, listening to the scratching sound it made. "You're not my son. But you have his essence. His genes. His mother is in you. You have his DNA."

"Cloning me won't bring him back."

"Yes, it really will. He would be identical in every way, and this time, I would get it right."

Has he been talking to George?

He finally looked at me for more than a second. "He wouldn't have you, though, would he? You were his world." He tapped the cane on the floor and turned abruptly, dropping back into his chair with a heavy sigh. "That hurt her so much, you know. That you were more bonded with a cat than you were with her. She would have been the one to go with you if she could."

Jo?

"Yes, Wick." Will touched my front paw with his finger. "I imagine it was very painful for her. But it was less about Wick, wasn't it?"

"Eh," he grunted. "You're here, you get to live. Good for you. I still want my son back."

"She was wrong, you know," Will said as he took his seat. "You wouldn't have been my anchor, either. I know she thought that. If you hadn't been the driving force in taking the meteor off course, she thought you could have been my anchor. I loved you both, but I always felt set apart. Wick was the only answer."

He knew.

"It will be different this time."

With a sigh, Will leaned back. "Whatever plotting you've been doing with the Engle family, it didn't work."

"I was told that it did. I've seen the report. She's pregnant."

"But not with my child or my clone."

As Will explained, the color drained from the old man's face. His defiance withered and his face was painted in defeat, his eyes rimmed in red. He listened to every word Will had to say about Dallas tackling Finn through the portal and the court case, and that the child she carried, the clone, was that of the man who had been his childhood enemy.

"Instead of replacing me, the world will now have another George Denton."

Old Finn's chair creaked as he turned it. He was searching his shelves for a particular picture, and when his eyes settled on it—Will in a karate uniform, the day he earned his black belt— he asked, barely a murmur, "Was I a good father?"

"I always thought so."

"I've always wondered. I thought the answer would be no."

"He adores you," Aisha said, her voice soft. "And we want to grow old together as happily as you and Jo are—"

"We weren't. I never had that." He barely heard her, instead listening to old memories whisper in his head. "He died, and we broke. She left me, after some time. Little Eli..." He swallowed. "Well, she's gone, in any case. More than a hundred years ago.

Possibly two. We didn't have the happily ever after. I was angry with her and felt relieved when she left. I saw her from time to time and loved her, but the trust, that changed. So, no, you don't want to grow old the way we did. Love like that tastes bitter."

"Did you ever find someone else?" Will asked though I wasn't sure he wanted the answer.

"How old am I now?" Finn wondered out loud. "Two fifty? Sixty? Maybe close to three hundred. I've lost track. I haven't been alone for all that time if that's what you mean. But I keep living, and they...don't."

"If you get what you want, that child will grow old and die, as well," Will reminded him.

"As long as he gets to grow old." He sucked in a deep breath. "I will not outlive another child, Dash. I don't have that in me. But I would be a better father, and I wouldn't send him away."

"Do you honestly think you have enough years left to raise him well into adulthood? Because I promise you, if my father died now, it would destroy me."

"Yes, well, I have news for you. He's not going anywhere."

"Will." Aisha reached for his hand. "Are you seriously thinking about this?"

Dude, you only wanted a baby with Aisha. Having one with your dad is kinda creepy.

"There would be conditions," Will said. Finn sat up straighter, paying attention. "For personal reasons, I won't consent until after she and I have conceived and delivered. We want a child of our own, and even considering that the clone you want would not be my offspring—I want my own child first."

Old Finn nodded.

"And should this be successful, you won't name him William, and you won't call him Dash. Regardless of his DNA, he will be his own person and deserves his own identity."

"Anything."

"And during the time you wait...I want you to seriously consider your options. You want to be a father again, Finn. It doesn't have to be to me. I'm still alive, and I've begun visiting this When. Whether you're in a direct line to me or not, you're still my father, and I'll want to see you. You don't need my clone to have me here."

"What, you want me to find some woman who thinks procreating with a man who's pushing three centuries is a good idea?"

"Hire a surrogate or use an artificial womb," Will said. "And if it must be a combination of my DNA that will make you happy, I know a woman who just might be willing to give you a solid sample or two."

"I can't see her, Dash, I can't—"

"You wouldn't have to. But think about it. Let *us* think about it."

"Let Will get to know you again first," Aisha said. "Prove to him you're not as off the rails as I think you are. Because honestly, I think this is all insane."

Old Finn looked right at Will. "She married you without knowing that much about this family?"

Will shrugged. "She loves me, anyway. And that's why I want this time to decide. We want a family of our own, and it comes first. Call off the cult, and I will seriously consider it."

Finn grimaced. "The cult. They're not the cult. The cult is filled with the strangest bunch of people you'll meet in any When. They think the stories are real and half of them think you're still alive."

Did he just hear himself?

I didn't think he did, and Will just let it slide.

28

During remodeling, Will made sure that the bedroom window seat would be big enough to cuddle on, but they were sitting at opposite ends instead of together. Their legs were touching, but Aisha had her arms crossed as if she were upset, and Will was resting his hands on his stomach, literally twiddling his thumbs. I watched him, wondering what the point was.

"That's driving me a little batty," Aisha said after a while. "I can't tell if you're waiting for me to say something or trying to draw my attention to your crotch." Before he could answer, she added, "One of the things I've generally appreciated about your level of maturity is that you've never whipped it out and wiggled it at me. All that twiddling makes me think you're about to."

He stopped twiddling. "That's a thing?"

"It's a thing. And I admit, get me a little bit drunk, and I'll think it's funny."

"I think I would be a bit self-conscious."

"We'll find out later." She sighed and unfolded her arms, drawing her knees up. "Just tell me why you're considering it, Will. Two days ago, the idea of someone else giving birth to your child upset you like nothing else. Now you're mostly on board with the idea."

"Two days ago it was a total stranger. Today it's my father, and it's not really my child."

"Does the idea that it's a clone really matter?"

"In this particular circumstance, I think so. He wants another chance, Aisha. I'm hoping he'll realize that he doesn't need me to do this, but if that's what it takes, why not?"

"Babies," she said. "It's that simple. I honestly want to be the only one having your babies. It matters to me."

"And a week ago you were willing to accept Dallas's child as mine."

"Because that baby wasn't a concept. It was real, and it was yours, and I don't think I can't not love a child of yours. But you have a choice in this. He wants to recreate his son, and that's a little bit creepy."

"He wants a do-over, Enzo. By the time he gets his way, he'll likely have changed his mind."

"Will, he's been planning this for *decades*."

"That was thinking I was lost to him forever. He's still Finn. I can be there for him from time to time."

"But he's not *your* father. I hate it for him, but he lost his William."

He gave a slight nod, and then took time to consider what he wanted to say. "We have spent several wonderful evenings with Jax and Aubrey in their later years. When we're sitting around that firepit, laughing with them and sharing stories about the kids, do you ever stop to think that those people are not really Jax and Aubrey?"

"No, of course not."

"And when I sat on my mother's deathbed, was that not still my mother?"

"Will, I get what you're saying, but—"

"That old man might not think of me as his son, but it's only to protect his heart. And the truth is that if my parents said they were having another child, the same combination of DNA that created me, I would be thrilled for them. I'm not sure this is much different. Same people, different When."

"Your parents wouldn't be trying to recreate you. They'd just be having another child."

"And I think that's all he wants. By the time I'm able to comply, I'm certain he'll understand that he doesn't need a copy of me. He just wants to be a father again. I can empathize with that."

"Will, you offered up your mother for this."

"I know. I did it because I'm certain she would be willing. He would have to keep her updated because the scientist in her will overwhelm any wish he would have for privacy, but her innate curiosities might compel her to do it."

"Is that fair to Finn?"

"That's a discussion they'll have to have if it comes to that. And this is all supposition for now. I won't do anything until we have a child of our own."

Her hand slid across her belly. "I really thought we'd be pregnant by now, Will."

He smiled and swallowed the blip of laughter that wanted to slip out. "We haven't been trying that long. But we can go see Mass. He did tell you he could knock you in up about two minutes."

"His poor wife," she snorted. "And I'm not ready to get clinical about it. I'm not even ready to start taking tests and checking my temperature or plotting things out on the calendar. I'm not keeping track. I just want it to happen."

"And if I start wiggling things at you?"

That made her laugh. "I'm not drunk."

"I'd say that I know a good bar, but I honestly don't feel like drinking."

She swung her legs over the side of the window seat. "How about we take a nice walk instead? We'll wander around downtown for a while and then stop and get some hot chocolate, and if we're lucky, the kids will be hanging around the bakery. We can pester them."

"I'm not eating a donut," he said.

"Oh, hon." She patted his leg. "You're eating a donut."

*

He ate a donut.

He drew the line at hot chocolate; one sweet thing at a time, he told her. He wanted coffee and agreed to the donut as long as she didn't try to get him to eat anything else sweet for the rest of the week.

"Meals are up to you this week," she said. "I'm getting the message, Bilbo. You *really* don't like my cooking."

"But I love that you try."

"Asshole," she chuckled. "I follow recipes, you know."

"Perhaps a better cookbook?" He wisely scooted his chair away. "I'll cook this week. There will be enough vegetables to make Jay whine."

Jay likes it when you cook. He gets excited because it won't taste like old socks.

"Jay is a hollow teenager," Will said. "He'll eat anything."

"Don't protect me from Wick's barbs. I know he wasn't praising my cooking."

"It's like she knows you, Wick."

"Hush. Just eat your donut and let me have this tiny victory."

There were no kids to pester, but Finn came out of the lab, and before he could head in the direction of home, Will texted him to come join them. Finn was eager to speak to them about meeting his older self, yet he was more excited about the idea of coffee and donuts and he made them promise to not tell Jo. "She's on a health kick. For some reason, that means I don't get anything fun."

Will bought him two donuts and agreed to keep it from his mother. "I guarantee, she has a secret stash of chocolate, Dad. In the history of her life, from the time she was twelve onward, she has never not had a stash. I can even tell you where it probably is."

"Well?" Finn asked around the wad of donut he'd bitten into.

"That lovely bowl of fresh fruit she keeps on the kitchen counter, no matter the When? It's a bowl within a bowl. Lift the top one, and underneath is a treasure trove of sugar."

"Dammit. How long as she been hiding that from me?"

"How old am I?" He chuckled. "I found it when I was six, I think. She knew it, too. It wasn't me she was hiding it from."

"Weirdest little boy ever," Finn said to Aisha. "Given a choice between a plate with sliced cucumbers and tomatoes and a bar of chocolate, he chose the cucumbers every time."

He used to eat junk. He liked cake. Pieces the size of his head.

"Good thing they can't understand you, Wick."

"He's ratting you out," Aisha guessed. She broke a tiny piece off her donut and set it on the table in front of me. "Cake, Wick? That has to be it. He used to inhale cake."

I ate the offered bite and then tried to get one from Finn because he still had an entire donut in front of him. While he broke it in half to dig out some of the soft, squishy inside for me, he asked about their meeting with Old Finn. I don't think he noticed that he'd given me nearly half the donut while they talked, not until Will reached out and dragged me away, warning that if I ate anymore, I would throw up.

That's a chance I'm willing to take.

"I'm still digesting that he's Liam Finnegan," Finn mused. "I've been in that office, and I've seen the volumes he has on display, but it never clicked. His lab is around the corner, and he's clearly doing biological research, but I assumed it was simply a new diversion. He'd exhausted his interest in physics and playing with time and had moved onto something new."

The notion came to him when he was three books deep into writing his tales of the Emperor: he could invent all the wishful stories the world could ask for, or he could find a way to have his son again. The technology was there; he only needed a small piece of Will to make it happen.

"He couldn't ask you," Will said. "He knew you wouldn't seek me out before the last effort to destroy the meteor, so he needed another way. His answer was to groom an employee and make her want to help him. In the end, he sent her granddaughter here with the intent to return, but when I appeared, and she didn't?"

Finn hated the idea that he would eventually turn into an ancient, lonely, and possibly ill old man. He didn't want to live that long, not without Jo. He wasn't as certain as Will was that she would volunteer her DNA to help the old codger have another child, a sibling to Will, but she would be interested in the outcome if she did.

Why didn't he just come find you? He knew where the portals were. He could have just popped over here, grabbed your coffee cup or something, and gone back without you even realizing.

They stopped talking and stared at each other for a minute.

"Maybe his transponder doesn't work anymore," Finn said.

"There may be cumulative effects to time travel," Will mused. "That might be worthy of a discussion with him. But, indeed, Wick has a point. Why not come to me himself? I would have believed his claim of being you. He doesn't look much older. He's clearly you."

"Well, how I look now. I wasn't even fifty when you left home Dash, and the last time you saw me before I came back with your mother, I was thirty. If he'd come, he would have seemed much, much older to you."

"Still. There has to be a reason."

Aisha's brain went in another direction. "Maybe he's just plain nuts."

"Ouch." Finn scowled. "I don't want to lose my mental faculties."

"You're truly not the same man," Will reminded him. "He's what you would become without Mom and with a mountain of grief weighing you down. Your future certainly won't be the same."

Finn thought about it for a moment. "Still. He at least surrounded himself with beautiful women. I suppose that takes some of the sting out of it."

"That's sexist, Dad."

"Well, if I'm going to be borderline evil, let me enjoy it." He drained the last of his coffee. "Don't do it, Dash. Don't give him any part of you. I constantly question how good a father I was, even now. I think every man does. But I did the best I could with the time I had, and you turned out damned well. He doesn't need a do-over. He needs to remember that he brought a remarkable human being into this world, someone who did a hell of a lot of good with the little time he had and was willing to sacrifice everything, and that was enough."

*

After Finn left, they stayed at the table, watching people come and go, silently. Will scooted his chair close to hers so that they could hold hands, but they didn't talk again until Zed and Sophia came up the stairs at the far corner of the Square. She was wearing his sweatshirt and he was in short sleeves, and they walked as close to each other as they could. Neither noticed us; they stopped once when a toddler ran in front of them and used it as an excuse to giggle and then steal a long kiss. They headed for the front door of the royal house, and when they were gone Aisha sighed and said that they looked very happy.

"Come on," she said. "Tell me when they make it legal. I know she's the one."

"Just because I know a thing, that doesn't mean it will happen this time around."

She poked at him. "Humor me."

"You can't say anything to anyone, you know that. Keeping their futures clear is important. Knowing is a burden, it truly is."

"I already know you're going to change that future for Zed at some point."

He nodded. "She is the light of his life, even this young. Losing her will crush him." With a deep breath, he added, "Unless things have changed, there will be a very quick wedding next July. Jax and Aubrey will forgo their birthdays and anniversary in favor of something they will treasure far more."

Her hand went to her mouth, hiding a smile. "I shouldn't be amused by my son's best friend getting his girlfriend pregnant."

"Indeed. I'm sorely tempted to physically pick him up and take him to see Mass and stop it before it happens, but…"

"But you know just enough to know how wanted and loved that baby will be."

"I can only judge by the things I read many years ago. I do know that his first child will go on to do wonderful things."

"Oh, I hope Aubrey and Jax aren't too upset."

He didn't think they would be. "Oz and Drew paved the way with their false alarm last year. I think Jax especially now grasps that there's no point in getting angry over something that will bring so much light into his life. And I look forward to him having to deal with Robert Lopez for the rest of their lives. I almost feel sorry for Zed, knowing who his father-in-law will be."

You like Lopez.

"Yes, Wick, I like Robert. But is he a bit of a blowhard and he cannot stop himself from outrageous flirting."

But he's happily married now.

"Being happy and content in his marriage does not change who he fundamentally is. And that person loves to charm the women around him."

He told Aisha that Robert was harmless and would take it well if she told him to back the hell off, but he would also be thrilled if she flirted right back at him. She heard him, but her brain was tripping over something else.

"You have no in-laws," she said, as if it had just occurred to her.

She hadn't had any when she was married to James, but he didn't bring that up. Instead, he lifted her hand and kissed her fingers, and told her he knew she missed her family. "Your parents would be incredibly happy for you, Enzo. Proud, too. Jay—"

Jay is running across the Square.

They both looked up. Jay and Zara were running toward them, holding hands and laughing as they tugged at each other. Jay was pulling her along, Zara was trying to get him to slow down. They were both flush with cold, cheeks bright red and breath coming from them like fog.

"My God, look how tall he's gotten," Aisha breathed when they were halfway across the Square. "Is he taller than you? He's taller than you."

Out of habit, Will stood when they reached the table and Jay mocked him for it. "You're making me look bad," he said, even though he held a chair out for Zara. "He thinks I'll learn by example. I still don't pop up when Mrs. B comes in."

"One should rise for their Queen," Will said, only half serious.

"Well, yeah, but I'm not sure one should jump up for Zed's mom. If she walks in wearing a crown, I'll get off my ass."

I barely paid attention after that. Will asked a lot of questions about their day and how school was, and I heard something about Zara meeting James and being really nervous about it, and Jay thought it was funny because James was more nervous than she was. They'd gone to an exhibit at the Modern Art Museum after school, I caught that. And they were going out to dinner, but Jay promised he wouldn't stay out late.

I watched Will and Aisha while they talked. He hung on every word, even when Jay was going on about James combing his hair for the tenth time, worried that he would look goofy when he met Zara. Aisha touched him a lot, her hand on his arm, and when she laughed, she leaned into him.

His comfort with touch didn't surprise me anymore. He craved it, and even when he slept some part of him was touching her. But when she reached over to brush a stray hair off his face, I felt something I hadn't before.

Her laughter settled on him like fine mist, and he left it to cling to his skin, undisturbed. There was a weight to those touches, and he bore it happily.

She was his anchor.

It didn't happen all at once; I'd hoped for it, and I wanted it for him, but it had been happening all around me and I hadn't noticed until that one moment. She touched him and I heard his soul sigh, and I knew.

Jay and Zara left for their dinner date, holding hands but not in the same hurry they'd been in before. Aisha waited until they were almost all the way across the Square and then asked him, "So, are they sleeping together?"

"Not yet. But soon, I imagine. Are you all right with that?"

She laughed. "I don't get an opinion, do I?"

"No. Do you want me to take him to see Mass and avoid any potential issues?"

"God, I don't want him to be this grown up yet. But yes, take him. Don't just suggest it, either. I'm pretty sure Drew has suggested it to Zed a dozen times, and he's relying on Zara to take care of things. Just drag his scrawny ass there and tell him it's time."

"I'll talk to Mass first."

"It hasn't even been a year, Will," she said with a heavy sigh.

"This time last year I was beating my head against the wall of George and thought Jay would never get what he needed."

"This time last year, I should have died," he mused. "It's been a good year, I think."

"Oh, hon, it's been a *great* year. Come on." She got up and tugged at his hand. "Jay won't be home, so you're off the hook for cooking tonight. Take me somewhere that has enough vegetables to make you happy, and then take me home and do things to me."

"That's decidedly non-specific. Can these vegetables be topping for a burger?"

"Bilbo, you can eat anything you want tonight."

*

We went to the diner, which meant I had to sit in a high chair but also meant I got bites of shrimp and steak, and I pretended not to notice when Aisha kicked her shoes off and ran her foot up and down his shin. Will pretended to not notice that he still had a guard trailing after him, but he couldn't help looking when she stepped into the path of a reporter and made him leave.

The questions that he'd heard being shouted across the street or the Square never had anything to do with Dallas Engle or why had she sued him. It was always the same question, phrased a dozen different ways: seriously, just *one* woman?

He'd watched a newscast with amusement when the story devolved from the results of the paternity test into a discussion about his love life. One talking head reminded viewers that the Emperor had not married until he was forty-three; the other reminded viewers that the Emperor and his bride had known each other in their teens and he had been heard recently professing that he'd loved her then. Surely shenanigans had occurred in their youth.

Either way, he was an oddity.

He didn't care what anyone thought. They could publicly declare him odd, stuffy, lost to archaic beliefs, and it didn't matter.

His soul was as happy as he was.

After we got home, I asked for a fire to nap in front of and curled up on my new, unspoiled rug. I didn't follow when they disappeared into the bedroom. If Will fell off, well, that was his problem now. I napped until Jay came home. He made snacks, and we sat together at the table and ate while he told me about his date—Aisha didn't need to worry yet; he was still thrilled about getting long goodnight kisses and wasn't anywhere near ready for more—and he spoke in a hushed voice, sharing his secrets.

He and Zed were making plans to take Zara and Sophia out on Valentine's Day, dinner out and then a movie at Sophia's apartment. I wondered if that would be the new hurdle that would get in Zed's way; maybe he wouldn't become a dad so early because he and Jay probably weren't hanging around like that in the last loop of time. Other Zed had probably spent things like Valentine's Day alone with Sophia, but my Zed wouldn't. They would double-date.

In the other When, Jay was probably still Jimmy, waiting to become himself, and the Emperor was days away from taking his last breath.

Half of me hoped things would change for Zed, the other half hoped it wouldn't.

After Jay cleaned up, washing our dishes before putting them away, he told me I needed to be quiet if Will and Aisha were sleeping, but if Will asked, I could be honest and admit he was a little late getting home. It was only a few minutes, but it might matter, and he wasn't going to ask me to lie.

He went into his room to call Zara, even though he'd taken her home half an hour earlier because the world would end if he didn't tell her goodnight one more time, and I went to Will and Aisha's bedroom door and listened. If they were still bouncing around, I wanted to stay out by the fire, because Will was getting more adventurous and I didn't want to witness him breaking himself.

It was quiet, though, so I went in and jumped on the bed. Will was on his back and Aisha's head was on his shoulder, but there was enough space for me to sit on his chest.

If she's asleep, we need to talk.

"I don't think she is, Wick. We can talk, anyway."

She might ask questions.

"And I have no secrets from her. What's the problem?"

She reached up and stroked my head. "Need me to leave, sweetie?"

No. But you can't repeat things.

"I won't keep secrets from her."

I know. Just yes or no. Do you think she's already pregnant?

"Yes."

She smells different. And you stopped talking about if you'd have a baby. Now it's when. And you didn't want to take her to a bar.

"Indeed."

You need to know something.

He waited.

I felt it tonight. I've felt it coming but tonight I really felt it.

"Something wrong?"

No. Something right. She's your anchor now, Will. Your soul told me.

"I've felt that, too," he said, voice soft. "That doesn't mean you're no longer one. You'll be my anchor as long as we're both alive."

Do I need an anchor?

"Wick." He shifted, trying to sit up without dumping me. "Do you feel like the connection between us has severed?"

No. But I'm so old, Will. What if I'm still here after you die?

"I can't imagine—"

Will time try to end me if I don't have an anchor?

"I wish I could tell you, Wick. I don't know."

"Come on, tell me," Aisha said, sitting up. "What's he worried about?"

"What happens to him without an anchor," Will answered, choking on the last words. "I don't know if he's as affected by time as humans are."

"Sweetie." She reached over to pet me. "You were here for a long time without Will. All those years with Jax, you were fine, weren't you?"

Jax might be an anchor, too. And Drew. Maybe I have options.

"I think we can have multiple anchors," Will said. "As I grow old, you might attach yourself to Oz and Drew's children, or Zed's or Jay's. If you need an anchor, you'll find one in them."

Or yours.

"Or ours."

I don't think I want to live forever. I won't, right?

"I don't know," he said again.

Promise me that when I say I'm done, you'll help me.

"Wick—"

I don't want to be like old Finn, angry and hurt because everyone I love left the world without me. I don't want to forget you again. I've forgotten so much.

You know Old Finn is more than three hundred. He spent four hundred in null space and that counts. What if I live that long? I don't want to.

"I can't even think about that, Wick. Not now. Not when—" He blinked, and tears spilled from his eyes. "The idea of you being gone is physically painful. I could easily live nearly two hundred years, you know. When I didn't die, one of the things I counted on was you being here with me."

"Oh, my God," Aisha breathed. "What's he asking you to do?"

Not today. Not even tomorrow. I want to live to see your baby and your baby's baby. But promise me. When I'm done, when I say it's time, you'll help me.

He swallowed hard.

If I were really sick and in a lot of pain, you'd do it.

"I know. If you were an ordinary cat and in pain, I would. But you're not ordinary, Wick. If you ever become that ill, I can take you home, and you can be cured."

Promise.

Aisha scooped me off his lap. "Sweetie, Will's going to outlive me, we've talked about this. I need you here for him."

Promise.

"All right, Wick." He conceded, but he wasn't happy. "But when you tell me you're done, I'm going to make damn sure of it first, all right? You can't just decide on a whim."

We'll be old, old men together, Will. I'll be here when you tell Jax goodbye for the last time. And Aisha. And Aubrey and even Oz and Drew. But I need to know that if I'm done before you are that you'll let me go.

"Goddamn, Wick. Yes, when we're old, old men, I will honor your wish."

Good.

I wiggled in Aisha's grasp until she set me down, and then I stomped up her chest until she laid back down, and when she did, I sniffed her face.

"I brushed my teeth, Wick. What the hell?"

I sniffed my way down her body, stopping just short of pissing Will off, and then draped myself across her belly.

October. Early.

"What the hell is he doing?" she asked Will.

"You smell nice."

"I smell like sex and sweat."

I slid off, and then pawed at her. *Tell her.*

"You're hungry? Maybe he hears your stomach growling."

"And maybe you're full of shit, mister." She jabbed him with her pointy finger. "You know what he's saying. What's Wick so—" Her hand went to the spot where I tapped my paw. "Will."

Oh, look. The lightbulb went off.

"No," she said, half breath and half hope.

"I was waiting for you to tell me," he said. "I keep track. And Wick...he says you smell different. He's guessing early October."

They both had tears in their eyes again, but at least this time it was happy tears and not *ohmygodwickdontdie* tears.

"I don't suppose you can sniff out gender," she said, tucking me under the chin.

"Doesn't matter," Will said, sliding his hand across her, pushing me out of the way. "Boy or girl, I'm turning into a pile of mush."

Maybe it's twins.

"Don't tell me you can sniff that, Wick, I won't believe it."

Or triplets. If it's triplets, I'm sleeping with Oz and Drew for a while.

"You can stop talking now. We're not having triplets."

You just jinxed yourself.

"You're sure about the dates?" she asked Will. "Maybe Wick is mistaken. And maybe you lost track. I sure as hell did, and—"

You guys took the whole Tree of Life thing literally.

"The park." He swung his legs over the edge of the bed and reached for a pair of shorts. "I'll be back."

She wanted to know where the hell he was going. This wasn't a time for snacks; if she was pregnant, he was damn well getting back into bed and cuddling.

"Two minutes," he said.

She huffed but nodded, and he went down the hall into their office. I watched from the foot of the bed as he came back, a small bag in hand.

"I bought these, just in case." He dumped the contents out on the bed. "Grab one and go pee on it. But I don't think I'm wrong, and I don't think Wick is, either."

Better make sure you know what color it's supposed to turn. Oz thought she knew and look how that turned out.

He grabbed one of the boxes she left behind. "Blue. This one should turn blue. If it's negative, it won't change at all."

We sat on the edge of the bed to wait. Jay came out of his bedroom to go into the kitchen but stopped when he saw us there, and he came over, lingering in the door, wanting to know if I'd ratted him out for being late.

Will didn't even get two words out before she came out of the bathroom, crying, blue stick in hand, and thankfully she'd put her robe on. She jumped at him, knocking him back onto the bed, and didn't realize Jay was there until after she'd sucked Will's tonsils halfway out of his mouth.

"Mom?" He was laughing, even if he was a little embarrassed. Then he noticed the stick she was clutching. "Wait, wait, wait, wait, wait. You're pregnant?"

"Little bit, yeah," Will said.

"Seriously? I actually get to be a big brother?"

Aisha was still crying and couldn't answer him, so all she did was bob her head.

"Fucking hell! That doesn't tell you if it's a boy or a girl, does it?"

"No, but if we decide we want to know, Mass can tell us. Do you think you want to know, Enzo?"

She couldn't answer.

"Yeah, she's not gonna be coherent for a while. And even if you find out, I mean, look at me. It might not stick. You could wind up with another me."

"That would be wonderful," Will said.

"But, you know—"

"It would be different this time, sweetheart," Aisha managed to say. "No George to stand in the way."

"I hope you get your daughter," Jay said softly. "I hope you get all the dresses and pink shit and that Will has to sit on the floor playing tea party with ribbons in his hair. I know you wanted that, with me."

"I wanted," she said, getting up to hug him, "a healthy baby. A happy child. And I hope you are, Jay."

"I'm happy. I swear."

"Then I got what I wanted."

"But I still want to see Will on the floor with ribbons in his hair. And maybe some makeup. Drinking pretend tea out of tiny cups while he makes conversation with five stuffed animals."

You'll do that, too, you know. You'll sit on the floor and pretend, too.

"Yeah, I think I will," he said when Will repeated it. "Brother or sister. We're having a motherfucking tea party."

Can we have a snack? We should celebrate with a snack.

"I just fed him," Jay said, even though he turned and headed for the kitchen.

It didn't matter. Will made hot chocolate for them—again, I was beginning to think it was the only thing he knew how to make—while Jay opened a can for me, and when I was done eating he and Jay were at the table, alone, because apparently the moment a woman knows she's pregnant she needs to pee a lot.

Dude. She just *went.*

"Speaking of babies," Will said when she was out of earshot. "Whatever you're thinking of with Zara?"

"We're not, I swear."

"But you will eventually, I assume."

"Kinda hope so. I mean, I really like her. But I haven't, you know..." He sucked in a ragged breath. "Not even, like, second base. I mean, she would be okay with it, we kinda talked about what we expect, but I'm not there yet."

"I'm taking you to see Mass. Just in case. And before you ask, your mother is well on board with the idea. Neither of us wants to embrace grandchildren right on the heels of having our own."

Jay chuckled. "Yeah, I've got way too much shit I want to get done before that happens. And seriously, all I want right now is to be an awesome big brother. Maybe kind of an uncle when Oz and Drew start having kids. But one of my own? Years away, Will."

"Good."

"Are you gonna be able to get used to me calling you something else? Because in a couple years, when the baby starts talking, she's gonna call you Daddy and will be really confused if I call you by name."

"We'll sort it out," he said.

Jay leaned back. "I had this talk with my dad. Like, before all that shit with the woman who sued you. I mean, about who you are to me, not about kids. If I'm having a little brother or sister who calls you Daddy, then I reserve the right to call you Dad, too. And not just because it'll be less confusing. But because you are. My other dad, I mean."

"James—"

"Is okay with it and understands. His words, not mine—I'm the lucky bastard with two fathers. It'll take some time because I've gotten used to calling you by name, but when that baby gets here? You're Dad. Our dad."

I went over to the fireplace and curled up on the hearth where I could still see them. Aisha came back, and they sat at the table late into the night, making plans and swearing each other to secrecy, not wanting to share with the world just yet.

Everything Will had ever longed for was in that apartment, and I could feel it pulsing around me. Not just the singing of his soul, promising me that Aisha would keep him anchored in time, but the pull of Jay and the baby, a settling that made me wonder if time wasn't letting him go, and leaving him at peace.

Yeah, I wanted to live long enough to see that.

Well, that and seeing him get horked on by a fussy three-month-old.

As I drifted off, I heard Will's grandmother in my head. People didn't have to understand me, they just had to know I was there. I heard Aisha laugh, Jay snort, and Will's voice rumble toward me, and I took a deep, deep breath.

And then, just in case Gram was right, I exhaled.

ABOUT THE AUTHOR, BECAUSE PEOPLE TOTALLY READ THIS STUFF WHEN THEY'RE DONE READING THE BOOK

Max Thompson is a writer living in Northern California with The Woman, The Man, and Buddah Pest. He's also a Feline Life Coach for Mousebreath Magazine, and writes the hugely popular blog The Psychokitty Speaks Out. He's 14 pounds of sleek black and white feline glory, and his favorite snacks are real live fresh dead steak, shrimp, and lots of cheese. He also appreciates that you've read this far, and would give you a cookie if he could.

www.ingramcontent.com/pod-product-compliance
Lightning Source LLC
Chambersburg PA
CBHW051432260626
47162CB00001B/55